WHAT THE STORMS OF WAR SCATTER, LOVE AND LOYALTY WILL BOND TOGETHER.

GABRIELE: Her love for the land that shaped her heritage reigned supreme . . . until the slave trade she despised shattered her family, her home, and the men who loved her.

ALEX: Born of Yankee wealth and Southern honor, he was a quicksilver renegade whose allegiance was only to himself . . . until he took a stand for loyalty and love.

JORDAN: Stricken by the vivacious Gabriele at first sight, he would be torn from her by duty and the Union Navy . . . only to be reunited within the ignoble confines of a Confederate prison.

TWILIGHT OF THE DAWN

"STIRRING!"

—Publishers Weekly

"DRAMATIC . . . Filled with romance and laced with Civil War adventure . . . True to the era . . . FASCINATING!"

—Baton Rouge Advocate

Continued next page . . .

"COLORFUL AND ENTERTAINING, an interesting story well-told!"

—*Anniston Star* (AL)

"The characters are not only warm and appealing, but true to their period and themselves. The dozens of small details . . . give the story that marvelous sense of authenticity that is [the author's] trademark."

—Jennifer Blake, author of *Love and Smoke*

"A well-researched picture of the ravaged South."

—*Booklist*

"Entertains and informs."

—*Chattanooga Times*

HIGH ACCLAIM
FOR THE NOVELS OF
ELIZABETH NELL DUBUS

ELIZABETH NELL DUBUS

ST. MARTIN'S PAPERBACKS

First published in Great Britain by William Collins Sons & Co., Ltd., as *The Twilight of the Dawn.*

TWILIGHT OF THE DAWN

Library of Congress Catalog Card Number: 89-30127

ISBN: 0-312-92303-1

Printed in the United States of America

St. Martin's Press hardcover edition published 1989
St. Martin's Paperbacks edition/January 1991

10 9 8 7 6 5 4 3 2 1

This novel is dedicated to
E. Ramòn Arango and J. Taylor Rooks,
whose many kindnesses to me and to my daughters
are deeply appreciated,
not only for the generous spirit
by which they are inspired,
but for the élan with which they are performed.

ACKNOWLEDGMENT

I should like to thank Robert H. Lister
and Fred G. Benton, Jr.
for providing me with books from
their personal libraries
that proved invaluable in researching the historical data
for this work.

The past is but the beginning of a beginning,
and all that is and has been
is but the twilight of the dawn.

H.G. WELLS
The Discovery of the Future

Chapter One

May 1860

A PATCH OF WATER, REFLECTING BACK THE SUN-GILDED MAY sky, caught the image of horse and rider as they cantered by—the girl's red-gold hair streaming behind her, the mare's tail pluming with the same fire. A narrow ribbon of creek wound in front of them, silver-rippled water a barrier in their path. The girl gripped the mare's sides more tightly, bent forward over her neck, and urged her on with heels dug into the sleek sides.

And then she felt herself lifted as her mount left the earth, and for one moment in time, as the mare ran through air, the rider's whole body became light, buoyant, filled with a sense of union with the day, with the animal beneath her, with the world that bounded the life of Gabriele Cannon.

On the far side of the creek, she turned the horse in a tight circle and urged her to jump again. Then the soaring, the feeling of possessing and being possessed by all that surrounded her. The fields on either side of her, green with the new cane. Bayou Teche, some twenty yards behind her, snaking its way southward, waters bubbling with spring vigour.

Far across the field, another horse appeared, its rider sitting tall, a dark silhouette against the grey-green rows. In the rows, figures moved. Gabriele saw the bright flash of hoes, the spots of colour made by the women's tignons.

She could just hear the chant the slaves used to set the rhythm of their work: it floated toward her through the soft air, the heavy voices of the men forming the foundation for the women's higher ones. For an instant, Gabriele sat poised on Brandy's broad back. Then she slapped the mare's rump, pulled at the reins to turn her, and galloped hard toward the bayou, recrossing the creek in a fluid leap and not slacking the horse's pace until they reached the Teche's bank.

Then she slid off Brandy's back and let the reins lie slack. As the mare bent to eat the sweet grass growing thick along the bank, Gabriele walked down the path to the boat dock, then leant against a post gazing idly at the water, before lying flat on her stomach, chin resting on her crossed arms, staring at her reflection in the water below.

Tall reeds made a frame for her face, circling the bright hair, deepening the colour of her green eyes, rippling across her fair skin. A sudden eddy of bubbles broke the surface, catching the spring sunshine and making brief rainbows across the water, and Gabriele jumped to her feet, following the path of foam to a cluster of mud-rimmed holes at the water's edge. Slowing only to grab a pole with a net slung from it, she ran across the dock to the grassy bank, pausing to tuck her skirt and petticoat into her belt and roll her pantaloons well above her knees before she moved cautiously forward, wading into the bayou with net poised.

A tiny shadow flitted through the water—the net came under it, and Gabriele lifted the crayfish from the water, quickly dumping it into a bucket hanging from a nail on the piling behind her. In another ten minutes she had over a dozen crayfish scuttling over the bottom of the bucket: encouraged by her success, she waded further into the bayou, so intent on her task that the darker water ahead failed to warn her of its depth.

She took one step forward, net outstretched, when her feet slipped from beneath her and she toppled backward into the water, just managing to retrieve the net before it floated beyond her reach. Struggling to gain footing in the soft bottom, she finally stuck the pole firmly into the mud and used it to get purchase. Then, just as she rose from the water, clothes clinging to her body and red hair hanging in limp strands, she heard the quick short toot of a steamboat whistle and whirled to see a packet coming around the bend. The water, stirred by the boat's passage, swirled around her, and after one frozen moment, she pulled her pole from the mud and struck out for shore, water-laden skirts dragging behind her.

Clambering up the bank, she turned to watch the packet pass, expecting to see the familiar face of Captain Fournet, whose vessel steamed past Felicity's dock twice each week. But the man in the wheelhouse was not Captain Fournet. Tall, with blond hair gilded by the sun's beams, he appeared to be the age of her brother Tom, and his blue eyes, staring at Gabriele through the large windows of the wheelhouse, held the same expression Tom's would if he could see his sister's state.

Gabriele's hand went helplessly to her face, touching the mud drying on her cheeks and brushing back her wet hair. The other hand pulled her wet skirt away from her body, trying to stretch it down over bare legs and muddy feet. Then the packet had passed, disappearing around the large curve in Bayou Teche that formed the farthest point of the southern boundary of Felicity Plantation.

A last shrill toot from the packet whistle, and then silence, with only the birds calling from the trees along the bank disturbing the afternoon quiet. Gabriele stared at the empty bayou as though the packet and its captain still steamed before her, and then, with a quick shake of her head, she returned the net to its place on the dock, picked up the bucket of crayfish, and headed up the bank. Brandy's soft whinny greeted her as she reached the top, and with bucket swinging from her hand, she ran toward the chestnut mare.

"I'm in for it now, Brandy," Gabriele said. "You better run like the wind so my clothes and hair can dry."

She removed the pair of shoes with stockings shoved into them and the sunbonnet slung over the mare's neck and, sitting on a nearby log, drew the stockings up over her mud-spattered legs and put on the shoes. Shaking her wet hair away from her face, and running her fingers through it in an attempt to comb out the snarls, she put on the bonnet, tying the strings beneath her chin and then rising, ready to ride.

She vaulted up onto the mare's bare back, bucket over her arm. Then, digging her heels into Brandy's side, she urged her forward. The mare's walk became a trot, then a canter. She ran up the road that led from the bayou to the first pasture, moving easily over rain-softened earth. They ran beside the pasture, and Gabriele, with a sudden shout, yanked the reins hard right. The mare's course veered; the three-railed fence bounding the pasture loomed before them, and Gabriele braced herself for the jump.

In one quick gathering of strength, Brandy left the earth, the top rail of the fence two feet beneath her. The cane fields, even green rows sliced by the dark bodies hoeing weeds, appeared as a blur—only the overseer's face, eyes widening a little before his hand automatically lifted his hat, came to Gabriele sharply. Then Brandy hit the ground, and Gabriele felt the jolt up her spine, tingling her neck. The mare regained her smooth canter and ran on, leaving Mr. Adams' startled face behind them.

Tall grasses wet from an early afternoon shower brushed stains across Gabriele's petticoats and left hard green burrs clinging to their lace as they ran on. The vast grove of oaks sheltering the house loomed into view, but Gabriele turned Brandy away from them, and from the solid white house lying beyond them, shimmering in the spring sun like a mirage, only its six massive Ionic columns anchoring it to the earth.

Gabriele reined Brandy in as they approached the paddock fence, walking her up to the gate and unlatching it so that they could go through it, and then carefully pulling it shut behind her. A large black man looked up from the horse he curried at her approach, eyes going from Gabriele's stained skirts to her mud-pocked face. His steady gaze reminded her of that other gaze, the blue one that had surveyed her so coolly from the packet window, and she tossed her head a little, sliding off Brandy and letting the reins slip from her hands.

"I—fell into the bayou, Samson," Gabriele said. "Getting these." She nodded toward the bucket still hanging from her arm.

"Yo' Auntie been looking all over for you," he said. "Sent Lucie down here to find you."

"Oh, Samson, you didn't tell her where I'd gone?"

Samson bent down and drew his brush gently up the horse's leg, waiting until he had finished before speaking. "I told Lucie I didn't rightly know where you'd gotten to, Miss Gabriele. But that Lucie, she got sharp eyes. Wouldn't surprise me if she saw the lie in my face."

"I'm sorry, Samson. I don't want to get you into trouble with Aunt Mat." She poked the dirt with her toe, wishing she had not succumbed to May's lure, that she had walked Brandy around the paddock in perfect decorum instead of leaping on her back, taking the fences in two good bounds, and then tearing over the pasture to the bayou as though she were ten instead of eighteen, Samson's shouts to come back ringing in her ears.

"It's one thing to cover up for you and Mr. Tom, Miss Gabriele. But when you go off by yourself—" Samson shook his head. "Mr. Tom, he fuss, too, if he hear about it." He moved around the horse and began to groom the other side, rising to peer over the stallion's back at Gabriele. "You better go along now. Lucie said something about a dress being ready for you to try on—"

"My costume for the ring tourney!" Gabriele said. She looked down at her ruined skirts and dirty hands. "If Aunt Mat sees me like this, she'll never let me go—" She felt Brandy's mouth nuzzling her neck and turned, putting her arms around the mare's neck and leaning her head against her. "Oh, Brandy, you've got to promise me the next time I want to do something crazy—you'll have sense for both of us."

Samson came up and took Brandy's reins. "I'll give her a good brushing, Miss Gabriele. And cool her down 'fore I let her drink."

Gabriele took two lumps of sugar from a box nailed to the stable wall and handed them to Samson. "Give one to Jupiter," she said. "Poor thing, Tom never gives him any."

"Mister Tom ain't much for spoiling Jupiter," Samson said, but he took the sugar and put it in his shirt pocket, then picked up the brush and began drawing it through Brandy's chestnut coat, loosening the drying mud.

Gabriele gave Brandy a last pat and then let herself out of the paddock gate, hurrying across the pasture to the shelter of the oaks. Screened by their thick trunks and low-hanging branches, she made her way up to the lawn around the house, peering cautiously from behind a tree to determine her course. She saw a woman's figure standing on the small gallery that stretched between two protruding wings at the back of the house and ducked out of sight, moving quickly from tree to tree until she came level with the formal garden on the right side of the house. If she followed a diagonal path, she would be hidden from the house, and could come up behind a gazebo built at the garden's far end, and from there through the garden and up a side staircase that led from her father's library to the second floor of the house.

The discomfort of wet, clinging clothes and mud stiffening on her arms and legs was matched by an inner unease: she could not shake the image of three pairs of eyes, all widened in surprise and disapproval. The blue eyes of the stranger, looking at her as though she were something fished out of the bayou just for his inspection. And then Adams, trying to hide his astonishment at seeing his employer's daughter riding like a hoyden in front of him and a field full of slaves. Even Samson, who had been a patient accomplice on so many of the hunting and fishing expeditions she and her brother Tom had organized when their aunt thought they were playing safely under their nurse's eye.

So intent was she upon her own condition that she had come within a yard of the gazebo before she realized there were people inside, and dropped to the ground, kneeling behind a large azalea bush and straining her ears in an effort to determine the identities of the man and woman she could see dimly through the wisteria vines blooming profusely over the gazebo's sides.

At first, even at that near distance, she could not make out either the speakers' faces or their words. Then a woman's voice, low and clear. "You can't know—you can't imagine—oh, Tom, tell me you'll stop it!"

"You know I will," the man said. "To even think of you in that situation is more than I can bear—" He broke off, almost choking on the last word, and Gabriele could see him reach out to take the woman's arm.

Gabriele, crouched beneath the azalea bush, uncomfortably aware of a small insect crawling down her neck, prayed that her brother Tom would not discover her. She had no idea what he and Veronique were talking about— whatever it was, it must be dreadful for them to be closeted in the gazebo, ignoring the rules that governed Tom's behaviour toward young female slaves.

She could see the flash of Veronique's bright green dress through the vines, and make out Tom's tall, lean form, standing close to Veronique now, bending forward as though to protect her.

Something about the pose bothered Gabriele, and she drew back even further under the bush. She felt as though she saw her brother and Veronique with different eyes: how could she see something—wrong—about the way they stood? Tom had always been Veronique's protector, just as he had taken care of Gabriele. He had made no distinction between the little octaroon girl and his own sister during the years of their growing up—wasn't it natural that she should come to him still?

Gabriele shook her head, trying to rid herself of the thoughts that plagued her. She looked at the couple in the gazebo again, and felt exactly as she had felt when she looked up to see strange blue eyes on her—Adams' familiar face, struggling with disapproval; Samson, barely able to hide his dismay. We are neither one of us doing very well with the rules today, she thought. And then, without warning, she sneezed. Once, twice, and yet another, loud, sudden noises that made Tom start as he looked around and demanded, "Who's there?"

"It's Gabriele," Gabriele said, emerging from the azalea bush and standing clear on the other side of the latticework from Tom.

"Gabriele! What the devil are you doing there, skulking about?"

"I'm not skulking, Tom. I wanted to—to get upstairs without Aunt Mat seeing me—"

Tom pressed his face close to the latticework and stared at her, eyes going from her drying hair to her ruined clothes. "I guess you did! What have you been up to, Gabriele? You look like a ragamuffin, sure enough."

"I—fell into the bayou," Gabriele said. She looked at Tom, eyes seeking permission to come into what seemed to be their private meeting. He frowned, then nodded, and went to sit on the bench built into the gazebo wall. Keeping to the side of the gazebo facing away from the house, Gabriele worked her way to the door and darted inside.

"Here," Veronique said, removing the light shawl draped around her shoulders and arranging it so that it covered much of Gabriele's dress. "This hides the worst of the damage. And your hair's almost dry—I think you can get safely upstairs."

"I couldn't help overhearing," Gabriele said, covering Veronique's hand with hers. "Veronique—are you in trouble?"

Veronique's eyes went to Tom's face, but she said nothing.

"Tom—what is it? Let me help!"

His lips, drawn into a tight line, pulled all the gentleness from his face, and his grey eyes, when he turned to his sister, looked dark and cold. "How much did you hear?" he said.

"Why, not much—Veronique asking you to stop something—" A possible answer formed in her mind, and she said, hardly able to get the words out for the terror that welled up in her throat, "You're not going to be sold!"

"Sold!" Veronique's ivory skin went even paler, and she sank onto the bench next to Tom.

"Whatever gave you that idea?" Tom demanded.

"Please—nothing—I only thought—"

"Then for God's sake, don't," Tom said. His anger spilled out over them, its hot edges sending out little fingers of fire that shrivelled Gabriele's skin. He saw her distress and gradually got hold of himself. "Sorry, Gabe." The use of the pet name calmed him further, and he reached out and took her hand. "It really would do no good for you to know what the problem is. Believe me, it wouldn't."

"I only wanted to help," Gabriele said.

Tom put his finger over her lips. "The best way you can help is to say nothing. And to go upstairs and get yourself in order before Aunt Mat sees you and we have a real ruckus."

"She's looking for me," Gabriele said, darting a glance at the house. "She wants me to try on my dress for the ring tourney."

"Then she must be looking for me, too!" Veronique said. "What will I tell her when she asks me where I've been?" The thin veneer of control she had assumed when Gabriele entered the gazebo broke, and she put her face into her hands, swaying slightly from side to side while from her lips came a low, steady moan.

"I'll tell her you were with me," Gabriele said. "I'll say I insisted you go with me to dig those wild lilies I want to put in the garden, and that I fell into a creek on the way—"

Tom and Veronique looked at each other, and Gabriele, catching the quick intensity that leapt between them, felt shut out. But when Tom spoke, his face had eased, and his grey eyes held the affection Gabriele always expected to see there. "Thanks, Gabe. That should do very nicely." He stepped to the gazebo door. "Looks safe. Go quickly, now."

"Yes," Gabriele said. The house, her cool, safe room— she could hardly wait to be inside it. She moved toward the door, glancing back to see that Tom had returned to Veronique. Inches of space separated them, but as Gabriele looked at them, she thought of the two faces of a coin—each looking out from a different perspective, and yet bound together by a solid core.

Tom: tall, lean, a shock of fine black hair combed low over his high forehead. Grey eyes burning like lamps in his thin face, mouth that moved from tenderness to laughter —a rush of love for her brother swept over her. Those bony shoulders had borne many a childish grief, and those lips had set seal over many a childish secret. No matter what he asks me, I shall do it, Gabriele thought.

And Veronique, ivory skin with its faint cast of gold, deep-set golden eyes unmasked now, shining with an emotion Gabriele did not want to read. Veronique did not wear the tignons that the other female slaves wore: her dark hair, dressed in a simple coil low on her neck, had a fine texture, and the light playing over it brought out its soft sheen. Slight of frame, Veronique stood not much taller than Tom's chin, but she moved with a grace that made her seem taller, and even the plain cut of her cotton dress could not conceal her delicately moulded body.

Gabriele let out her breath in a long sigh—the small sound rippled against their stillness, and Tom and Veronique turned to look at her as though surprised to find her still there.

"We must go," Gabriele said.

"Yes," said Veronique.

Together they left the gazebo, hurrying down the walk toward the house.

"You take the little stairs," Veronique said as she opened the small door set next to the big chimney that rose up through the three floors of the house. "I'll go up the back ones and see if I can divert Mrs. LeGrange."

"I promise you, Veronique. When I wear that splendid costume you're making me for the ring tourney—I shall behave like the most proper lady there ever was," Gabriele said, following Veronique through the door.

Veronique gave Gabriele a quick smile, then vanished through the door that led to the hall. Gabriele stood blinking her eyes as the dimness of her father's library closed around her. The staircase Veronique had referred to occupied one corner of the room; steep and narrow, it spiralled tightly upward, giving Oliver Cannon access to and from his library without having to use the main halls of the house.

"I wish you weren't at that convention way off in Charleston, Papa," she whispered. "Something's wrong, and we need you here to fix it." She mounted the stairs slowly, climbing past shelf after shelf of books, random titles bringing her father so strongly to her mind that she almost expected to hear him speak.

I wonder, she thought—I wonder, if Papa were here, would Veronique have gone to him? Somehow, she did not think so. Veronique seemed to avoid Oliver Cannon: her duties did not take her near him, and the only times it was necessary for him to see her was on the occasions all of the house hands gathered. And sometimes, not even then. Since Veronique's talent for dressmaking became known beyond Felicity's gates, other families hired her, and she disappeared for weeks at a time, returning briefly to sew for Aunt Mat and Gabriele before being sent somewhere else.

If it were not that Papa makes money on her work, I

would almost think he sends her away on purpose, Gabriele thought, opening the door at the top of the stairs a crack to survey the hall. She knew her father thought he had made a mistake allowing Veronique to grow up with his daughter and son. She had heard him say so to Aunt Mat, just a few weeks ago, before he went away.

"A case of heart winning out over head, Mat," Oliver Cannon had said. "But when she came here with you—she was so tiny, so frail—"

His words had reminded Gabriele of Veronique as she was then, a small, golden girl with big, solemn eyes who was finally cheered by Tom's constant good humour and patience and Gabriele's mischievous games.

"It's my mistake, too, Oliver," Aunt Mat had said. "I could have insisted she live out in the Quarters instead of with Abigail closer to the house—"

"Well, what's done is done," Gabriele had heard her father say. She had huddled against the door, knowing she should not listen, but unable to tear herself away. "She has talent, and presents herself well—I suppose the fact that her education is better than that of some of the ladies she sews for doesn't give her too much difficulty—"

Aunt Mat's knitting needles clicked, sharp, staccato sounds making her even-voiced words sound angry. "Now you did that, Oliver, all by yourself. I won't take any blame for it. No, nor for the way you stuffed Gabriele's head with all that Greek and Latin—or the way you reared her as though she were another son."

"I've made no mistake there, Mat," Oliver Cannon said. "She's as lovely a young girl as any father could wish for— and thank God, she's sturdy enough so the first illness won't carry her away—"

He had said no more, but Gabriele knew what he would do next. He would rise from his chair and go stand before the portrait of her mother that hung over the front parlour mantelpiece, staring at her as though the very power of his sorrow could bring her back to him. Her death when Gabriele was barely three had changed the course of

Oliver Cannon's only daughter's life: she would not be brought up like a hothouse flower, he vowed, but would ride and hunt and fish alongside her brother until she had the strength to resist the ills her mother could not.

Well, and in such an irregular household, where I studied along with Tom, it did not seem at all strange for Veronique to learn with us, too, thought Gabriele—she saw Veronique appear at the top of the back stairs and go knock softly on Aunt Mat's door, then vanish inside. Taking advantage of the opportunity presented her, Gabriele flew down the hall, darting into her own room and leaning against the closed door with her breath coming fast.

She heard footsteps, and voices, and hurried into her dressing alcove, sliding the curtain that fronted it along its smooth rod. Her door opened and she heard her aunt's voice. "Gabriele, are you here?"

Gabriele thrust her head out through the curtains. "I'm just changing, Aunt Mat—I fell into the creek—"

For a long moment, Aunt Mat's grey eyes held Gabriele's green ones in a steady gaze. "So Veronique said," she said at last. With a half-frown, Aunt Mat pulled her watch forward and snapped it open. "Hurry up, then. I want to see how your dress looks, and I've got a dozen things to do."

"Yes, Aunt Mat," Gabriele said. "I'll be right there."

"See that you are," Aunt Mat said as she closed the door and went down the hall.

Gabriele pulled off her stained clothes and began to wash her face and arms, puzzled by the way Aunt Mat had behaved. She didn't fuss at all, she thought. Could she possibly have believed Veronique? A slow blush rose from her throat to her cheeks. Of course Aunt Mat had believed Veronique. Her own code would never allow her to use a slave to avoid trouble for herself—she would not think that her niece could do it.

It is because I don't like to think that Veronique is a slave, she told her reflection. I treat her as I would a friend, someone in league with me against the foolish rules that keep getting in our way.

Now she did hear her father speak, heard him with such force that she actually pulled the curtains back, knowing they would reveal an empty room, but still feeling him there.

"And that is what you must not do, Gabriele," he had told her. "You cannot treat Veronique as a friend. You may treat her kindly—you must treat her kindly—but to pretend that she is your equal, to pretend that her life has anything in common with yours—this is not friendship, Gabriele, but self-deception of the worst kind."

"She could be my friend if she were free!" Gabriele had said.

"Free? What nonsense is this?"

"Why is it nonsense, Papa? She has a skill that earns money—it goes to you now, but if she were free, she could keep it—I'm sure she would do very well!"

"Whose idea is this, Gabriele?" her father had said, eyes suddenly sharp.

"Why—no one's. I only just thought of it—but it's a good one, Papa! She could go to New Orleans—they always need good modistes there—and we know so many people. We could tell them about her—" Even now, she could remember how exhilarated she had felt. Of course, how easy! She had taken her father's hands, sure of his answer. "Oh, Papa, how happy she will be!"

"Gabriele. You must never even mention this idea to Veronique, do you understand?"

She would not let the finality she heard in his voice end her hopes, and she begged and pleaded until her father, as near to real anger as he had ever been with her, said, "Gabriele, you must not say another word. Not today, not ever. What you propose is completely out of the question for many reasons, none of which I am disposed to go into with you."

Standing in her dressing alcove in fresh pantaloons and petticoat, Gabriele felt the same shiver that had shaken her when she saw her father's eyes. Not cold and angry, but disturbed—unhappy—she had not been able to bear that she had made him feel that way, and she had gone into his arms, sobbing, until he had said, in a voice much more like his own, "My dear child. Your concern for Veronique does you credit, but it really must not go any further than being as kind a mistress to her as you possibly can be. As for the rest—I will not make you any promises. But I will at least . . . consider Veronique's lot."

And then he had gone to Charleston where the Democrats were meeting to decide who they would run for president, and Veronique had gone off to the Flemings on the other side of St. Martinville to sew, and had not returned until two days ago, shutting herself up at once in the sewing room to work on Gabriele's dress.

The thought of the splendid green- and pink-striped dress she would wear to the ring tourney in New Iberia in a week's time finally drove every other thought from Gabriele's head, and hastily completing her toilette, she left her room, almost running down the hall to the sewing room door.

She paused on the threshold, concealed by the half-closed door. She could see Veronique, seated in a low chair with a mass of pink- and green-striped silk spilling over her lap. Aunt Mat stood with her back to the door, arms folded across her chest, back straight.

"I'm not saying I believe Mrs. Fleming," Aunt Mat said. "Still—the charge she makes in this note is quite serious, Veronique."

"If there were any truth in it, you would not have heard a word about it," Veronique said. She stood up, holding the silk against her like a flag. "I don't even look at the male members of the households where I sew, Mrs. LeGrange. And if they look at me—well, there's not very much I can do about that."

"Don't be insolent!" Aunt Mat said. She tapped a folded note against her palm, and Gabriele stared at it, wondering what awful thing it contained.

It must have to do with that horrid Michael Fleming, she thought. He's teased Veronique and she would have none of it—good for her, but oh, how awful that she couldn't just slap his face!

"I have certainly never seen you behave with anything but perfect decorum, Veronique," Aunt Mat said. Her voice had softened, sounding as though she wanted to apologize—but whether for thinking for even an instant that Veronique might have done something to bring Michael Fleming's unwelcome attentions on her or whether for the unhappy circumstances that made such an affront possible Gabriele could not guess. She stirred restlessly, and her hand rattled the door-knob.

"Gabriele?" Aunt Mat said, turning.

"Coming," Gabriele said, and making sure her face reflected nothing of what she had just heard, she darted into the room, took the half-finished dress from Veronique's hands, and lifted it against herself with a cry of delight.

"It's just as I imagined it," she said. "Oh, Veronique, it's going to be splendid!"

"I'm not sure about the way the neckline falls," Veronique said. "If you'll just try it on—"

"Of course," Gabriele said. She stood while Veronique unfastened her dress and drew it over her head, feeling the cool touch of Veronique's light fingers. They moved quickly, impersonally, as though Gabriele were a mannequin, and when the costume settled around Gabriele's waist, Veronique picked up a pincushion and, sticking a few pins in her mouth, began to pin up the bodice.

"It's much too low!" Aunt Mat said. "Heavens, Veronique, she's hardly covered!"

"I know," Veronique said. "But if I move this drape here —and take another tuck here—" Her fingers touched Gabriele's breasts, drawing the silk up higher. Gabriele looked in the mirror, seeing the expanse of white skin rising above the curving neck, feeling a quick, hot flush flood her cheeks.

Veronique stood at her side, and the long mirror framed

them. Gabriele, a little taller, her figure a little fuller, though with a waist as slender as Veronique's. Creamy skin against red-gold hair, ivory against black—she doesn't even look Negro, Gabriele thought. If she wore a dress like mine to the ring tourney, no one would ever even know.

Her eyes sought Veronique's, searching for the old affection. She knew better than to say—"Oh, I wish you were going, too!" She had not made such a gaffe for years, not since the time she first said it, as she and Tom got ready to go to a picnic on a long-ago summer day, and Veronique had to stay behind. I see you as you are, she thought, willing Veronique to read her mind. To me you are a person, not a slave. A flicker of acknowledgement in Veronique's eyes—then a sudden glint of anger, quickly suppressed, before she spoke to Aunt Mat.

"Is that all right, do you think, Mrs. LeGrange?"

"Yes—I think so," Aunt Mat said. "Look here, child— yes, that's much better." She took out her watch again. "I've got a dozen things to do, Gabriele. Now that the neckline's right, I'll leave the rest of the fitting to you, Veronique."

"Yes, Mrs. LeGrange."

"And the bonnet? You've got that underway as well?"

"The idea of it," Veronique said. She picked up a bonnet form and held a bunch of tiny pink roses under the brim. "I thought roses here—the bonnet itself of the silk—with a pale green veil."

"Very fetching," Aunt Mat said. "Well, Gabriele, you can stop worrying yourself sick over this ring tourney. With this costume to wear, you will certainly have at least one young gentleman asking to ride for you."

"If only it isn't Harold LeBoeuf!" Gabriele said, and for the first time since she had entered the room, saw Veronique smile.

"If Harold LeBoeuf asks to ride for you before anyone else does, you will of course say yes," Aunt Mat said. "This whole ring tourney is creating a great deal of commotion, and I won't say I won't be glad when it's over."

"I shan't," Gabriele said. "I can't wait for it to happen—but I know that once it starts, I'm going to want each minute to take at least two hours, so it can go on and on and on—"

"We can't stop time," Aunt Mat said. "Which means I had better go meet with Letha. Finish up here and then do your practising, Gabriele. And be sure to work on that new music your father sent, or you'll never have it mastered before he gets back."

Gabriele looked at Veronique, ready to exchange a glance that meant—have you ever in your life seen anyone with so much energy? But Veronique, bonnet form on the table beside her, was bent over the silk, carefully cutting pieces to match the shape of the brim.

"Yes, Aunt Mat," she said.

The door closed behind Aunt Mat, and Gabriele stood watching Veronique. The thin hiss of the silk as the scissors cut through it, the light click of metal on wood, were the only sounds. Gabriele looked from Veronique to her reflection in the mirror. How calm I look, how composed! And yet inside, this unease, this feeling of having forgotten something, or left something behind . . .

"Veronique."

Veronique looked up at her, the light at her back making her eyes dark and still.

"I couldn't help overhearing what Aunt Mat was saying about Mrs. Fleming—" Veronique's expression made Gabriele blush again, and she spoke faster, feeling the cut edges of the silk prickle against her skin. "I seem to be—listening to a lot of private conversations today—I don't mean to—if they weren't about you I wouldn't—but, Veronique—did that horrid Michael Fleming—say something to you?"

"He told his mother I said something to him," Veronique said. She bent her head so that Gabriele could not see her face, but her tone had already told Gabriele all she needed to know.

"How could he lie like that! It's too dreadful, Veronique —you must never go there again!"

"Unless I am sent," Veronique said. Gabriele heard the faint emphasis on the last word and went to Veronique, taking her chin in her hand and making Veronique look at her.

"You won't be. I promise." Then—"Is that what you and Tom were talking about?"

Veronique's eyelids closed, making her face a sculpted mask. "No."

"So there is more trouble—oh, Veronique, what's happened to us?" She sank onto a low stool near Veronique's chair, staring at the face which now seemed so distant, so strange. "Everything seems so—so all to pieces. Tom would never behave as Michael Fleming behaved to you— he is supposed to be a gentleman! How could he do it?"

"If you had not been listening, you would not even know it had occurred," Veronique said. She touched Gabriele's cheek, then stroked it gently. "It is over and done with—you mustn't think about it any more."

"How can I not think about it, when you are so unhappy?" Gabriele said. She rose and took off the costume, handing it to Veronique. "I am not so foolish that all I think of is ring tourneys and pretty new clothes—"

"Of course you're not," Veronique said. She put the costume aside and helped Gabriele into her dress. "But there is really nothing you can do about any of my—troubles—so why should you have to think about them?"

"You don't mind Tom thinking about them. Veronique, you trust him. Can't you trust me, too?"

Veronique looked at her, the smallest flicker at the back of her eyes acknowledging their old bond. And then again that glint of anger, quickly suppressed. "I—went to Tom because in Mr. Cannon's absence he is the master of this place," Veronique said. "You have no power that I know of —of what use is it to come to you?"

Veronique's word ate at the edges of Gabriele's pride,

crumbling her until she stood quite small. "None, of course. None at all."

She brushed at her eyes, but not quickly enough to hide her tears.

"I'm sorry," Veronique said. "My temper gets the best of me. And I forget you have always been—my friend."

"And I shall continue to be!" Gabriele said. "I know I have no real power here, Veronique. But there are more ways of doing things than by simply ordering them done. And I am not inexperienced in using those."

"Yes, of course," Veronique said. "Well, then, I am very fortunate to have—a friend at court."

She speaks to me as Aunt Mat does, Gabriele thought as she left the room. As though I am a child who does not understand anything—who makes up fairy tales with which she hopes to conquer the very real dragons in this world. She went down the stairs briskly, her thoughts energizing her walk. I will not be a child. I will not be sent back to the nursery every time something unpleasant occurs—and I will speak with Papa again about setting Veronique free, just as soon as he gets back.

She went into the parlour and searched through her music for the new Louis Gottschalk composition her father had sent from New Orleans on his way to Charleston, studying the opening chords before settling down to play. Papa must understand what is happening here—Veronique's unhappiness will spread to all of us, just as it has already spread to Tom. He has always been able to carry his own sorrows—it is those of others that are so hard for him to bear.

But how bravely he has always done it, she thought, remembering the many times when her brother's compassion had made a grief or disappointment of her own seem lighter, less durable, because of his constant willingness to call part of it his share.

And not just my grief, my disappointment—she saw him as she had seen him an hour earlier, standing close to Veronique. Felt again that discomfort, the dark thread through the afternoon. Because we are older now—no longer in the no-man's land of childhood, where rules could be suspended and games freely played. Nor are we yet adults, able to choose our own paths—

Another image—her white throat, rising from exposed breasts quickly covered with shimmering silk. And then another—one never seen, only imagined, quickly thrust away—slave girls crouching half-naked on a block, the auctioneer's gavel slamming down the last time. She felt again the hard blue gaze of the stranger on the boat, Adams' astonished look. Slowly, she began to play, concentrating on the cool, liquid music, letting it solace the heat in her soul.

Then the music, the quiet expanse of the room around her, made her feel peaceful again—closed away from ugliness and disorder in this serene glass cage. No one would dare break through it, no one would dare do her harm. Beyond it, girls like Veronique stood defenceless, looking in at her in her safe, smooth world. Her fingers paused on the keys, and she stood, pulling the piano lid shut. All those rules—rules Aunt Mat lived by, rules Gabriele had never understood—like rods, reinforcing her cage—keeping danger out. Some other knowledge hovered at the edge of her mind—she groped for it—and then the clatter of horses' hooves on the drive pushed it away.

She went to one of the long windows that gave onto the gallery running across the front of the house and peered out. Two riders trotted up the drive: two young men, one blond, the other dark-haired, both tall and long-legged, with well-set shoulders that spoke of health and vigour, and quick, lively expressions that testified to confident enthusiasm in the world and their place in it. She leaned forward—there seemed some other similarity, a more subtle one—the cast of a chin, the lift of a hand, the way a mouth curved—these men were, if not brothers, close kin; shadow images of each other, one dark, the other fair, both intent now on the house they approached.

Just then Tom burst into Gabriele's view, racing

through the front door to stand on the top step of the short flight leading up to the gallery, both hands out-stretched. He shouted a name, a name Gabriele did not stay to hear. Because although she was certain she had never seen the dark-haired man before, the blue eyes of the blond man were all too familiar. With hands pressed against her cheeks, she ran from the parlour and up the stairs. She had almost reached the landing where the arms of the staircase met when Tom's voice stopped her.

"Gabriele! Gabriele, look who's here! Alex St. Cyr, my old friend from college, come all the way from New Orleans to see how we live in the country. And he's brought his cousin with him—"

Reluctantly, she turned and looked down at the three men standing at the foot of the stairs. Tom had his arm flung around the shoulder of the dark-haired man whose deep-set brown eyes dominated his face—then that was Alex St. Cyr. Slowly, with one hand poised lightly on the banister, she descended the stairs, trying to ignore the first flash of recognition she saw in the blond man's face. His eyes opened wide—that same surprised look—the same quick appraisal—and then the walls of the cage settled around her. She could see him adjust his thinking, could see manners control his eyes.

A blur of introductions—Alex St. Cyr, bending over her hand, murmuring something she did not even hear. And then the other one, Alex's cousin Jordan Scott, taking her hand and shaking it in the American fashion, only the tiniest light of surprise at the back of his cool blue gaze.

"Just think," Tom said. "Their packet docked in New Iberia not two hours ago, and they rode straight here!" He turned to Alex. "But you should have brought your luggage, as though we'd hear of you staying in the hotel! I'll send for it right away—"

"If you're sure we're not imposing," Alex said. He clapped his cousin on the back. "Now you'll see how the plantation system works, Jordan. Felicity's as good an ex-ample as any you could find."

"Are you an economist, then?" Tom asked.

"I'm in the shipping business," Jordan Scott said. "Like the rest of my family. But as a New Englander, I'm naturally interested in observing everything that I can."

"Well, you'll find no Simon Legrees here, Scott," Tom said.

"I wouldn't expect to," Jordan said. He smiled, and Tom relaxed.

"Sorry. I shouldn't assume your opinions until I've given you a chance to express them—"

"Which he will do at length, but not, I hope, in my presence," Alex said. "Come, Jordan, we'll make Miss Cannon think her new houseguests a dreadfully dull lot."

He moved restlessly, slapping his riding crop against the top of his polished boot. He seemed to charge the hall with energy, every tiny movement seeming to vibrate through the room until the surfaces of vases and prisms vibrated, too. Gabriele looked from Alex St. Cyr to Jordan Scott. He stood quietly, the small trace of perspiration across his brow making his fair skin glow. Solid, almost rooted, as though once he settled into a place it would take a great deal to move him from it.

Gabriele shivered, as though whatever it was that vibrated from Alex could move through her, too. Some power here, something between them—"I'll go tell Aunt Mat," she said. "And see that the rooms in the *garçonnière* are made up for you." She turned away and went back up the stairs, feeling that they must all be watching her. But it did not matter: she had found her way back inside her safe glass cage, and from behind its clear shield she could watch them, too.

Chapter Two

THE MOVE OF THE BAGGAGE FROM THE HOTEL IN NEW IBERIA TO the *garçonnière* at Felicity was quickly effected, and Aunt Mat enlisted Gabriele's aid to put the finishing touches on the rooms prepared for their guests.

"Of course Alex St. Cyr is accustomed to comfort," Aunt Mat said, critically eyeing a vase of roses she had just set on a table in the *garçonnière*'s lower room and shifting it an inch to the right. "And if he follows in his father's footsteps, he likes luxury and beauty as well."

"Oh, do you know Mr. St. Cyr's family?" Gabriele said. She was glad of the small tasks that kept her hands busy: she felt as though Alex St. Cyr's restlessness had conveyed itself to her as a permanent condition, and she felt sure that Aunt Mat had already concluded that her niece's agitation could be traced directly to the presence of their two guests.

"I've known Hector St. Cyr since I was a girl," Aunt Mat said. "He was quite the bon viveur—and I don't think he's changed a great deal since he married." She laughed suddenly, a bright, young-sounding laugh that changed her face, making it for the moment less plain. "Hector was forever getting into scrapes, and although his charm usually made the ladies forgive him, I think his behaviour finally wore a little thin with the men." She read Gabriele's face and added, "Oh, nothing really wrong or serious. But foolish things that made more . . . solemn gentlemen less ready to trust Hector's—sense of purpose."

"This is Mr. St. Cyr's father—"

"Yes—his mother is a Yankee, strangely enough. How surprised we all were when Julia Scott accepted him! So strait-laced herself—it seemed an improbable match."

"And a Yankee, you said."

"Julia was born in New Orleans—but her father came from Boston. Established himself in New Orleans right after the Purchase in 1803—he came from a family that has had shipping interests in the East for decades—I imagine Jordan Scott is a nephew from that branch of the family."

"So you know Mrs. St. Cyr?"

"I've met her," Aunt Mat said. "A pretty enough lady, but quite cold, to my way of thinking. And very different. Takes an interest in the shipping business, I'm told, and spends part of every day down at the office."

"That does seem a strange choice for a bon viveur, doesn't it, Aunt Mat?" Gabriele said. She kept her eyes on the tray of cheese and biscuits and wine she had just placed on a lowboy, hoping her aunt's pleasure in discussing such an interesting topic would keep her from remembering that such information was not always granted to a young girl's ears.

"Oh, well," Aunt Mat said, her voice soft with gentle indulgence. "Hector has always known how to make his own happiness—and of course, it's pretty plain what each saw in the other. Hector's family arrived in New Orleans soon after Bienville founded it—the St. Cyrs are part of everything that goes on, and of course that would be quite attractive to a new arrival. And while one doesn't comment on these things, there is no question that the St. Cyrs' house in town was badly in need of repair and renovation when Hector and Julia married. I've not seen their plantation, it's north of St. Francisville and they use it only as a country place to get out of New Orleans in the fever season, and for Hector's hunting parties, but if the New

Orleans house is any example, Olympia must be a show-place, too."

Aunt Mat stopped short, pulling her watch forward and snapping it open with the familiar gesture. "Here I am running on and there are still a dozen details to be seen to before dinner. Come along, Gabriele, Samson will be back with their baggage, and you mustn't be here when our guests settle in."

Gabriele walked the short distance that separated the *garçonnière* from the main house in silence, mulling over the information she had just heard. Now that she knew a little about Alex St. Cyr's family, she could picture his tall, slim form dancing a fast polka or leading a partner in a graceful waltz. She could imagine his dark eyes flirting with young ladies, his lips making pretty speeches under-lined by that lazy smile. And how well the trappings of New Orleans' Carnival season would suit him, the masks that made all the men mysterious, and the fantastic cos-tumes that let them assume identities not their own.

"Papa has friends in the New Orleans Carnival Krewes, doesn't he, Aunt Mat?" Gabriele said.

"Why, yes—but what made you think of such a thing?" Aunt Mat glanced at her niece, and then back at the *gar-çonnière*. "Of course—our guests from New Orleans. They are attractive young gentlemen, Gabriele, and of course Mr. St. Cyr is Tom's very good friend. But there will be many young gentlemen in New Orleans this winter when you have your season—and some of them from families to whom we are particularly close."

As we are not to the St. Cyrs. The words seemed to hang in the air between them, and Gabriele said no more. The other piece of knowledge, the one she had almost grasped before Alex St. Cyr and Jordan Scott's arrival drove it from her mind, fell into place. The safe glass cage that protected her here at Felicity would extend to New Orleans, separating her from that city's cruder aspects with its shining shield. But now she realized that there would be another effect. Not only were undesirable people and things kept away from her by her world's iron-lace walls—but she was kept most effectively in.

Alex led the talk at dinner, at first telling stories about people he and Tom had known at the University of Virginia, but then asking questions about Felicity and their life there with such evident interest that Tom soon took over.

"Don't think we have no sophisticated entertainments," Tom said. "There's going to be a ring tourney in New Iberia next week, and I'll warrant you'll see riding there such as even the ones in New Orleans can't match."

"A ring tourney? Really?" Alex said. He turned to Gabriele, seated across from him. "And will you be one of the fair ladies from whom a knight may ask a favour, Miss Cannon?"

"She's been looking forward to it for weeks," Tom said. "Now, don't deny it, Gabriele. I've seen you jousting with the ring I set up—as though you'd rather be a knight, after all!"

"Miss Cannon would be wasting herself if she is anything other than the fairest lady there," Alex said. He bowed slightly, keeping his eyes on Gabriele's face until she bowed in return. "The horses we hired from the stable are all very well to get about on, Tom, but hardly fit to enter a tourney. Can you find us better ones?"

"You can have any horse in Felicity's stable except my own Jupiter," Tom said. "And Brandy, of course, unless Gabriele offers her."

"I should prefer to think my victory came from my own skill and not because my lady's horse knew more than I did," Alex said. His eyes laughed at Gabriele, and she looked away. How could Tom have blurted out that he'd seen her jousting! It is because I don't act like a lady, she thought. Every time Tom looks around I'm doing something disreputable—she sat straighter in her chair and sipped her wine, fixing her attention on what Alex was saying to her aunt.

"Now—we'll need costumes. Mrs. LeGrange, surely you have an old trunk somewhere filled with all kinds of trappings that we can turn into knights' garments. I have grown up believing that such a trunk is indispensable to a well-run house in the country—please, don't disappoint me."

"You are your father's image, Mr. St. Cyr," Aunt Mat said. "Hector was always way ahead of everyone else when it came to frivolity and games—"

The merest shadow darkened Alex's eyes, and then he laughed, raising his wine glass in a mocking toast. "Then I must thank him. Had he not taught me so well, I might spend my days in some useful and tedious occupation. As it is—I shall devote myself to earning the right to crown the tourney's Queen of Beauty."

"That's rather hard of you, St. Cyr," Tom said. "Come into a fellow's territory and try to take all the glory." He turned to Jordan Scott. "With two of you to contend with, I'm going to have to be on my mettle to even show."

"Thank you, but I have no intention of riding," Jordan said.

His voice, coming after a long period during which he had said nothing at all, startled them, and Alex, after turning to stare at his cousin, said lightly, "Oh, come now, Jordan, don't make us beg. Of course you'll ride."

"No, I will not," Jordan said.

A look passed between the two cousins that Gabriele, sitting across from them, caught before they suppressed it. She could not read it exactly—not anger, nor yet hostility —a kind of challenge?

Alex looked away first, laughing and saying in a voice that reminded Gabriele of the way his eyes had looked the moment before, "All right, then, don't ride. But I shall." He lifted his wine glass again and looked around the table. "I should like to propose a toast to your sister, Tom," he said. He waited for Jordan and Tom and Aunt Mat to raise their glasses, then said, his eyes fixed on Gabriele, "To

Miss Gabriele Cannon, who shall reign as Queen of Beauty at the ring tourney, and who reigns as Queen of Felicity now."

Light from the chandelier overhead shimmered against the glasses, turning each segment of the deep-cut designs into rainbows. Beams of light bouncing off glass—Gabriele felt her heart catch, as though something more solid than light had struck her. She groped for something to say, but Alex saved her. Turning to Aunt Mat, he bowed. "And to Mrs. LeGrange, whose hospitality so well fulfils the promise of this house."

"I'm glad you are pleased, Mr. St. Cyr," Aunt Mat said. "It's been a long time since I spent any significant time in New Orleans, but I hope we have not quite forgotten civilized ways."

Alex glanced around the room and shook his head. "Mrs. LeGrange, there are few houses in New Orleans or indeed anywhere in Louisiana that can match Felicity for beauty and style. Tom took us about before dinner, and I constantly upbraided him for allowing me to think, when we were at the University together, that he hailed from some simple farm."

"Oh, *Tom* will never be accused of exaggerating," Aunt Mat said.

The weight she put on that name pulled some of the light from Alex's face: a pause, and then he said, "I should say he will not. He has admitted that you, Miss Cannon, can 'play the piano a little.' Given Tom's propensity for making things less than they really are, I look forward to hearing a virtuoso performance."

Aunt Mat looks exactly as someone looks when she has set her cap for a gentleman and been rejected, Gabriele thought. But why is she so cross with Mr. St. Cyr? He is Tom's good friend—and she knows his family—

"Well, Miss Cannon? Will you play?" Alex said.

"You won't hear a virtuoso performance," Gabriele answered. "But I shall be happy to play if it will give all of you pleasure."

"Splendid!" Alex said. "I am much more soothed by music than by sober discourse—though Jordan tells me that Boston ladies often spend their evenings in just such a serious pursuit."

"Good conversation is to be treasured, Mr. St. Cyr," Aunt Mat said, "since it is not always easy to come by." She gave the signal to rise, and Jordan went to hold her chair. Alex came around the table to Gabriele, bending near her as he helped her rise. "I shall turn the pages for you, Miss Cannon. I do not play an instrument myself, but I made certain to learn to read music well enough so that I might assist those fair ladies who do."

"And those who are not so fair, Mr. St. Cyr?" Aunt Mat said.

"Ah, Mrs. LeGrange, those ladies usually play so well that they demand someone far more knowledgeable than I," Alex said.

"You're incorrigible, St. Cyr," Tom said. "For a stuffy old fellow like me, it's one of your greatest charms."

" 'Stuffy old fellow,' " Alex repeated. "I should rather have said—good, sensible chap." He clasped Tom's shoulder, and when he spoke, Gabriele heard a true emotion in his voice. "The best friend I've ever had—what good fortune I found you!"

"We're a good pair, all right," Tom said. "It's great having you here, St. Cyr." He turned, suddenly aware of his other guest. "And you, too, Scott. I'm looking forward to getting to know you better—and as it happens, you couldn't have come at a better time. We're neither planting nor harvesting—I've a bit more free time than I normally would. Though with Father away in Charleston, I keep occupied."

"You're most kind," Jordan said. "But we are down here for business reasons, Mr. Cannon. And while I don't want to appear ungracious—most of my time, I'm afraid, will be spent in work."

"But not tonight," Alex said. "Come, Jordan, we've

been promised a concert. You like music, you know that you do."

"Very much," Jordan said. He glanced at Gabriele, and she felt a flash of sympathy. His cousin can be overwhelming, she thought. Just look at how he has arranged this evening to suit his wishes—

But when they adjourned to the front parlour and Gabriele settled herself to play, Alex made himself so agreeable, singing while she played until the others joined in, that she found Jordan Scott's silence almost an affront, and at first remained very conscious of him, sitting off in a chair by himself, seemingly ignoring them all.

Then the pure joy of playing, of having a man as attractive as Alex St. Cyr, no matter how frivolous and lightly-meant his attentions, sit beside her, glancing at her as he turned each page, made her forget Jordan Scott, forget everything, in fact, until Aunt Mat rose and looked at her watch.

"Look at the time!" she said. "Gabriele, it's time you went up."

"Could we have just one more?" Alex said. He held out a sheet of music yellowed with age. "This is one of my favourites—I'd so like to hear it played."

"What is it?" Gabriele asked. She took the music and opened it, and then involuntarily looked at the portrait of a young woman hanging over the mantel across the room. "It's my father's favourite, too—our mother used to play it, and he would sing with her."

"I'm sorry," Alex said. "I would not have asked you to play it—"

"But I should like to play it," Gabriele said. "My memories of my mother are few—but they are sweet. I don't mind thinking of her."

"You are fortunate," Alex said. She looked up at him, surprised at the darkness in his voice. Before she had caught more than a glimmer of pain in his eyes, it had fled, chased by the smile with which he opened the music and said, "Then play on, Miss Cannon, play on."

Her fingers sought the opening chords; as they found the melody, she began to sing:

> " 'Believe me, if all those endearing young charms,
> Which I gaze on so fondly today,
> Were to change by tomorrow, and fleet in my arms,
> Like fairy gifts fading away,
> Thou would'st still be adored as this moment thou art,
> Let thy loveliness fade as it will—' "

Alex took up the verse, their blended voices backed by the piano's resonant notes. Time had texture, and pattern. The smooth, cool feel of the ivory keys under her fingers. The light touch of the spring breeze, bringing the scent of sweet olive and roses into the room. The music soared, floating out of the room to challenge the stillness of the sleeping gardens and the silent trees. When they finished, a moment of quiet followed, as though they could still hear the last notes echoing in the air.

Jordan Scott broke the silence, rising and coming toward her. "You do indeed play beautifully, Miss Cannon. And your voice has a natural sweetness that would hardly be enhanced by formal training. Thank you, you have made this a most enjoyable evening."

"There, Jordan, I knew you had pretty speeches packed somewhere away in your steamer trunk," Alex said. "Now, Miss Cannon, don't look at me as though you'd like to scold. Jordan needs a bit of jollying up—his seriousness quite frightens Creole ladies."

"I did not intend my words to be taken as a pretty speech," Jordan said. "But as a compliment sincerely meant." He held himself rigidly, as though braced for another assault, and Gabriele felt again that quick flash of sympathy.

"I took it exactly as it was meant, Mr. Scott," she said. She kept her eyes from Alex St. Cyr's face, but she could feel him grow still beside her as she spoke. "My father says that we must often search for sincerity among words spoken in abundance—but that in the scant speech of some, there lies much truth."

"I should like to know your father, Miss Cannon," Jordan Scott said. "From all I have heard of him, he is a reasonable man—and certainly we need as many of those as we can muster."

"I believe I sense a political discussion in the making," Alex said. He rose from the piano bench and bowed. "Since you and Miss Cannon are ready to retire, Mrs. LeGrange, may I bid you good night?" He glanced at Tom. "I think I'll take a stroll in the garden, if you don't mind."

"Of course," Tom said. "Jordan?"

"I'm rather tired," Jordan said. "I'd like to retire."

"Then I'll walk with you to the *garçonnière,*" Tom said.

The ladies left first: as she went upstairs with Aunt Mat, Gabriele could hear Tom and Jordan Scott talking as they walked down the hall to the back entrance that gave onto the path to the *garçonnière.* The ladies' exit—and perhaps his cousin's absence, for Alex had stepped through one of the long windows out onto the lawn—seemed to have loosened his tongue. She heard his deep voice, the New England vowels and harder consonants making it sound alien, cutting in over something Tom said, energetically making some point.

Just before she got into bed, she stepped out onto the gallery fronting her room and walked to the end that overlooked the garden. A bright glowing fire, a faint plume of smoke disappearing into the night mist—and Alex St. Cyr's dark form, sitting on a marble bench.

How amazing today has been, she thought, standing in the shadow of a pillar so she could not be observed. Here I woke up in a small, dull world—and now it has opened up and let these two gentlemen in. And then she thought of something, a happy thought that made her smile. Her worries about the ring tourney were over. Her knight had already asked for her favour—and thank heaven, she was saved from Harold LeBoeuf.

* * *

"From here you get the best view of the place," Tom said as Alex and Gabriele joined him on top of the Indian mound that rose to a height of some thirty feet, wild flowers pushing their way through the clam shells lining its sides. Their horses grazed at the foot of the mound, and a breeze blew up from Bayou Teche, lifting Gabriele's hair and blowing it around the confines of her bonnet.

"The Indians named the bayou—teche means snake in their language," Tom said. "They thought a great snake lived beneath its waters—I gather many of their rituals were intended to appease it."

"Superstition is a powerful force," Alex said. "I don't know if your slaves have much belief in voodoo, but in New Orleans, it's a constant part of their daily lives."

Tom picked up a loose shell and skimmed it toward the bayou, watching it skip across the surface and then disappear beneath it. "They've got a strange mixture of Christian faith and a kind of voodoo, I guess," he said. "There's a woman over at the Robins' plantation who calls herself a *traiteur,* which is a kind of faith healer, as well as I can gather. But the slaves stay away from here—it's a burial mound, and they won't have anything to do with something connected with another people's dead."

"Tom and I used to play up here when we were children," Gabriele said. "Scaring each other with tales of ghosts of Indians who would come scalp us to keep us from digging up their treasure."

"Is there treasure in this mound?" Alex asked.

"I'm sure it has pots and trinkets—the usual belongings sent to accompany the dead into the other world," Tom said. "Interesting how similar many of the Indians' burial rites are with the Egyptians—though not nearly so advanced, I suppose."

"When Tom takes on what I call his schoolmaster look, I know I am in for a lecture," Alex said. "You know, for a while I thought he might follow the urgings of his professors at Virginia and live out his life in the groves of

Academe—what, Miss Cannon, didn't he tell you? They thought Tom had the makings of a fine classics scholar—they very much wanted him to study abroad, and then join their faculty."

"Why, Tom! And you never said a word," Gabriele said.

Tom picked up another shell and threw it, using the movement as an excuse to turn his face from Gabriele's stare. Alex, quickly reading Tom's reaction, touched his arm and said, "Sorry, old man. I didn't mean to give away a secret."

"It's nothing so important as a secret," Tom said. The shell sank beneath the bayou waters and he turned back to them, face smooth and smiling. "If it had been important, I'd have given it more thought, wouldn't I?"

"Of course," Alex said. "Who would shut themselves up in a stuffy college when this delightful world awaits them at home?"

"I would," Gabriele said. "At least for a few years—I can't tell you how I envied Tom when he went off to Virginia—"

"Really, Miss Cannon? Well, perhaps you would have been like your brother, and reaped a fine harvest. I'm afraid that except for the few odd verses of Homer rattling around in my head, I retained very little for all the time I spent there."

"Gabriele probably knows as much Homer as you do," Tom said. "In fact, I'll wager she can pick up whatever passage from the *Iliad* you choose."

"Can you?" Alex said. A different sort of interest infused his face as he glanced at Gabriele, and then, watching the bayou as though the lines had been inscribed on its brown waters he began to recite: " 'They arose with a mighty sound, rolling clouds before them. And swiftly they came blowing over the sea, and the waves rose beneath their shrill blast; and they came to deep-soiled Troy, and fell upon the pile, and loudly roared the mighty fire . . .' "

Gabriele recognized the passage at once and took it up, conscious of the way Alex's head turned when he heard her voice, and of his eyes, fixed now on her face. " 'But at the hour when the Morning Star goeth forth to herald light upon the earth, that star that saffron-mantled Dawn cometh after, and spreadeth over the salt sea, then grew the burning faint, and the flame died down. And the Winds went back again to betake them home over the Thracian main, and it roared with a violent swell.' "

"Capital, Miss Cannon!" Alex said at the end of the stanza. "Tom has told me that you've had a very different upbringing from that of most young ladies; I should say it has had a happy result."

"Most of the time," Gabriele said, suddenly blushing as she remembered the spectacle she had made of herself not far from this spot only yesterday afternoon.

"I shall brag on you to my cousin Jordan," Alex said. "His view of Southern society is a gloomy one, and his opinion of the Creole ladies he has met is hardly flattering."

"Oh, but then your mother is so well-educated herself," Alex said. "I imagine Jordan's mother and sisters are of the same type."

"Educated, you mean? I don't know, I have never met any of my Boston relatives save Jordan himself. You are right about my mother; she is quite intelligent and educated as well, but her education has built walls through which nothing may penetrate and behind which very little change seems to occur." He looked from Tom to Gabriele, the self-mocking smile twisting his mouth. "You are too polite to ask how my father responds to such— rigidity. But you see, my mother's inflexibility does not bother my father because nothing bothers him. He is a fine fellow to dine with and sample wine with, as you know Tom, having met him. He can give you the name of the best tailor in New Orleans, the best horse at the Metairie Track—Jacques runs his affairs, that very competent octaroon whose Parisian education well prepared him for taking charge. This leaves my father free to be the eternal bon viveur in New Orleans, and to play at country gentleman when he goes up to Olympia, much in the manner, I suppose, that Marie Antoinette played at being a milkmaid at Versailles, but not, I fervently hope, with the same dismal results."

Alex's outburst shocked them; while Tom's intimacy with Alex was such that this speech did not surprise him, Gabriele's presence changed the situation, and, desperate for a new topic, he seized on the steam packet coming down the bayou, shielding his eyes with his hand, and saying, "Look, Alex. Is that one of yours?"

Alex glanced toward the bayou and shrugged. "I think so. With Jordan to run our new inland route so competently, I hardly have to trouble myself with it at all." He laughed shortly, and turned away from the passing vessel, swinging his riding crop across the tall grass. "There he is, grubbing away in the New Iberia office, and here I am, enjoying good company and a beautiful day. Who am I to change such a happy situation?"

"There's time before luncheon to practise for the tourney," Tom said. "I rigged up some poles in the paddock, with one of Gabriele's embroidery hoops to serve as the ring. Let's have a couple of goes at it, shall we?"

"And will you join us, Miss Cannon?" Alex said. "Though I confess I should hate to find you as proficient at jousting as you are at Homer's verses—"

"I can't deny I did try it, since Tom told you so," Gabriele said. "But I do wish you wouldn't tease me about it, I don't take well to teasing—I'm sorry—I just don't."

"But, Miss Cannon—please forgive me! I'm afraid the lovely open feeling of the countryside—my very great affection for Tom—I'm sorry. I let myself be carried away, and now I've offended you," Alex said.

"Of course you haven't," Gabriele said. "If young ladies forget their upbringing, they can't complain when they're teased. I only ask that you forget it, please—and let me be comforted that you will."

"You misunderstand me, Miss Cannon," Alex said. "I find it so refreshing to meet a young lady who is not always anxious about what people think that I expressed an admiration I very naturally feel. I promise you, I will let the wonderful image I have of you tilting pell-mell toward that beckoning ring fade, overpowered by others lovelier still."

"There, now, Gabriele, you've had your head turned by one of New Orleans' most experienced practitioners," Tom said. "Come now, St. Cyr, that's my sister you're talking to. She hasn't had her first season yet, so go easy on those pretty words."

"As you say," Alex said. He moved a little away from them, staring out over the fields, whip slapping against his boot top with the same display of restlessness as the day before.

"How many acres is Felicity?" he said.

"About five thousand," Tom answered. His voice still sounded strained, made harsh by the annoyance with which he had spoken to Alex, but he walked toward his friend and stood beside him, looking at the expanse of green.

"As much as that!" Alex said. "My father's plantation would fit into a fourth of it!"

"But Olympia's not a working plantation," Tom said. "Your father uses it for pleasure—whereas we plant every possible acre here."

He was completely back to normal, shoulders relaxed, voice eager as he talked, and Gabriele walked over to stand next to him, glad to have so impersonal a subject at hand.

"No wonder you couldn't become a professor," Alex said. "With this to be responsible for—" He gestured at a distant field, where slaves could be seen moving up and down the rows. "Not just the land—but the people it takes to work it."

"We have two hundred and thirty slaves," Tom said. "And, yes, they are a great responsibility." He sighed, and Gabriele took his hand and squeezed it. He's thinking of Veronique, she thought. I wonder—has he ever spoken of her to Mr. St. Cyr?

Something in Alex's tone focused her attention back on him—he sounded hard, almost angry. "Jordan will take you to task for every one of them," Alex said. "Like any proper Bostonian, he is a complete Abolitionist, a position my mother also embraces."

"But you must own slaves?" Tom said.

"My father does. And he treats them like either pampered pets or irresponsible children. My mother's servants are freed men and women—this situation makes for an interesting household, I assure you."

"A miniature of the dilemma the nation finds itself in," Tom said.

"And without much more expectation of solving it," Alex answered.

"What? Have you no hope that the delegates to the Democratic convention can find a way out of our difficulties? Certainly my father left for Charleston determined to help the moderates prevail."

"A consummation devoutly to be wished," Alex said. "The alternatives if they do not are hardly comforting."

"You do not sound very sanguine, Alex."

"How can I, when our own Governor Moore has made it plain since his inauguration last January that he sees little hope the Union can stand?"

"Your father and mother manage," Tom said, smiling a little. "The nation can follow their example."

"Yes, of course," Alex said. He turned to Gabriele. "Let me help you down the mound, Miss Cannon. The grass is still damp and the footing is treacherous." He offered her his arm and they walked in silence towards their horses, grazing in the grass. When they reached Brandy, Alex made a step with his hands, holding them so she could mount. "And you, Miss Cannon, what is your opinion? Do you think the Abolitionists and the pro-slavery factions will ever settle their differences in a manner that will allow us to go on with our lives?"

"How can they, Mr. St. Cyr? If the Abolitionists have their way, all the slaves will be free—and my father says

they are not ready for it, that to free them all now would
be the wrong thing to do."

"I'm afraid the Abolitionists are interested in nothing
less," Alex said. "At least, to hear Jordan speak."

"My father is a convincing speaker," Gabriele said. "And
he is not alone in his views. I am confident some good will
come out of Charleston—if for no other reason than that
it must."

"I do not share your confidence, Miss Cannon, but that
is a general fault of my disposition, I believe. An unhappy
cynicism that of course affects my view."

She watched him swing up onto his horse's back, and
followed him as he started toward home. Tom came up
beside her, slowing Jupiter's long stride to match Brandy's
pace.

"A complicated fellow, St. Cyr," Tom said. "They used
to call him Mercury at school."

"Mercury? The messenger of the gods?" Gabriele said,
watching Alex take the first fence.

"No—the element. You know—quicksilver." He shot a
glance at her, marking his words. "Shining and wonderful
to look at—but almost impossible to hold in your hand."

Tom's words stayed in Gabriele's mind as she went to the
parlour and began running through her scales. The syllables of Alex's nickname picked up the rhythm of the notes:
Quick-sil-ver, quick-sil-ver. She ended the last set with a
crash of keys, then turned to the Gottschalk music with
relief.

So absorbed did she become that she was not aware that
Jordan Scott had entered the room, standing quietly in
the doorway until the piece ended. The sound of light
applause made Gabriele spin around, wondering who
could be behind her.

"Mr. Scott!" she said, rising and closing the piano. "I
thought your business would detain you all day." How
tired and hot he looks, she thought as she crossed the

room to him. And no wonder—he has been working while we played.

"I thought so, too," he said. "But it seems one of the packets broke down and will not be here until tomorrow, so my interview with its captain must wait until then."

"Then perhaps you'll join Tom and your cousin," Gabriele said. "They're out in the paddock practising for the ring tourney—you may find it better sport than you imagined, and change your mind."

"Thank you, no," Jordan said. "I went to one in New Orleans. In my view, watching my peers dressed up like knights and grabbing a ring off a hook is a waste of time—and as far as winning the thing—I'm not convinced that means anything more than that a man has a good horse and knows how to ride it."

"What else should it mean, Mr. Scott?" Gabriele said. "It's all meant in a spirit of fun—"

"A spirit I'm dismally lacking in, I'm afraid," Jordan said.

"You are too intelligent to be dull," Gabriele said. "Just because your diversions are different from your cousin's—"

"What do you know of Alex's diversions, Miss Cannon?" Jordan said. His blue eyes held hers, and she found herself wanting to look away.

"Nothing, of course. Only what I know of New Orleans, and of the entertainments available there—" She broke off at the sound of voices and footsteps in the hall.

"That must be Tom and Mr. St. Cyr now, finished with their practice and ready for lunch," she said. "They'll be happy to see you—we missed you on our tour."

"Then perhaps I may ask for a separate one," Jordan said. "If you have not ridden too much today."

"I am sure Tom will oblige you—"

"I would prefer that you did, Miss Cannon."

She heard the voices coming closer, knew that at any moment Tom and Alex would gain the door. "Then of course, Mr. Scott. But we'll have to wait until it is cooler

—Aunt Mat doesn't allow me out in the hottest part of the day."

"So, Jordan," Alex said, coming into the room. "I thought the charms of business would wear thin when compared to the pleasures here."

"You're quite wrong, Alex," Jordan said. "A packet broke down, forcing me to postpone until tomorrow what I would have done today."

"What a pity," Alex said. "I know how it appalls you to have to waste time."

"I shan't," Jordan said, looking at Gabriele with a smile. "Miss Cannon has graciously agreed to repeat for me the tour that I missed—as you know, my interest in the plantation system is great, and I think I could hardly have a better guide."

"I agree," Alex said. He bowed to Gabriele, then took Tom's hand. "I'd quite forgotten until this very moment—but I promised to carry a message from my mother to a friend of hers who lives in town. I should probably start now—no, don't bother about lunch, I'll dine at the hotel. Until later, then?" He bowed again, and turning, walked swiftly back down the hall.

Gabriele looked after him, wondering why she felt as though the laurels of victory had just been dashed from her hand.

"I'll ride a little way with you, Jordan," Tom said. "When you go on your tour. I want to show you the irrigation ditches we were talking about—"

He held out his arm to his sister. "There, Gabriele, you see just exactly what I mean. You can't know what Alex will do from one minute to the next—the only certain thing is that the minute you're sure of him—he will do something else."

But then he might change his mind about the ring tourney! she thought, almost speaking aloud. Oh, how perfectly dreadful if he does—I just know I will have to accept silly little Harold LeBoeuf. As though Jordan read her thoughts, he said, "Yes, that's true. Alex has a very changeable mind. But I must say that when he has given his word —there is no doubt he will carry it through."

"Oh, yes—in anything he considers important, no one could be more punctilious about carrying it out." Tom laughed, and Gabriele heard his affection for Alex conquering any vexation he might feel. "The problem, of course, is that the things most people agree are important —St. Cyr almost never does."

Chapter Three

"IT'S—OVERWHELMING," JORDAN SAID, REINING IN HIS HORSE and staring at the expanse of fields all around them. "So much land!"

"Felicity is one of the largest plantations in Louisiana," Tom said. He had ended up accompanying Jordan and Gabriele on the entire tour—listening to his animated explanations of everything they saw, Gabriele could almost believe that Tom had truly wished to spend the afternoon going over exactly the same ground as he had that morning if it were not for the glance he shot her way when she had said, after the first half-hour, "You needn't trouble yourself to come any farther, Tom. I can answer Mr. Scott's questions, I'm sure." The look had said, Not unchaperoned, you won't. As a result she had become unnaturally silent, hardly responding even when Tom let a question fall to her, until finally, with another look at her, this one full of exasperation, he had taken over duties as host and guide.

"How many hands does it take to work this much land?" Jordan said. Rain clouds piled up in the west scudded ahead of a brisk breeze, a breeze that lifted the blond curl that lay on Jordan's forehead and tossed it lightly, making him look suddenly much more open, much less removed and stiff. The same breeze blew Gabriele's hair back from her face and belled her skirt gently: as though it also cleared her lingering annoyance, she closed the small distance between her and the two men, guiding Brandy to a standstill beside Jupiter.

"We have two hundred and thirty slaves," Tom said. "Though some of course work in the house—and others have special skills. Samson, for instance, is in charge of the stable. I suppose on any given day, we have about a hundred and eighty slaves in the fields."

He interpreted Jordan's look. "There are always a percentage who are sick," he said. "Sometimes they really are ill, sometimes they just don't feel like working that day. We have to pretty much take Samantha's word for it. It's not worth risking sending someone who really is sick into the fields just because a good half of the time it's only an excuse to stay in bed."

"Samantha's the nurse," Gabriele said. "She isn't really —I mean she hasn't worked in a hospital or anything like that. But she knows folk medicine—how to use herbs and things—and of course Aunt Mat has taught her a lot."

"And one overseer manages all those people? That's astonishing—you'd think they'd—well, I may as well say what I'm thinking—you'd think they'd overpower him and run away," Jordan said. His cheeks turned red, and Gabriele could almost feel his reluctance to embarrass himself and his hosts any further. She turned away, letting her gaze roam to the far horizon. They had crossed the road that ran in front of the house, entering the fields that stretched for 5,000 acres on the other side. Jordan's questions from the first had been different from Alex St. Cyr's. Alex had of course asked very little—Felicity might be one of the largest plantations in the state, but the system used to run it was no different. Alex had been primarily interested in geographic features of the land; or really, to be completely honest, Gabriele thought, his primary interest was plainly in—us.

"Well, Scott," she heard Tom say, "it's not that easy for slaves to run away, this far south. Which is why, of course, one of the most effective ways to keep slaves farther north in line is to threaten to 'sell them South.' ' "

"I'm sorry," Jordan said. "I'm afraid my eagerness for first-hand knowledge is overcoming my manners—"

"Not at all," Tom said. "You feel very much as I should feel, I imagine, were I given an opportunity to examine the conditions of the crews on one of your ocean-going ships—or to see how mill and factory workers manage to live on what they are paid in New England."

"Tom!" Gabriele said.

"It's all right, Miss Cannon," Jordan said. "None of us —certainly not the Scotts—are innocent of the misery of those on whose backs we make our fortunes. And I would be the worst sort of hypocrite if I tried to deny that one great corner of the foundation of my family's fortune came from the slave trade."

Tom's face changed, the tension that had darkened it vanishing as quickly as though the still steady breeze had carried it away. "Well, you're an honest fellow!" he said, giving Jordan his hand.

"So are you," Jordan said. He smiled, taking Tom's hand and shaking it firmly. "I'm glad we can speak openly —you've no idea how many times I've bitten my tongue almost through since I came down here."

"You carry the onus of an entire region's actions with you when you enter a New Orleans parlour," Tom said. "Your hosts look at you and see, not a pleasant young gentleman upon whose manners they can depend, but a rapacious Yankee who would deprive the South of the backbone of her economic security—"

"And I am afraid I am just as guilty," Jordan said. "For when I am in the presence of people who—own slaves—I can't help it—I feel quite—isolated—as though there is some mental bridge they have crossed that I can't even see."

"We've crossed no bridge," Tom said. "At least, Gabriele and I haven't. The very education our father gave us to enlighten us makes it difficult to support slavery as an idea." He held out a hand to Gabriele. "Gabriele will tell you how many hours we have spent discussing this dilemma."

"But what is your dilemma?" Jordan said. "If you are opposed to slavery—then how can you have slaves?"

"How can I have something I was born into? And before you shake your head at me, Scott—think of what you have said about your own fortune. I doubt that you approve of the conditions on ships, in factories—but you don't walk away from a business that profits by them."

"I hope to change them, of course," Jordan said. "I have only just entered the business—a year in the Boston offices, and now this time in New Orleans—and I have no say-so at all. But I will, Cannon. I will."

"And so will I," Tom said. "But those changes will take time. If all compromises fail and the Union dissolves—the resulting chaos will make ordered change almost impossible."

"Do you think there would be war?" Jordan asked.

"That is the worst possibility. But even at best—would the United States continue to trade with those that broke away? I doubt it. And although we could build up our ties to England and France—they are already strong—we could hardly survive if we could not exchange our products for your finished goods."

"That is one of the clearest analyses of the situation I have yet heard," Jordan said. "Those are your father's views as well?"

"Certainly," Tom said. "And he hopes they will prevail at the Democratic convention."

A cloud of dust came into sight from a distance down the road, and the sound of voices came faintly to their ears. Tom peered down the road, then said, "Here are some of our people now, Jordan. Finished their work and heading home."

"Finished?" Jordan looked at the sky. "But the law allows you to work them as long as there is daylight—"

Tom gave Jordan a long, cool glance. "You're well informed, Scott."

"I—try to be," Jordan said. .

"Then you'll have read about the task system?" Tom said. "It's what we use here."

"No—I haven't."

"Between them, my father and his overseer determine what a reasonable amount of work per day for each hand is. That is set for them—and when they have completed it, they may go back to the Quarters to do as they like."

"Then you are both benefited," Jordan said. "You because they work more consistently—they because they earn a little leisure."

"There is also the benefit of knowing we have not driven our people into the ground," Tom said. Tom sounded, not vexed, but as though he now answered Jordan under some great duress. His eyes turned ahead, where, as the cloud of dust moved closer, they could see a group of some twenty or so slaves.

They neither of them want to see the slaves pass, Gabriele thought.

"Come, Mr. Scott," Gabriele said. "If you wish to see the sugar mill we should start right away. Those few hours of daylight are barely long enough to ride there and back."

"I think I have taken advantage of your generosity long enough," Jordan said. "The mill is not working, of course —perhaps you will renew the invitation to see it during grinding season in the fall?"

"As you wish," Gabriele said. She looked away from Jordan's eyes, from a clear blue look that seemed to ask her to forgive his discomfort. It is those slaves, she thought. He has probably never before been near so many—he is bracing himself, he cannot think what he will do.

And indeed, as the first rank drew abreast of them, she could see Jordan's body stiffen, and his head turn away. Then, with an almost visible act of will, he shifted in the saddle so that he saw the slaves pass him as though in a parade on review. Men and women, their skins shading from *café au lait* to ebony, some tall with massive bones, some thick-set and flat featured, bare feet sending up puffs of dun-coloured dust that clung to their rough-woven cotton garments of much the same hue.

Heads bobbed as the slaves passed them, some of the women making awkward half-curtsies as they saw Gabriele and Tom. Gabriele felt the stiffness in her own body, she thought the smile on her face must have been pasted there, so tightly did it draw against her skin. Each time a slave bobbed or curtsied she nodded back, occasionally addressing one of them by name.

"How's your baby, Margaret?" she said to a young woman passing by.

"Doing wonderful," the woman said. She stopped and stepped out of the ranks, coming to stand at Gabriele's side. "Miz LeGrange, she sat up with him most all night last week when he got the colic so bad. But he's fine now."

"I'm—glad," Gabriele said. "You must bring him up and let me see him—"

"Yes, miss. I bring him."

The last little group of slaves had already gone by, and the woman ran after them, feet slapping against the dirt road. The breeze died, dropping to earth as though it were an animal running to cover. A veiled light, coming from behind the darkening clouds. A thick stillness— motes of dust settling into the road bed. And then the first big drops of rain, splashing against the dust, making dark marks on its smooth surface.

"We'd better run!" Tom said, wheeling Jupiter around and motioning to Gabriele to go ahead. The three horses pounded up the road, fleeing ahead of the chasing rain. They came up fast upon the slaves, and Gabriele saw them scatter, running to each side of the road in a frenzy of arms and legs and staring eyes, then standing silently as a sheet of rain came over them.

By the time they reached the house, the three of them were drenched, soaked to the skin with water even running down inside their boots.

"I'll take all three horses around to the stable," Tom said. "You go on in, Gabriele—you, too, Jordan."

"I'm wet already," Jordan said. "Another little bit won't hurt me."

"Then go ahead," Tom said. "I'll lead Brandy."

Gabriele stood watching them from the shelter of the gallery, standing well back from the blowing rain. They vanished around the corner of the house, and she turned to go inside. Lamps had not yet been lit: the house looked cold and uninviting, as though all life had gone from there. You are tired and soaking wet, she told herself, opening the door and going into the hall. The great curved arms of the staircase rose before her, shining white through the gloom. They rose into darkness—she felt that when she went up them, she would move into something unknown—some alien place quite removed from her familiar home.

Your mind is providing fancies to match the discomfort your body feels—such nonsense you allow yourself to think! She went quickly across the floor, almost running up the first few stairs.

Then a figure appeared on the landing where the two arms met: a woman holding a lamp. "Miss Gabriele? Miss Gabriele, look at you!"

"Oh, Lucie!" Gabriele said. "Yes—I got caught in the rain—I've dripped all over the rug, I'm afraid—"

"You come get dried off," Lucie said. She moved ahead of Gabriele, lighting her way down the upstairs hall. "Now what can I do with your hair?"

Gabriele felt ease come over her. The familiar rituals would soon enclose her. Lucie would carry off her wet clothing, she would towel herself off with a thick, warm towel. And then she would sit at her dressing table, her new silk wrapper soft against her skin, while Lucie fussed with her hair—and it would be time for dinner, another evening with Jordan Scott and Alex St. Cyr.

The rain fell steadily, darkening the trees beyond the upper gallery rail. Gabriele's room, softly lit, scented by a great vase of roses set on a table near her bed, made a centre of warmth and promise. She felt a rise of excitement when she thought of the hours ahead. Then, at the very edge of her consciousness, a dark blur. Such a long way they had to walk, she thought. They'll still be out there in all this rain.

Alex seemed abstracted at dinner, initiating little conversation and entering minimally into that of others. Only when the entrée had been served did he come to himself, looking down the table at Aunt Mat and apologizing. "Forgive me, Mrs. LeGrange, I have not been giving either this excellent dinner or the company the attention both deserve—but I spent an uncomfortable afternoon, and the effects of it are still upon me."

"I'm sorry to hear that, Mr. St. Cyr," Aunt Mat said. "Did you find your mother's friend unwell?"

"Not at all," Alex said. "She herself seemed in good spirits and perfect health—but by the time my visit was over, she had reduced her hapless daughter to the point of tears, and myself to a state of embarrassment and chagrin."

"What on earth do you mean?" Aunt Mat said. "That seems a strange way for a hostess and mother to behave!"

"Oh, I think the mother instinct outweighed any other," Alex said. "It seems I am considered a good match —and so both the daughter of the house and myself had to suffer a great deal of well-intentioned comment meant to make it plain to me that if I seek a wife—my search need go no further than that house."

He picked up his wine and sipped, then glanced at Tom. "A wonderful Bordeaux—your father's cellar must rival ours. Ah, don't look at me like that, old fellow. You know me well enough to know that I was kindness itself to that poor girl—but what a tightrope I had to walk between kindness and giving her hope!"

"And do you think she agrees with her mother's judgement that you are a good match, Mr. St. Cyr?" Aunt Mat said.

"I imagine anyone who would take her out from under her mother's control would be a good match, Mrs. LeGrange, as long as he gave her some respect for her individuality—"

"But you do not think this young lady would be a good match for you?" Aunt Mat spoke to Alex, but she looked at Gabriele. See how freely this young man talks, the look said. And be warned.

"How can I have any idea? She had no opportunity to present herself as she really is—the virtues her mother enumerated make her an ideal mistress of a household—a hostess of some competence and skill—and I believe she is accomplished enough in some of the finer arts to create an aesthetic atmosphere as well—but as to what sort of wife she would make, I am sure I don't know. Nor will I ever attempt to find out, for even the most urgent commands from my mother will not induce me to enter that house again."

"You must have been exposed to such maternal . . . concern before," Tom said. He smiled at Jordan, inviting him to ease the tension Alex's vehement speech had caused. "I imagine things are not much different in Boston, are they, Scott? An eligible gentleman calls at a house where there is a daughter of marriageable age—and from all that he sees and hears, here resides the most perfect lady that ever lived."

"I did not go out in society much," Jordan said. "I like quieter pursuits, and remained within the confines of a circle of families with whom I had grown up. So of course I already knew all the daughters, as well as they knew me. There would be no point in putting on airs, any of us, under those circumstances."

"It is not airs I am talking about," Alex said. "It is the deliberate trotting out of a human being and putting her on display, allowing her to be—bid on—with her life being awarded to he who makes the most acceptable bid."

"Is that what you think of marriage, Mr. St. Cyr?" Aunt

Mat said. "You are even more cynical than your father, for he at least had some sentiment at your age!"

"I think Alex has sentiment, Aunt Mat," Tom said, "or else he would not feel so strongly. And it is true that some mothers are more—open about the ends they have in mind than others. It is uncomfortable, for both the young lady and the gentleman concerned."

Gabriele had hardly moved from Alex's first outburst through all that had ensued, but now she stirred. The slight forward movement put her into the full circle of light from the chandelier: candle-glow burnished her hair, picking out the deeper colour and turning the tendrils curling around her face to gold. "What you describe sounds so horrid, Mr. St. Cyr, that I think I am forever put off from any situation which even approaches 'being put on display.' I wonder if I even want to go to the ring tourney, dressed up like a medieval lady, and playing such an elaborate game."

"But, Miss Cannon—present company is always excepted from any such conversation—you can't think my comments could ever apply to you—"

"And why not, Mr. St. Cyr?" She could not keep her cheeks from showing the strength of her emotion, nor her eyes from sparking with green fire. His dark eyes almost frightened her, she felt as though she sat, not at her own dinner table, but in some strange and dangerous place. Then she straightened her shoulders and willed her voice to be calm. "Why would your comments not apply to me as well as to any other 'hapless young lady' of my age?"

"Because you are not like other young ladies of your age, Miss Cannon," Alex said. "By both your admission and your conduct, you reveal a quite different view of how your life should be. As for the ring tourney—it is, as you say, an elaborate game. We will all be on display—and believe me, those of us who tilt at that small ring run far more risk than those who sit, beautifully garbed, in the stands."

"At any rate, Mr. St. Cyr," Aunt Mat said, signalling for

the plates to be removed, "your view of the way our society arranges for young people to meet is your own, and I doubt that it would be supported by anyone else."

Alex bowed, a slight smile accompanying his reply. "I am sure you are right, Mrs. LeGrange. I am so often not supported in my views by any other opinion that I am fast reaching the point at which I will either not express them —or give up having them at all."

He again fell into silence, creating a distance between himself and the rest of them that even Tom's efforts could not close. When Aunt Mat and Gabriele left the gentlemen to their brandy and cigars, Gabriele followed her aunt to the parlour with relief. The informality of last night seemed years away, the ease with which she and Alex St. Cyr had sung an impossible accident that would not happen again. She preferred not to play, she said, when the men came to join them. The hours on horseback had fatigued her, if they would excuse her, she would retire.

Rain still fell, a gentle soft rain that should have lulled her to sleep. But somehow, it did not. I am mistaken about Mr. St. Cyr, she thought. At first it seemed Mr. Scott was the observer—that bright blue gaze piercing through to the heart of every question—while Mr. St. Cyr's glance seemed to graze only the surface, darting away as something else caught his fancy. Now I see that Mr. St. Cyr's eyes are like great dark holes into which everything he sees disappears, to be changed, transformed, by his own particular view—

No wonder he makes pretty speeches and pretends to loll about. He wears a mask so that he can go about among us, examining us so critically from behind that smiling face! Now she wished that Alex St. Cyr would live up to his nickname, would change his mind about riding in the ring tourney, would, when the day came, be far away. Harold LeBoeuf is younger than I am, Gabriele thought, turning her pillow to the smooth side and trying vainly to sleep. And his behaviour is often silly. But there is one thing about him—there is nothing more to Harold than one sees and hears. And right now I think that is probably a very good thing.

The world had been created new by morning, the rain leaving every leaf, every petal, fresh and free of dust. Gabriele carried her coffee out onto the upper gallery, sipping it as she breathed in the fragrance of roses climbing over the rail. A clatter of wheels drew her attention to the drive in front of the house, and she turned to see Samson bringing the carriage around, every inch of it shining, the horses that pulled it prancing in the cool air.

The Jumonville wedding. Of course, how could she have forgotten? She should be getting dressed right now. By the time she re-entered her room, her maid had already returned with her breakfast, and stood waiting for Gabriele to decide on her dress.

"Heavens, Lucie, I'd forgotten all about that wedding," she said as she sat down and began to eat. A slight frown on Lucie's face made her remember something else, and she quickly crossed herself.

"Abigail say Miz LeGrange, she want to start out by ten. We have to go fast to get you ready by then."

"I think the ivory—no, I can't wear something so close to white. Maybe the lavender—or the blue—"

"Abigail say yo' aunt say you to wear the blue dress." Lucie laughed suddenly, a quick white line of strong teeth. "Yo' aunt don't want you to outshine the bride, Abigail say."

"Bother!" Gabriele said. She dribbled fig syrup over the last biscuit. "We're only going because Mr. Jumonville and Papa work together—I don't think I've spent more than six hours with Miss Jumonville in my entire life."

"Plenty people be there," Lucie said. "Come on, Miss Gabriele, we got to get you dressed." She waited while Gabriele bathed her face and arms, then handed her fresh undergarments. "Jonas say Mr. Tom's going to take those two gentlemen." Lucie's eyes slid over Gabriele's face. "So you got plenty reason to be pretty, Miss Gabriele, even if you ain't the bride."

"I don't ever want to be a bride if I have to do it the way Miss Jumonville is," Gabriele said. She saw Lucie's surprise and tried to sound less angry. "Oh, Lucie—you must have heard. You always hear things long before I do—and hear lots more, besides."

"I hear Miss Jumonville marrying somebody from pretty far away," Lucie said. "Sit down, Miss Gabriele, let me brush out yo' hair."

"Yes, a man at least twenty years older than she is, and with several children besides!" Gabriele said.

"Man cain't help it if his wife, she die," Lucie said, pulling the silver-backed brush through Gabriele's loose hair. "Your mama, she died."

"But Papa didn't go out and marry somebody half his age!"

"He had his sister," Lucie said. "Now if Miz LeGrange husband, he hadn't died—yo' Papa would have had to have somebody, Miss Gabriele."

"I don't care," Gabriele said. "I can't see how Miss Jumonville can even think of marrying someone that old —and going off to be mother to a lot of children she doesn't even know! Why, the oldest one isn't much younger than she is herself—"

The brush strokes became harder, and Gabriele knew Lucie thought she had gone too far.

"Miss Gabriele, look at it sensible. The Jumonvilles, they don't have the kind of money your papa got. And those girls—Abigail say they smart—but, Miss Gabriele, a young man, he wants pretty. Later, he might care about smart—"

"It's disgusting, Lucie, that's what it is. Instead of being an honourable spinster, Miss Jumonville will—sell herself—"

Lucie laughed, a great peal of laughter that seemed to shatter against the mirror's glass. "Well, Miss Gabriele, you might be saying what's so. But I will tell you one thing—if she is selling herself—she can be proud of the price."

"I'm sorry," Gabriele said. "I shouldn't have such—thoughts. And if I have them—I should at least hold my tongue."

Lucie curled a lock of Gabriele's hair around her finger. "I won't say nuthin'," she said. "One thing—the money your Papa has, and pretty like you are—when gentlemen come courtin', the shoe be on the other foot."

Their eyes met in the glass, Gabriele's wide with question, Lucie's dark with knowledge. A slow imperceptible nod of Lucie's head, and she smiled again. "It's like we say, Miss Gabriele. You got the world in a bottle and the stopper in yo' hand."

Gabriele's spirit suddenly matched the morning. Last night's mood vanished, melted in her bright reflection in the glass. "I'm afraid the blue dress has an awful grass stain on it, Lucie," Gabriele said. "I didn't see it when I last wore it—but I can't wear it today."

"Miss Gabriele, that dress don't have no grass stain—" Lucie looked at Gabriele, then down at the dress. "Oh, I see it now. Yes, Miss. You better wear another one—now which one do you have in mind?" .

"The lavender," Gabriele said. "And the cream lace shawl Papa brought from Brussels to cover up the neckline until after dark."

"That poor bride, won't nobody look at her," Lucie said as she settled the lavender gown over Gabriele's head.

"Well, she won't care," Gabriele said. She stood, staring at herself in the mirror, a little smile she couldn't remember ever having seen before on her face. She turned and looked over her shoulder at the gratifying way the ruffles on the dress fell. "She's getting married today—her husband will look at her, that's all that should matter to her."

Tom stood with Alex and Jordan near the foot of the stairs as Gabriele went down. Tom and Jordan talked with great animation, Alex stood staring at a portrait on the wall. His head turned first, and he gazed up at her, swallowing her image into that dark hole. Then Jordan turned and saw her; he smiled and came to stand at the foot of the stairs.

"You make missing a day of work to go to a wedding well worth it, Miss Cannon," he said. "The bride herself can hardly be prettier."

Alex took a step forward, but he still did not speak. And Gabriele, goaded by the memory of all Alex had said the night before, laughed, touching Jordan's wrist lightly with her fan. "I don't think it will matter, Mr. Scott. From what I understand, the bride in this instance is not required to be pretty. She is only required to be smart."

"You mean this marriage has been arranged," Alex said.

"So my maid Lucie tells me," Gabriele said. "And if the slaves speak so about it, poor Miss Jumonville's courtship can have had no privacy at all."

"Then my observations were not far wrong," Alex said. "About the sorry state relations between men and women have fallen to."

Gabriele, standing between Alex and Jordan, flanked by her brother Tom, felt a small surge of something she could not yet identify—a feeling kin to that when she and Brandy leaped all fences, took miles of pasture and open road in their free stride.

"I am not sure we can call Miss Jumonville's marriage evidence of that," Gabriele said. "I believe she thinks she has made a good bargain. And who are we to say that she has not?"

"But you would never make such a bargain," Jordan said. "Would you, Miss Cannon?"

Tom stepped closer, offering Gabriele his arm. "That is not a question my sister will ever have to consider answering, Scott," he said. "Even if she were tempted—my father and I are here to make certain that she does not."

"You surprise me, Jordan," Alex said as they followed Tom and Gabriele toward the front door. "Surely you know that bargains are between those who must make some kind of trade. Such a notion has no application when what is at stake is a—prize."

"Here, come stroll about with me," Dorothea Robin said to Gabriele. "It seems ages since I saw you, although it has only been—what? A month?"

"Since you went to visit your cousins," Gabriele said. She moved off with Dorothea into the shelter of an arbour and stood idly surveying the other guests dispersed about the Jumonvilles' lawn. "Did you have a pleasant visit?"

"Very," Dorothea said. "I was sorry to return. I met such delightful people there—but tell me about your guests! They are splendid looking! So attractive, and they present themselves so well."

"There is not a great deal to tell," Gabriele said. "Mr. St. Cyr is Tom's old friend from college. Mr. Scott is Mr. St. Cyr's first cousin, down from Boston to work in their shipping office in New Orleans."

"How placid you sound, Gabriele! As if having two such guests were not enough to make your head spin!"

"Yours may spin away as much as it likes," Gabriele said. "As for mine, it is usually steady."

"And mine is at the moment impervious to accidental charm," Dorothea said. "When we have a moment, I will tell you about one gentleman in particular whom I met— but, look, there is the bridal couple now, I believe they will soon leave."

"I'm glad you didn't say the happy couple," Gabriele said. "How can Miss Jumonville do it, I wonder? She can't love him, do you think?"

"How can she do it? Very easily," Dorothea said. "Mr. Forbes has over two thousand acres planted in cotton, and several large houses as well. His wife will live in luxury— and he seems kind, Gabriele. There is not an ugly line in his face."

"If she were thirty! But she is not! Oh, Dorothea, how can she give up—"

"Romance? You read entirely too much Tennyson and

Walter Scott," Dorothea said. "Miss Jumonville cannot eat romance for breakfast, nor wear it against the cold."

"Her father is sufficiently wealthy to provide for her—"

"What? Live on in his house when she can rule Mr. Forbes'?" Dorothea shrugged, smiling at Gabriele from the eminence of being two years the elder. "It is different for you, Gabriele. Your father is one of the wealthiest men in the South—and you are his only daughter. Now Papa has four of us to give dowries to—naturally, my sisters and I enter the lists with not quite your advantage."

"You sound exactly like Mr. St. Cyr, Dorothea, whose cynicism is shocking! Will you stand there and tell me you don't believe in love?"

Dorothea's smile changed, and Gabriele thought she must be remembering the particular gentleman of whom she had spoken. "I believe in love, Gabriele. I hope I shall have it." She shrugged again. "But if I do not begin marriage with it—I am sure it will come in time."

A large carriage with a liveried driver and a footman riding behind circled around the drive and came to a stop. "Come, let us go nearer," Dorothea said. "They are getting ready to leave."

Gabriele stared at Mr. Forbes and his bride. In her travelling dress, the new Mrs. Forbes seemed smaller, diminished now that she had taken off her bridal gown. She stood near her family, clinging to a sister's hand. "And Mrs. Forbes? Will she find love?"

Dorothea glanced in the direction of Gabriele's gaze. "Not everyone has your notions, Gabriele. They cannot afford to, something they learned long ago. I am sure Mrs. Forbes knew very early that she must earn her way into a good marriage by skill and competence in domestic affairs. Mr. Forbes will live in a well-run establishment again, Gabriele. He will show his wife his gratitude by treating her with generosity and kindness, as any gentleman would. Her life may look—circumscribed to you. But I don't think she would agree with you, no matter how tearful her parting from her parents now."

"I—dropped my fan somewhere in the grass," Gabriele said. "Go ahead and I will catch up to you." She turned away before Dorothea could speak, eyes on the ground as though truly searching for her fan. Dorothea must be right, she thought. But if the kind of love I speak of cannot very often exist—why do poets write of it, and why do authors like Walter Scott make it the centrepiece of their tales?

She heard a sound, someone crying, and looked up, eyes hunting for the source. A small cluster of Negroes, standing near the fence—a man and a woman, a few little children—and a girl of about fifteen, sobbing on the woman's neck.

But what is it? Gabriele thought, involuntarily moving forward. Then from behind her came a voice. "Ellen! Ellen, where in the world have you gone?"

The girl's head came up, and looked toward the voice. In her expression, and in the faces of her family around her, Gabriele knew the truth. Ellen would go with Mrs. Forbes to her new destination, a present from Mr. Jumonville to his newly-married child.

"There she is!" Mr. Jumonville said. He came abreast of Gabriele, nodding as he went on by.

But you know this is the way of things, Gabriele told herself.

Yes, I know this is the way of things, she thought, turning slowly away to go join the rest. I have always "known" it with my head—but now, I think, I am beginning to know it with my heart.

Chapter Four

THE CLEAR HIGH CALL OF A TRUMPET SOUNDED OVER THE NEW Iberia racetrack, and brightly-coloured pennants set on tall poles around the field danced in the light breeze. Gabriele, skirts billowing around her, could hardly keep still: as yet another knight appeared at the far end of the oval track, she leaned forward, almost rising out of her chair in her effort to see who it might be.

"Oh, Aunt Mat, it's as though everything Sir Walter Scott wrote about has been transported before our very eyes!"

Aunt Mat's eyes went from Gabriele's flushed cheeks and excited eyes to the knights on their prancing horses. "Be sure you take it no more seriously than you take his stories, Gabriele. If you are crowned the Queen—that will be pleasant for you. If you are not—it is but one afternoon, after all."

"I don't take it seriously at all," Gabriele said. "It is just a play, a wonderful charade—oh, look, here comes Tom!" She half-rose from her place, waving to the grey-garbed knight passing before them. "Doesn't he look grand, all grey and silver!"

"He looks as well as any," Aunt Mat said, allowing the tiniest bit of satisfaction to colour her tone. She settled back in her chair, taking a fan from her reticule and waving it rapidly to and fro. From behind its shield, she could exchange comments with her nearest neighbour and good friend, Mrs. Walter Robin, who, with her four daughters, occupied the next box.

The parade of knights continued, a shifting pattern of plumed headpieces and beribboned lances that stirred the crowd to even higher excitement. In every box containing a young lady of appropriate age, a special excitement ruled. Although most of the knights had already chosen their ladies, and almost no one would be surprised at the identity of the knight approaching her box, still, in the last minutes before the knights completed their parade, a delicious tension filled the air. Minds and hearts could change—a knight could be delayed—or someone could ride out of nowhere, cutting out the expected champion with his own request.

Jaime Robin rode by, bowing to his mother and sisters, and then to Aunt Mat and Gabriele. More knights, some they recognized, some they did not know. And then Tom again. Tom! But that meant all the knights had circled past her—all but Alex St. Cyr.

A stir in the box next to Gabriele caught her attention, and she turned to see a knight bowing in front of Dorothea, who was smiling as she handed him a scarf she drew from her neck, and tying it so that it fluttered from his sleeve. A knight approached the box on the other side—and the one beyond that. "Oh, where is Mr. St. Cyr!" she said, realizing she had spoken aloud only when Aunt Mat looked her way.

"Perhaps his business kept him longer than he thought that it would," Aunt Mat said. "He was meeting Mr. Scott at the steamship office, was he not?"

"Yes, but he did not expect that meeting to last even an hour—" Quick-sil-ver. Quick-sil-ver. The words rang in her head. "Well, this is, as we agree, only a game. If Mr. St. Cyr is detained—I shall simply enjoy watching the other knights ride."

A horseman separated himself from a cluster of knights and started in their direction. Despite the splendour of the rider's garments of scarlet and green, Gabriele recognized Harold LeBoeuf. *He cannot mean to ask me if he may ride for me. He mustn't.* She turned to Aunt Mat, her back deliberately positioned in Harold's line of approach.

And then her breath caught in her throat, and the words she had been about to speak died as she watched a new knight enter the track. He stood poised on his jet-black horse while the Herald checked the list of entries, the gold bands on his black tunic glittering in the sun. As the Herald waved him on, the knight leaned over and spoke: the Herald looked about the field, then raised his arm and pointed. The knight's head, magnificent in a gold headpiece topped with black plumes, turned, following the Herald's arm. He nodded and rode slowly forward, making straight for the Cannon box.

"But that is not Mr. St. Cyr?" Aunt Mat said.

"No—Mr. St. Cyr's costume is blue and silver—and look, there he is now!"

Alex, mounted on a pale grey horse, silver bands gleaming against the tunic of deep blue, had entered the track almost on the strange knight's heels. Now, after one quick glance at the dark knight drawing steadily nearer to the Cannon box, Alex spurred his horse forward, coming up behind the other knight, passing him, and reining in triumphantly before Gabriele a good three seconds before the other knight arrived.

He swept off his headpiece, bowing low over his horse's neck. "Miss Cannon, would you do me the honour of allowing me to ride with your favour as a sign of my fealty and respect for all to see?"

She raised her eyes to his, expecting to see the familiar cynical smile. But he looked serious, intent, as though the English ballads played by the musicians had bridged centuries, and the racetrack were truly the greensward at King Arthur's Camelot. *Why, he does know how to play,* she thought, lifting her hands to her bonnet and finding the long pin with which Veronique had secured the veil. She removed the pin and held the strip of pink chiffon to the knight before her. He took it, looped it around his arm and knotted it twice. The breeze picked up the veil and sent it streaming behind him, and Gabriele, following it, looked right into Jordan Scott's blue eyes.

"Mr. Scott!" she said. "I thought you would not ride—"

"I had a change of—mind," he said. "May I also ride for you?"

Alex shifted in his saddle, the movement making his tunic shimmer and his headpiece gleam. "Don't say no on my account, Miss Cannon," he said. "You will double your chances for being Queen—and my cousin and I will have particular reason to ride well."

"Then, yes, of course," Gabriele said. She reached into her sleeve and withdrew a lace-edged handkerchief with her monogram worked carefully in pale blue thread. "Here," she said, putting it in Jordan's outstretched hand.

She saw his posture change, some small relaxation, and knew he had thought she would refuse. "I am not the most skilful rider," Jordan said, fixing her handkerchief to his sleeve. "But I doubt that any knight here has a greater desire to win." And then he turned to join the other knights, all of whom now wore their ladies' favours fluttering from their sleeves.

Harold LeBoeuf was the last knight in the train, wearing the yellow scarf of the youngest Robin girl tied to his scarlet sleeve. As he passed Gabriele, he reared his horse and made what Gabriele knew he intended to be an elegant bow. She bowed back, smiling at him with such warmth that his cheeks turned red, and he sprinted across the field, drawing up with a flourish at the end of the line.

I am too hard on him, she thought. He is young, and of course lacks polish. But if gentlemen like Mr. Scott and Mr. St. Cyr can treat me as though I am already an accomplished lady—then I can be friendly to him, and not make it more difficult for him to grow up.

A burst of music—a military-sounding air, all blaring trumpets and quick-beating drums. As the volume grew, the knights finished their parade and gathered at the top of the track, ready for the tourney to begin. The flash of sunlight on their lances, the sound of horses' hooves, the clatter of metal on metal as a lance crashed against a shield, made the field a storybook illustration come to life, and Gabriele sat transfixed, feeling as she had in those long-ago days of childhood when she and Tom played at Knights of the Round Table, jousting at targets Samson devised for them, and even floating Gabriele on the bayou as the tragic Lady of Shallott.

Three short blasts from the Herald's trumpet broke through her daze, and with everyone else in the grandstand, Gabriele turned toward the starting line where the first knight appeared, ready to ride.

"Sir Gawain," the Herald proclaimed, and all eyes fixed on the rider and his brightly-clad horse.

"That's one of the Fournets," Aunt Mat said. "My, he rides well!"

"He will have to, if he is going to secure the ring," Mrs. Robin said.

Gabriele looked down the field at the small gold ring swaying from a crosspiece on a long golden cord. She thought of her own efforts, in the paddock at home. Tom had rigged up two poles, then suspended a third between them, dangling one of Gabriele's embroidery hoops from it on a string. Using the broomstick with a nail driven in it Tom fashioned to practise with until the blacksmith could make him a lance, Gabriele had learned first hand how small a six-inch ring could be when approached from two hundred yards away on a horse pelting along as fast as she could.

Sir Gawain proved equal to the challenge: he rode toward the poles at full gallop, and passed his lance through the small gold ring, lifting it from its hook and circling around to come back to the top of the field. The crowd cheered, and some of the younger boys, too young to ride themselves, but eager partisans of a chosen knight, tossed their hats in the air and let their spirits out in exuberant cartwheels that took them dangerously near the horses' hooves.

Four times more Sir Gawain rode forward, and four times more he hooked the ring, but on the sixth attempt, his lance passed through empty air.

The crowd cheered as Sir Gawain left the field, then turned its attention to the next knight in line.

Mrs. Robin called to Aunt Mat, and she leaned toward the Robin box to hear something her friend whispered behind her fan, then turned back to Gabriele.

"Just imagine, Gabriele! Mrs. Robin says that Mr. Scott bought his costume and the use of that horse from Etienne Levert—simply stopped him as he rode up to the field, and asked him for both, as cool as you please!"

"And Mr. Levert agreed? I wondered how Mr. Scott had gotten himself up so quickly—but imagine getting his outfit from Mr. Levert!"

"Oh, well, I'm sure he gave Etienne a good price," Aunt Mat said. "It does seem odd—I can't put my finger on just why—Yankee impulsiveness, I suppose—"

"Or Yankee ingenuity," Mrs. Robin said. "As for Etienne—I suppose he sees nothing strange in letting someone else ride that prize horse of his and parade around in finery he bought to wear himself." She looked past Aunt Mat at Gabriele. "Mr. Scott must have wanted to ride very much—I wonder he didn't decide earlier, Gabriele."

"He works very hard," Gabriele said. "And has many demands on his time. I imagine some business appointment was changed—and he discovered he had time to come to the tourney after all—"

"I wouldn't have thought he had so much boldness," Aunt Mat said. "But I'm glad to see it. I admire a young man of serious purpose, of course. But a little frivolity as leaven—that is always desired."

The Herald announced the next knight, who rode forward eagerly only to miss the ring on his first pass. Several others rode in rapid succession: a few achieved their objective once or twice, with one lifting the ring four times before returning empty-handed.

When Tom came up, the crowd, its appetite whetted now, called his name, and the same pack of young boys ran alongside the track as Tom galloped forward, urging him on. As Jupiter carried Tom faster and faster toward the poles, Gabriele's hand grasped her fan so tightly that its ribs marked her palm. But Tom's practice stood him in good stead, and he carried the ring away eight times before Jupiter stumbled and Tom's lance passed just under the shining ring through empty air.

Two more knights tried their skill, but none approached Tom's mark. Then came Harold LeBoeuf, making up in enthusiasm and vigour what he lacked in style, and carrying the ring away six times before he failed. Now only Jordan Scott and Alex St. Cyr were left: word had spread throughout the crowd that each wore Gabriele Cannon's favour on his sleeve, and a stir of excitement rippled over the grandstand as the two knights waited to be announced.

Each deferred to the other—for a moment, it seemed as though the Herald would have to decide who rode first. Then Alex bowed to his cousin and rode forward, signalling to the Herald that he was ready to begin.

"Sir Lancelot!" the Herald said, his trumpet's blast announcing the knight's advance.

Lancelot—the chosen knight of the fair Elaine, Gabriele's favourite lady in King Arthur's court. Could Alex have known that? Gabriele looked at her brother, far down the field. No matter—he rode for her now, a tall blue and silver figure on a pale grey horse, racing toward the golden ring with silver lance held high.

Gabriele did not have to count how many times Sir Lancelot sailed through the poles and bore the ring away. The crowd's mounting noise counted for her. As Sir Lancelot surpassed Tom's mark, and succeeded yet again, a quiet settled over the crowd. They watched in silence while Alex rode three times more, each time coming away with the ring upon his lance. Only on the fourteenth attempt did Alex fail; as he rode back to the starting point, the crowd broke its silence with a cheer, and Dorothea said to Gabriele, "You are certain to be crowned Queen. No one can defeat Mr. St. Cyr but his cousin—and he rides for you, too."

Jordan's try seemed almost anticlimactic, as far as the audience was concerned. The Queen of Beauty would be Gabriele Cannon—who cared who placed the crown upon her head? But when the Herald called, "Sir Tristram!" Gabriele bent forward to watch him as though all the important issues were still his to decide. She watched Jordan set his horse in motion, golden lance held in one gloved hand. He rode well, hooking the ring with a sturdy deliberation and measured approach quite different from Alex's dashing grace and reckless style. It proved equally effective, for Jordan succeeded twelve times in a row, riding as though this task had been set him by some hard schoolmaster, and stopping only when the twelfth ring slid down his lance.

"One more and they will be tied!" Dorothea said. "An amazing turn of events, Gabriele!"

She could not speak. She understood Alex St. Cyr's entering the tournament, there could be no reason for him to do anything else. But Mr. Scott had made his excuses, and they had been accepted. Now, with his last-minute appearance, he had created a stir—people looked at her and whispered behind their fans, commenting on this stranger who so little understood their ways that he would buy Etienne Levert's costume and rent his horse.

Mr. Scott does not understand that if this event is not important enough to prepare for—it is certainly not important enough to enter at the last possible time, she thought. *His behaviour is bringing undue attention to me, and to himself. I hope he loses, for his cousin, even if he is unpredictable, at least understands our rules.*

She sat back, determined to give no outward appearance of interest in Jordan Scott's fate. But he did not need her attention, or, if he did, he gave no sign. Only when he drew level with their box as he made his next run down the field did he glance to the side—and at that moment, as Gabriele looked toward the field, Jordan caught her glance and held it, ignoring the ring swinging in a slow arc against the blue sky.

Still he rode toward his target, with his lance held high. But the moment of distraction had destroyed his aim: the horse veered to the right, carrying the point of the lance past its gold prize. Sir Tristram jerked his head around to look back at the ring swinging on its cord, not reining in his horse or turning him as he reached the fence bounding the track. At the last instant, when it seemed the horse must collide with the fence, Sir Tristram yanked the reins and turned him, slowing him to a trot and regaining control.

He joined Sir Lancelot at the top of the track, riding through a jubilant crowd. The Herald placed the crown between them: Sir Lancelot held it with his right hand, Sir Tristram with his left, and they rode toward Gabriele together, lances cutting a bright path. Tom, as the knight with the next highest number of wins, fell in behind them, with the full company of competitors forming a colourful train.

Sir Lancelot and Sir Tristram dismounted, Lancelot retaining the crown for a moment, then both sharing it as they drew near. Mr. Scott looks like a little boy who has been taken to a circus for the very first time, Gabriele thought, and she almost forgave him for the talk he had caused, remembering that he had no experience with this sort of entertainment and had carried the day on a field in no way his own.

And Mr. St. Cyr—she turned to study her other knight. Mr. St. Cyr looks as though he spends his days in exactly this sort of amusement, she thought. As though nothing suits him quite so well as an elaborate game.

"Your bonnet, Gabriele," Aunt Mat whispered, and Gabriele abandoned all thought, giving herself to the moment, determined to savour it to the last. She untied her bonnet and removed it from her head, handing it to Aunt Mat with her eyes still on the knights.

The two hands holding the crown moved slowly forward, and Gabriele felt the flower- and ribbon-bedecked circlet settle on her head. Alex's hand brushed against her cheek as he lifted the ribbons so they could stream back over her shoulder—the merest brush, the drift of wings of a butterfly. Then Alex extended his left arm and Jordan extended his right, helping Gabriele to rise, and guiding her to a gaily decorated marquee set up on the far side of the track.

The other knights found their own fair ladies, and brought them to be presented to their queen. While the rest of the gathering strolled about, visiting friends or taking refreshment under another marquee, Gabriele and the ladies of her court set tasks for their knights, or begged to be regaled with glorious tales.

"You mustn't disappoint me, Sir Tristram," Gabriele said. "All the other knights have spoken of their valour—now surely there is something you can tell!"

"I would not make so bold in this company," Jordan said. "But if I can borrow a mandolin, I will sing you a story instead."

Someone handed him the instrument, someone else made room for him to sit on the grass, and with a rippling succession of chords, Jordan began singing an old English air. "'. . . He fell in love with a nice young girl, Her name was Barb'ry Ellen . . .'" His voice, clear and strong, gradually overpowered the chatter around them, and he soon sang to a silent circle of listeners who, when he had finished the ballad, begged him to sing again.

"But you sing so well!" Gabriele said. "To think you have never joined in when I play after dinner at home—"

"It is the costume," Jordan said. "It tempts me to deeds I would otherwise never have the courage to try."

"Then here is another one," Gabriele said. "And it includes you, Sir Lancelot. As I listened to Sir Tristram—

and remembered how well you sing, too—I could not help but think how pleasant it would be to hear you sing a duet."

A tiny flicker in Jordan's eyes, a twist of a smile on Alex's face—and then Alex nodded his head. "As you wish, my lady."

"Sir Tristram?" Gabriele said.

"But of course."

He fingered the mandolin, striking soft chords. Then, with a glance at Alex, he said, "Do you know 'Greensleeves'?"

Alex nodded, and they began, their voices carrying past the marquee out over the crowd. Shadows lengthened now, and the sky turned a rosy gold, softly lighting the young faces gathered beneath the marquee.

A perfect moment, Gabriele thought. A time to be remembered. One of those amulets life sometimes gives us as proof that doubt and fear are ephemeral, and that only love and beauty are real.

Gabriele woke to rain, heavy streams of water rattling on the roof, gushing through downspouts to splash into the two great cisterns at the back corners of the house. A milky light lay behind the shutters like a thin grey lining, too pale to brighten the room. She knew she was happy. At first, she did not remember why. Then her eye fell on the ring tourney gown, hung to air before Lucie put it away. The crown, fragile petals bruised now, lay on her dressing table, and her green silk slippers, shimmering faintly in the pale light, stood neatly on the floor. A rush of memories, of the high, clear call of the trumpet, of hooves striking the soft earth of the field, of a shining lance piercing a shimmering ring, came over her, and she sat up, letting the sheet fall from her bare shoulders, and reaching out a hand to ring for her maid.

She dressed quickly, hardly able to stand still long enough for Lucie to arrange her hair, and hurrying down the main stairs as though the butler would remove breakfast if she were even a minute late. But she composed herself before entering the breakfast room, where Tom and Alex sat talking over plates of eggs and fried ham, supplemented by a silver basket of Letha's biscuits surrounded by preserves and jam. Both rose when Gabriele came into the room; Alex held a chair for her, and she slipped into her place with the delightful feeling that no matter how hard it rained outside, inside it would be a bright and beautiful day.

"Imagine being out in this," Alex said, gesturing toward the rain beyond the window. This room, set between the dining room and the butler's pantry, looked out over the formal garden, and following Alex's gaze, Gabriele saw rain dripping down the statues and cascading from an overflowing fountain centring the design.

"Thank goodness we don't have to be," Gabriele said. "And thank goodness we have guests—otherwise, on a day like today, my aunt would tell me to mend all my gloves or sit at the piano for hours learning a very long and difficult piece."

"I hope one guest will require as much attention as two, Miss Cannon," Alex said, accepting another cup of coffee from Gabriele. "My cousin Jordan Scott, in an unaccountable display of Yankee perseverance to duty and devotion to work, has ridden into New Iberia, there to board one of our packets and accompany it as far as the point where the Teche connects to Six Mile Lake." He sipped and looked at Gabriele over the rim of his cup. "I say unaccountable, because I cannot imagine a young man in his right senses leaving Felicity where now the acknowledged Queen of Beauty reigns."

"But someone must see to your business, Mr. St. Cyr," Gabriele said. "And if you are not to do it, I suppose it must be him."

"Ah, dear lady, don't rebuke me," Alex said. "It is only when I find myself in a team harness that I balk—I work well enough alone."

"Then you should form no partnerships, Mr. St. Cyr,"

Gabriele said. She poured hot milk and black coffee into Tom's cup, carefully watching the double streams join. "Such an arrangement is fair to no one—not to your partner, and not to yourself."

"Some partnerships are more agreeable than others," Alex said, but then, from the end of the hall giving onto the back gallery came a high, shrill scream, followed by shouts and sounds of running feet. Again the scream— Tom leapt from his chair and dashed out of the room, Alex fast behind him. Gabriele sat staring at the empty doorway and then, knocking her chair over in her haste to rise, followed quickly on Alex's heels.

Tom reached the gallery first, with Alex and Gabriele gaining the threshold to see, half-blocked by Tom's body, two women fighting, the dark face of one contorted like an ebony mask, the light face of the other drawn with revulsion and fear.

"My God—it's Veronique!" Tom cried, and started forward with hands outstretched to stop them. But even as he moved toward them, something metallic flashed in the darker woman's hand: Veronique, seeing the knife thrust coming, pulled long-bladed scissors from her apron pocket and ripped them across her opponent's face.

"Devil!" the woman shrieked, and plunged the knife into Veronique's chest.

"Don't look, Miss Cannon," Alex said, turning to shield her.

But she pushed past him, crying, "Veronique!" as Tom's hand closed on the other woman's wrist, and he tightened his grip until the tense fingers relaxed and the bloody knife clattered to the brick floor.

"God help you, Colette, if you've killed her," he said to the slave cowering at his feet. He made a compress of his handkerchief and motioned to a nearby slave to hold it against Colette's face, then went to kneel beside Veronique.

She lay slumped on the floor, ivory skin faintly grey, golden eyes dark with shock and fear. Gabriele knelt beside her, wrapping her shawl around Veronique's chest, pulling it tight to staunch the blood and making her lie flat. "You must be very still, Veronique. So as to slow the flow of blood and help it stop."

Veronique lifted her head as she struggled to speak, but Gabriele put her hand gently over Veronique's lips. "Shh," she said. "Don't try to talk. Tom will take care of everything—you lie still and rest."

Two slaves stood at the edge of the gallery, frozen and still as though under some dark spell. When Tom moved to confront them, they shifted slightly, and Alex felt a terrible tension emanate from them as they looked from Colette to Veronique.

"How is the bleeding, Letha?" Tom said to the tall, lean woman who held the compress against Veronique's cheek. Letha looked up, her high cheekbones and great hooked nose thrown into strong relief against the pale grey rain.

"It's almost stopped," she said.

Tom's foot struck the scissors that Veronique had dropped, and he bent and picked them up, looking from their blood-stained tips to Veronique, and then back at the men standing at the edge of the porch.

"All right, Samson, what happened?" he asked.

"It's still that same thing, Mister Tom. Colette, she mad 'cause Zeke, he want Veronique 'stead of her."

Gabriele looked down at Veronique. Her eyes, tightly closed, made narrow slits from which a trickle of tears escaped, and a low moan came faintly from her lips.

Tom's arm shot out and he grasped Colette's shoulder, whirling her away from Letha so he could look into her face. "Damn it, Colette, is this what comes of our kindness to you?"

Colette stood before him, blood drying on her cheek, with only a few drops still oozing from the long cut that crossed it. The pose of her body had changed: she no longer cowered, but stood defiantly before them, every taut line of her body a statement they did not have to hear to understand.

"I ain't forgot any kindness," Colette said. "I wants to have healthy hands for you—I can do that if I live with Zeke."

"We should have sold you," Tom said. "You've been nothing but trouble since the day you came here—"

"Trouble! She the one that make trouble," Colette said. "Put a spell on Zeke to make him want her—why else would he want that yellow gal?"

Gabriele shivered and drew back against the gallery wall. She wanted to close her ears to Colette's thick ugly words —she could almost see them leaving dark marks across the clean surface of their lives.

Colette bent low, putting her face close to Veronique. "She can't make strong babies. All she's good for is to sew them clothes—"

"If I had you punished as I ought, you would be good for nothing for weeks, Colette," Tom said. "But you know I won't have you whipped—you count on it."

Colette's head lifted slightly, one hand moving to her thrust-out hip. She said nothing, pulling her lips into a narrow line. One corner drooped, just tracing the edge of an arrogant smile. "If you lets me live with Zeke, I don't care if you has me whipped, Mister Tom."

"Mr. Adams and I will decide how to punish you, Colette," Tom said. "Now go back to your cabin and don't leave it—do you understand?"

"I understand," Colette said. Her eyes slid from Tom to Veronique, and back again, a long, slender arc that made Gabriele suddenly afraid.

"Letha, take Veronique into the office and put her to bed on the cot. Let me know if we should send for the doctor—and Zeke, you stay here. I want to talk to you."

"Yes, Mister Tom," Letha said. She lifted Veronique carefully, easing her to her feet and supporting her as she began to walk. Slowly, they moved down the gallery, disappearing inside the plantation office door.

Samson put his big hand under Colette's elbow, almost lifting her off her feet. "I see she go right back to her

cabin, Mister Tom. You want me to get somebody to
watch her?"

"No," Tom said. "If she even starts up toward this
house—I'll shoot her down where she stands."

He turned away, his face so white Gabriele knew that he
could barely contain his rage. "I've got to find Adams," he
said to Alex and Gabriele. "Wretched business—I'm sorry,
St. Cyr. This is hardly pleasant for a guest."

"Can I help?" Alex said quietly.

Tom looked into his friend's face, and his own face
eased. He took Alex's hand and squeezed it, then slowly
shook his head. "It's bestial, isn't it? To reduce what can
be the greatest source of human joy to—that."

He turned and watched Samson half-pull, half-carry,
Colette into the thick curtain of rain, their bare feet suck-
ing softly in the thick mud. "Aunt Mat would want my
hide if she knew you witnessed this, Gabriele," Tom said.
He sounded exhausted, and Gabriele saw all over again the
scene in the gazebo: the connection between it and what
had just happened could not be more plain.

"She asked you to stop it," Gabriele said. "Veronique—
in the gazebo—she asked you to see to it that she does not
have to—marry Zeke."

"You must forget that, too, Gabriele," Tom said. "Now
more than ever—"

"Are you sure I can't help?" Alex said. "I don't want to
intrude—but you seem to be in a terrible mess—"

"It's one I have to take care of," Tom said. "As for
helping—believe me, if there were anything you could do,
I would let you know."

"See that you do," Alex said. "Now let me be clear on
this—as I understand it, Mrs. LeGrange is not to know
that Miss Cannon was anywhere near—"

"That's right. I hate to ask you to be party to a deception—"

"It's necessary, I agree," Alex said. He looked down at
Gabriele, the smile on his lips not yet reaching his eyes. "I

fear you must play another game today, Miss Cannon, but one less pleasant than being a queen."

"If you mean that I must pretend I don't know what happened to poor Veronique, I don't know if I can," Gabriele said. "It is so horrible—so dreadfully wrong—"

"But you must, Gabe," Tom said. "I can't be worrying that you'll slip and tell Aunt Mat—"

"Of course she won't," Alex said, offering her his arm. "Miss Cannon, I propose that we go back to the morning room and finish our meal. And if you aren't hungry—then you can satisfy another appetite of mine." He guided her gently toward the door, avoiding the bloodstains gleaming on the brick floor. "I have an insatiable curiosity about other people's families—I want you to tell me all about yours—including those ancestors so disreputable you pretend you don't descend from them at all."

His voice, light, even, flowed over her as he took her down the hall. He kept up a stream of questions, ignoring her silences, and gradually getting her to talk. By the time they were seated again, her pulse had returned almost to normal, her cheeks no longer felt hot. She looked across the table at Alex, sipping coffee with the familiar indolent smile. How perfectly his nickname suits him, she thought. He is like quicksilver—one moment full of concern for Tom's problems, the next moment flirting with me. Then he shifted position, and a shadow fell across him, darkening the expression on his face. No, I am wrong, she thought. His mood has not changed. He is still worried about Tom—he proves it by looking after me.

Chapter Five

I MUST HOLD MY END UP, GABRIELE THOUGHT, THOUGH I hardly have the heart to make talk. Her eyes roved the room as though searching for a topic and fell on a painting hanging on the wall behind her guest.

"You know Adrian Persac's work, of course," she said. "There behind you is his vision of our house."

Alex turned and examined the painting. "We have one of his at Olympia, using that same device of cutting out figures from magazines and gluing them into place. I asked Persac once why he didn't either leave people out of his pictures or paint them in himself—but he said this method suited him and his clients did not seem to mind."

"People rarely mind anything that flatters them," Gabriele said. "Not that Persac makes houses look better than they are—I suppose I was thinking of a certain portrait artist who paints his sitter's most idealized self."

"Then he would have to paint you as you appear every moment, Miss Cannon," Alex said. "There is no way to idealize perfection—it is there."

"Please don't speak that way," Gabriele said. "I—am not able to—bear it."

"But forgive me, Miss Cannon!" Alex said. "I did not mean—"

"No, you did not mean it," Gabriele cut in. "At least—you meant to say something pleasant, it is what gentlemen are supposed to do. And I daresay I should listen, and practise receiving pretty speeches from my brother's good friend. But I am still *distraite*, Mr. St. Cyr—I can't get what happened to Veronique out of my mind. I see her still—that awful wound—the horror in her face—"

"Yes—a terrible thing to have happen—"

"It is bestial, just as Tom said."

"But then—that is the condition of all slaves, is it not? Which is why so many people oppose it."

"Oh, yes," Gabriele said. "They oppose it in principle— at least, they say that they do. But they continue to own them—" She saw the expression on his face, and nodded. "Yes, I know. My father owns over two hundred slaves. But he does intend to free them, over time."

"That will be difficult, Miss Cannon, if other planters in this region do not hold your father's view. They will worry that their own slaves will rebel to be free, too, and perhaps unite against Mr. Cannon until he changes his mind."

"You do not know my father, Mr. St. Cyr. Once he is set on a course of action, he rarely changes his mind— unless better and more complete information persuades him that he should."

"A reasonable man," Alex said. "I always thought so, from things you wrote to Tom."

"Things I wrote to Tom?"

"When we were at Virginia," Alex said. He coloured slightly, and turned his attention to his plate. "He used to —read portions of your letters to me—"

"But I am astonished, Mr. St. Cyr! Of what possible interest could my letters be? Full of country news and family doings—"

"That is just it, Miss Cannon. I have never had a sister —no one to write of such small events as a neighbour's new child or the arrival of a new Paris gown."

His colour deepened, as though he confessed to some great sin, and Gabriele felt suddenly sorry for him.

"Then I'm glad that my letters brought you some pleasure, Mr. St. Cyr. Though if I had known Tom shared them—I should probably have been too intimidated to write at all."

"There is something I must tell you, Miss Cannon. Something Tom does not even know—"

"I have no secrets from my brother," Gabriele said. "As he has none from me." Even as she spoke, she thought of Tom and Veronique as they had stood when she came upon them in the gazebo. But that is not a secret, she thought. At least—not any longer.

"You may tell him this if you choose to," Alex said. "But it is you I want to tell." He looked past her into the still-pouring rain, then back at the bright room. "I—read your letters to Tom, all of them. When he was away from our chambers—it was despicable, I know—but the bits and pieces I heard were like the beginning of a story—I—I had to know the end."

"Mr. St. Cyr—but—why would you risk your—honour —to read letters not meant for you?"

"Honour, yes," Alex said. He brought his eyes around to her face. "Some need stronger than honour impelled me, Miss Cannon. I can explain it no better than that. As though the love and trust and sweetness of words meant for your brother somehow eased my soul."

"I am sorry you did not have a sister, Mr. St. Cyr," Gabriele said softly. "For she would certainly have been proud to have a brother like you, and would have sent letters by every post."

"If I had had a sister, Miss Cannon, I fear she would have modelled herself after our mother—and then I should have had no letters at all," Alex said. He caught himself, and stopped, mouth twisted in the now familiar cynical smile. "But I am taking advantage of your goodness, Miss Cannon, and burdening you with trifles not worth your time. I have some books to go over—if you will excuse me, I will go out to my rooms and set to work."

"And I have a stack of correspondence to see to," Gabriele said. "Which I now face with a little more confidence, since you have been kind enough to let me think my letters pleasant to read."

Alex came around the table and took her hand, holding it as Tom did, as though it were some small, fragile thing he must protect. "Now I have seen true generosity," he said. "You are ignoring the infamy of my act—and thanking me for it instead."

"If reading my letters to Tom is the worst thing you have ever done, Mr. St. Cyr, then you are still worthy to be a knight," Gabriele said. His smile rewarded her: he seemed almost restored to his usual easy ways, bowing over the hand he held and taking his leave after arranging to meet her later that day.

She settled down to her letters, dividing them into stacks to organize the task. This stack invitations to be accepted, that one invitations to be refused—this thin stack letters that must be answered, giving detailed accounts of family news. She glanced at the calendar hanging near her desk. I must enter the invitations we are accepting, she thought, mentally imagining the neat entries that would carry her through a summer of house parties and expeditions to the resorts lining the waters of the Mississippi Sound.

And then my season in New Orleans—she laid down her pen, her thoughts automatically going to Alex St. Cyr. What books can he be working on, she wondered, remembering his remark about working very well alone. Perhaps I am unfair to him. Just because his ways are not those of his cousin doesn't mean that Mr. St. Cyr always shirks his share.

It is as though he pretends to be more frivolous than he is—she remembered something else, a bitter comment Alex made in answer to a question arising when they toured the plantation that first day.

"What is your view of slavery, Mr. St. Cyr?" Gabriele had asked. "Are you like your father, who owns slaves but pretends that they are pets? Or do you follow your mother's lead?"

She could still hear the short, harsh laugh that had accompanied Alex's reply. "I have no view," he had said. "With such a wealth of opinion available between my parents to have one myself seems—*de trop.*"

That answer had annoyed her then, but now it gave rise to pity. To walk a tightrope between father and mother— to dread that by supporting one parent's view he would lose the other's esteem. No wonder he hides behind flippant comments and facile smiles, Gabriele thought. But there is a danger there, I wonder if he sees it? By acting as though he takes nothing seriously, he is at risk of never being taken seriously himself.

Nor must I, she resolved, picking up her pen. Aunt Mat is right, there will be many young gentlemen in New Orleans this winter, whose families we know, and who do not present such enigmatic faces to the world. Nor, she added in the honesty of her heart, such attractive ones, I'm sure.

She made quick work of the invitations, and turned to the letters, answering first one from a cousin living now in Savannah. I shall write her all about the ring tourney, Gabriele thought. She has attended many there, she will be pleased to hear of my triumph. But even as her pen raced across the page, as she described the lively scene, the daring knights, another event intruded into her mind.

And what would this cousin think, I wonder, if I wrote about Colette and Veronique? A dreadful fight—a woman debased. But our letters never refer to such: we avoid recording these things, deceiving ourselves that if we look past them, they will cease to exist.

It seemed more difficult to write her letter now, as though the words she put on paper made a lie. The splendid gown she had just described, made by Veronique's skilful hands—to read about it, her cousin would not think past the dress to its maker. And why should she? Gabriele thought. When do any of us, surrounded by comfort and luxury, think past the meals to those who prepare them, or past the hot water in our pitchers to those who carried it up long flights of stairs?

She drew another sheet of stationery before her and continued to write. "And so the entire occasion gave me the greatest pleasure, marred only by an unhappy incident this morning when one of the field slaves made a completely unwarranted attack upon Veronique, whose talents had fashioned my beautiful dress. I am quite wretched about it—" And I am not supposed to know. Slowly, her hand crumpled the paper and dropped it into the wastebasket at her side.

The door behind her opened, and she looked around, almost expecting to see her aunt. But Tom burst into the room. "Father's home!" he cried. "The Southern delegates bolted the convention—he's just arrived!"

"Papa!" Gabriele said. She rose and ran to her brother, everything else forgotten in her joy. "Oh, Tom! What wonderful news!"

"He went to change," Tom said. "But he'll join us for lunch—"

"I must speak to Letha," Gabriele said. "With Aunt Mat spending the day with Mrs. Robin, we'd planned a very simple meal—"

"Father's tired, Gabe. He won't want very much."

"Still," she said, "Letha would be upset if I did not warn her he is home. You know she likes to please him—"

They stepped into the hall, where the sound of the front door being opened made their heads turn. Jordan Scott walked past the slave who opened it, mud staining his trousers and water dripping from his hat. He looked upset, as though he, too, had had something unpleasant with which to contend, and Gabriele remembered words she had forgotten in her happiness that her father was home.

The Southern delegates bolted the convention—that's what Tom had said. She stood staring at Jordan Scott, thinking of her father's opinion expressed to his children on his last night home. "Pray that the Southern wing of the party prevails," he had said. "Slavery and secession must be the central issues of this presidential campaign—and if the Democratic party cannot agree on the candidate to carry them—then it is almost certain the Union will be split."

"You've heard the news, Scott?" Tom said, going to greet their guest.

"The Southern bolt? Yes," Jordan said.

"You are distressed," Tom said.

"I—can't help but be."

"Perhaps it is not as bad as we fear," Tom said. "Father will tell us all about it at lunch."

"You might prefer I take my meal alone," Jordan said.

"Alone? Don't be absurd! We wouldn't hear of it, would we, Gabriele?"

"Of course not," she said. She went to Jordan, smiling warmly to put him more at ease. "The Union still holds, Mr. Scott. We are not yet under separate flags. But if we cannot even dine together because of politics, I'm afraid there's little hope the nation won't divide."

She left Tom and Jordan in the hall, hurrying away to tell Letha her master was home. I don't see how they shall ever sort out this muddle, she thought. To talk of splitting the country, as though the Mason-Dixon line truly were a knife, and could cut cleanly through the two regions, putting all who detest slavery on one side and on the other all those by whom it is embraced. Why, even in our small region, planters disagree. There are those like Papa who wish to gradually free all the slaves, hiring them to work—and there are those who see no difference between the animals in their barnyards and the men and women who till their fields.

The bestial condition of slavery—that is the term Mr. St. Cyr used. And Veronique must not remain in it any longer—I must speak to Papa again, Gabriele resolved. And this time, I will not let him refuse.

She held herself a little straighter, unconsciously holding her head in a regal pose. When she entered the pantry,

Letha looked up and crossed herself, exclaiming, "Gracious, Miss Gabriele, you gave me a fright. You look so like your sweet mama that for a minute, I thought you were her ghost."

Even Oliver Cannon's obvious pleasure at being with his family once more did not dispel the grave air with which he took his place at the luncheon table, and Gabriele sank into her chair at his right with a feeling of disquiet, certain that everyone else in the room waited to hear her father speak with the same sense of dread.

He signalled to them to bow their heads, and then said the familiar words with which they began each meal: "Bless us, O Lord, and these thy gifts which we are about to receive through thy bounty, through Christ Our Lord." But then he added something, letting each word fall as solemnly as though tolled by a bell. "Please guide us in the months ahead so that we may act with charity, with wisdom, and most of all, within thy grace. Amen."

Gabriele heard soft echoes of the same sigh that released her held-in breath, and looked up to see the same anxiety she felt marking the faces of her brother and their guests. "You fear the worst, sir," Tom said. "That is plain."

"I wish I did not," Oliver Cannon said. "Those who went to the convention determined to bring about just this result are jubilant—those of us who hoped that reason could somehow prevail see no cause to celebrate. When the Southern Democrats walked out of that hall in Charleston, we said in effect that our loyalty to the South's cause is greater than our loyalty to the Union—our action might be the beginning of the end of a noble dream."

He looked around the table, accurately reading the question posed by four pairs of eyes.

"You are wondering, all of you, why I joined the bolting members if my sentiments are not wholeheartedly theirs."

"It does seem, sir, that if you had remained—you and

others who hold your more moderate views—reason might have still prevailed," Tom said.

"Had the convention not already been aligned along regional boundaries that might have been possible," Oliver Cannon said. "As it was—the Northern delegates entered with their own firm agenda, just as we did. We determined fairly quickly that the two agendas had little in common, and were not likely to, no matter how long and heated the debate."

"So it came down to Abolitionists on one side and slave-holders on the other?" Alex said. "That is a familiar division, one I confront daily in my own home."

Oliver Cannon peered at Alex over the top of his spectacles, and took a sip of wine before he spoke. "You are too intelligent to believe the issue is that simple, St. Cyr," he said. "The debate over slavery is the emotional one, the one that enlists supporters to strengthen both sides."

"Yes, the sight of a whip striping a slave's back can make more converts than hours of argument," Alex said. He held up a hand before his host could speak. "I know your overseer avoids the whip, relying instead on disciplinary methods less brutal and cruel. As Tom said so justly to my cousin the day we arrived here—there is no Simon Legree at Felicity, and I cannot imagine that there ever would be."

"Were the other issue not so important, Mr. St. Cyr, the emotional one could be resolved," Oliver Cannon said. "The bills known collectively as the Compromise of 1850, authored by Henry Clay and supported by such Northern leaders as Daniel Webster himself were agreed upon by our Congress—that should have been the end of the matter, but of course, it has not been! Which is why the other issue, the issue of secession, is so important—and why it is the thing we must settle, and settle soon." Oliver Cannon signalled to the butler to pour more wine, holding his own glass meditatively as he spoke. "Whether a state having freely joined the Union can freely leave it—that is paramount."

"But you spoke of a noble dream, sir," Jordan said. "I thought you meant this nation—this experiment in a democratic government—"

"Do you call what we have democracy, sir? When the populous North rules us in Congress, piping the tune by which we must dance? I do not believe the men who founded this nation would call it so—your Abolitionists go farther than our own Constitution, and with little right that I can see."

"But you know that you believe the slaves should be freed, Papa," Gabriele said. "How many times have I listened to you speak of that—"

"Yes, that is exactly what I believe. Freed over a period of time, gradually assimilated into a free society—by the end of the century, I think we would have seen all the slaves freed, paid for their labour whether in the fields or in town."

"By the end of the century! That is forty years away!" Jordan exclaimed. He had the same heated look that he had worn at the ring tourney, but instead of reminding Gabriele of a little boy at his first circus, he looked instead like a man determined to have his say. "Excuse me, Mr. Cannon—I am very new to your household, and I realize that my Yankee origins should make me subdue my speech—"

"Of course they should not," Oliver Cannon said. "The opinions of all of our guests are welcome here, so long as they are expressed civilly, with the rights of others in mind."

"I have been at Felicity only a short time, sir," Jordan said. "But long enough to know that none of you are unconscious of the ills of slavery—" Jordan broke off, intercepting a look Alex gave Tom. "I'm sorry—did I say something wrong?"

"No—continue," Tom said. But he could not keep his eyes from going to Gabriele, and she knew that at that moment, three people at the table could think of nothing but the particular ills that had overtaken Veronique.

"Well, then—you are kind people, concerned about your slaves—you speak of eventually freeing them. So what I don't understand is—why don't you free them now?"

"All at once?" Tom said.

"Why not?"

"In the first place, Jordan," Alex said, "for some years now Louisiana law has forbidden freeing slaves. That is not to say there are not ways around it—a slave 'earns' his freedom by the simple device of his master adding up the money he makes for him until it matches the price the slave would bring."

"You have told me you use the task system here, Tom," Jordan said. "Then you know the value of each slave's work. Why can't they work themselves free?"

"But, Scott, use your head!" Tom said. "Free all the slaves on this one plantation? What kind of chaos would that create, do you think?"

"Why should it create any?" Jordan said. "I am not trying to be contentious—but really, I don't see why it should."

"If you had been here longer, it would be easier for you to understand," Gabriele said. "Imagine the discontent on other plantations if our slaves were free. There could be insurrections at the worst—and at the best, work slowdowns leading to more losses than we usually suffer from such things."

"Then you put yourself in an untenable position, Miss Cannon, one I don't see how you can bear. On the one hand you decry what the institution does to those who must live in it—but on the other hand, you are not willing to act boldly to bring it to an end."

The terrible emotions of the morning, pushed under the surface and held there by Gabriele's joy in her father's return, rose up stronger than ever as she listened to Jordan Scott speak. She knew she must answer him, but she knew also that her last control would break the moment she opened her lips. The silence stretched on: it had just reached the point of becoming unbearable when Alex, who had been silently watching the others talk, leaned forward.

"Don't be perverse, Jordan. You understand perfectly well this dilemma you pose. I have heard you rave against the conditions of the crews on the great Scott ships—but I have yet to see you do anything that will help them crawl out of their miserable holds."

"Our crews are free men, Alex. The slaves of the South are not."

"Free?" Alex threw back his head and laughed, that same harsh sound Gabriele remembered. "Oh, I grant you that legally they are free. No one can actually sell them—but they are bought, Jordan, over and over again. Bought for low wages and given scandalous living quarters—not only in ships, but in factories all over the North."

Although Jordan sat next to Tom, he seemed distanced from them, as though his views had separated him after all. When he spoke, the natural enthusiasm that had warmed his voice was gone, and he sounded formal and cold. "As you know, Alex, I have those same concerns. And you have heard me say I intend to work unceasingly to bring such conditions to an end."

"I believe, Jordan," Alex said, the merest veil of courtesy softening what sounded to Gabriele very much like contempt, "that our host and his family hold the same good intention, and would indeed begin to put it into practice were it not for the unfortunate interference of those who, having long since pocketed their slave trade profits, are now free to criticize us."

"I see I shall have no lack of discussion, even if I have left the convention," Oliver Cannon said. "Of course you bring up an oft-debated question—whether the economic slavery of workers in the North is as heinous as the legal slavery in the South—or whether it can be exonerated on the grounds that the workers up there are—free." He rose, coming to Gabriele and holding out his hand. "Come, my dear, and walk with me to my room. I am still weary from my journey and will take a rest." He tucked Gabriele's hand through his arm and they took leave of the others: a silence fell, and their voices drifted back down the hall.

"I have learned the new Gottschalk piece, Papa," they heard Gabriele say. "I shall play it for you when you come down again—it is very nice, and I think of you each time I play it—"

"I look forward to that," Oliver Cannon replied. "And to hearing all about the ring tourney. Your brother assured me you made him and your aunt very proud."

Then the listeners could hear no more: Alex spoke first, looking at Tom with a smile. "Well, old fellow, you're a lucky man. But I suppose you know that?"

"Because of my father, you mean? Yes, he gives me a great deal to live up to."

Alex smiled again, and nodded, but Tom saw the quick flicker in his eyes. He did not mean I am lucky to have a man like that for a father—he meant I am lucky to have a sister like Gabriele. He almost said—you envy me Gabriele. But Jordan's presence silenced him, he had no wish to enter into a personal conversation with Jordan sitting there.

"I have some business with Adams," Tom said. "If you will excuse me?"

"And I must go out again," Jordan said. He hesitated, then went to stand in front of Tom. "We haven't known each other very long," he said. "But I believe we have grounds for mutual trust."

"I agree with that," Tom said.

"Then take this offer as it is meant. If your family will be more comfortable without me here—I will move into town today."

"Good heavens, Scott, do you think my father has never been disagreed with before? Or challenged in his own house, at his own table? You are civil, you tramp on no one's rights—of course you are not to leave, we won't hear of such a thing."

"I will," Alex said. "Unless you both promise me that

we shall not talk only of politics. I have heard every point that can possibly be brought up on either side of those issues—and whether it is slavery or secession, I have had my fill."

"But even old arguments have a new point now," Jordan said. "The turn of events in Charleston brings us closer to the brink—Alex, don't you realize that by this time next year there may be no Union at all?"

Alex still sat at the table, and now he leaned back in his chair, sipping the wine the butler had just poured in his glass. "I must remember to ask your father about his cellar, Tom. Each wine I sample is better than the last—" He looked at Jordan, his eyes seeming to measure just how high a degree his cousin's anger had reached. "I confess I am not that devoted to the Union, Jordan. The prospect of its dissolution does not then fill me with dismay."

"Not care about the Union! Are you mad?" Jordan said. Tom felt that neither man saw him: the sparks that flew between them came from an old, banked fire, that burst into new life each time either of them gave it fuel.

"Louisiana has not been part of it very long," Alex said. "Not yet fifty years—a very short span as nations go."

"I realize New Orleans and Louisiana are very different from, say, Boston, or my native state," Jordan said. "But surely this difference would not affect a decision of such magnitude as leaving the Union!"

"The Revolution that birthed this nation began in Massachusetts," Alex said. "But Louisiana at that time was still ruled by Spain. And while the British were defeated here a Spanish general led mainly Spanish armies, with very few Americans in the ranks, and some Acadian militia to fill out his troops. No, Jordan, as you well know—the French families of New Orleans have not rushed to welcome Americans to their doors."

"I won't believe that simply because New Orleans society has great affection for its French and Spanish roots it will decide to leave the Union as readily as its members decline an invitation to dine—"

"In some instances, my dear cousin, they would leave the Union more readily than that. Some families' invitations command instant acceptance—having a power that the Democrats in Charleston seem to have lacked."

"You will never be serious, Alex, not if your life depends upon it!" Jordan said.

"And you will never be frivolous, even if your happiness demands that you should," Alex answered.

For a moment the cousins stared at each other: then Jordan bowed and left the room.

"I'm sorry to expose you to that little scene, Tom," Alex said. "We like each other well enough, Jordan and I, but we do not always see things from the same point of view."

"An interesting point, that, about Louisiana not being part of the Union from the first. I knew it, of course—but I had not really considered its effect."

"I probably make more of it than it is," Alex said. "But we have had many flags fly over us, Tom. Yet another would not be so unusual, you know."

"Unlike the states which came out of the original colonies—whose fields are marked with monuments to the war for freedom's dead—"

"I hope the call for such monuments is past," Alex said. "Of all the methods for solving difficulties, war must rank as the worst." He rose and approached Tom. "And this morning's problem—is it over?"

"For the time being," Tom said. "I shall speak with Father—he must understand that something permanent has to be done."

"I'll take her off your hands if that will help," Alex said. He saw Tom's face and grasped his hand. "What have I said? Tom—what?"

"You mean you'd—buy her," Tom said.

"Well, of course! Take her to New Orleans—let her join my father's pets. Or whatever you suggest, Tom. Don't glare at me, old fellow! I only mean to help!"

"There can be no question of—selling Veronique," Tom

said. "Please don't even suggest it—if my father heard you, he might see that as a very good idea."

Alex's eyes changed, and he drew closer to Tom. "Is there something I should know?" he said.

"No—nothing."

Alex sighed, taking a cigar from his pocket and slipping off the band. "Come out and have a smoke," he said. "It'll clear your head."

"It will take more than a cigar, I'm afraid," Tom said. But he followed Alex out on the gallery, where they stood smoking, staring out into the rain.

Gabriele napped briefly, and then woke, possessed by a sense of great unease. The house, surrounded by the blanket of soft, thick rain, seemed isolated from the usual markers of time and space, and she rose from the daybed and hurriedly dressed herself, leaving her room and entering the silent hall in search of human companions.

The downstairs presented the same gloomy aspect as the rooms above; her father's study door was shut, and she dared not disturb him; there was no sign of either Alex or Tom. I'll go see Veronique, she thought, and turned to the back of the house, tiptoeing stealthily so that no sound would give her away.

A breath of cool, damp air enveloped her as she stepped outside, and she stood for a moment, watching the rain cascade through a downspout that emptied into a cistern set at the back corner of the house and listening to the rain's steady murmur against the cypress shingles of the roof. Then she walked down the gallery to the office door, drawn to the woman lying inside as though pulled by an invisible cord. The door to the office stood half-open, and as Gabriele approached, a woman appeared suddenly on the threshold, blocking her way.

"Why, Abigail! You startled me!" Gabriele said, discomfited by the presence of her aunt's maid. "I wanted to see if Veronique is in need of something—Letha has some nice soup—"

"I'se seeing to her, Miss Gabriele," Abigail said.

"I want to see her," Gabriele said, moving forward. But Abigail's set expression did not change, nor did the solid pose of her body yield.

"You got no call to see her," Abigail said. "Yo' aunt, she tell me good if I let you in."

"Abigail—" She faltered and stopped. She could almost see Aunt Mat's stern eyes turned on her, backing up every word Abigail said. "All right, then," she said. "I won't—disturb her. But let me know if there's any change."

"Yes, Miss," Abigail said. Her mouth curved in a small smile, pulling taut the scar that ran the full width of her right cheek and ended at the corner of her mouth. Gabriele stared at the familiar mark, thinking of the explanation Aunt Mat had always given for the wound on Abigail's face.

"An Indian attack, when Louis and I first went west," Aunt Mat said. "Poor Abigail, we'd only been in Texas a week and I was certain she'd never stick it out." Now, as she went back inside the house, Gabriele wondered if Abigail had been scarred instead in just such a low conflict as had occurred here. The thought depressed her further, and when Alex St. Cyr loomed out of the dimness of the hall, she greeted him with relief.

"I don't think the rain will ever stop, do you, Mr. St. Cyr? I'm afraid you'll find the country very dull if we cannot enjoy the outdoors."

"I am quite accustomed to our climate's limitations," Alex said. "And far from disliking the rain, I appreciate the opportunity it provides for whiling away the afternoon in pleasant company."

"That's very kind of you," Gabriele said. "But I don't feel at all pleasant. I feel out of sorts and ruffled—"

"Then let me divert you," Alex said. "Tom is closeted with your father and I am completely at your service."

"Divert me from reality, Mr. St. Cyr? A rather large order, even for you, considering the kind of reality we have been handed today."

"I never say the right thing to you, do I?" Alex said. They had moved slowly down the hall and stood now in the double doorway leading to the drawing room. Alex surveyed it, his eyes going from the cream velvet draperies with puffage spilling over the floor to the Aubusson rugs brightening the wide-boarded polished floor with gardens of colour and design, then to the furniture carefully chosen for both beauty and craft, the dark wood frames of chairs and sofas setting off the pale silks and brocades that covered them.

"It's very strange," he said, eyes coming back to her face. "This house, this room—they are very like the houses and drawing rooms I frequent in New Orleans as a welcome guest. But the words that are appropriate there bring me only difficulty here—" He stopped and stared up at the portrait of Gabriele's mother hanging over the marble mantel that centred the wall.

"She died when you were very young," Alex said.

"I was three."

"A terrible loss. You must have grieved very much."

"I miss her still," Gabriele said. "Not as a person—I have little memory of her at all. But the love we might have shared—the time we might have spent together—"

"I understand," Alex said, turning to face her. "I feel very much the same way."

"But your mother is alive!" Gabriele said.

"Yes. And yet—when I listen to other men speak of their homes—their parents—then I have a sorrow that is a shadow of yours, Miss Cannon."

"All parents are not alike, nor should we expect them to be," Gabriele said.

"Still," Alex said, "I wonder if many are as different as mine?" Taking a position nearer the hearth and again looking up at Mrs. Cannon's face, he said, in a voice so low that except for its intensity Gabriele could hardly have heard him, "I have grown up a chameleon, Miss Cannon. To suit my mother I should have to devote myself almost entirely to business, though I have been given to understand that after a suitable marriage is entered upon, I may of course spend some small portion of my time on domestic affairs. My father believes with all of his energy that to go to business is perhaps the most useless way a gentleman can spend his time, as well as being of course the most *déclassé*. As for a suitable marriage—while he does not say so, it is clearly apparent that his own marriage is suitable but for one reason. The influx of my mother's money, from that shipping business my father so abhors, has made it possible for the St. Cyr style to carry on."

Gabriele gripped the back of a chair, steadying herself against it. "Mr. St. Cyr—I should not be hearing this—"

Alex's eyes swung from the portrait to Gabriele's face. The look in them surprised Gabriele: she had expected to see anger, or perhaps embarrassment—she was not prepared for the sorrow that gazed out of Alex's dark eyes, and with a feeling of being suddenly overwhelmed by matters she did not understand and emotions foreign to her, she made a quick apology and almost ran from the room.

Gabriele had no opportunity to speak with her father alone until late that afternoon. She had waited at the top of the stairs until she heard Alex St. Cyr leave the house, then had gone to her piano and played upon it softly, ending with the new music her father had yet to hear.

He had come to her there, sitting near the piano and signalling her to begin the Gottschalk piece over again, and then they settled in the alcove overlooking the garden for their first tête-à-tête since his return home.

"It's good to be home," Oliver Cannon said. "And to have such a good report of my daughter as I've been given today." He circled Gabriele's waist, drawing her closer. "I'm sorry your world can't always be filled with ring tourneys and balls, my pet. My deepest sorrow is that with all my might, I cannot avert the dark days ahead."

"Do you really think it will come to war, Papa?"

"I'm afraid it will," he said. His hand tightened on her waist, and he looked at her with shadowed eyes. "War is a terrible way to settle a difference—but unfortunately, each new generation has to learn that lesson all over again."

"But surely the war will be far away!" Gabriele said.

"Why do you think so, Gabe?"

She looked past him at Felicity's lawns, shrubbery dark against the spring-green grass. She knew each inch of the grounds; each flower bed, each path, each statue, each carved bench. Her mind's eye roved past the formal lawns and gardens to the paddock, the stables, the barns and outbuildings, to the slave quarters beyond. And then the fields, the great expanse of land, rich soil pin-pointed by the first green spikes of cane. "Because I couldn't bear it if war came to Felicity," she said. "I could not."

"Ah, well," Oliver Cannon said, his voice softened to hide his fear. "There is still much work to do, and I have not completely abandoned hope that we can effect a solution. The Southern Democrats will meet in Baltimore at the end of this month to choose our candidate—the rest of the party will meet there, too, nominating theirs. And who knows, Gabriele? In the three weeks between now and then, sufficient delegates might consider the seriousness of this split and be willing to compromise."

"Do you really think so?"

"I hope so," her father replied.

That's not at all the same thing, she thought, but I shall press Papa no more. I must speak to him about Veronique quickly before someone comes in or I lose my nerve.

"Papa—I am sure Tom told you what happened this morning—Colette's attack upon Veronique, I mean."

Oliver Cannon rose and turned to the window, presenting his broad back to her gaze. "It distresses me more than I can tell you that you witnessed such a scene, Gabriele. Your brother has been strongly chastised—he will protect you better in the future, that I promise you."

"Protect me!" She flew up and confronted him, grasping his arm and looking into his face. "Papa, I need no protection—it is Veronique who does. And I beseech you —send her to New Orleans. Set her up in business. Please,

Papa, do this for me and I shall never ask for anything ever again."

"But you are all wrought up," Oliver Cannon said. He disengaged her hand and then clasped it in his. "My dear child, what is this you are proposing? Haven't we discussed it before, and haven't you agreed it is impossible?"

"I never agreed," Gabriele said. "I only—stopped asking. Because I was sure you knew better—and I did not know what awful things are part of Veronique's lot."

"I don't wish to speak of this, Gabriele."

"But I do." She looked away from her father, gazing at her mother's portrait as though to draw strength. When her eyes came back to his, she thought she saw the smallest glimmer of sympathy there, and heartened, she pressed her case. "I have thought for a very long time and I have said so to Tom that we did no kindness to Veronique by treating her so differently from all the other slaves. And I have never understood it, nor has anyone tried to explain. But she can't take her place among them now, Papa, can't you see that? How can you even think of asking her to?"

"You remember when Veronique came to Felicity, don't you?" Oliver Cannon said.

"Of course. When Uncle Louis died out in Texas and Aunt Mat came to live here and brought some of the people from their place."

"Yes. Abigail, of course, and a couple of men. And a little girl just a year older than you, so light-skinned at first I wouldn't believe she wasn't—white." Oliver Cannon stopped speaking, staring in his turn at his dead wife's face. And then, as though every word cost him great effort, he said, "Your aunt explained that Veronique was the daughter of a quadroon who had vanished from the ranch leaving no trace. The father of course did not come forward— but Mat is certain he was white. The child could hardly be left to fend for herself—and so although both Mat and I had serious reservations—I allowed Veronique to be brought up on our place."

"I don't understand. What reservations? Veronique is

intelligent, quick—and for a long time, a playmate of imagination and gentleness whose presence I still miss."

"I see I shall have to speak much more plainly than I would prefer," Oliver Cannon said. "Veronique is also beautiful, Gabriele. And because of her light colour—she creates problems for herself."

"She creates them! Oh, be fair, Papa! It is men who create her problems, and if you do not release her from this terrible bondage, I fear you will be no better than those who take advantage of her position with no shame nor sense of disgrace."

For a moment she thought she had gone too far. And then the emotion in her father's face changed; the angry light left his eyes, and he came to her and held her close, tears running down his face.

"How like your mother you are," he said. "And how right to chide me. I will release Veronique, Gabriele, I promise you."

"Oh, Papa! Thank you!" she said, and pressed her lips against his moist cheek.

"The task is not yet done," he said. "And don't deceive yourself that it will be easy. The law forbids my freeing her —I can get around that simply enough, I think. But the larger problem is still to be solved, Gabriele. I agree with you that Veronique has the skill to be a very proficient modiste, and I have no doubt she will be able to support herself very well. But she has grown up in the country, New Orleans will be a big and dangerous place—we must go slowly, and make sure that when we let our little bird out of her cage, we do not send her into the jaws of a waiting tiger."

"I will do whatever I can to help," Gabriele said. "As will Tom, I know. He is very fond of Veronique, Papa—"

At those words Oliver Cannon's eyes grew stern again, and his lips made a narrow line. "I believe Tom has his work cut out for him helping Adams run Felicity since I am away so much," he said. "We shall leave Tom out of this, Gabriele. I shall take care of everything myself."

The sound of voices in the hall announced the arrival of Tom and their guests, and Oliver Cannon moved to the doorway to welcome them while Gabriele tugged the bell-pull that would signal Jonas to bring in her father's favourite Madeira that she had already made certain had been decanted and set out on a tray.

I shan't worry over Veronique any more, she told herself. Once Papa makes a promise, he will go to the ends of the earth to see that it is kept.

She went forward to join the others, feeling as though she had put a week of living into one short day. I will have to be more careful, when I talk about Veronique, she thought. Papa looked so odd when I said Tom was fond of her—and yet he praised my concern. But all those years we played together—shared games and toys—neither he nor Aunt Mat seemed to object to Tom acting as brother to us both. Cannot men and women have the kind of friendship to which Papa's favourite Greek philosopher aspired? One which seeks the ideal, the spiritual—she saw Alex St. Cyr's eyes upon her, and quickly turned her head.

It must be so, she would have it so. She could meet Jordan Scott and Alex St. Cyr as friends, with no thought of anything more. Else how could she meet any man? No, it is too absurd to think that all love is of but one kind. When I have learned more about myself—when I can tell the difference between the pleasure being admired and flattered gives me, and a sturdier emotion that seeks the pleasure of the other rather than my own—then I will consider loving a man in a deeper way.

But even that is not what Papa fears when he thinks of Veronique, she thought. His eyes betrayed him. He does not conceive that Tom could be in love with Veronique, could wish to bring that love to its happy end. He fears that Tom will succumb to something else—the impulse that made Michael Fleming insult her—the lust that drives Zeke.

She tried to banish that flash of insight, and succeeded in pushing it deep into her mind. But when she approached the men, and Alex came to meet her, she wondered, as she looked behind his easygoing surface to the shadow of sorrow in his eyes, if he could look at her through this same clear glass, and see places in her that had never before been exposed to the light.

Chapter Six

OLIVER CANNON'S PRESENCE INCREASED THE TEMPO OF THE house: his first full day home he rose early, despatching Jonas before breakfast to area planters and property owners with invitations to a meeting called to determine the region's position on the course Louisiana should next take.

At breakfast he seemed preoccupied, focusing his attention on his food, although Gabriele noticed that he did not eat much of it. "I am still weary from my journey," he said when she inquired about his lack of appetite, and draining his cup of coffee, he rose and beckoned Tom to follow him to his study for a morning of work. Alex and Jordan left right after breakfast, too, Alex to travel down to the place where the Teche met the Atchafalaya River and Jordan to go with a packet steaming the other way.

"Although to tell you my true opinion, this seems a ridiculous time to start a new venture," Alex said to Gabriele when Jordan left them alone for a few moments before they departed. "We will be building a sacrifice for the gods of war—and that is something I have absolutely no interest in doing."

"Papa says New Iberia is a very important inland port," Gabriele said.

"It is," Alex said. "Which will make it a prime target if war comes." He saw her face and immediately looked chagrined. "I am a fool," he said. "Please forgive me, Miss Cannon. You have had enough to contend with without worrying about a very remote war."

"Papa doesn't think it will be remote, if it happens," Gabriele said. "He saw how much the thought of war here frightened me, so he acted as though it might not happen at all—but I know that already he is thinking about it, and preparing for it as much as he can."

"Preparing for war," Alex said. He paced slowly to the end of the front gallery, staring into the rose garden and at the gazebo gleaming in the morning sun. Gabriele followed him, standing at his side quietly, aware as though she saw it through Alex's eyes of the rare beauty of the roses, now in their first full bloom.

"There is one very effective way to prepare for it," he said. "And that is to get well out of the country before it has time to start."

"Out of the country—I don't understand—"

"Sell everything and go live abroad. Accept the fact that this experiment in democracy has not been able to endure even a hundred years, and remove to an older society whose people have learned that adaptability and compromise are the rules by which they survive."

"You can't mean that, Mr. St. Cyr."

"Why not? Your father is a wealthy man, Miss Cannon. I don't presume to guess his worth, but Tom has told me enough and I have observed enough to know that between this plantation and his holdings in New Orleans, his fortune would sustain your family in London or Paris in the highest and most luxurious style."

"Sell Felicity? Abandon the place where all of our family traditions and sentiments began? Papa would never do that—not if armies camped at the gate!"

"No—no, of course he wouldn't," Alex said. "I continue to make inappropriate suggestions, Miss Cannon. I wonder if I shall ever stop."

"And I continue to respond to your conversation as though I had never heard a new idea in my life," Gabriele said. She remembered her resolution to know Alex St. Cyr as a friend. "It is because—it is because you are so much more knowledgeable than I am—so experienced—I feel—very young and not a little silly, Mr. St. Cyr. Of course I don't like feeling that way. And so I—bristle at you."

"*You* feel silly, Miss Cannon? You? And here I have been feeling like the greatest sort of fool—either being fussed at by Tom for flattering you, or having you look at me with those great green eyes as though I were some strange insect who had better be carried off to be stuck on a pin—" His shout of laughter rang out over the garden, a sound so open, so happy, that Gabriele knew she had said exactly the right thing.

"Then may we be friends, Mr. St. Cyr? As you and Tom are friends?"

"Perhaps not quite as Tom and I," Alex said. "I cannot abandon all my old ways—I reserve the right to flatter you, a boon I would never ask of Tom."

"I insist that you do," Gabriele said. "I have to practise, you know. Before my season in New Orleans you can provide me with the armour I will need against false beaux."

"Then give me your hand on it," Alex said. "I must say, Miss Cannon, I feel immensely better now—you're very good to put things right between us."

"They were never wrong," Gabriele said, "but only perhaps needed—defining."

"Exactly," Alex said. His hand covered hers, and he shook it warmly, smiling down at her with clear and happy eyes. "But I think I am not nearly as experienced as you, Miss Cannon. Perhaps in length and frequency of exposure to relations between men and women—but not in an instinctive awareness of what is right."

They heard horses' hooves on the drive, and walked toward the front of the house where they found Jordan in the saddle ready to go. Alex swung up on his horse, taking the reins from the groom's hand. "I shall look forward to this evening, Miss Cannon," he said. "My first spent in the company of my new good friend."

She saw the glance Jordan gave them, blue eyes going from his cousin to Gabriele. "I have decided to stay in New Iberia at least the next few days," Jordan said, drawing their attention immediately to him. "I know your family's hospitality can be relied on, no matter what the political climate is. But I need to sort out in my own mind how I feel about what happened in Charleston—and I can do it better if I am alone."

"You're not even a Democrat," Alex said. "I should think you'd be pleased that the party is splintered—it should give the Republicans an easier task."

"It's not that," Jordan said. "It's the—irresponsibility of factions who have put the entire nation in jeopardy that I cannot condone."

"Do you mean my father, sir?" Gabriele said. "If you do, say so!"

"One man does not make a faction," Jordan said.

"But he is part of one!"

"As I said, Miss Cannon—these are things I must work out in my mind—alone."

"I see nothing for you to work out," Gabriele said. "You term the behaviour of the men who bolted the convention irresponsible—but irresponsible to whom, Mr. Scott? They believe—my father believes—that they obeyed their most sacred charge—that of taking care of the people they represent!"

"Do they represent the slaves?" Jordan said. "Other than technically, I mean. I know a slave counts as three-fifths of a person when congressional apportionment is being made—but did the Southern delegates to that convention consider them in any real way?"

"You heard my father," Gabriele said. "States' rights are paramount to him at this point—once that issue is decided, he and other moderates will continue to work on the one that occupies you." She saw Alex stir, and lift his head as though to speak. "But I detain you, Mr. Scott. You will be late for your work." She bowed and turned to go into the house: from the silence behind her, she knew they had not moved. A thought struck her, and she turned back. "One thing you might do when you ride into New Iberia this morning, Mr. Scott. Regard the fields on either side of you—think of the labour required to plant and care for them. And then come up with a speedy and effective way to free the slaves who work them now. When you do, come tell us, please."

The ease she had felt with Alex had vanished, but she would not blame Mr. Scott. He is honest, anyway—and willing to bear the consequences of his convictions, which, as Papa always says, is the mark of an honourable man. Still, it is dreadful that our little house party has so quickly fallen into disarray. A small casualty, I know—but a bad omen nevertheless.

"Is this how it will be now?" Gabriele asked Aunt Mat. They sat in the sewing room taking Gabriele's summer clothing from a trunk: surrounded by flimsy voiles and lace-trimmed ruffles, it was difficult to imagine that an event in Charleston could disrupt the summer's pleasures, but if Jordan Scott's behaviour were a straw in the wind, Gabriele foresaw uneasy times ahead. "Will people allow their politics to interfere with normal friendships? Dictate the invitations they issue and those they accept or refuse?"

"Now, Gabriele," Aunt Mat said, holding up a lavender voile dress and shaking out the skirt. "Mr. Scott is rather an extreme case, don't you think? He is Boston-bred and born, an Abolitionist, a Republican—we do not know many of those!"

"But many families we do know have Northern connections," Gabriele said. "Were educated there—have relatives there—"

"Even so—some people are more politically inclined than others, Gabriele. Those who go to the extreme, who are excessive in the way they state their views—they should not go about in polite society anyway. As for Mr. Scott— he himself is not extreme, he behaves very well. I appreciate his delicacy. After all, Gabriele, your father is one of the leading figures of the state! By Mr. Scott's tact, he has removed any embarrassment to Oliver his presence might have caused."

"It is too unpleasant, Aunt Mat, and I hate to even think about it. The merest sign of a division—and already our hospitality is subjected to rules we have not made!"

"Nothing about the situation is pleasant, Gabriele, nor has it been for a very long time." Aunt Mat sighed, her hands poised over a shawl. "Louis and I did not have slaves in Texas, although we could have. Except for Abigail. I wish I were still there, Gabriele. I should have stayed and made our dream come true instead of turning tail and running home."

"But what would we have done without you, Aunt Mat?" Gabriele said. "Oh, that sounds selfish—if you would have been happier there—then of course I wish you had stayed—but without Uncle Louis? Away from all who love you?"

"I probably should not have been happy," Aunt Mat said. "At any rate, the speculation is useless, for I did not stay." She touched her lips to Gabriele's forehead lightly, then rose and looked at her watch. "And I have known happiness here, Gabriele, happiness and—love."

"I am glad," Gabriele said. "Felicity could not have gone on after my mother's death had you not come."

"And it won't go on today if I don't go downstairs," Aunt Mat said. "Zeke and Colette will announce their plans today—they must wait a month to marry, as your father always requires—and despite Colette's prior history of disobedience Oliver and I have decided to mark the announcement with a small fete."

Gabriele bent over a dress as Aunt Mat spoke, wondering how much Aunt Mat really knew. It is always the same, she thought, as Aunt Mat left her alone. I am told things in just this oblique way—so that if I have heard any rumours, I will have information sufficient to put them to rest. And I have heard nothing—I will have all that they think I should know.

Alex St. Cyr would not treat me so, she thought. Nor, I

think, would Mr. Scott. I must take full advantage of Mr. St. Cyr while he is here, learning as much as I can from him—as for Mr. Scott, I can only hope he forgives my rudeness. No, he will not call it rudeness. He will call it forthrightness—since he is a walking example of how people possessed of that characteristic behave, he will not fault it in me.

Still, her conscience bothered her as the morning wore on. She made herself face the possibility that her speech had been occasioned as much by Alex St. Cyr's presence and her desire to impress him as it had been by any other cause, and when she finished her work in the sewing room, she wrote a note to Mr. Scott, dispatching it to New Iberia when Jonas sent in their mail.

"Please forgive my impetuous speech," she wrote. "I meant what I said, of course, but I could have said it more gracefully, and without putting you in the wrong. My tutor often warned me that my temper overtook my reason far more times than it remained in control: if he were here now, he would be quite chagrined, as I am, that I have gotten no better with age. I should so like to talk with you about all of these things—your view is not the one held by my father, but that does not mean it should not be explored. Come dine with us, please, and move back as our guest if you will. As for solving the dilemma of slavery—it has not been solved these more than two hundred years since the first ones arrived, and I know that neither you nor any of us will solve it in just one day, as I so rudely challenged you to do. But perhaps if those of us who have not yet assumed our property, and the power attaching thereto, look into other avenues, other modes—there may be hope for all of us, slaves and masters alike."

Her spirits restored, she went to meet her family for lunch. Tom appeared, but their father did not. "His tiredness persists," Tom said. "He is resting in his room and will have his meal on a tray."

"Papa works much too hard," Gabriele said. "As if managing Felicity and the properties in New Orleans were not

enough, now he must embark on another long and fatigu-
ing journey with only weary hours of argument at its end."

"We will pamper him while he is home," Aunt Mat said.
"By tomorrow we can have a proper dinner to welcome
him. Gabriele, I depend upon you to help me make
plans."

But by the next evening, Oliver Cannon's favourite
dishes were the farthest things from anyone's mind. Tom
tested Jupiter to the limits of his endurance galloping hell-
for-leather to New Iberia for the doctor, while Oliver Cannon lay in a semi-conscious state in a darkened room, his
sister and his daughter at his side.

Yellow fever. The two words, pronounced by Dr. Delahaye after he examined Oliver Cannon and met with the
family, sent Gabriele to her brother's arms, from which
shelter she stared at the doctor with large, frightened eyes.

"But—can he get well, Dr. Delahaye?" she said, running
her tongue over lips that seemed suddenly dry.

"People recover from yellow fever," Dr. Delahaye said.
"Their own resilience—some resistance their body pro-
duces that unites with our efforts—"

"Oliver is already tired," Aunt Mat said, lips pressed in a
grim line. "He's been wearing himself out in Charleston,
batting heads with men just as stubborn as he is and with
no success." Her normal steady voice changed, fear and
anger raising its pitch and charging it with fire. "To what
avail these martyrs to principle, these sacrifices on the altar
of Right! In the end, it is always the same. The good suffer
and the evil triumph, for their energy is not dissipated by
concern for anyone but themselves."

Dr. Delahaye took Aunt Mat's chin and turned her face
so that she had to meet his eyes. "Now, Mrs. LeGrange,"
he said, "this won't help your brother, will it?"

Aunt Mat stared at the doctor, rebellion still a hot flag
in her eyes. Then she shuddered, as though she, too, met
a stubborn opponent and conquered him. When she
spoke again, her voice was the one that had marked the

days of Gabriele's growing up, the voice that accepted duty and took joy where it could be found without any conscious search for either. "You're right, of course, Dr. Delahaye," she said. "Now tell me what to do."

"The first thing to do is to get Samantha up here to nurse him," the doctor began, but Aunt Mat rose, every line of her body affirming her resolve.

"I will nurse my brother," she said. "You will only be wasting valuable time if you try to dissuade me."

Dr. Delahaye glanced at Tom and Gabriele, and then back at their aunt's face. But in that one glance Gabriele read all his fears: that not only her father, but her aunt, would fall victim to the disease and that she and Tom would be left with neither.

For that moment, her own fear became enormous, a feeling greater than any she had ever had to endure. And then Tom, as though he read her thoughts through the quick tensing of her body, the faster beat of her pulse, held her closer. "Buck up, Gabe," he whispered. "Father needs our strength, not our weakness."

"I can help," Gabriele said, standing taller and moving slightly away from Tom. "Not with the actual nursing—I know I can't do that." Her lips trembled, and she fought to maintain control, taking a leaf from Aunt Mat's book even while she wondered how her aunt managed it. "But I can take over many of Aunt Mat's other duties—"

"You can rely on both of us, Aunt Mat," Tom said. "Whatever needs to be done."

"Of course I can," Aunt Mat said quietly, and the affirmation in her voice carried them through that difficult hour and through the weary ones that soon followed.

The first reorganization of the household into a hospital occurred quickly, with the only difficulty being Alex's refusal to move to the safety of town.

"I'm not a fatalist, Mrs. LeGrange," he said. "But I do believe that if I were susceptible to yellow fever, I'd have gotten it in New Orleans long before I'd get it here. I admit there are duties I get out of if I can—but I have yet to leave a friend in trouble, and I am not leaving Tom."

"I won't waste energy arguing with you, Mr. St. Cyr," Aunt Mat said. She started for the door, then turned her head. "It won't be a bad thing to have you here," she said. "Tom and Gabriele will need cheering—I will entrust that to you."

"I shall do more than that," Alex said. "Our packets make the trip from New Orleans thrice weekly—if there is anything you need, make a list and I will see to it that the goods are delivered to your dock."

"I'll call on you if the need arises," Aunt Mat said. "Now I must see to my brother."

She bustled out of the room, her usual energetic movements heightened to an almost frantic state that frightened Gabriele more than Dr. Delahaye's serious words. "I have never seen Aunt Mat so agitated," she said. "I know yellow fever is a dangerous illness—but Papa is strong, he will have such good care—surely he will soon be well!"

She looked up to see Alex watching her, an expression of such deep concern in his eyes that, shocked, she realized in that instant that he was certain her father would die. The fear that she had somehow held at bay came over her, and she felt herself sinking toward the floor. Only Tom's arms braced to catch her saved her, and when she came to again, she found herself in her own bed.

A shadowy figure sat at the shuttered window; Gabriele sat up and strained to see who it might be. Then she recognized Veronique and lay back again. She had neither seen nor spoken to Veronique since the day Colette attacked her: Abigail had taken her back to the cabin they shared near the house to complete her recovery. I will tell her what Papa has promised, she thought. That will make her glad.

And then she remembered her father's illness, and sat up, calling out, "Veronique—is my father—better?," knowing instantly she did not want to hear the reply.

"He is the same," Veronique replied. She rose and approached the bed. The bulk of her bandage under her bodice made her move stiffly, and she held her arm awkwardly, as though to avoid pain. She lit the lamp set on the commode beside the bed and leaned down to peer into Gabriele's face. "How are you feeling?"

"Fine," Gabriele said. "I am so ashamed of myself—causing such a commotion. I never faint!"

"You," Veronique said, handing Gabriele her robe. "Can you imagine how I feel? How—disgraced?"

"None of that was your fault, Veronique—we all know you did nothing to provoke that horrible attack."

"No—nothing," Veronique said. She kept her head down, but Gabriele did not have to see her face to know how Veronique must look. All light gone from those golden eyes—and only the darkness of fear and humiliation left.

"They are to—marry," Gabriele said. "Zeke and Colette. When the month of waiting is over—"

"Then I wish them joy!" Veronique said.

"I don't blame you for being bitter—but I have good news for you, Veronique. I spoke to Papa about you, just the day before he fell ill. He means to help you, he promised me he would—"

"Help me," Veronique repeated.

"I asked him to free you," Gabriele said. "I think he will."

Now she could see Veronique's expression, but she could not read what it meant. Even as Veronique thanked her, and seemed to be less tense, something in her eyes tinted her gratitude with a darker feeling—what is it? Gabriele wondered, and then realized she had spoken aloud.

"I'm sorry," she said. "You look so—as though you're not sure you can trust what I just said."

"I can trust you," Veronique said. "And I can trust your father. You to intercede for me, him to—do what he thinks is best."

"Then what makes you unhappy? Papa will get well—and soon you will be free!"

"I should not be so stubborn," Veronique said. "But I have this strange desire to—make my own decisions. Not to always have someone else control my life—my future—"

"That's what freedom is, Veronique. That's what Papa will give you—"

"But he is not the one who took it, is he?" Veronique said. "And that being the case—is he the one who can indeed set me free?"

"He believes he can," Gabriele said. "That is good enough for me. I don't understand this opposition, Veronique. Papa has lawyers, they know what to do."

"Of course you don't understand. How can you? I hardly understand myself." She took up a hairbrush and began to pull it through Gabriele's curls. "You think my freedom is curtailed by a piece of paper that defines me as a —slave. That may be so. If your father effects his wishes—well, then I shall see."

She met Gabriele's eyes in the mirror. Veronique's eyes had gone blank, the veil slaves used to conceal thoughts and moods and attitudes from masters and mistresses who preferred to think they had none.

"Don't look at me like that, Veronique! I hate it—it is as though you have gone away somewhere I cannot follow—"

"I'm sorry," Veronique said. "I was thinking—and see, I have let myself become distracted from what your aunt wished me to tell you. She is gathering the house servants in the back parlour to say the Rosary for your father at five. If you are strong enough, she would like you to attend."

"Of course I am," Gabriele said. "Let us hurry—I don't want to make my aunt wait."

As she knelt beside Aunt Mat, watching the beads slip through her fingers as she recited the prayers, Gabriele shivered and tried to dislodge a thought that seemed stubbornly fixed in her head: that this gathering seemed to foretell a funeral, and that the prayers lifted to Heaven seemed ominously like prayers said for the dead.

A note arrived from Jordan Scott the next morning, requesting permission to call. Gabriele sent an immediate answer, and when the appointed hour arrived, greeted him in the front hall. "We'll go out to the gazebo if you don't mind," she said. "We are keeping the house as quiet as possible for Papa—he is so sick, as I'm sure you know."

"Yes, Alex told me. I am distressed beyond all measure, Miss Cannon. When I recall my effrontery the night we first met—already he must have been succumbing to the fever. I hate to think that I added to his strain."

"Nonsense," Gabriele said, walking with him across the gallery and down the broad white steps. "Papa thrives on stimulating conversation—and he has never yet run from anyone just because they held views opposite to his own."

"Is he—any better?" Jordan asked as they reached the path that led through the rose garden to the gazebo beyond.

"No," Gabriele said. That one syllable seemed to take all her breath, and she could say nothing more.

"It is kind of you to allow me to call, Miss Cannon. But I fear you will overextend yourself—your anxiety is too great—"

"Please don't go!" Gabriele said. "Tom works like a demon, determined that no task Papa might think is necessary is left undone; Mr. St. Cyr has gone to see about goods Aunt Mat asked him to order—and Aunt Mat of course is in with my father—oh, don't leave me alone, Mr. Scott!"

"But of course I won't," Jordan said. "Here, let us sit in the gazebo and you shall tell me about the statuary around the garden. You have some very fine pieces—Italian, are they not?"

"Yes—Mama and Papa chose them on a trip to Europe the winter before she—died," Gabriele said, hurrying past the dread word. "She designed the garden herself—when a rose is replaced, it is always an exact replica of the one in her plan."

"I don't mind telling you that the life I have found at Felicity surprised me very much," Jordan said. "I expected to find sophistication and culture in New Orleans—but out here in the country—well, it does not flatter you I know, but I thought to find rural people of little education or grace."

"We are accustomed to being thought backward by those who don't know us, Mr. Scott," Gabriele said. She smiled at him with a tinge of her old mischief. "You are fortunate you come from Boston. If you came from a less renowned place in New England, I might have expected you to be like Natty Bumpo, or some other of Cooper's men."

"I might do better if I were," Jordan said. "If they had the courage to face wild Indians, I'm sure they could take Creole parlours in their stride."

"Oh, Mr. Scott!" Gabriele said. "You will never get on in that city if that is your opinion! The idea of it taking courage to listen to charming ladies entertain you—that must be a notion you brought from the North."

"It does take courage," Jordan said. "Not for you, of course. Alex says you will be a belle this winter, and I'm sure of it. As for him—he sails through the most complicated social encounters as easily as I can straighten out our office books."

"But Mr. St. Cyr is born to it," Gabriele said. "You are mannerly, Mr. Scott, I am sure you never give offence."

"Oh, not offence," Jordan said. He leaned back against the latticework, seeming completely relaxed for the first time since Gabriele had met him. "But I am forever assigning people to the wrong branches of families, or bringing up a relative they have for some reason removed from their rolls—I arrive on time for dinner to the chagrin of my hostess, who seems to have counted on everyone being a half-hour late—and then, most hideous crime of all, I dare to question young ladies about their reading habits, a process guaranteed to bring their conversation to a halt."

By the time Jordan finished speaking, Gabriele's spirits had taken a definite turn. She could just imagine this sober young Yankee in a Creole gathering—trying to follow the chatter of the ladies, and getting hopelessly lost.

"You must not bring up anything serious at a general soirée," she said. "But talk about the latest entertainment, or brag about your new horse."

"Now you are teasing me, Miss Cannon," Jordan said, "but I don't mind, because I am at least making you smile." He studied her a minute, seeming to turn something over in his mind. "I should like to strike a bargain, Miss Cannon—one harder on you, I fear, than on me."

"What is it, Mr. Scott?"

"You asked in your letter if I would instruct you in my political views—if you still wish it, I will do so gladly. But in return, Miss Cannon, I want you to teach me to become a beau."

"A beau, Mr. Scott! What a singular request!"

"You think I cannot learn to do it? To say flattering things and gracefully retrieve a lady's handkerchief or fan?"

"Of course you could learn it," Gabriele said. "But why would you want to? That's what I don't understand."

Jordan glanced away: Gabriele thought he looked in the direction of the *garçonnière,* where Alex still stayed. "Call it part of my Louisiana education," Jordan said. "I don't know how long I will remain in New Orleans now—but as long as I am there, I might as well do the thing right."

She caught his reference to the unstableness of any Northerner's position in the South just then, but did not pick it up. Far pleasanter to take this hour of surcease, to idly chatter and give Jordan Scott his first lesson in how to flirt.

"We will begin with introductions," Gabriele said. "Now—let us say that you and I are meeting for the very first time—"

By the end of the lesson, Jordan had revealed a natural

wit that would, Gabriele told him, stand him in good stead.

"A neat turn of phrase—an epigram—scatter these through your conversation, Mr. Scott, and you will be welcome anywhere."

"You don't demand all this," Jordan said. "Why can't all young ladies be just like you?"

"Ah, but I am not 'out' yet," Gabriele said. "That makes a difference. When we meet in New Orleans this winter, I shall expect to see an accomplished beau. But for now, Mr. Scott—what I really want is a friend."

The sudden anxious concern in his eyes broke through her poise. The silent house behind her seemed too much like a tomb, and her worry for her father pushed all levity aside. "I am so afraid, Mr. Scott," she whispered. "So terribly afraid."

"I will come every day if that will help you," Jordan said. "If only there were something I could do!"

But over the next few days, with all the good will in the world he could do no more than anyone else. Oliver Cannon lay alternately burning with fever or wracked with chills while his family anxiously waited for some sign that the fever would abate. On the fourth day, Oliver Cannon slipped into a coma which Dr. Delahaye and Aunt Mat knew was almost certainly a prelude to death. Even then, Gabriele refused to believe her father would not recover. She cut every rose, ruthlessly snipping even the tightest buds, making a bouquet for Samantha to put near her father's bed, and slipping notes of love and encouragement under his door. Tom tried to warn her, taking her for a stroll in the garden at sundown, speaking gravely of their father's condition, trying to help her be prepared.

There is no preparation for that loss; when death came, Gabriele fought it, refusing to accept her aunt's solace or her brother's love. She broke away from their restraining arms, ran down the steps and out to the stable, where she threw herself on Brandy's back, hurtling through the open doors, bounding over the paddock fence, and galloping over the fields as though if she could run fast enough, she could lure death from her father's side and beat him still.

May conspired with her: in a world filled with blooming flowers and greening fields, with birdsong and busy squirrels, how could death prevail? Her father could not be dead. She would not listen to those who said that he was. Hope filled her: when the doctor came, he would tell them they were wrong, that while Oliver Cannon lay locked in coma still, a stronger pulse beat beneath the waxen mask, and recovery hovered, waiting to take command.

She finally pulled Brandy to a stop, slipping off the mare's sweaty back and releasing her hold on the flowing chestnut mane. Here on the Indian mound near the bayou a stronger breeze stirred, finding a tunnel between her neck and hair, slowly cooling her so that she felt her blood stop pounding, and the brisk colour in her cheeks begin to fade.

Here, standing quietly, silence so thick around her that she might inhabit the world alone, she found it harder to deny death's power. Her eyes strayed to the grove of oaks, the distance making their mighty branches and flourishing leaves dark green blots against the sky. The house lay hidden beyond the trees, but its presence seemed near. As though her spirit had left her body standing in the afternoon sun, as though it had left the fresh breeze and the shrill cry of the blue-jay behind, she felt the deep stillness of her father's sick-room close around her. Dark, so dark, shutters pulled tight against the light, bed swathed in a white mosquito net—and her father's form, motionless and silent upon his bed.

She did not know from where the image came, she did not consciously remember her mother's death, nor her own infant self clinging to her nurse while in the parlour people from miles around gathered to mourn. But she knew with cold certainty that her father, too, was dead. For one moment more her heart held on to the hope her mind denied. Then it gave in, collapsing before the weight of death. A spasm jerked through her, catching her off-balance, and making her reel. She crumpled to the ground and lay against the rough shells, face cradled in her arms while she finally gave herself up to grief.

Tom found her there, weeping. He came and sat beside her, holding her against him until she had no more tears. And then he helped her down the small slope, lifted her onto Brandy's back, and rode beside her all the way home. Neither spoke; they had no need of words between themselves, and both knew, with weary acceptance, that in the days ahead many words would be required, and that as a shocked and sorrowing countryside came to mourn their father's death, they would have to offer comfort to those who came to comfort them, assuring everyone, and perhaps also themselves, that Oliver Cannon's death did not mean the end of wise leadership and balanced judgements, but could serve as a rallying point for them all.

Only when they had almost reached the stables did Tom speak. Reaching out a hand to his sister, he said, eyes dark and intent, "Gabriele—it is up to us now, you know. To keep Felicity going as it has always been—to hold our ground and our principles—to show the world the legacy of decency and honour which our father leaves."

"Oh, yes, Tom," she said. She could feel a surge of strength, a renewal of vigour. She had a challenge now, something fine and good to carry her through the next awful hours, the next terrible days. She would not think beyond them; death had its own rituals, and by the time they were observed, a path would have emerged and duty would have declared itself. The girl who threw herself on the ground and wept was only a very small part of her, after all. There was another girl inside, the one who had followed Tom fearlessly no matter where he led. That girl could carry this burden, that girl would not shirk. And if the other one, that sentimental person who felt she could not bear this blow, tried to weaken Gabriele's resolve, she would not be heard.

For many years, Gabriele had tried to show her father

that she honoured her mother's memory in every thought and act of her own life. Now she had a larger and harder task, for she must demonstrate to the world that mourned him that part of Oliver Cannon lived on, not only in his son—but in his daughter as well.

The men who would have come to Oliver Cannon's meeting came to his funeral instead, borne in a stream of carriages and buggies and horses bearing the people of the region who came to offer comfort and share in the family's grief. Although Gabriele had heard people speak of her father's position and influence since she was a very little girl, until she stood in the parlour between her brother and aunt and listened to the callers praise him, she had not realized the magnitude of his name.

Tales of aid he had provided, stories of wise decisions he had made. And always, the same words, repeated over and over again—"Besides all that, he was one of my most beloved friends."

At times she thought she would not be able to bear up under these constant reminders of what she had lost. Until Alex, who had scarcely left Tom's side since his father's death, took her outside for a breath of fresh air. Walking her up and down the back gallery, steadying her with his hand, he said nothing for a long time, waiting until she had her emotions well under control.

Then, just before they went back inside, he paused, looking as though he were trying to decide exactly which words he wanted to use. "Look," he said finally. "What I am about to say may be poor comfort to you—the words I would normally use in these circumstances do not seem at all sufficient to fit this case."

"You are very kind," Gabriele said. "Everyone is . . ." Her voice trailed into silence, and she gazed past Alex into the grove of oaks, so lost in her own grief that she had little consciousness of anything he said.

"Miss Cannon," he said, taking her hand in his. "Listen to me, please."

She did look at him then, lifting eyes dulled by pain and reddened by tears and loss of sleep. She looked so vulnerable, so unable to defend herself against this recent blow, that Alex's nerve almost left him: what if he only caused her more pain?

"All right," she said. "What is it, Mr. St. Cyr?"

"I only want to say—dash it, I've no practice at this, Miss Cannon, I'm used to glib phrases and worn clichés—"

The faintest smile touched her lips, and put a brief light in her eyes. "You are trying to divert me, Mr. St. Cyr, and you are almost succeeding. Now, please—what is it you want to say?"

He still held her hand; now he took the other one, and holding them tightly in both of his, he bent close to her. "Only that no matter how dreadful a loss you suffer now— just think how terrible it would have been for you to never have had a father like yours at all."

She could feel her heart close against an assault of pain, and she leaned forward and kissed Alex's cheek. "Thank you," she said. "Yes, of course. That gives me a perspective to which I can cling." She took the handkerchief Alex offered her and blotted the tears from her face. It is true, she thought, walking with him to the door that would take them inside. I have not really lost Papa—we have been too close, we have meant too much to each other for me not to believe he will walk with me all my days.

Then, as Alex guided her to stand once more near her father's bier, another thought caused a fresh wave of pain. This pain, though, came from her sympathy for him, not herself. Remembering all she had been told about Hector St. Cyr, and contrasting that to the praise of her own father still echoing in her ears, she knew that if she had to choose between this grief and the one Alex must carry, she would take her father's death, coming as it did after a lifetime of love and care.

And later, when they returned from the plantation cemetery, gathering wearily to eat the food Letha had prepared, Jordan Scott came to Gabriele. "It is presumptuous for me to say anything about your father—a man I had barely met," he said. "But I must tell you, Miss Cannon, I cannot remember ever hearing anyone praised more highly or more sincerely—what a long shadow your father cast with his life!"

"Yes," Gabriele said. "And now we shall never know— would it have been long enough even to stop a war?" She shook her head, holding her handkerchief against her eyes. "I should care about that—it should matter that our region, our state, has lost such a leader—but I don't, Mr. Scott, I don't!"

"We shall not be here much longer, Alex and I," Jordan said. "But I want you to promise me that if you ever need a friend—you will send for me, knowing I will come to you as fast as I can."

"I'm sorry I won't see you this winter," Gabriele said, trying to smile. "You will cut a wide swath in New Orleans with your new skills—you must write and tell me how it all goes."

"You won't be there? Of course not—I'm an idiot, Miss Cannon. Then I shall have to come here. Your brother has asked me to hunt—and there is that promised tour of the sugar mill."

She knew he tried to divert her, to make her think of returning to a normal routine. But despite her grief and distraction, she had observed the hesitancy with which some of their friends and neighbours greeted Jordan, formally acknowledging the introduction but then hurrying away to somebody else. Not all, of course. Some, when they heard his Boston intonation, made some polite observation before turning the conversation to the event that had drawn them all there. And it would be different in New Orleans, where the St. Cyr name opened doors for all their connections. Still, she thought, when the long day finally ended and she could escape to her room, there's no point in thinking a friendship with Mr. Scott will progress as it would have if we both lived on the same side of the Mason-Dixon line.

"I realize that what we ask is difficult, and poses serious problems," Mr. Robin said to Tom. He glanced at the other men gathered in Oliver Cannon's study the day after the funeral. "But we have talked among ourselves and we all agree—you must take your father's place at the convention in Baltimore. There is no one else who can."

"I'm honoured, but hardly agree," Tom said. Unconsciously, his body fell into a pose of his father's: half-sitting on the corner of the big desk, one leg cocked over the other knee, a hand rubbing his head. "There must be any of a dozen men who could perform that duty far better than I."

Again Mr. Robin glanced around the room, as though seeking affirmation from the men convening there. "It is not a question of duties, Tom. It is a question of your name. The Cannon name is well-known and respected. We believe that the presence of your father's son in our midst will do much to strengthen the moderate cause."

"If you put it like that, then of course I will go," Tom said. He passed his hand wearily across his neck, rubbing it as though that would relieve the tension caused by the last few days. "But I shall have to start immediately if I am to reach Baltimore in time—"

"Can you?" Mr. Robin said. "I know it is a lot to ask—"

Tom smiled. "I seem to have no other choice." Already, his mind raced. Adams could get along without him: Felicity's overseer was among the most competent in the region, and this time between planting and harvesting was probably the best time for Tom to be away. His father's will had not yet been read, but that could be accomplished quickly. And then, as far as Tom knew, the only duties left were the many letters his aunt and sister would have to answer, and the callers they would receive.

"I shall be glad to go to Baltimore," he said, rising and shaking Mr. Robin's hand. "And I promise you I shall try to live up to your expectations, though I have no illusions about filling my father's place."

"Good man," Mr. Robin said. "We'll leave you now—I realize your family needs you. But I should like to meet with you later today to discuss the various issues, Tom."

"I'll ride over around four o'clock," Tom said. "By the time I see you, I should have myself well-organized for the trip."

He saw his visitors to the door, then sought out Aunt Mat. Filling her in quickly, he said, "We should probably get Delahoussaye out here to read the will tonight, Aunt Mat. I imagine it will be pretty pro forma, but I'd feel better about leaving you if I knew we had all that straight."

Aunt Mat sighed, and Tom felt a jolt of surprise. He could not remember hearing Aunt Mat sigh; her constant energy kept her moving steadily, the rapid rhythm of her walk was never broken by a ragged breath. "You're exhausted," he said. "And now I propose leaving you to see to everything—I shan't go, Aunt Mat. I'll tell Robin it's not possible—"

"Nonsense," Aunt Mat said. "Give me a few good nights' sleep and I'll be right as rain, Tom." She paused, looking out the window as though she could see her brother's grave from where she stood. "Sleep won't ease my pain—but it will make me strong enough to bear it." She put her hand on Tom's shoulder and patted him. "Go along to Baltimore, Tom. Gabriele has shown amazing maturity these last hard days—I can rely upon her now in ways I wouldn't have dreamed of just a short time ago."

"I do think I should go," Tom said. "No matter how reluctantly."

"And so you should," Aunt Mat said. "Your father would be the last man to want you to remain here when the South needs you somewhere else."

"Duty before desire," Tom said, thinking of the sacrifices in his father's life.

Mr. Delahoussaye, Oliver Cannon's lawyer, read the

will that night after dinner; its terms could not have been simpler, nor Cannon's affairs better arranged. "A very proper document," Delahoussaye said, peering at Tom and Gabriele over his pince-nez. "Typical of all your father's doings—I wish all my clients would follow his mode." Then he summarized the will's contents for them, going slowly to make certain they understood.

Oliver Cannon's holdings, both Felicity and his New Orleans properties, were to be held jointly by his two children, each sharing equally in the income produced, and mutually enjoined to maintain their aunt. "The house goes to whichever of you makes a marriage that would be best supported here," Delahoussaye said. "The other will then receive money or property equal to the value of the house —but I take it this is a decision still some time ahead?"

Satisfied by their expressions that neither concealed an engagement, he picked up the will and scanned it again. "There is a list of the New Orleans properties which I will leave for you to peruse at your leisure," he said. "Tom, your father had perfect confidence in your knowledge of and your ability to manage the plantation's affairs. I suggest that you and I meet with the overseer—Adams, isn't it—as soon as possible to inventory movable property and to list the stock. Oh, I forgot—you leave for Baltimore tomorrow. Well, no matter, it can wait until you return."

"I will help you," Gabriele said.

Mr. Delahoussaye stuck his glasses back on his nose and looked at her through them. "I wouldn't dream of troubling you, Miss Cannon," he said. "You will have quite enough to do inventorying the contents of the house, including jewellery, plate and the like."

"Be assured, Mr. Delahoussaye," Aunt Mat said, "that the contents of this house, both personal possessions and furnishings, are inventoried each year, and that the list is checked carefully each quarter."

"And so I will have time to work with you and Adams," Gabriele said.

Mr. Delahoussaye allowed the smallest bit of annoyance

to colour his voice. He stopped shuffling papers, rapping the sheaf he held against the desk with a sharp, quick sound. "It can really wait for your brother," he said.

"But it really doesn't have to," Gabriele said.

"Let her work with you, Delahoussaye," Tom said. "Gabriele knows a great deal about Felicity already—and it won't hurt a bit to have her learn a lot more."

"Whatever you say, of course," Delahoussaye said. "Now if there are no questions—"

"What about the slaves?" Gabriele said. "Doesn't my father say anything about them?"

"They are part of the movable property, Miss Cannon—"

"Like the ploughs and mules."

"Miss Cannon—"

"Does he—free any of them?"

"He originally intended to do so, yes."

"And now?"

"He changed that intention with a codicil to the will written in early April of this year. Here, I'll read it to you."

Gabriele closed her eyes, trying to hear her father's voice behind the lawyer's measured tones.

" 'This codicil is written because of the unrest and uncertainty our region faces. To free the abovementioned slaves now would be sheer folly, for I would turn them loose into a world possibly about to be turned upside down. Therefore, it is now my will that no slave be freed upon my death. When circumstances change, and I know the kind of world in which they will live, I will write another codicil, again freeing those slaves whom I think can bear it.' "

"But—but did Papa expect to—die?" Gabriele said.

"My dear Gabriele," Mr. Delahoussaye said. "All wills are written in the knowledge that the writer will someday die; few are written with expectation of that occurring soon. Your father was simply a very wise and responsible man. He changed his will frequently in order to keep pace with what he determined his family's needs to be—and also, of course, to keep pace with his property's increasing value. It is in that spirit this codicil was written."

"He meant to free Veronique," Gabriele said. "He promised me he would—the day before he took ill."

"Veronique?" Delahoussaye looked at Tom. "You seem surprised, Tom. Had your father not told you of this wish?"

"No—but there was hardly time."

Delahoussaye tapped the will with a long finger. "This codicil is clear. He wishes no slaves freed."

"But they are ours now—" Gabriele began, until a look from Tom silenced her.

"Technically, yes, they are," Delahoussaye said. "But the will must be probated—the succession executed—and with Tom away there will be an inevitable delay."

"Do you mean we can't free Veronique?" Gabriele demanded.

"I cannot advise you to dispose of any property until the estate is legally yours, Miss Cannon," Delahoussaye said. His abandonment of her given name warned Gabriele that she could get no farther: allowing herself an unhappy glance at Tom, she fell silent until the last few matters were concluded, and they bid the lawyer good night.

"What can you mean, Gabriele, that Oliver said he would set Veronique free?" said Aunt Mat as soon as the door closed.

"I asked him. And he agreed," she said.

"But to do what? She could not stay here!" Aunt Mat looked almost wild, as though she expected to be told that Veronique would move into the house that very night.

"We spoke of setting her up as a modiste in New Orleans," Gabriele began. Then Tom's face stopped her. He looked as though he would explode, as though whatever emotion gathered behind lips set to repress a too-quick response and eyes struggling to conceal shock would overpower him at any moment. "But we had not gotten very far—"

"Well," Aunt Mat said. "We all have enough on our

minds without you stirring up something new. Tom off tomorrow for heaven knows how long—and as Mr. Delahoussaye said, Gabriele, you own nothing yet."

"I'm not trying to make trouble," Gabriele said.

Tom's face softened, and he put his arm around her, holding her close. "Of course you aren't, Gabe. But Aunt Mat is right. We own nothing yet. And until the estate passes legally to us—we can do nothing for Veronique."

"But later—when we are in possession—you will agree to free her, won't you, Tom?"

Aunt Mat's eyes fastened on Tom's face, but Gabriele looked at her aunt. She is afraid, just as Papa was, Gabriele thought. But her fear is different. Papa did not think Tom would marry Veronique—Aunt Mat is afraid that if she is freed, despite all the laws against it—he will.

Chapter Seven

NARROW SLICES OF HOT BLUE SKY MADE CHINKS OF LIGHT through the shutters' slats, reminding Gabriele of the smothering heat that lay over New Orleans like a wet canvas sail. Every time she had to leave the high-ceilinged rooms of their house on Esplanade Avenue, she longed for Felicity and its canopy of trees, and the breeze that came up from the bayou late in the evening, sending a breath of coolness into the open windows, making it possible to sleep.

She had not slept well since she and Aunt Mat arrived in New Orleans in mid-July. At first she told herself that grief for her father kept her awake. Then she blamed the unusual circumstances of being in the City in mid-summer for her lack of sleep, and finally she made the terrible heat the culprit, coming down each morning with deeper rings under her eyes, and with another layer of colour faded from her cheeks.

Now she heard the clock on the landing strike four and sat up, relieved that the household would begin to stir, and she could leave these damp sheets and still air for the cooler rooms downstairs. She put out a hand and rang for Veronique, vowing that now Tom was back from his journey, she would urge him to work with her to set Veronique free.

It cannot take that long to execute the succession, she

thought, rising and slipping on a light batiste robe. And although Tom's mind is taken up with politics, he will not overlook our responsibility to Veronique. Gabriele had seen Tom only at dinner last night, and then the conversation had been all of the presidential campaign, and how its outcome would affect the prospects for union and peace.

"Louisiana's leaders may have paid homage to our father's memory, but they didn't follow his advice," Tom said. "Moderation and compromise have been tossed from the South's lexicon—where at first we had only two Democratic conventions and two presidential nominees, we now have three—and God knows another splinter group makes any kind of agreement with the North more impossible than ever before."

It had taken Gabriele a while to get the splinter groups and their nominees straight: now she named them on her fingers, determined to get them right. "Let me see now. The Southern Democrats—the ones that bolted the Charleston convention to begin with—have nominated John Breckenridge, and Tom thinks he's a good choice. The main group Democrats nominated Stephen A. Douglas—whom Tom thinks well of but says won't get any support in the South at all—and now another group of Democrats who apparently aren't pleased by either of those nominees have formed the National Constitutional Union party, and want a man named John Bell for President."

She sighed and leaned forward to look in the mirror, pinching her cheeks until her fingers brought faint colour up. "I can't help but think," she told her reflection, "that the very men who are warning everyone else how serious this election is are not taking it nearly seriously enough themselves. They're going to cause a war if they keep on like this!"

The door behind her swung open, and Veronique entered, carrying a glass of lemonade on a silver tray. Every time Gabriele saw Veronique, the scene with Aunt Mat, just before they left Felicity for New Orleans, played again in her mind. Lucie had succumbed to a summer fever two days before they were to depart, leaving Gabriele without a maid to accompany her. It seemed perfectly natural to take Veronique: she could find everything she needed to make their mourning clothes in New Orleans, and see to Gabriele's needs as well. And, Gabriele had thought, although I will say nothing about it, since Aunt Mat seemed so surprised at the idea, I can do a little research about setting up Veronique in business, once she is free.

Aunt Mat had been adamant. Veronique should not go. When pressed for reasons, she had none. When asked who else might attend her niece, she could suggest no name. By the end of the interview, both Aunt Mat and Gabriele had been on the verge of tears, frustrated and angry. And then, Aunt Mat had given in. Even a few months ago, Gabriele would have backed down. But she had stood her ground, overlooking Aunt Mat's reluctance and never mentioning it again.

And so they came to New Orleans, and Veronique put her things in the small room next to Gabriele's own. Aunt Mat kept busy with her own affairs, receiving condolence calls from a wide circle of friends, and one day visiting her husband's relatives at their home on Bayou Lafourche.

"Now that Tom is here, Veronique, we can move forward with the legal matters that must be completed before we can set you free," Gabriele said.

"I don't let myself think about it very much," Veronique said. She went to the armoire and took out a black afternoon dress. "I've waited this long—I can wait a few months more."

"Months! It won't be months," Gabriele said. "Tom and I are the only heirs—and I will tell you one thing, Veronique. When I saw the size of Papa's estate, and realized how much he paid his lawyers—I assure you, they will expedite this as fast as they can."

"The only heirs—" Veronique said, and then stopped.

"What do you want to ask?" Gabriele said, taking off her

robe and sponging her throat and arms with water faintly scented with cologne.

"I shouldn't ask you—it's none of my business—"

"Oh, for heaven's sake, Veronique!"

"Your father—did he leave anything to Mrs. LeGrange?"

Gabriele took the towel Veronique handed her and blotted herself dry, then took up a puff of lambs' wool and pressed it into powder held in a crystal jar. She paused, powder-laden puff in her hand, looking at Veronique. "No —he didn't. He enjoined Tom and me to maintain her— but he didn't leave her anything outright." Gabriele dusted the powder over her shoulders and throat, watching the thin white cloud rise around her. "I suppose she has money of her own—I've never really thought about it."

"I don't think she does," Veronique said. She set the dress aside and came to style Gabriele's hair. "Abigail talked about it, right after Mr. Cannon died. She was hoping he'd left Mrs. LeGrange something—she said she doesn't have anything of her own."

"But she must!" Gabriele said. "She and Uncle Louis had a big ranch in Texas—a great herd of cattle—I always thought they did very well."

"Abigail says she thinks the money went—and that's why Mrs. LeGrange came back when he died."

"Do you mean that if Aunt Mat did not live with us— she would have nothing? Would have to somehow scrimp a living? But my father would have helped her—"

"I shouldn't be going on like this," Veronique said. "Abigail was so hopeful that there would be some money now —I'm sure Mrs. LeGrange has told her there will not."

Gabriele watched Veronique put the last jet comb into her hair, then stood up and held out her arms for the black dress. "I'm not playing the devil's advocate, Veronique—but what difference would it make if Papa had left Aunt Mat some money? She has everything she needs and wants—he has never denied her a thing! As Tom and I won't. Why, one of the first entries in Papa's household accounts is the personal allowance he makes to Aunt Mat, to do with just exactly as she pleases. Tom and I will continue that, of course—what more could she want?"

"I don't think she could want any more," Veronique said, fastening up the dress. "But then, I'm not Abigail."

"It's all very vexing," Gabriele said, picking up a lace collar and holding it against her dress. "If Aunt Mat wants more money, all she has to do is ask. She must know that!"

"I knew I shouldn't have brought it up," Veronique said.

"You can bring up anything you like," Gabriele said. "There are no barriers between us—"

"Bless you," Veronique said, leaning down and giving Gabriele a swift kiss. "Now, let me fix that—" She picked up a jet brooch and used it to hook the lace collar, standing back to see the effect. "Very proper," Veronique said. "Even a New Orleans lawyer will be impressed."

"I don't care about impressing him," Gabriele said. "I just care that he does what I want."

Gabriele waited until the end of their meeting with Mr. Guillot, the lawyer who took care of Oliver Cannon's New Orleans affairs, to bring up the subject of Veronique. "There is something else I wish to discuss," she said, glancing at Tom. "It is what I told you the night before you left for Baltimore, Tom—about Papa wishing to free Veronique."

"Gabriele—you and I have not even discussed that—"

"But there is no reason why we should not find out the legal technicalities while we are here, is there? That should make our decision all the more easy, Tom."

Mr. Guillot looked up from a list he held in his hand. "Did you say Veronique?"

"Yes," Gabriele said.

"There is no one here by that name," Mr. Guillot said.

"What?" Gabriele reached across the desk for the list. "Could I see that, please?"

"But of course." He gave her the paper, then settled back in his chair, hands making a temple under his chin. His expression needed no clarification: clearly he had been subjected all too often to the wishes of clients who had no basis for what they said.

"Her name isn't on here," Gabriele said, handing the list to Tom. "But how could that be?"

Tom ran his eye over the page, then turned to the next one, hunting for her name. "You're right—it isn't. But why wouldn't it be? Unless—of course, that's it. Veronique didn't belong to Father, Gabriele. She belongs to Aunt Mat."

"Aunt Mat? Then why didn't she say so—the night I said what Papa had promised to do? And why did he promise to free her?"

"Is that exactly what he said?"

"Of course it is," Gabriele said. "Wait a minute—let me think." She closed her eyes, bringing the scene with her father near. "He said he would release her." She opened her eyes. "Yes, I'm sure of it. He said he would release her."

"He must have intended to speak with Aunt Mat," Tom said. "And considering the love and trust between them— I suppose he thought Aunt Mat would agree."

"It seems strange that he didn't simply tell you this woman did not belong to him—that he had no power to do anything, one way or the other," Mr. Guillot said.

"It doesn't seem strange to me," Gabriele said. "Despite the fact that my father saw to it I received an education equal to that of many men, I'm afraid that when it came to matters like this one—he still kept things from me, as one would from a child."

"Gabriele!" Tom said. "How can you speak of our father that way?"

"Oh, Tom, I am not attacking him—you know that I am not! It is the way things are—a young lady in my position is protected from all kinds of knowledge—much of it simply out of custom, with no real purpose at all. I think it was in that vein that Papa answered me. He believed he could do what I asked—he did not think it mattered if I knew all the details."

Tom sat back in his chair, fiddling with the watch hanging from his vest on a heavy gold chain. "I can't say I don't know what you mean, Gabe. Even I ran into that kind of wall from time to time—" He looked up at Mr. Guillot. "There's no point in taking up your time on this question, sir. Obviously, we must speak to our aunt."

"Just so," Mr. Guillot said. "Even if she says yes—there are legal manoeuvres that will have to be made. Technically, it is against the law now to free a slave—"

"I'm sure you know all the manoeuvres, Mr. Guillot. No matter how expensive they are," Tom said.

A small smile briefly warmed the formal chill of Mr. Guillot's face. "You may count on it," he said.

"If there's nothing else, we'll bid you good day," Tom said. "And keep you informed, of course, as to what our aunt says about Veronique."

"There is a matter—but it is of personal interest only," Mr. Guillot said. "If you have a few moments?"

"Of course," Tom said.

Mr. Guillot sat back, his hands again forming a temple under his chin. "You travelled throughout the South after the Baltimore convention, I believe, meeting with leaders in other cities?"

"Yes—as the youngest and most inexperienced man in any meeting, I listened a great deal more than I talked—and I have to say that I found myself both disappointed and frightened to find that among those present at any conference table, Reason seemed to be an unwanted guest by many there, with Emotion invited to take a high seat."

"Oh, yes," Guillot said. "Reason always receives short shrift when someone wants to make room for that fellow called War."

"Will there be a war?" Gabriele said. "You all say so—and yet you do nothing to make such madness stop!"

"Madness," Guillot repeated. "Now you have said it, Miss Cannon." He picked up a pamphlet from his desk and scanned the heavy black type. "The author of this practically insists on war," he said, tossing it onto his desk. "Nor is he alone. Broadsides of this nature fill the streets, spreading their inflammatory poison."

Tom retrieved the pamphlet, holding it so Gabriele could read it, too. "Thank God Breckenridge will not support such sentiments," he said. "Which is why I intend to devote a great deal of time and effort towards his election."

"That is the difference between us," Mr. Guillot said. "You in your youthful hope work to make things better— I, as an old cynic, prepare to flee."

"What?" Tom said.

"I am consolidating my investments, preparing to sell all I can—and move my assets abroad."

Tom grew very still, watching the lawyer's face as though he hoped for something more. Then he said, sounding very young and unsure, "And yourself. Will you move, too?"

"Not for a while," Guillot said. "Perhaps not at all. It depends upon what happens." His thumbnail flicked the property list. "I am not advising you to follow my example, Mr. Cannon. You asked me what my position as a private person is, and I have told you. I am, after all, a bachelor with only the most remote family ties. My assets are easily sold. Your situation is more complex—and perhaps the single most important factor is your youth, yours and your sister's. It is one thing to take steps to preserve a certain order for the latter part of one's life. It is another to—how shall I say this?—abandon a position before one has even really secured it."

"We have time," Tom said. "War will not come tomorrow—and, depending upon the election, it may even be averted."

"We will hope so," Guillot said. He rose to escort them to the door, pausing as he opened it. "Your father had great pride in and affection for you both," he said. "I can see why." And then, as though this intrusion of sentiment had been a breach of his own code, he bowed, turned on his heel, crossed his threshold and vanished inside.

"An odd sort of gentleman," Gabriele said. "I hardly know whether I like him or not."

"He's all right," Tom said. "And he's smart. If there is no obstacle to freeing Veronique—he'll know just exactly what to do."

"I shouldn't have sprung it on you that way, Tom," Gabriele said as he helped her into their carriage. "But I wanted to go forward with it—I'd no idea anything stood in the way."

Tom picked up the reins and guided the horses into the street. Automatically, Gabriele held her scented fan in front of her face, breathing in its perfume to cover the stench from garbage rotting in the streets. That made her think of Alex, and of a comment he had made a day or so before.

"New Orleans may be a grand lady," he had said as they strolled through the Quarter late one afternoon. "But she needs to pay more attention to her toilette."

"Oh, Tom," she said, "I haven't had time to tell you what a faithful friend Mr. St. Cyr has been. Not only while we remained at Felicity, and he popped in on several occasions when his packet came by, but here. We arrived last week to find a great basket of fruit awaiting us, with flowers sufficient to fill every vase. And Aunt Mat had hardly taken the dustcovers off the furniture before he sent his card around."

"One can always count on St. Cyr to do the right thing," Tom said, yanking the team's reins to avoid running over an urchin dancing in the street. "And Scott? Has he been around?"

"Mr. Scott went back to Boston—something about a new line of ships. He is to return soon, I think."

"Poor fellow," Tom said. "I wouldn't want to be in his shoes." He read his sister's inquiring glance and went on. "Well, he knows now that the South is not filled with irrational beings, all determined to pull the wreckage of the Union around our heads. And of course he knows, too, that increasingly our right to leave a Union we feel oppresses us is a great force that will probably push all other considerations aside. He may focus on the slavery issue as much as he desires—but he is an honest man, and the longer he stays among us, the more he will feel compelled to at least look at the other one."

"But still—his loyalties would lie with the North?"

"I don't doubt that at all," Tom said. He turned the carriage into the alley running behind their house. "Which is why I don't envy Scott his dilemma. His intellectual honesty demands he explore every view—but the ties of his heart demand he support only one. Whereas you and I? There is no division."

Gabriele waited while her brother came around to help her get down. Then, with her hand in his, she searched his face. "Truly, Tom? Are you that clear on this cause?"

He looks just like Papa, Gabriele thought, that same determination, that same high resolve.

"Yes," Tom said. "I am." He tucked her arm through his and started across the carriageway to the house. "I don't agree with everything I heard in Baltimore, and at the other meetings since—I don't agree with those men who held up all Northerners as vicious beasts bent on the destruction of the South. That's entirely unreasonable, as unreasonable as Northerners who think all slave-owners torture and brutalize their slaves."

He opened the door and Gabriele passed ahead of him into the cooler air. "But we cannot escape the fact that as things stand, injustice against the South is perpetuated by a Northern-controlled Congress. I won't believe our forefathers ever intended such to be the case—in my view, their behaviour abrogates the Constitution, which is in itself an attack upon the Union as it was meant to be."

"Such views leave—little room for dissension, Tom," Gabriele said. She caught sight of her face in a long mirror hanging in the hall. Who is that pale ghost, she thought, all swathed in black?

"Do you disagree with me, Gabe? Where is the flaw in my argument? With what do you not agree?"

"Oh, I agree," Gabriele said. "But I understand now what you mean about Mr. Scott—he will be uncomfortable here."

"Perhaps he will decide to stay in Boston," Tom said. He sounded disinterested, and Gabriele remembered the small distances that had existed between some of the mourners at her father's funeral and Jordan Scott.

"Perhaps he will," she said. Then, as a familiar figure approached them, she caught Tom's arm. "There is Aunt Mat," she said. "We must ask her about Veronique."

"Wait, Gabe," Tom said. "I need to know more about this—I don't want to ask Aunt Mat to do something I know nothing about."

"Why—what is there to know? We will free her—and she will become a modiste."

"As easily as that, Gabriele?"

"It will take effort, I'm sure. And money. We've plenty of money, heaven knows." She remembered the system under which Veronique worked. "And some of it she has earned!"

"But is that what she wants to do, Gabriele? Where would this business be, for example? Have you thought of that?"

"Here in New Orleans, of course," Gabriele said. "There is a large freedmen community here—" An idea struck her. "And there is Mr. St. Cyr's factor—the octaroon—what is his name?"

"Jacques Lamont?"

"Yes. He must know everyone—efficient in business, an octaroon like herself—" She spoke without thinking, only half-looking at her brother's face. What she saw there frightened her, and she tightened her hand on his arm. "Tom—don't you want what's best for Veronique?"

His features relaxed gradually, and the light that had frightened her faded from his eyes. "Of course I do," he said. He lifted her chin with his hand. "But, Gabriele, are you sure what you suggest is—best?"

"No," she said. "I am not. I only think it—possible."

Tom sighed, releasing her. "All right. Aunt Mat went into the parlour—let us go to her."

Aunt Mat sat in her usual chair, the one known as Oliver's empty at her side. She seemed to be dozing, but she opened her eyes and sat up alertly when her niece and nephew came in.

"Well, so how did it go at the lawyer's?" she said.

"Very well," Tom said. He flung himself down in his father's chair, and Gabriele saw a slight frown cross over her aunt's face. "What a lot of property there is, Aunt Mat! I'd no idea!"

"Your father increased his own inheritance many times over," Aunt Mat said. "And did very well by your mother's, too."

"But he didn't own Veronique," Tom said.

"What?"

"Her name is not on the list of slaves—"

"Nor should it be," Aunt Mat said. "Veronique belongs to me."

"We should have always known that—she arrived with you and Abigail—but somehow—growing up with her—I suppose Gabe and I began to think she had always been at Felicity."

"And since she is mine," Aunt Mat said, "I think what happens to her is a decision I will have to make."

"Aunt Mat," Gabriele said. "I would never have spoken so impulsively that night before Tom left if I had realized that it is up to you to free Veronique—it's just that Papa had promised—he said he would release her—I thought he meant he could."

"He probably could have," Aunt Mat said. "I have not

always followed Oliver's advice—but for many years now, I have."

"Then you will free her? Oh, Aunt Mat!" Gabriele said, flying to her aunt and kissing her on both cheeks.

"You are not thinking, Gabriele," Aunt Mat said. "Your father's will made it perfectly plain that he did not wish any of his slaves freed in these uncertain times—and I am certain that if he were here to be consulted, the same advice would apply to Veronique."

"Aunt Mat!" Gabriele said. "Do you mean you will not free her?"

"I mean that I intend to follow my brother's counsel," Aunt Mat said. "And I suggest that you do the same." She rose and looked at her watch. "Mr. St. Cyr sent his card around just after you left—he wishes to call upon us this evening, so we had better have our meal."

Gabriele stepped in front of Aunt Mat, blocking her path. "But that night—why did you not say then that you owned her? Or in all these weeks since?"

"Gabriele, I had barely buried my brother after nursing him for days—a will had just been read, a will that while it had no surprises—made certain things very clear." She shook her head as though dislodging something clinging there. "Then you spring this idea on us—this idea of setting that girl free—I blurted out the first thing that came to my head. I don't even remember what I said, how could I, as exhausted and grief-stricken as I was then? Then later —well, I think I hoped you had remembered that codicil to your father's will, and put the entire matter to rest."

"Then there is no hope for Veronique?" Gabriele said, speaking softly to keep them from hearing the trembling of her voice.

"Hope! What is hope, Gabriele? If you mean is there a chance she may have a life different from that she was born into—I really don't know. At this moment, and taking into consideration all that Tom has told us—I am not sure any of us will keep the life we were born to. And until that is more certain—there is nothing I can do for Veronique."

She swept past Gabriele, black skirts whispering against the floor.

"Oh, Tom," Gabriele said when Aunt Mat had left the room. "What shall I say to Veronique? Like a fool, I told her what Papa said—she expects to be freed, Tom, very soon!"

She could not remember when her brother had been really angry with her, but he was now. She braced herself for whatever Tom would say, telling herself that no words from him could be worse than the ones with which she upbraided herself. But after one frozen moment, when his grey eyes blazed from his pale face, Tom uttered an oath and strode from the room.

Gabriele stood looking after him, then dazed, turned slowly, taking in every detail of the parlour as though an answer to her problem lay hiding behind a brocade chair. I can't tell her. But I must. She clenched her hands, not even feeling the fingernails biting into her skin. Her eye fell on her father's favourite chair, and she went and huddled between its arms as though her father held her. My wretched impatience, she thought. It gets the better of me every time—but this time, it is not I who must suffer, but poor Veronique.

The sound of the bell calling her to dinner made her jump up, and with a hasty pat to her hair, she hurried to join her brother and aunt. Aunt Mat was just entering the dining room when Gabriele arrived at the door, only the small tight line at the corner of her mouth betraying the earlier scene.

"There you are, Gabriele. But where is Tom?"

"I—don't know, Aunt Mat," Gabriele said. "He only just left the parlour—I'm sure he will join us soon."

At that moment, Tom entered, looking hardly less *distrait* than he had a few minutes before. He held his aunt's chair, then Gabriele's, taking his own place in silence.

There is no possible topic of conversation, Gabriele thought, and indeed the meal progressed in the silence with which it had begun, each of them too absorbed or upset to think of talking. When the maid came in to tell them that a gentleman had arrived and waited for them in the parlour, they rose in one move, each walking quickly toward the door.

"I shall greet Mr. St. Cyr and then retire," Aunt Mat said. "This August heat exhausts me—I am sure he will understand."

He knows something is wrong, Gabriele thought, watching Alex's face as they entered the room. She watched him bow over Aunt Mat's hand, listened to the solicitous inquiries he made. "But of course our city heat is terrible," he said. "Not a breeze anywhere—except at the lake. Perhaps you will allow me to escort you and Miss Cannon to Milneberg some afternoon soon, Mrs. LeGrange. It is only a quarter-hour away—and affords much pleasure as well as a good breeze."

"I am hardly in the mood to seek pleasure, Mr. St. Cyr," Aunt Mat said. "And I can think of no place where mourning would be more inappropriate than at a restaurant on the lake."

"I should like to go, Mr. St. Cyr," Gabriele said, ignoring the look on her aunt's face. "I have worked very hard these last days—and I am more than ready for just the sort of diversion you suggest."

Alex looked from Gabriele to Aunt Mat, then glanced at Tom, whose expression gave him no clue as to what course he should take. "Perhaps Tom will help me arrange an excursion," he said. "Something small, with a private pavilion as our destination, so you, Miss Cannon, will not have to bear the brunt of public curiosity—"

"I shall leave it to you, Tom," Aunt Mat said. "Good night, Mr. St. Cyr. Good night, Gabriele."

"Good night, Aunt Mat," Gabriele said. For the first time that she could remember they did not exchange an embrace; Aunt Mat's rigid back spoke of no softening, and Gabriele was still far too upset to think of taking the first step.

Tom waited until his aunt's footsteps vanished up the stairs before turning to his friend. "Sorry about all that, Alex, but we've had—a difficulty here, and we're all still quite disturbed."

"It's all my fault," Gabriele said. "No, Tom, I shall tell Mr. St. Cyr what happened—you would not be hard enough on me—oh, if you knew how dreadful I feel!"

She had thought facing Veronique would be difficult, as well it might. But as she told the story to Alex, as she saw the expression he tried to conceal, she knew that to have to reveal to him her thoughtlessness, her foolishness, was the hardest thing she had yet had to do in her life. "You are disappointed in me, Mr. St. Cyr," she said when she had finished and Alex still did not speak. "And you are right to be—I talk about thinking things through and being careful to look before I leap—now I will have to tell Veronique that this promise I held out to her cannot possibly be kept."

"I am not disappointed, Miss Cannon, you misread me," Alex said. "Sorry—yes, that describes my feeling. I am sorry that your first generous impulse as the mistress of your own property has met with such little success."

"But you do understand? She does not belong to us?" Gabriele said. "If she did—oh, I know Aunt Mat's position has some merit—Papa did leave instructions that none of his slaves were to be freed. But he could not have meant Veronique! She didn't belong to him—"

"Would Mrs. LeGrange sell her, do you think?" Alex asked. The energy Gabriele sometimes felt coming from him so powerfully filled the room: Alex sprang from his chair and clasped Tom's hand. "To me, Tom. And then—I could set her free."

"I don't know," Tom said. "I hadn't thought of that possibility—"

"Then think of it!" Alex said. "Look, I'll write her a note and make the offer now."

"We'd better think this through," Tom said. "And not

rush in without a sound plan." He didn't look at Gabriele, but he didn't have to. Aunt Mat's temper normally stayed under tight control: in such a well-run household, very little ever happened that she had not made provision for, and it had been years since her niece and nephew had needed anything but the mildest reminder to keep them true to the way in which they had been brought up. But since her brother died, Aunt Mat had changed. Her surface calm was thinner, much more easily disturbed.

"Tom's right," Gabriele said. "And if I had thought of anything or anyone besides my own feelings, I'd have known better than to confront her like that."

"What's done is done, Gabriele," Tom said. "But if you will excuse us, I think St. Cyr and I had best talk alone—we'll go smoke in the garden, Alex, and think this thing through."

"Of course," Gabriele said. "Oh, I hope you can make Aunt Mat do as you wish! It has been bad enough for Veronique—but now, with freedom held out to her—and then snatched out of her hands—"

Alex crossed the space between them in two long strides, taking her hand in his and looking down at her with a look so intense she almost pulled away.

"There is one thing about being frivolous, Miss Cannon, and that is this. Frivolity and play strengthen the imagination—if there is anything I do well, it is to come up with good plans."

"A simple one will do," Gabriele said. "Persuade Aunt Mat to sell Veronique—then set her free."

"Yes," Alex said, exchanging a glance with Tom. "Well —to work, Cannon. And by the way—so long as we are planning—we might plan that excursion to the lake."

"As you say," Tom said.

He kissed Gabriele's cheek, and followed Alex out of the room.

"Oh, Tom—" Gabriele called.

He looked over his shoulder. "Yes?"

"Should I wait until morning to—tell Veronique?"

His eyes darkened, and she saw pain glitter there, tiny bits of mica against a field of grey. "That won't be necessary," he said. "I've already told her myself."

Chapter Eight

I WON'T RING FOR VERONIQUE, BUT WILL GET READY FOR BED BY myself, Gabriele thought, going slowly up the stairs. But with each step her shame grew: as bad as it was to have given Veronique hope before she had solid grounds for it, to avoid facing her would be worse. She braced herself as she entered her room, intending to immediately ring Veronique's bell. She did not have to: Veronique waited there, a slender figure standing at the window looking into the garden below. The lines of her body, her face when she turned to Gabriele—all told how hard she had been hit.

"Oh, Veronique!" Gabriele said. "I'd give everything I own if I had just waited to say something until I was sure!"

"I—know you did not mean to—hurt me," Veronique said. "And Tom helped me. He reminded me that you have never wanted anything that you did not receive."

"Then this should have been something I wanted," Gabriele said. "This terrible disappointment should have come to me, whose fault it is."

"That's not the way things work," Veronique said.

"Is there anything I can do? Oh, Veronique, if there is!"

"Give me wings," Veronique said. And then she set about her duties, her face making it clear that she had nothing more to say.

We'll neither of us sleep, Gabriele thought as the door closed behind Veronique. Both lying awake all night over something Aunt Mat could so easily fix. And why won't she? She does not really like having Veronique at Felicity— you'd think she'd be happy to have her well away, safe in New Orleans making her own life. Any attachment Veronique thinks she feels for Tom would weaken, once she were here. And his concern for her, rooted in his sense of justice, his compassion for those whose position is less secure and happy than his own, would settle into friendship. Why can't Aunt Mat see that by refusing to free Veronique, she is doing just what will push Tom's emotions over the edge?

She sat up, realizing the truth of that thought. Yes— yes, that is just what will happen. Up until now, Tom has not really been in love with Veronique, no matter what Papa or Aunt Mat feared. His affection for her has come from his own nature—he could no more stop caring about her welfare than he could mine. But now Veronique is a particular victim, not just one of a mass of slaves. If Aunt Mat had set out to make certain that Tom would devote his whole being to Veronique's happiness, she could not have found a better way.

And what went on in the garden? Did they try to determine the price Alex would offer for Veronique? How does one set a price on a woman like Veronique? Her skill would account for a portion, of course—but what else? She tried to banish the thought, seeing already the dark byways to which it led, but she could not let it go.

If someone set a price on me, what would I bring? Take Miss Jumonville—she had a small dowry—but she married a wealthy man. She remembered Dorothea Robin, discussing the bride. A well-run home, children reared correctly —and Mr. Forbes, cherished by his dependent wife. And what else had Dorothea said? Oh, yes. Mr. Forbes would be kind and generous in return, as any gentleman would.

Mrs. Forbes' path is as set for her as though she were a slave, Gabriele thought, lying down again. Yes, she is "free" in ways slaves are not, and there is no question that her life has more than its share of ease—but still—she had few choices. To remain at her father's as a spinster—or to go to Mr. Forbes.

A thought formed at the edge of her consciousness, and she lay very still, waiting for it to take shape. Aunt Mat. Aunt Mat had been married, yes. But for fifteen years now she had led the life of a spinster, living in her brother's house. And with no money, if what Veronique said was true. What could have happened to it? That great ranch in Texas—all those cattle . . . I am distracting myself. Let me focus on the main thought. Yes, that's it. I'm sure of it. Aunt Mat has so little left—she supervises our home, and yet others make the decisions governing it. She will never sell Veronique, not if Alex St. Cyr offers the highest price. She must have something she can control—unfortunately, what she has now is Abigail and Veronique.

Gabriele hoped that she was wrong, that her judgement about her aunt came, not from rational thinking, but from worry and fatigue. But the next morning, when Alex St. Cyr called on Aunt Mat to make his proposal, it ended just as Gabriele had thought that it would. Aunt Mat had no intention of selling Veronique. Not today, not ever.

As though that were not bad enough, she suspected Alex's motives, calling Tom into her room and speaking so bluntly that Gabriele, listening on the other side of the door, could hardly believe what she heard.

"I suppose this purchase was part of a scheme to set Veronique free," Aunt Mat said.

Gabriele could not hear Tom's reply: he murmured something, and then, after a moment, Aunt Mat spoke.

"I thought as much. Well, Tom, I have known you too long and trusted you too much to think you are deliberately trying to go against me. You are misguided, you think you know what is best for Veronique, without taking into account that older and wiser heads just might know a little more than you."

"Father told Gabriele he would release Veronique," Tom said.

"Yes, that is what she told us," Aunt Mat answered. "I

am not saying that Oliver did not say that—Gabriele is a truthful girl, if a little—impetuous. But the fact remains that my brother did not have an opportunity to speak to me, Tom. I have no idea what his intentions were, and I cannot act on what I do not know."

"Aunt Mat—you've made your decision. Do we have to belabour it?" Tom said. Gabriele could imagine how he looked from the way he sounded. Face drawn, eyes blazing, lips set against the slowly building anger—

"I won't say much more, Tom. Only this. If Mr. St. Cyr had purchased Veronique—and then set her free—what would happen next?"

"Why—we would follow Gabriele's plan. Set Veronique up as a modiste."

"A modiste," Aunt Mat said. "Nothing else?"

"What are you implying, ma'am?" Tom said.

The anger has spilled over, Gabriele thought. Oh, why does she prolong this when it is so painful for them both?

"Mr. St. Cyr has a reputation in New Orleans, Tom, as I'm sure you know."

"A reputation, Aunt Mat? You had better make that a little more clear—"

"He is older than you are, Tom. He has been on the New Orleans scene for several years now—and every season, he leaves behind at least one broken heart."

"Are you saying St. Cyr deliberately makes a lady fall in love with him, and then throws her over?" Tom said.

"How else would you account for what I am told?"

"I'll tell you how," Tom said. "Mothers whose daughters have not been successful in getting him to the altar—and who see that great fortune slipping through their grasping hands! Alex does not fall in love easily, ma'am—though that is something I know you won't believe. As for deliberately flirting until his victim succumbs—that is to accuse him of dishonourable behaviour. I refuse to hear another word!"

"Very well," Aunt Mat said. "If you don't care what people say about your friend, it is nothing to me. But the identity of the man who wished to purchase Veronique entered heavily into my decision, Tom. It is all very well to say she would be set up as a modiste—but there are too many cases where a girl of Veronique's—background—has been set up as something else instead."

I can't believe Aunt Mat said that, Gabriele thought. The silence inside frightened her—Tom was so angry— and then she heard her brother's voice.

"It will be better if we both forget you said that, Aunt Mat. I will lay your suspicions to a mind wearied by grief, and to your natural desire to—protect Veronique. But as a consequence—I must take steps also to protect my friend. I shall suggest to Alex that he confine his calls here to Gabriele and to me. He will not ask for an explanation— he sees more than his easy surface would suggest."

"You propose to allow your sister to continue to be in his company, and without me there as a chaperone?"

"Chaperone? Really, ma'am, you surprise me. If St. Cyr is really the devil you think him to be—he would find a way around you. No, I will not prevent Gabriele from seeing him if she so chooses. They are good for each other, whether you believe it or not. He does not flirt with her, Aunt Mat, any more than I would."

"Tom—" Aunt Mat said, sounding for the first time unsure.

"Gabriele needs to be exposed to men of more sophistication than the ones she meets at home," Tom said. "Especially now, when she will not have her season because of Father's death. Time spent with Alex will make her more discerning when the suitors you and I both expect come to call—she is, after all, a great heiress now, and I imagine every eligible man in the state is already making his plans."

Tom's last words made Gabriele forget everything that had gone before. What was this he was saying? That men who did not even know her would come ask for her hand? Like Miss Jumonville, she thought. Like—a slave on an auction block. She waited to hear no more, but fled to her room, thinking as she closed the door behind her that the old axiom was true: those who listen in stealth rarely hear anything good.

She came down at noon to find that Aunt Mat had gone away, finally accepting the invitation pressed upon her by an old friend to spend a few days at her summer home across the lake.

"I—am sorry she did not think to tell me goodbye," Gabriele said. "It seems strange—"

"Aunt Mat and I had a confrontation this morning," Tom said. "It was highly unpleasant—we both said a great deal more than we should."

"I know," Gabriele said. "I heard—most of it."

"Gabe! Listening at doors?"

"And how else am I to know what goes on? How would you like to be kept out of everything, told only what people think you should know?"

"Calm down, Gabe," Tom said. "I am too upset to even care—and in a way, it makes it easier, for now you know what Aunt Mat said about Alex."

Gabriele turned her head, staring at an arrangement of wax flowers in a bell jar as though she must memorize each petal and leaf.

"Well—you did hear what she said?" Tom said.

"Yes."

"Gabe, there's not one word of truth in it! Alex is too honourable to ever lead a lady on! You remember that day he came back from New Iberia—so disturbed because he felt he had been put in a situation where it was almost impossible to steer a fair course—"

She looked at Tom, letting the sincerity with which he spoke filter through her pain. "I have always found Mr. St. Cyr—honourable," she said. "He pretends to be frivolous —but he really is not."

"Pretends!" Tom said. "There you have it. It is precisely what Alex does, although I have told him his mask redounds against himself."

"Well, we shall not be in New Orleans much longer,"

Gabriele said. "So my opportunities to be—corrupted—by him will be few." She went to her brother and leaned her head against his chest. "Oh, Tom, it is so horrid for Aunt Mat to feel that way. I don't, of course—and I shall be glad to see Mr. St. Cyr."

"But she's taken some of the joy out of your meetings," Tom said. "And there is no question—she has sown a seed of distrust." His arm came around her and he patted her back, soothing her as her father used to do. "Overcome that little seed as fast as you can, Gabriele. Alex has a real regard for you—"

"As I do for him!"

"Good. Then let us say no more about it. I'm glad Aunt Mat is gone for a few days—we've planned our excursion to the lake for tomorrow—and she will not yet be home."

"I feel—disloyal going against her wishes," Gabriele said.

"But you are not going against mine," Tom said. "I am the master of the household now, Gabriele. You are perfectly justified in doing as I ask."

"Yes, of course," Gabriele said.

The bell rang to announce lunch, and she took Tom's arm. But as they walked toward the dining room, Gabriele could not suppress the thought that rose unbidden in her mind. She and Tom shared equally in all their father's property—yet he was the master of the household, just as he said. And somehow, that arrangement did not seem quite fair.

A stiff breeze off Lake Pontchartrain ripped Gabriele's parasol from her hand, sending it tumbling across the grass like a wayward hoop. Alex dashed after it, retrieving it in one gloved hand and sweeping his tall hat from his head with the other. "Careful, Miss Cannon," he said as he gave her the parasol. "The wind will take this yet."

"I'm so grateful for cool air that I'm almost ready to let the wind have it," Gabriele said. "It's astonishing—New

Orleans is stifling, and here, only five miles out from the city, the air is so fresh."

"Which is a primary reason for Milneberg's popularity," Tom said, looking at the large crowd thronging the area of restaurants and dance pavilions. "A fifteen-minute ride on the Lake Pontchartrain railroad—and you're in a different clime."

"I would like to see some of the attractions," Gabriele said, "but I think we had better go on to the pavilion you have reserved. I am so conspicuous in this black dress—"

"The pavilion is just past that hotel," Alex said. He offered Gabriele his arm and they moved slowly across the sand, threading their way through the crowd that strolled about with seemingly no purpose other than to enjoy the breeze off the water on this sultry summer evening.

The sudden crack of gunfire made Gabriele jump, and she looked in the direction of the noise with a stifled cry.

"It's only a shooting gallery," Alex said. "Don't be alarmed."

Tom glanced toward the booth where a young boy hefted a rifle to his shoulder. "I wouldn't mind having a go myself—see if the eye I trained in the swamps down home holds true here."

"I can escort Miss Cannon on to the pavilion if you want to stop," Alex said.

Tom looked from Alex to Gabriele, then back at his friend. "I think I will," he said. "You don't mind, Gabriele?"

"Of course not," Gabriele said.

"Then I'll meet you at the pavilion," Tom said, striding off across the sand.

Gabriele and Alex moved forward: she thought he quickened his pace a little, and guessed that he wished to get her safely inside.

They had almost reached their destination when a man walking the opposite way called Alex's name, tapping his shoulder with a malacca cane. "Well, St. Cyr," the man said, his eyes going from Alex to Gabriele. He removed his hat and bowed in her direction, and she answered him with a slight nod of her head. "We missed your father at the meeting last night. I hope he is not ill?"

"My father is quite well, thank you," Alex said.

"Then why did he not join us?"

"Since I am entirely ignorant of the event my father missed, I can hardly offer an excuse," Alex said. There was no overlooking his cold reserve, and the man stepped back as though he had been slapped.

"The Washington Artillery met to determine which presidential candidate we will back," the man said. He looked at Alex through narrowed eyes. "Am I to presume your father has no opinion he cared to pursue?"

"You may presume anything you like, sir," Alex said. "Now if you will excuse me—this lady is waiting." He turned away with the merest nod; Gabriele took his arm and they walked in silence, Alex's tension communicating itself through the taut muscles she felt even through his sleeve.

Not until they were seated in the pavilion at a table commanding a view of the open water did Alex relax, smiling at her in the familiar way. "Now we are comfortable," he said. "Shut away from intrusions we can do very well without."

"The gentleman seemed to—annoy you very much," she said.

"A man whose membership in the Washington Artillery is through a collateral rather than a direct line," Alex said. "He has always resented my father, whose family arrived soon after Bienville, whereas that gentleman's antecedents did not come until after the war of 1812."

"I am very glad, then, that my ancestors arrived as early as they did," Gabriele said. "Else you might put us with those new arrivals you seem to disdain."

"I disdain no one, Miss Cannon," Alex said. "It is useless to think badly of people's behaviour, and easier to avoid meeting them at all."

He watched while the waiter opened a bottle of champagne and then poured it into cut-crystal flutes. "That gentleman is not happy because although my father almost never lifts a finger to make himself agreeable to anyone outside of his own tight sphere, he is welcome everywhere—as why would he not be? He belongs to every organization in the city open only to families of certain credentials and descent—he has a magnificent cellar, an excellent chef—and the hunting parties at Olympia are renowned for both the company and the game."

The words, idly spoken, seemed to mean little in themselves, but the look in Alex's eyes said otherwise.

"You are not proud of your father, are you, Mr. St. Cyr?"

"Proud?" Alex shrugged and looked out at the white-capped waves. "Everything he has he has inherited or been given—except, I suppose, his famous charm. There is little to be proud of in that."

He turned back to her, light from the low-hung sun staining his face. "But I like him well enough, Miss Cannon, never think that I do not. I have learned not to expect from people what they cannot give—that makes it much easier to get along."

"Yes—I'm sure it does," she said. She wished that Tom would hurry. Aunt Mat's words seemed fixed in her head; at the slightest pause in the conversation, they demanded her attention, filling the silence until she found something to say.

"What is it, Miss Cannon?" Alex finally said. When she did not answer, only looked away from him, colour coming up in her face, he leaned back in his chair, seeming in that small gesture to put a much wider distance between them. "It is what your aunt told Tom," he said. "And the consequences of their—conversation."

"Yes," Gabriele said.

"I cannot defend myself, Miss Cannon. I cannot say young ladies' hearts have not been broken colliding with this smooth facade. I can say that I have not—wished them to. If there is anything I don't want to be responsible for, Miss Cannon, it is some foolish young lady's heart."

"I am sure of it," Gabriele said. "But Tom did not think before he spoke—to tell Aunt Mat that you would not call upon her—I don't think that decision is properly his."

Alex picked up the linen-wrapped bottle and tilted it over Gabriele's glass, watching the golden bubbles rise through its slender shape. He filled his own glass and replaced the bottle in the silver cooler standing at his side. "She will not miss me, Miss Cannon," Alex said. "It might perhaps be a little awkward—but in time, even that will pass."

"I have never sided against Aunt Mat," she began, but Alex's eyebrow, raised in a mocking black curve, stopped her.

"Of course you have," he said. "Tom constantly told me of scrapes the two of you got into that pitted you against your aunt's rules."

"I was a child then," Gabriele said.

"And now you are an adult, come into her property and in quite a different position." He looked at her, and again she felt that she was being pulled into the centre of his eyes. "She will have much to divert her, in any case, as soon as the train of suitors arrives at Felicity's gates."

"Please don't say that!" Gabriele said. "If you knew how I detest the prospect!"

"What? Do you mean you do not wish to be courted, to be told that you are the most adorable creature inhabiting the earth?"

"I did not say I did not wish to be courted, Mr. St. Cyr." She picked up her glass and sipped the champagne. "I said I do not want to receive a train of suitors who come to Felicity, not because they know me, but because they know the extent of the Cannon estate."

Alex lifted his glass, bowing in a silent toast. "My sentiments entirely. Which is why I do not defend myself against reports such as the ones that so disturbed Mrs.

LeGrange. I have not found that the number of invitations I receive diminishes—quite the contrary, I'm afraid."

"Well, St. Cyr, you have a good opinion of yourself!" Tom said, coming up behind Gabriele. He took the chair between them and filled his glass with champagne. "But you have good reason—all the attributes that make any gentleman greatly in demand—"

"Thank you, but I think my attributes can be reduced to two," Alex said. "The Scott money and the St. Cyr name."

"I feel just the same way, Tom," Gabriele said. "And I promise you—I won't stand having a series of gentlemen I have never met taking up my time with thinly-veiled proposals meant to unite their property with mine."

"Gabriele—what are you talking about? What series of gentlemen—"

"Can you deny you told Aunt Mat the selfsame thing?" she cried. She searched for her handkerchief, and felt one pressed into her hand.

"Gabe—Gabe—confound it, you misunderstood!"

"I didn't," she said through the thickness of the damp cloth.

"Alex—help me."

"I'm not sure I can," Alex said. "Sorry, Tom, but in a way Miss Cannon is perfectly correct. Gentlemen who do not know her, who have to make sure of her name, *will* send cards and will ask to call. Now you know that is the case—why pretend otherwise?"

"But she doesn't have to marry them! By God, if it makes you this unhappy, I don't care if you never receive them at all!"

She looked over the handkerchief, examining her brother's face. "Do you mean that, Tom?"

"Well, of course I do! What is Felicity, some public hotel people can stroll in and out of at will? If you don't want to see someone—just refuse."

"Aunt Mat will fuss, Tom, you know she will. And you'll be off politicking for Breckenridge—I won't have anyone on my side."

Tom patted her hand, smiling now that her crying had stopped. "Gabe—I've told you. It's all right with me if you don't want to play the game as it's written. But if you're going to make up a new one—I think you better be able to play it without anyone else on your team."

His lips smiled indulgently, the big brother giving in to another of his little sister's whims. But his eyes looked different—something had gone out of them, but she could not see yet just what.

"I have an idea, Miss Cannon," Alex said. His voice seemed to float between them, slowly drawing their attention to him. "If the game gets out of control—and you must take drastic measures—announce that you are considering accepting my suit—and must put off everyone else until that decision is made."

"I say, Alex!" Tom said.

"Oh, Tom, Mr. St. Cyr is just showing us how far we have carried this," Gabriele said.

"I meant it, you know," Alex said. He smiled, and turned to Tom. "Come, Cannon, don't scowl. Miss Cannon understands me well enough. She knows I should enjoy the protection such an announcement would give me more than she would."

"I won't say I don't agree with you that the whole process of matching people leaves a great deal to be desired," Tom said. "And frankly, I wish a solution to the problem were as easy as those frivolous ones you propose—"

"Take heart," Alex said. "If the elections go against us in November, our whole world will turn upside down. And then marriages once considered most unsuitable can take place without anyone caring at all."

Tom's eyes darted to Alex's face, still with that curious blank stare. Then something moved at the back of them—a flash of emotion Gabriele could not read before it was as quickly gone. "Ah, well, let us hope we don't have to tear one thing apart to build another up," Tom said. He picked up his menu, using it to screen his face. "So—what are we having? Alex, what do you recommend?"

The evening settled back into a smooth groove, with Alex alone entertaining them with stories at first, but with Tom gradually joining in. As they left the pavilion to catch the return train, Gabriele saw a small group of people leave the lighted walkways and disappear into the woods.

"Where could they be going?" she said. "Look, there!"

Alex and Tom looked in the direction she pointed, just catching sight of the group as it vanished into the trees.

"I imagine they're searching for Marie Laveau," Alex said. "You've heard of her, of course. She's supposed to be the voodoo queen."

"And she lives out here?" Gabriele said. "Why did I think she had a house in the French Quarter?"

"She does," Alex said. "On St. Ann Street. But she also has a house out here—it's where they celebrate the major rituals on June 23. St. John's Eve," he said, answering Gabriele's puzzled look. "It has some great significance for the followers of voodoo, though I really couldn't say what it is."

"It's all frightening to think about," Gabriele said, drawing closer to Tom. "Although the slaves at Felicity pretend they have nothing to do with it—every once in a while I catch sight of the *gris-gris* some of them wear hidden beneath their clothes. They always tuck it back, of course, and give me that blank-eyed look. There's no point in talking to them about it—they would pretend not to understand what I meant."

"That woman over at the Robins' who says she's a *traiteur* doesn't help," Tom said. "Mr. Robin won't take it seriously—but if she were mine, I'd make her either stop her nonsense or I'd sell her off the place."

Nothing could be seen of the small party that had entered the woods: the branches, black now that night had come, seemed to make a solid wall beyond which nothing could penetrate. Gabriele tried to imagine what they would find if they indeed reached Marie Laveau. And why would anyone risk such a meeting, given the terrible deeds voodoo worshippers claimed?

She shivered slightly, and leaned closer into the shelter of her brother's arm. "I hope they don't find her," she said. "I know people scoff at voodoo, and deny it has any power—still, there must be something to it. We have all heard of slaves who had had death curses put on them, and who did indeed die."

"There can be many explanations for that," Alex said. "Not the least an hysterical condition in which the victim persuades himself that he is to die—and literally brings it about."

"But if there had been no curse—the victim would never have had the idea," Gabriele said.

"Now you are being morbid," Tom said. "But look, there's our train. Let's forget all about voodoo and have a pleasant journey back, or I shall have to sit guard opposite your door to keep nightmares away!"

The trip went swiftly: in not more than half an hour, they had reached New Orleans and been driven by Alex's coachman to the Cannon house. Gabriele immediately went upstairs, leaving Alex and Tom to smoke and talk. A pleasant evening in all, Gabriele thought, despite some small bumps. Poor Tom—he tried to pretend he did not think of her, but how obvious that Veronique and her troubles are still uppermost in his mind.

Then she thought of Alex, feeling a quick rise of happiness when she remembered all he had said. Aunt Mat is quite wrong about Mr. St. Cyr, she thought. She believes he does not take marriage seriously, but on the contrary, I believe he takes it more seriously than anyone I have ever met.

Gabriele woke late the next morning to a house empty of the usual sounds. She rang for Veronique, but no one appeared, and when, having dressed and made her toilette quickly, she hurried downstairs, she found Tom and Alex in the study, both looking serious, and both jumping up when Gabriele came through the door.

"What is it?" Gabriele said. "Tom—what's wrong?"

"Nothing," Tom said. "Why do you ask?"

"Oh, Tom, as though I don't know you," Gabriele said. "You and Mr. St. Cyr both look as though you are plotting to blow something up at the very least—"

"I shall blow up nothing, Miss Cannon," Alex said, bowing. "It is hot enough as it is without creating more heat." He glanced at Tom. "In fact, I have tired of New Orleans in August, and leave today for Olympia."

"Today! But—this is very quick!"

"I warned you, Gabe," Tom said. "At college we called Alex Quicksilver. Now you see why."

"Of course it will be cooler there—much more pleasant than here," Gabriele said.

"Yes, Olympia is known for being pleasant, Miss Cannon. You must pay us a visit some day."

He went to Tom and clasped his hand. "I hope I am back before you leave the city—if not, send me your schedule so we may correspond."

"I'll see you out," Tom said.

"Let me bid you goodbye, Miss Cannon," Alex said. "And if you are gone when I return—perhaps I may call at Felicity?"

"That will be difficult with Tom gone, Mr. St. Cyr. Since this wedge has been driven between you and my aunt—"

"Send your card around when you are down that way, Alex," Tom said. "I'll speak to Aunt Mat. Such a tempest in a teapot, anyway!"

"When hurricanes are brewing, these smaller storms become attractive, Tom," Alex said. "Since they are possible to control." He took Gabriele's hand, holding it a moment before letting it go. "I will call, then, Miss Cannon."

"Yes—of course."

She watched them leave the study, and heard them begin to talk in low voices as soon as they gained the hall. They are plotting how to save Veronique, she thought, but I won't ask Tom to tell me one word. But, oh, how I long to know!

Tom proposed a final tour of their New Orleans properties, a venture that would take the better part of the day. And while we are gone, Veronique will complete her escape, she thought. She kept glancing at Tom as they slowly progressed from one building to the next, wondering at his calm face. He and Mr. St. Cyr, if I am right and they are helping Veronique escape, are committing a grave crime—and yet he is as tranquil as if he has nothing to hide.

She tried to mention Veronique once, but the name died on her tongue, and with a sense of following a story in which she had no real part, she put a distance between herself and the event she knew had occurred.

She will go to Olympia with Mr. St. Cyr, Gabriele thought. There to be one of his father's pampered pets— but, no, surely between them Tom and Mr. St. Cyr can do better than that—it is freedom Veronique wants, not just an easier place. Oh, why couldn't Tom have told me about this, and let me help him plan? I might have come up with something, something with less risk.

She dreaded the next few hours, the deceit Tom must practise, the silence she must keep. And when they returned at the end of the day to find Aunt Mat home, refreshed and ready to overlook the disturbances that had cracked the smooth surface of their lives, Gabriele felt she could not bear it. She sat down to dinner with Tom and Aunt Mat, knowing that Veronique's room was empty, and wondering who would sound the alarm. Should she, when she rang for Veronique tonight and she did not appear? Would Tom? She could hardly eat, and when at last the moment came, she wondered if she could support Tom through it, and not give what she suspected away.

"Oh, by the way, Aunt Mat," Tom said when they had finished their dessert. "I ran into young Favrot yesterday— he said his mother wants to know if Veronique can do some sewing for her—some sort of emergency, I gathered —their regular seamstress is sick."

"We shan't be here much longer," Aunt Mat said. "But of course if Louise Favrot needs a favour—such an old and dear friend—ring for Veronique, will you, Gabriele? I'll see how her work is going. And perhaps in the morning she can go round to Louise and see how much time her work would require."

Gabriele felt that she could not possibly cross the distance to the bell-pull on the wall, but Tom's eyes urged her, and she rose and gave it three hard tugs. The butler would hear it in the kitchen and relay the signal up to Veronique, using the central pull in his pantry that rang in all the slaves' rooms.

When Veronique did not appear, Aunt Mat told Gabriele to ring again. When still no one came, Aunt Mat pushed the foot-bell under the rug in front of her chair that would bring in the butler. Eli came quickly, already knowing what Aunt Mat would say. "I rang for Veronique, Miz LeGrange. But she don't answer—I don't know where that girl could be."

"Send Abigail up to find her," Aunt Mat said, her lips drawn tight and thin. When Eli had left, she shot a glance at Tom. "Sulking, I suppose. That's what comes finally, no matter how kind you try to be."

Tom said nothing, nor did Gabriele. They sat in silence, listening to Abigail's footsteps on the stairs. I wish it were over, Gabriele thought. I wish I could be in my bed—or away from here. She remembered what Veronique had said to her—I wish I had wings. Then Abigail appeared on the threshold, the scar on her cheek seeming darker and longer, as though the news she had for them had already begun to work change.

"She ain't nowhere, Miz Mathilde. Not in her room—not anywhere."

"What do you mean, Abigail? She has to be somewhere!" Aunt Mat said.

"Yes'm, I know, but that somewhere—it ain't here."

"Very well, Abigail. Thank you—go wait for me in my

room, I'm extremely tired and will soon want to go to bed." Aunt Mat waited until Abigail had left, then turned to Tom. "Where is she?" she demanded.

"You mean Veronique? I've no idea, why would I?" Tom said.

Gabriele recognized Tom's expression, and one glance at Aunt Mat's face said she did, too. He would say nothing he did not want to say. It did not matter how long she questioned him, nor what threats she made. When Tom Cannon got that look on his face, you might as well accept the fact that you would have to find out what you wanted to know from somebody else.

Aunt Mat's eyes dropped away from Tom's steady gaze, and then shifted to Gabriele. "Gabriele? Is there anything you can tell me about Veronique?"

"No, Aunt Mat," Gabriele said. Her eyes met her aunt's, and she saw her aunt blink. I am such a poor liar, Gabriele thought. Thank heaven I don't know anything!

"She seems to have—run away," Aunt Mat said, sounding almost disinterested. "Well, if that's the case—we shall have to take steps to find her. The usual advertisements—I shall of course offer a large reward." She rose, surveying their faces. "But it is too late to do anything tonight—I am too tired, and I don't suppose twelve more hours will make any difference, do you, Tom?"

"I've no idea," Tom said. He had the same look on his face, walling her out. He stood and bowed to Aunt Mat. "I have an engagement," he said. "And since you already know what you intend to do about getting your—property back, then I shall not offer either aid or advice."

He is hurting her, Gabriele thought when she saw Aunt Mat's face. Oh, how right I was when I knew that if something were not done, Veronique's unhappiness would spill into each of our lives.

"And you, Gabriele? Have you an engagement, too?"

"No, Aunt Mat. I'm very tired—I intend to go right up to bed."

"I will send Abigail to you when she has finished with me," Aunt Mat said.

"Thank you," Gabriele said, and with only a slight, frightened glance at her brother, followed her aunt out of the room.

Chapter Nine

AUNT MAT LEFT EARLY THE NEXT MORNING WITHOUT STATING her purpose, but Gabriele assumed she would visit newspaper offices to place advertisements for Veronique's return. And a printer, to order the kind of flyer posted by owners of runaway slaves to broadcast their escape.

Gabriele could imagine what those advertisements and flyers would say. "Runaway—a female slave. Age 19, octaroon. Well-formed, slender. Height about five feet four inches, weight 120 pounds. Skilled seamstress. Is called Veronique. Large reward offered for information leading to her return—"

I must put this at least temporarily out of my mind, she thought, going into the parlour and opening the piano. She began the usual scales, but found that she could not concentrate on them, and turned to a book of simple melodies her father had always liked to hear her play.

Tom found her there when he returned from some errand of his own; she was weeping quietly over an Irish lullaby Oliver Cannon had used to sing to her. He sat down beside her and pulled her against his chest, holding her without speaking until finally she raised her head.

"I miss him so, Tom," she said. "At first I thought it would get easier as time passed—but my grief seems to grow instead."

"I know," Tom said. "And I am partially to blame,

Gabe. I am not measuring up well to Father's legacy—just look how badly I have mishandled this whole thing about Veronique."

"You did not refuse to sell her," Gabriele said. She watched Tom carefully, wondering if he would tell her about the escape.

"No, but I should have been easier with Aunt Mat instead of throwing Alex's offer at her the very next day—of course she could see through it, anyone could."

"Concern for others very often blinds us to the wisest path to take," Gabriele said. "I started the entire wretched business by flying ahead with my eyes closed and my mouth open—saying everything I knew without thinking of what might lie ahead."

"Yes, and now we are at sixes and sevens with Aunt Mat —I am not happy about her stubbornness with regard to Veronique, and my blood still boils when I think how she spoke of my best friend—still, I owe her better treatment than I have given her. Father would never have acted as I have, Gabriele."

"Oh, Tom! How can you berate yourself? You have had no time to grieve for him—off to Baltimore days after his death—travelling across the South—and coming here to be plunged into the middle of this mess! I am proud of you, Tom, and I know Papa would be, too. As for Aunt Mat—I believe I understand a little of her feelings, Tom, though that does not make me like her decision any better."

"Feelings! Her feelings in this matter are strange, Gabriele. To think a man I have as much affection for as I have for Alex could contemplate anything so base as what she described—and to think that Veronique, who grew up under her tutelage just as you did would consent to such a thing! Why, she would beg in the streets before she allowed herself to be—supported in that way!"

"But don't you see? That is why Aunt Mat won't sell Veronique—or set her free. She feels responsible for her, she does not believe Veronique could avoid such a—liaison —if she were not under Aunt Mat's care."

"Don't say another word, Gabriele, or the desire to be reconciled to Aunt Mat I am trying to develop will die before it is born," Tom said. He stood up, rubbing the back of his neck. "I'm all tied in knots, Gabriele. What I wouldn't give to be back at Felicity, with nothing more onerous ahead of me than a good long ride with you!"

"Sit on that stool and I'll work the kinks out, as I used to do for Papa," Gabriele said. She took a position behind him and began to massage his tense muscles, feeling them gradually ease under her hands.

"What a treasure you are, Gabriele," Tom said. "I'm glad you're set against those suitors we anticipate coming to court you—it will take an extraordinary man to deserve you."

She responded to his words with a kiss on his cheek, the shy happiness in her eyes telling Tom how much his praise meant.

"You will bring great joy into your husband's life, Gabe," Tom said, returning her kiss.

"I don't know," she said. "From all I have heard, what most men are looking for is someone who can manage their household—bear and rear their children—and, of course, bring a dowry to enrich their joint holdings. Almost any properly brought-up young lady can do that, Tom. As for joy—I have never heard of that being considered at all."

"That doesn't matter, Gabe. You saw our father's devotion to our mother, as fresh fifteen years after her death as though she still lived. Such devotion came from a marriage that brought great joy—it is what I demand for myself, and I advise you to accept nothing less."

"But how shall I know, Tom? How will you?"

"You just will," he said. He rose and held out his hand. As she took it, she looked up into his eyes. He has not told me how I will know who will give me joy, she thought. But plainly, he has already discovered that for himself.

Aunt Mat returned for lunch and reported the results of her morning to Gabriele and Tom.

"I went to see Mr. Guillot," she said as they began eating a cold soup. "I thought he could better handle this business than I—and indeed, he will place the usual notices and post the usual flyers. But he is not sanguine of success."

Gabriele could see that Tom had no intention of entering this conversation, and so asked, "Do you mean he thinks Veronique will not be found?"

"Exactly," Aunt Mat said.

"But Louisiana is so difficult to escape from," Gabriele said. "We are so far south—and there is no free territory anywhere near—"

"If Veronique were a field hand, she might be found," Aunt Mat said. "But a girl of her colour and skills—well, Mr. Guillot reminded me that there is a large free population of octaroons in New Orleans. If she makes her way to them, he believes she will slip in among them—and that will be the end of it."

"Oh, I hope so!" Gabriele said. "I'm sorry, Aunt Mat, you know how I feel—"

"Yes, we are all too much aware of how we all feel on this subject," Aunt Mat said. "And I for one would like to have no further discussion of it." She turned to Tom, waiting until he looked up and met her gaze. "Tom, I said some rather harsh things about your friend. I—apologize."

Gabriele watched a battle go on in Tom's eyes, and looked at him steadily, willing him to remember his earlier resolve to bury his differences with their aunt.

"I—accept your apology, Aunt Mat," Tom said. "And I beg your pardon for the rash things I said."

"Thank you, Tom," Aunt Mat said. "Of course I forgive

you—we are neither of us accustomed to being without Oliver's counsel—we are bound to make mistakes."

"Yes," Tom said. "Well, I'm glad that's settled, Aunt Mat. I leave tomorrow to join Breckenridge's campaign in the northern part of the state, and I imagine you will return to Felicity very soon."

"Yes—we should book our passage today so we may leave by the end of the week," Aunt Mat said. She looked at Tom a little uncertainly, then said, her eyes on her plate, "I thought we might ask Mr. St. Cyr to dine with us before you go. That would mean this evening—shall I send him a note?"

"St. Cyr is up at Olympia," Tom said. "Seeing to his father, who broke his leg training a new hunter. I don't know when he'll be back."

"Oh," Aunt Mat said. "But he left very—suddenly. He was just here—"

"I think falls from horses do occur suddenly," Tom said. He seemed more cheerful, as though he himself had taken an obstacle with surprising ease. "At any rate, he summoned Alex to entertain him."

Aunt Mat said, "Then we'll not see him again."

"I believe he will call at Felicity when he inspects his packets, ma'am," Tom said. "In any case, I extended that invitation—"

The smallest change of expression on Aunt Mat's face told them that she realized Tom had asserted authority over her, but when she spoke, she changed the topic, and did not refer to either Alex or Veronique again.

They did have a caller before they left New Orleans: Jordan Scott, back from Boston, came to see them on their last afternoon.

"I am sorry to have missed your brother, Miss Cannon," he said. In his pale blue coat and cream trousers, he looked unruffled and cool, as though he had managed to bring some of Boston's cooler weather along in his bags. "He is enthused about his candidate then."

"Oh, yes," Gabriele said. "He will be away most of the

time between now and the election in November, urging others to vote for Mr. Breckenridge."

"And you, Miss Cannon? What are your plans?"

"We leave tomorrow for Felicity, Mr. Scott. And then—" She looked into Jordan's clear blue eyes, remembering the first time she had come under that observant gaze. "Oh, Mr. Scott, you will find it hard to countenance, since you know that my true nature is somewhat less dignified than the world requires—but I have been warned by my brother that I can expect gentlemen to call on me, every one of them with matrimony on his mind." She laughed at the expression on Jordan's face. "I see you regard that prospect with as much enthusiasm as I do myself, Mr. Scott. Tell me, if I lived in Boston, would the same sort of procedure be practised?"

"I suppose," Jordan said. "But, Miss Cannon—do you mean to accept one of these suitors?"

"Certainly not!" Gabriele said.

"But among them will be some gentlemen you know, surely—they will come from families in the vicinity—"

"Like Jaime Robin or Harold LeBoeuf? Oh, Mr. Scott, believe me, I have met no one there whom I could even consider marrying—in fact, the whole topic causes me so much distress that I would appreciate your abandoning it —please."

"I'm not sure this one will suit you any better," Jordan said. "You said just now I knew your nature to be less dignified than your society requires—"

"You saw me emerging from the bayou, Mr. Scott!" Gabriele said. "Dripping wet, barefoot—a disgrace!"

"Yes—I have never been so surprised," Jordan said. "A placid bayou—the tranquility of the passing scene—and then, there in the water—a nymph with red hair!"

"If Brandy had been anywhere near when you walked into our house—believe me, I'd have leapt on her back and gotten out of there! What a terrible moment that was for me, Mr. Scott."

"I knew it was—yet I could not assure you that you could depend on me never to refer to it again—"

"Well, you are safe enough now," Gabriele said. "With all that has happened since then, to worry over a silly incident like that seems absurd."

"Silly—yes—and yet—did you not feel it, Miss Cannon? Some charge in the air—a feeling of suspense—as though a book had just been opened—a story just begun—"

"You need no lessons in flirting, Mr. Scott," Gabriele said, frowning slightly. "You are doing quite well."

"I am not flirting, Miss Cannon, but telling you what I felt. It is what made me enter the ring tourney, and risk making a fool of myself."

Gabriele rose and moved away from him, her eyes shadowed by the disappointment she felt.

"If you tell me that you fell in love with me the moment you saw me, I shall leave the room instantly, Mr. Scott."

"No—no, I would not say such a thing," he said, rising also, but maintaining the distance she had set between them.

"Then what, Mr. Scott? You confuse me—"

"I hardly know myself. A connection, some intertwining of our lives—" He paused, and Gabriele saw how unsure he suddenly felt.

"Yes, of course, Mr. Scott—such a coincidence occurring in the life of someone who reads as much as I do— well, I could hardly ignore the drama inherent in such an event!"

"You're not teasing me? You do feel that we are meant to have some impact on each other's lives?" Jordan said, taking a step toward her.

"Why would I tease you?" Gabriele said. "As for impact —I cannot go so far as to say that—but already, in just the short time I have known you, and in the few conversations we have had—you have affected my thinking, Mr. Scott."

"And you mine!" Jordan said. "Come, sit down with me again, Miss Cannon. There is so much I want to say! My trip home to Boston—"

"Oh, yes, I should have asked you—did you have a pleasant visit with your family? They must have been very happy to have you with them once more."

Jordan smiled, waiting until Gabriele took her chair before seating himself. "I received a royal welcome, you may be sure. Everyone wanted to know my observations of the situation here—uncles who barely noticed me at all a year ago hung on every word."

Gabriele shook open her fan and began wafting it slowly to and fro. She saw Jordan's eye follow the rhythmic movement, then come up to her face. He looked bemused, as though he had lost track of what he had just said, and quickly, increasing the speed with which she fanned herself, Gabriele brought him back to the topic at hand. "So what did you tell them?"

"What?" He shook his head, then looked at her, eyes now wide awake. "My family? Well, I told them what I think. That the situation here is quite serious—and that if one of the Southern Democrat candidates does not win the election, it will grow steadily worse."

"Do they agree with that?"

"They do not think a Southern Democrat possibly can win—so of course they were not happy to hear how high feeling is running in the South."

"In the South! I see no lack of fire in Northern rhetoric, Mr. Scott!"

"I won't deny that," Jordan said. He leaned forward a little, the small breeze from her fan stirring his hair. "In my own family, we run the gamut of opinion, from my father who attempts to remain open-minded to my great grandmother whose major fear is that some New Orleans belle will entrap me, and that she will never see me again."

"You had a lively trip," Gabriele said, determined that she would spend no more time discussing courtship and marriage with Mr. Scott. Something about the way he looked at her from time to time, as though he understood very well the nature of the connection he thought their lives might have, and withheld it from her for reasons neither of them could control.

"Lively, yes. And very busy." He sighed, blotting the moisture on his forehead with his handkerchief. "Is it always this hot in August?"

"At least this hot," Gabriele said. "You came to Louisiana from Boston when? Last October? Then I fear you are in for a shock. The heat will not abate until well into September. I'm glad we go to Felicity tomorrow—I don't know that it's cooler in the country, but it always seems so."

"May I call on you there, Miss Cannon? I shall still be taking the inland route with our packets from time to time —and I stored up so much to tell you while in Boston! I kept seeing things through your eyes—I seemed to know just how things would strike you, I could almost hear you make some original comment—" He broke off, not looking at Gabriele, but studying the shining surface of his shoes as though he expected to see his future there.

"Don't fall in love with me, Mr. Scott," Gabriele heard herself say. And then they looked at each other, both so shocked that neither could speak. Jordan regained his composure first.

"Why—why do you say that, Miss Cannon?"

"It will be a useless enterprise—"

"Do you mean you could not—love me back?"

"No—I mean exactly what I said. It will be a useless enterprise."

"Because of the political situation—"

"Yes, of course."

"Miss Cannon, you surprise me—I'd no idea you were so—practical. I thought you a romantic—an idealist—"

"I hope I am both," Gabriele said. She stood up, closing her fan and moving toward the door. Jordan came to his feet in an instant, looking so confused and unhappy that Gabriele held out her hand. "Mr. Scott," she said gently. "Already your grandmother worries that you will marry a Louisianian and thus be alienated from your family—"

"My grandmother has worried about who I would marry since the day I was born!" Jordan said. "I am the eldest son, she sets a great store by that—"

"Well, and she would be very unhappy if she thought you had decided to fall in love with me," Gabriele said. She saw his face and shook her head. "No, Mr. Scott, you are not in love with me, I will not allow you to say that you are. You are perhaps intrigued—because, as you have said, you rarely meet—'a nymph with red hair.' And I think you are grateful, because I have treated you kindly, and you feel at ease with me—please, Mr. Scott, don't ruin a perfectly good friendship!"

He looked at her hand, the fingers entwined with his. "How well they look together, don't you think?" he said. Then he drew himself up a little taller. "You may be right, Miss Cannon. I have never been in love before, or even near it—so I could be wrong about what I—feel. In any case, you have my word on it—I shall never be the one to bring this up again."

"Then let us shake hands on that, in the good American way," Gabriele said. "And let me promise you, Mr. Scott, that when you come to Felicity as my friend—you may come as often as you like."

After Jordan was gone she went up to see to the closing of her trunk. But as absorbed as she soon became in the last details of leaving New Orleans, she found herself thinking from time to time of Jordan's exact words. "I shall never be the one to bring this up again." Which left a door open, if she ever cared to walk through.

Among the stack of letters waiting their attention was an invitation from the Robins for Gabriele and Aunt Mat to help them celebrate their thirtieth wedding anniversary at an afternoon fête.

"I'm glad we arrived home in time," Aunt Mat said. "I

should have been disappointed to have missed this—the Robins are such good friends."

"Yes, it will be good to see Dorothea and the others," Gabriele said. "I do hope we get a good rain, though, to help break this heat."

And indeed, the country seemed no cooler than New Orleans: the air hung heavy with moisture, a trap for dust and pollen that made breathing difficult and energetic movement impossible. Sitting on the gallery just as dawn broke, watching the slaves file slowly from the Quarters to the fields across the road, Gabriele imagined the hours ahead of them in that stifling heat and asked Aunt Mat to tell Adams to make sure the hands had sufficient rest throughout the day, and that water barrels were carried to them in the fields.

With Tom away, Gabriele and Aunt Mat ordered the lightest food possible, and Letha took to getting up hours before the sun rose to build her cooking fires and bake her breads and meats so that the hottest fires would not be needed later on in the day.

As though the still, heavy air were a weight gradually pressing the ceiling of the sky closer to the earth, confining them in an increasingly smaller space, everyone at Felicity grew restless and irritable, with even mild-mannered Lucie going around with her lip poking out.

Veronique's disappearance had created a reaction that made Gabriele uneasier than if there had been open talk about it. It simply did not come up. Abigail must have relayed all that had happened in New Orleans to, at the very least, Letha, and undoubtedly Lucie as well. But none of them said a word. As though, Gabriele thought, the conspiracy of silence by which they protect themselves and each other whenever wrong-doing occurs operates even when they can have no possible knowledge that would help Aunt Mat in her recovery.

And so she greeted the diversion of the fête at the Robins' gladly, happily anticipating the company of young people, and admitting to herself that it would be a relief to turn Aunt Mat over to her own friends.

Gabriele and Aunt Mat had achieved a state of balance on the trip home: the tranquillity of the packet journey, the ease of the hours they spent on the deck, watching the scenery change, gradually worked upon them, and by the time they had again installed themselves at Felicity, Aunt Mat once more held the reins of the household firmly in her hands.

Still, Gabriele did not look at Aunt Mat in the same way as she had only a few weeks before. The aunt she thought always made decisions based on justice and reason had failed her: Aunt Mat might not have many faults, but the one she had revealed had cost them all a great deal, and Gabriele found that confidences did not spring as easily to her lips as they once did. More and more, she wished to keep her thoughts and feelings to herself.

The Robins' house provided as much protection from the heat as could be obtained, set as it was on a slight rise and built in the West Indian style, with a high, deep-pitched roof, halls and windows placed to cross-ventilate every room, and with trees screening it from the western sun. For once, as guests gathered in the high-ceilinged rooms or under marquees set up on the lawn, the terrible heat did not form the main topic of conversation.

Gabriele sought out Dorothea as soon as they arrived, and found her sharing a swing with a young man Gabriele did not know.

"Gabriele, may I present Paul Levert?" Dorothea said, and the way her voice changed when she said his name told Gabriele this must be the gentleman Dorothea had met at her cousin's earlier that year. "This is Miss Cannon, Mr. Levert," Dorothea said. "My good friend I have spoken of so often—but, come, tell us the news!"

"New Orleans in August is hardly attractive," Gabriele said. "We had a great deal of business to attend to, and since we are in mourning, of course did not go out." The excursion to the lake did not seem worth telling: that would lead to a discussion of Mr. St. Cyr and Mr. Scott, and although Dorothea's curiosity would be subdued by Mr. Levert's presence, Gabriele felt that she did not want to talk about either gentleman at all.

"But what is this about Veronique?" Dorothea said. "Bess told Mama that she heard that Veronique had run away!"

"Now how would your cook know that?" Gabriele said. "Our own slaves haven't even mentioned it—at least, not to me!"

"You know how they get word out," Dorothea said.

"Yes," Gabriele said. Another subject I don't want to discuss, she thought, and murmuring an excuse, hurried away.

She seemed unable to take much interest in any of the other guests, and the eagerness with which she had dressed to come soon wilted, leaving her feeling disconsolate and peculiarly alone. Taking a cup of punch, she sat on a bench in the shade, watching the bright scene, and wondering why she had so little desire to take part. Her eye fell on Dorothea, still attended by Mr. Levert.

How strange love is, she thought. I have always looked up to Dorothea—she is so intelligent, and has such good sense. Yet Mr. Levert does not appear extraordinary in any way—a pleasant-seeming young man, but of no particular force. And how pale his eyes are, they quite fade into his face! Oh, you are ridiculous, she scolded herself. As though the shade of his eyes matters in such a serious business as falling in love.

She saw Harold LeBoeuf change course so that his path would bring him to her bench, and hastily rose, opening her parasol and walking toward a refreshment table set out on the lawn. The long twilight would soon end: already Mrs. Robin had ordered candles set in tall holders to be lighted, and some of the guests were preparing to start home.

Gabriele walked between two rows of crepe myrtles whose brilliant pink foliage defied the August heat. The sky, dyed by the sun, matched the petals' colour; the world glowed with heat, threatening at moments to burst into crimson fire.

Then the thunder of sound—horses' hooves pounding on the drive—a man shouting—she could see the disturbance his words caused rippling through the crowd, breaking up the small groups and tossing them forward until they thronged around the man who pulled his horse up in front of Mr. Robin, and gave his awful message again.

"Michael Fleming's been murdered—and the slave who did it got away. We've got patrols out—but we're warning people to be very careful—Joseph has killed one man, and he won't hang any higher for killing more."

Cries of disbelief—of shock—a woman fainting—someone else beginning to weep—and then Mr. Robin, waving his hand for silence, waiting until the crowd grew quiet.

"All right—I'm sorry to have our party end this way—but I know all of you want to get home right away—so Mary and I bid you Godspeed—please, be on your way."

People were already making their way toward their carriages, bodies held tensely as though the murderer hid behind every tree. Mr. Robin saw Gabriele and came toward her. "You and Mrs. LeGrange had better stay here, Gabriele. With no man in the house—well, I'd feel better if I had you safe under my roof."

Aunt Mat did not need persuading. She wrote a note to Mr. Adams and gave it to Samson, telling him to drive straight to Felicity and to stop for no one.

"But why?" Dorothea said. "Why did Joseph—is that his name?—why did he—kill Mr. Fleming?"

The man who had ridden in to warn them looked at Mr. Robin and then quickly away. "Couldn't say, Miss Robin," he said. "You know how it is—slaves just go crazy from time to time—some hide out in the woods for a while, some try to escape, and some—get violent."

"It's horrible," Dorothea said. "Horrible!"

"You ladies go on inside," Mr. Robin said. He motioned

to his overseer, standing quietly nearby. "All our boys in, Wallace?"

"Yes, sir. All in safe and sound."

"And you've let the dogs loose?"

"Yes, sir. They're running patrol."

Mr. Robin sighed. "All right, then. And you—you're armed?"

A smile flickered over Wallace's face. "Yes, sir," he said.

"Good. Jaime and I will get our shotguns and then we'll set the watch." He glanced over to Dorothea and Gabriele, who stood listening, and frowned. "Dorothea. Didn't you hear me tell you to go inside?"

"Yes, Papa," Dorothea said. And with a despairing look at Paul Levert, who remained at Mr. Robin's side, she took Gabriele's hand and almost ran toward the house.

"Let's go up to my room," she said, once they were inside. "I don't want to listen to Mama and my sisters fretting—Felice has no nerve at all, she's such a scaredy-cat she'll probably get hysterical at the least noise."

"Aren't you afraid, Dorothea?" Gabriele asked as they hurried upstairs to Dorothea's room.

"What? Of that slave? Of course not! He'll never make it as far as this, Gabriele. We're miles from the Fleming place. And even if he did—he wouldn't get past the dogs. They're vicious—Papa won't let any of us out of the house when they're loose. Then the patrols will be riding the roads—and Papa and Jaime and Wallace, and I guess maybe Mr. Levert, will be armed to the teeth guarding the house. Goodness, Gabriele, that slave must have been crazy to have killed Michael Fleming when he has absolutely not a prayer of getting away."

"I should be sorry Mr. Fleming is dead, but I'm not," Gabriele said. "If we knew the whole story, I'm willing to wager we'd find out that slave had severe provocation— Mr. Fleming is—was—a very unpleasant man."

"Provocation! What provocation could justify *murder*, Gabriele? You better not let anyone hear you talk that way —they'll say you're dangerous, Gabriele."

"He insulted Veronique, earlier this summer, when she was sent to sew there," Gabriele said. "And then lied to Mrs. Fleming about it, to make it look as though Veronique had—enticed him."

"I can't believe my ears," Dorothea said. "Gabriele—these are *slaves* we are talking about. Do you realize how outnumbered we are? Do you realize that the slightest sign of softness, the slightest relaxation of rules, could put us all in danger of our lives?"

"I won't believe someone would just up and murder Michael Fleming for no reason at all. I know when Tom heard—" She clapped her hand over her mouth at the expression on Dorothea's face.

"When Tom heard that he had insulted Veronique?" Dorothea said. She looked at Gabriele coolly, examining her as though this were a girl she had not met before. "Mama always said your father made a terrible mistake, letting her grow up with you and Tom the way he did."

"Perhaps you'd better explain that remark, Dorothea," Gabriele said. She felt cold, chilled to her fingertips, as though Michael Fleming's death had opened a crack in the earth, and air from an ice-bound cave had rushed over her.

"It gave Veronique false expectations, to be pampered that way," Dorothea said. Gabriele's coldness shook her. She was not accustomed to being challenged; as the eldest of four daughters, she expected her words to be taken almost as a command. "Don't look at me that way, Gabriele! It's most unbecoming—and be careful before you say to other people that your brother is overly concerned with what happens to Veronique. Not everyone knows Tom as well as his close neighbours do—if you aren't careful, Gabriele, people will think he made away with Veronique himself."

With an effort of will so great she could feel her back muscles strain, Gabriele kept her expression from changing as she turned and moved toward the door. "It's late," she said, when she stood well beyond the glow of the lamp. "I had better go to my aunt—she will be wondering where I am."

Aunt Mat and Mrs. Robin sat together in Mrs. Robin's room, talking in low voices, with curtains drawn and every lamp lit.

"There you are," Aunt Mat said when Gabriele knocked at the open door. "Now don't let your mind dwell on all this, Gabriele. He'll soon be caught and taken off to jail— these things happen, and as I just told Mrs. Robin, somehow, they seem to have the same effect as lancing a boil. A certain amount of pressure drains—and then we're quiet again."

"Until the next time," Gabriele said. She faced her aunt, knowing that what she said would be almost as disturbing as Joseph's crime. "I'm glad Veronique is out of all this, Aunt Mat. And wherever she is, I hope to God she finds no Michael Flemings there."

She didn't wait to hear Aunt Mat's shocked reply, or to see Mrs. Robin's astonished face. She left the room and went down the hall, walking through the doors that led out onto the upper gallery to lean against the sun-warmed brick wall. A line of torches made a barrier of flame all along the drive, and she could see a dark figure marching in their glare.

She tried to imagine what Joseph must feel, the heat of anger that had made him strike Michael Fleming gone now, chilled by fear. Did he hide between cane rows, hoping to get help when the first slaves went out to the fields? Did he flounder through the swamps, dreading that each step would take him into quicksand, or within reach of a snake? Did he hear the hounds baying as they nosed their way along his path? Or did he cower in darkness, waiting for the doom he knew must come—but rejoicing that if he went to hell, at least he had sent Michael Fleming there as well?

Chapter Ten

Now another topic joined Veronique's escape as one never to be mentioned: Michael Fleming's murder and Gabriele's unaccountable speech. The slave, captured by midnight and in jail by dawn, could be left to the wheels of justice, which would deposit him either on the gallows or in the penitentiary at Baton Rouge. Of greater concern was the effect of the killing on other slaves: Adams took certain steps to ease the tensions at Felicity, granting the field hands a half-day off, and allowing them to get up a dance.

"They're settling down, ma'am," he reported to Aunt Mat several days after Fleming's death.

"Still," Aunt Mat said, "with Tom not home—I want extra measures taken, Mr. Adams."

"Don't lose your nerve, Mrs. LeGrange," Adams said quietly, and Gabriele saw a quick lick of fear on her aunt's face.

"Every time something like this happens, it brings back the fear I had to face down in Texas," Aunt Mat said. "First Indian raids in the early years—and then later—the Mexicans."

"The slaves aren't armed, Mrs. LeGrange, and they won't be," Adams said. He held up a hand. "Yes, I know cane knives can be used as weapons—but, believe me, I've got them under control." He studied Aunt Mat a minute, and then said, "Tell you what. Until you feel better—I'll keep the dogs out at night."

"Thank you, Mr. Adams," Aunt Mat said. "I don't know what's the matter with me—there have been—incidents before, and I never had this—concern."

"It's been a long summer," Adams said. "With too much happening for us to handle. Mr. Cannon dying like that—"

"Yes," Aunt Mat said. "You're right. It has been a long summer. I shall be very glad to see it end."

A cool spell early in September heartened them all, even though, as Aunt Mat said to Gabriele, "We shall be prostrate with heat again next week. But in the meantime—I've taken advantage of this good weather and invited my old friend Edith Maraist and her son Phillip to dine with us tomorrow. You might remember meeting Phillip, Gabriele, although he has been away at school in the East for several years, and then took a year abroad."

"How old is Phillip?" Gabriele said, giving Aunt Mat a cool, green look.

"About Tom's age," Aunt Mat said.

"And not engaged?"

"I have not heard that he is," Aunt Mat said.

Gabriele rose and walked down the room, standing before her mother's portrait and staring at it for a long while before she spoke. Then she turned, waiting until Aunt Mat reluctantly met her gaze.

"How did Papa and Mama meet, Aunt Mat? I don't believe I ever knew—"

"Why, in the usual way," Aunt Mat said. "Your mother was in New Orleans for the winter—your father was of course at every reception, every ball—"

"How did you meet Uncle Louis?"

"In the same way," Aunt Mat said. "But, Gabriele—you will not be in New Orleans this winter—you will not meet young gentlemen in that way—and so we must do as well as we can. Edith and her son are visiting in the neighbourhood—what can be more natural than to invite them here?"

"You really don't understand, do you?" Gabriele said. She looked back at her mother's portrait, the happy, serene face. "What does she remind you of, Aunt Mat?"

"Your mother? Why—what do you mean?"

"If you did not know her—but had to describe that portrait. What would you say?"

"Gabriele, what are you getting at?"

"Please, Aunt Mat. How would you describe my mother?"

"Why—as a lovely young woman. A young woman of obvious breeding—of great beauty—of a happy disposition—what do you want me to say?"

"Is there anything in that portrait that reminds you of a slave ready to be auctioned?"

"Gabriele!"

"Is there, Aunt Mat?"

"How can you speak of your mother that way? Oh, I wish your father were here! Without Oliver, without Tom —you are uncontrollable!"

"No, there is nothing of the slave on the auction block about my mother, because her courtship was conducted with dignity—it was *personal*—Papa fell in love with her because he could do nothing else!"

"Are you saying that you will feel like a—like a slave on an auction block if the Maraists come to dinner? How can you have such wicked thoughts, Gabriele?"

"How? *How*? Think, Aunt Mat, think! Think of the things you implied to Veronique about Michael Fleming. Think about the things you intimated to Tom. Think of marriages like Miss Jumonville to Mr. Forbes—and think of your opinion of Mr. St. Cyr. How can I think anything else, but that everything I hear about courtship and marriage makes it a business arrangement, and little else. With some of the—the items being traded things I don't wish to even imagine!"

Aunt Mat rose, her face so rigid with anger and disgust

that Gabriele wondered if they could ever look kindly at one another again. "I don't know whether this comes from being allowed to read so widely, or whether it comes from running wild with your brother, Gabriele. But if I had had any idea you harboured such—ideas—I would have—" But for once, Aunt Mat's resources failed her. Leaving Gabriele to hold the field, she fled to her room.

She regained her forces quickly, however, sending a note by Abigail telling Gabriele to remember that Aunt Mat was her legal guardian, and that if Gabriele refused to accept an invitation to dine with her aunt and the Maraists, then she would be ordered to appear.

That afternoon was the first of many when Gabriele took her problems to her father's grave, sitting on the marble bench next to Oliver Cannon's tomb and weeping her anger and confusion away. In the dim coolness of the cemetery, shaded by oaks, screened by arbours heavily covered with vines, she could admit how badly she had allowed herself to behave, and wait in the stillness for some answer to come. The air touching her skin, soft and cool instead of harsh with heat, the whisper of leaves and the low mournful coo of the doves, found their way past hurt and rage and fear, bringing to her spirit the first healing grace.

"Oh, Papa!" she said, kneeling beside his grave and tracing the letters of his name with fingers wet with tears. "What am I to do? If you were here, you would know how to manage this discreetly, so I never saw the machinery that puts this young man and that young lady in just the right place! It is the obviousness of it that I despise—the being put on display, with everyone knowing that is exactly what is going on!"

And then her saving humour made her smile, and she could almost hear her father laughing with her as she said, "Because to be honest, Papa—I should not mind seeing a few gentlemen this fall. But with you and Tom gone—and with Aunt Mat so blunt!—how can it be managed so *I* am the one calling the tune, not them?"

She felt better now: she had defined the problem, and could set out to solve it. Not emotionally, but rationally, discarding one answer after the other until finally she knew she had found the one that would work.

"Thank you, Papa," she said. "For teaching me to think —for trusting that I could do it—" Tears threatened again, but she blinked them back. If she were to win the day, she must meet Aunt Mat as a responsible young lady, not as a weeping child.

The apology was the most difficult part, because although Gabriele knew that what she had said was shocking —she also knew that to her, at least, it was right. But she had not borne fish hooks in her thumbs or stinging nettles on her bare feet for nothing: Tom had trained her well, and when Gabriele chose to be stoic, no matter how hard the obstacle, she could conquer it.

"I must forgive you, Gabriele, it is my duty," Aunt Mat said. "As for forgetting—that will take a long time, I fear. You said terrible things, things I never expected to hear from your lips—"

"Aunt Mat—I've said I'm sorry. Please—can we—just go on?"

"I would very much like to," Aunt Mat said. "I hope to enjoy the dinner tomorrow, not have indigestion at every bite!"

"Then will you hear me out, please? I have devised a plan, one I think we can both accept."

"A plan? What can you be up to now, Gabriele?"

"Just this," Gabriele said, sitting at Aunt Mat's side. "You wish me to entertain people who wish to call here. And while I reserve the right not to see—just anyone—I will be perfectly happy to see—certain ones."

"Certain ones? Gabriele—"

"Aunt Mat. If you and Tom expect my name to rank high on the list of eligible young ladies, then I must assume that it does. But—if that is the case—should not a high-ranking young lady be allowed to be a little—particular about whom she receives?"

I have struck exactly the right note, Gabriele thought, watching the first relaxation in her aunt's face.

"Well—of course you would not be expected to welcome gentlemen who come with no introduction at all—"

"But, you see, Aunt Mat—you are the one who knows what kind of—credentials my father would have wanted a suitor for my hand to have. And I wondered if you could perhaps—screen them. And then advise me as to which ones I should see."

"And you will accept my judgement?"

"Of course, Aunt Mat. I—did a lot of thinking this afternoon. And I realize that even if my parents did meet in a crowd of other people—that crowd had been very carefully selected." She raised her eyes to her aunt's, and saw agreement there. So Aunt Mat did know what she meant—might have learned it in a harder school, because while the Cannon features sat well on a man, they made a woman plain.

"Still—the presence of other people—the nature of the occasion—made certain private screening possible." Gabriele lifted her head, looking in that moment so like the young girl Oliver Cannon had fallen completely and constantly in love with the night he met her that the last of Aunt Mat's pride succumbed. Honore Delery Cannon had been the kindest, most generous woman Mathilde Cannon had ever known: she had been, in fact, the only beautiful woman in whose presence Mathilde had not felt homely, had even felt—pretty.

"I understand," Aunt Mat said. "Well, let us to cases. What shall we serve the Maraists, Gabriele?"

The pleasant task of planning their menu, a challenge they mutually enjoyed, dispelled any vestige of ill will between them. When Gabriele sat down at the piano to play for an hour at the end of the evening, she could with a clear conscience play the song she always thought of as her parents' own: "Believe me if all those endearing young charms . . ."

And Aunt Mat, half-dozing in her chair while she listened, sent up a prayer of thanks that all disturbance at Felicity seemed to have come to an end.

Their dinner for the Maraists went well. Phillip proved to be an amiable young man, and also a wise one. He picked up the subtle signals Gabriele sent, and when he went away, Gabriele knew that when they next met, Phillip would be a dancing partner, a supper partner—but that he would not give a minute's thought to being anything else.

As September drew to a close, each week brought letters from gentlemen who would be houseguests at nearby plantations or would be seeing to business in Franklin, New Iberia or St. Martinville, and who, trading on "the long-time association of my father with Oliver Cannon" or "my mother's happy memories of her girlhood friendship with Honore Delery," asked to pay their respects. On the last day of the month, Aunt Mat called to Gabriele as she passed by the morning room where her aunt sat busy at her desk.

"I don't know whether to laugh or scold you, Gabriele," Aunt Mat said when Gabriele entered the room. She held up the letter she had just finished reading. "I have become so expert at screening prospective visitors that I shock myself. I am quite cold-blooded, I'm afraid!"

"I would say particular," Gabriele said, and kissed Aunt Mat's cheek. She took the chair opposite, marvelling to herself at the change in her aunt. How agreeably they had got on these last weeks, with not a single difficult moment to mar their harmony. "Now tell me—what standards do you hold these gentlemen to?"

"Family, of course," Aunt Mat said. She saw Gabriele's expression and laughed. "No, I won't bore you with all the delicate gradations of background and behaviour that go into such a deliberation—as you grow older, such recognitions will come to you—and one day, to your complete surprise, you will find yourself tracing family lineages and connections with all the expertise of a practised hand."

"If I could master all the monarchs of England and France, I should be able to manage that," Gabriele said. She settled back to enjoy herself, thinking that to listen to Aunt Mat on this subject was almost better than a play. The intrigue and drama—the weight one factor had when measured against another—the inevitability with which certain decisions were made, no matter how reluctantly!

"And then, position or wealth, but preferably both," Aunt Mat said. "Because of the extent of the Cannon holdings, it is not easy to find people who can match your property, Gabriele—I am perfectly willing to accept someone of considerably less wealth if his position in the state's leadership is such to offset that. But there is absolutely no point in even considering a gentleman whose property and position make him dependent upon you. Such unions rarely work out, Gabriele, for reasons I am sure you can understand."

"You make me think I am to form a dynasty," Gabriele said idly. "This reminds me of nothing so much as the arrangement of marriages among Europe's royalty, Aunt Mat!"

"But what did you think it was, child?" Aunt Mat said. "When you struck out against this system so angrily—I thought at least part of your protest was rooted in those egalitarian ideas which you have tasted so widely—but which perhaps you have not had time to fully digest."

"Egalitarian ideas? If you mean those this country was founded upon—"

"Not wholly," Aunt Mat said. "I don't recall which of those gentlemen said it—precise quotations have never been my forte—but one of them said something about a natural aristocracy—"

"It was Thomas Jefferson," Gabriele said. "As a matter of fact, what he said was something to the effect that there is a natural aristocracy among men—founded on virtues and talents."

"Ah, well, it comes to the same thing," Aunt Mat said. "If a society is to persevere, Gabriele, it must make certain that its strengths are perpetuated and its weaknesses weeded out. By matching strength to strength, opposing this weakness with that force—we achieve people who can maintain our economy, and its political structure as well."

"But not as a nation, it would appear," Gabriele said. "Well, Aunt Mat, I am astonished. This all goes deeper than I thought—I must hope that if the process you follow is modelled on that devised by European states, I have a happier fate than some of their poor ladies—such as Marie Antoinette and Mary Queen of Scots."

"I thought we were doing all this so you would not lose your head unwisely," Aunt Mat said, so pleased with her mild joke that she did not see the cloud forming in her niece's eyes.

The two callers Gabriele had hoped to see did not come after all. Jordan Scott wrote from New Orleans in mid-September that the affairs of the central office in that city absorbed all of his time, and that the luxury of trips to inspect the success of the inland route had to be forgone for a time. And in the next post, Gabriele received a letter from Alex, who remained at Olympia, where, he reported, his father's leg mended slowly, but his temper being completely recovered, they spent the time pleasantly enough.

"I shall be sorry not to see you at Felicity, as I would have had I followed my plan of spending at least some time on our inland route, but I am not sorry to be out of New Orleans. Guests report to us that nothing is talked of but the election, and that while the receptions and dinners given to support the various candidates are elaborate and well up to the highest standards, still, one must pay for one's supper by listening to endless political persuasion, and since I selected my own candidate a long time ago, I should be rendering a false coin."

Will Mr. St. Cyr vote for Breckenridge or Bell? Gabriele wondered, thinking that it would seem natural for him to support Tom's choice. Still—he is called Quicksilver, and for good reason, as I have learned. She reread the letter, searching for the slightest hint that would give her word of Veronique, but saw nothing. Nor did Tom's letters, hastily scrawled at the end of a day of campaigning, refer to her. As though the earth truly opened and swallowed her, Gabriele thought, and then remembered the depth of Alex St. Cyr's dark eyes. If she were not safe—they neither of them would be where they are. Tom would be searching for her everywhere, not to return her here, but to make sure she has not come to harm. And Mr. St. Cyr would be right there with him—there can be no question of his loyalty to my brother, or the devotion he feels.

She wandered out into the gazebo, and sat there, thinking how delicately the pink and white roses that still bloomed there balanced the first early camellias. How young my parents were to build such a house, she thought, letting her gaze rest on it. Their wealth made it possible of course—here is tangible evidence of the kind of foundation money can build. But there are other things that make a more lasting foundation, I believe, and they none of them appear on Aunt Mat's list. Things like loyalty, and honour, and devotion. She stopped, realizing that she had just attributed some of these qualities to Alex St. Cyr. And he has the others, too. Family and property . . . She rose and walked among the roses, snipping those ready to cut to carry to her father's grave.

Mr. St. Cyr is proof that men do exist who can measure up to several standards, she thought. Those which will carry out society's objectives—and those which meet more human needs as well. My father was such a man—no wonder I have such expectations! As she made the familiar walk down to the cemetery, she realized that if Aunt Mat had her own set of yardsticks, Gabriele had now found her own. A man like my father—I will settle for nothing less. Sober of purpose, honourable beyond any doubt—loyal to those to whom he is committed—and capable of openly receiving and giving love.

None of the gentlemen she had met thus far could stand beside that yardstick and meet its measure. Even friends like Alex St. Cyr and Jordan Scott had failings—Alex lacked purpose, and Jordan's reserve kept him from freely expressing himself. As for loyalty—in Jordan's case, this would prove a double-edged sword. For if Jordan abandoned his family's political views to embrace those of the South for emotional reasons, would this not indicate a character in which loyalty could be superseded by more volatile feelings?

The same could be said of Alex St. Cyr. His two parents held totally opposite views: since their marriage did not appear harmonious in any aspect, their political differences could only drive them apart. Already, he avoided stating firm opinions that would put him squarely on one parent's side. No, if he were ever forced to make that choice, the resulting unhappiness would bode ill for his then entering any other commitment. If the lady did not doubt him, then he must doubt himself.

Gabriele did not come away from these musings particularly happy; she had not realized what ground she broke when she first confronted her aunt. But now that she saw the extent of the territory she had opened, she resolved that in the best traditions of her father's and brother's teachings, she would not shirk until she had mapped it all.

Adams was waiting for her when she got back to the house. "I've had a letter from Mr. Cannon," he said. He saw her confusion and added, "From your brother, Miss Cannon."

"Oh—yes—"

"He plans to arrive in New Orleans just before the election on November 7—he asks me to tell you that you will have to go there earlier than that to sign the bills of sale when we ship our sugar."

"I? But could not Mr. Guillot? He must have our power of attorney—"

"Mr. Cannon says he prefers a family member to be present, and since he will be delayed, he wants you to go." He could read her thoughts, and said, "Here is his letter.

You see where he says he is so busy he did not have time to write twice—"

Gabriele scanned the page, nodding. "Yes, it's a wonder he remembered the sugar harvest at all, with all this on his mind. Very well, I shall make my arrangements at once." She looked up from the letter. "I doubt that my aunt will find it convenient to leave just now—but we have sufficient relatives in New Orleans who can act as chaperones until my brother arrives. I myself do not see the need for such a person—but for my aunt's sake, the conventions must be observed."

Adams rose, taking Tom's letter and then pausing as though there were something else he wanted to say. Then, with a slight bow, he said, "Folks always say you favour your mother, Miss Cannon. But just now—that could have been Oliver Cannon talking to me."

The familiar rush of pain swept over Gabriele, accompanied this time by something new—a sense of fulfilment, as though the promise she had made to her father that her life would honour his had worked its way through the morass of grief and loss to hold to the sun.

"Travel *alone*?" Aunt Mat said, when Gabriele went to tell her the new plans. "Gabriele—you can't."

"I shall not be alone," Gabriele said, "but on a packet full of other passengers, most of whom I will certainly know. Aunt Mat, this is what Tom wants—there is no time to write him that I cannot go—what else can I do?"

"It is just like Tom," Aunt Mat grumbled. "Half of the rough spots in your nature come from the harum-scarum way Tom would enlist you in his adventures, whether they were proper for a girl or not."

"I think, Aunt Mat," Gabriele said, "that travelling to New Orleans to see to the profitable sale of our sugar hardly comes within the definition of a harum-scarum adventure, do you?"

"I suppose not," Aunt Mat said. "But I shall send Samson into town at once to telegraph our cousin Emma to meet you at the dock in New Orleans and stay with you at the hotel." She looked over her glasses at Gabriele. "That is—you won't open the house, will you?"

"Not for so short a time. I imagine Tom will be very anxious to get back to Felicity once the election is over— he has been away such a long time!"

Between going over business details with Adams and supervising Lucie's packing of her trunk, Gabriele had little time to think of anything else. But once on the packet, as the distance between it and Felicity's dock widened, a thought that had lain just beneath the surface of her consciousness floated up in full view. Surely Mr. Scott would take time off from his duties to call on her—and surely Mr. St. Cyr's father's leg had healed sufficiently to release his son.

The first two days in New Orleans went quickly as Gabriele and Mr. Guillot completed the transactions concerning the final sale of Felicity's harvest. Miss Emma Fontenot, Aunt Mat's cousin, had barely recovered from her shock that Gabriele had travelled from Felicity unaccompanied by anyone but her maid before she had to assimilate the idea that when Gabriele left the St. Louis Hotel in the mornings, she went, not to shop or to her modiste, but to a bank to do business.

"Well, they say that if we do not elect a moderate Southerner, our world will crumble about our ears," Miss Emma remarked at breakfast the third morning. "So I suppose I should be able to bear these signs that the edges have already begun to weaken."

"I own half the property," Gabriele said. "It makes sense that I should understand how to manage it."

"Oh, I'm sure it does," Miss Emma said, putting a liberal spoon of blackberry preserve on her plate. "But in my day, a young woman who filled her head with such things was a rarity, Gabriele." She sighed, apparently remembering past glories. "Of course, your dear aunt was a bit ahead of her time, too. I remember when she married Louis LeGrange, we all thought it so fortunate for him that he had found a wife with such a good head on her shoulders. Louis was smart, but just the least little bit—well, not flighty, I wouldn't say that—but maybe a bit more willing to take a risk than others."

"I never knew him," Gabriele said. She sipped coffee, wondering if her conscience would allow her to probe deeper into Miss Emma's store of information and deciding that it would not. Still, it might be permissible to prime the pump . . . She picked up the coffee pot and refilled Miss Emma's cup, pushing the jug of hot milk closer. Miss Emma buttered a croissant and broke off a tiny piece, spreading it with the preserves.

"Very handsome, Louis was. But you'll have seen pictures? And popular—everyone liked him, you know—so witty, and amiable—oh, yes, Mathilde Cannon made quite a catch."

"Is that the way their marriage was regarded?" Gabriele said. "That she had done—better than he had?"

Miss Emma's pale eyes widened. "Oh, my dear—I don't mean to imply—after all, Mathilde had her portion of the Cannon money. And very accomplished, as you know. Only—"

"Only not pretty," Gabriele said.

Miss Emma's lashes, fluttering down to hide her eyes, the blush that put faint colour into her cheeks, told Gabriele the rest of the story. She finished her coffee, then said, smiling so that Miss Emma would not fear she had betrayed her friend, "Tell me—did he deserve my aunt?"

"Deserve?" That one word, spoken in a voice that showed little comprehension of what Gabriele meant, hurt Gabriele more than anything else this silly little spinster had said.

"As you say—notions change, Miss Fontenot. Look at the time! If I don't hurry, I'll be late."

She must have been pretty enough, Gabriele thought as she went down the stairs and out onto the street. You can still see remnants of it, faded as she is. So why did she not marry? Was it because prettiness wasn't enough, and whatever else was needed she could not provide? Silly woman! Aunt Mat is worth ten of her, even if she does go off on tangents every once in a while.

The sight of a familiar figure striding down the street ahead of her brought her to a full halt. Tom! It couldn't be—he would have come to her immediately—she hurried forward, anxious to correct her mistake. I will catch up to him and see that it is not he, she thought. Then the man in question stopped to let two ladies pass out of a shop, and there could be no doubt. Tom Cannon, in New Orleans, and not coming at once to his sister—not even sending word!

Then Gabriele knew why Tom had not let her know he had arrived. She saw it in every line of his body as he started walking again. He's going to see Veronique, she thought. Only a moment did she hesitate, and then, with pounding heart, she followed him.

At first she found it difficult to keep Tom in sight while at the same time keeping herself concealed. Soon she realized that Tom's urgency prevented him from paying attention to anyone else; he strode ahead of her looking neither to the left nor to the right, barely halting his pace at intersections, but plunging almost under the wheels of passing carriages as he hurried along.

Gabriele's breath came short, and she almost despaired of keeping Tom in sight when she saw him turn into a narrow alley running between two streets. She hastened on, peering cautiously, ready to draw back if Tom waited there.

But it was empty, occupied only by a large grey cat that opened one yellow eye and looked at Gabriele before going back to sleep. A stiff breeze blew down the narrow passage, tossing dust and dry leaves up against Gabriele's skirt. She drew her cape around her; as she stood irresolute, a man emerged from a door midway down the alley, pausing a moment to pull on his gloves and settle his hat more firmly on his head, and then moving toward her.

As he drew near, Gabriele saw that he was an octaroon,

nattily dressed, with a silver-knobbed cane hanging from his well-tailored arm. He walked with the kind of grace Gabriele associated with the dancing master who had taught Tom and her the steps and deportment of the ballroom, and she watched almost in fascination as he approached.

His eyes, almost black against his light skin, met hers. He lifted his hat and bowed: in that instant, Gabriele felt something close to recognition, despite the fact that she knew she had never seen him before. Not until he had passed her did she realize the source of this feeling: it came not from her knowledge of his identity, but from his knowledge of hers.

The danger of her position suddenly asserted itself. If Tom were to emerge from whatever house sheltered him and find her spying on him, the consequences would be ones she had no wish to face. Turning, she retraced her steps, taking a route that would bring her to Mr. Guillot's office, where the lawyer impatiently waited for her to arrive.

"I'm sorry I'm late," she apologized. "An unexpected delay—" She waited while he took her cape and hung it on a rack in the hall, then followed him into his office. "You —haven't heard from Tom, have you?" she asked, bending over the papers she had come to sign.

"From Tom? Why, no. He's not due in until tomorrow, is he?"

"That is my understanding, yes," Gabriele said.

"Election eve—well, he times his arrival well. All New Orleans will be a madhouse—almost as bad as Carnival, I fear."

Gabriele signed her name by rote, trying to keep her mind blank until she could leave Mr. Guillot's observant eye. Somehow she maintained her composure, exchanging routine pleasantries once their business had been completed, and assuring Mr. Guillot she would remember him to Tom. And on the walk back to the hotel, she managed to keep her face calm, holding the thoughts that raged behind it well under control. But when she reached the hotel, and could take refuge in her room, she sat staring into the street in the direction from which Tom must come if he were to appear that day.

If he does not—oh, if he does not, what can it mean! she thought. I have no evidence Veronique lives in that alleyway—but who else could it be? An hour went by—three quarters of another—and then, turning the corner and striding toward the hotel came Tom, looking at ease now, as though whatever worry had sent him hurrying through the streets earlier had been relieved.

How can I meet him? Gabriele thought. Surely he will see what I know—no, what I suspect—in my face. She turned back to the window, and saw that she had been given a reprieve. She would not have to meet Tom alone: he had been joined by Alex St. Cyr. She overlooked the fortuitousness of Alex's appearance, and the implications it gave about his involvement in Veronique's escape. With one other person present, she could hide her feelings, and by the time she and Tom were alone, she would have managed to conceal them long enough to make it possible to continue the deception.

But as she prepared herself to give Tom the joyous greeting he would expect, she felt a new source of sorrow. She and Tom had never had secrets from one another, not about matters in which they were both concerned. She could understand his not telling her how he and Alex helped Veronique escape. She might have given them away, Veronique's safety had to be considered before anything else. But if he did not tell her now where he had just gone—then something would open between them, not yet a chasm, not that—but the first crack in the perfect trust with which they had lived all their lives.

When she heard a knock on the door of the parlour of her suite, she hastened to open it, listening to her voice cry Tom's name as though she did not know he had arrived in the city, and then greeting Alex St. Cyr, treating them both to a spate of questions that turned the conversation into a direction Gabriele considered safe.

Watching Tom and Alex in those first few minutes, Gabriele decided that both had changed: Tom had more of Alex's restlessness, while Alex had become more calm.

"Goodness, Tom," she said as he paced up and down the room as he talked. "You might still be campaigning—you talk to us as though you are making a speech."

"I do, don't I?" Tom said, flinging himself onto a low settee. "But it's practically all I've done in the last months —it will be a hard habit to break."

"Will Breckenridge win, do you think?" Gabriele said.

"I've no idea," Tom said. "If Bell weren't in the race— but he is. He'll split votes with Breckenridge, which might mean a victory for Douglas."

"Any Democrat will be better than Lincoln," Alex said. "Now that the day of reckoning is upon us, I imagine that many of the Democrats who supported splitting the party in April will regret it when they are presented the bill."

"You sound as though you think Lincoln will win," Tom said.

"His party is running one candidate—ours is running three," Alex said. "The odds are all his, Tom." He rose and clapped Tom on the shoulder. "But you at least have worked to prevent his election. I, typically, idled my time away at Olympia, decimating the game population and playing my father at interminable games of chess—other than that, I have nothing to show for the last few months."

"I imagine you have something to show for it," Tom said, meeting Alex's gaze for the briefest moment. Then, as though he could feel Gabriele's curiosity, he turned to her. "Well—and so what have you been up to, Gabriele? Besides holding court for a train of suitors—how I wish I could have been there to see you!"

Alex's eyebrow curved, a peak of interest, but he said nothing, only taking a chair close to Gabriele's and looking at her intently.

"Heavens," Gabriele said, "there really isn't anything to tell—"

"But you did have callers, I think?" Tom said. "Aunt Mat wrote about a Mr. Harrison—and didn't you mention a Mr. Foret?"

"Then you have heard all that is noteworthy about both gentlemen," Gabriele said. "As for any others—let me put it this way. For some reason the presence of an eligible heiress put a number of gentlemen on the *qui vive* to change her happy state—and Aunt Mat at first could be found firmly on their side. By using a little diplomacy, I was able to make her my ally instead—I have now received all the gentlemen I intend to, and though Aunt Mat still wishes that I would marry some suitable person—she has lost her first enthusiasm. Any declarations she makes in the future about allowing this foolishness to continue will be easier to overcome since I have been amenable to her wishes this fall." She rose, facing Tom and Alex and giving them both the same cool look. "Now—that is all I care to say on the subject now—or ever. May we agree on that?"

"Do you mean no one pleased you at all?" Tom said.

"Does that surprise you, Tom? When you consider the standard any man I might think of marrying must meet?"

"Father, you mean," Tom said.

"And you." She went to him and put her arms around him. "Oh, Tom—having grown up in a house with men like you and Papa—how could I love anyone not cut of the same fine cloth?"

"You couldn't, of course, Miss Cannon," Alex said. "Nor should anyone expect you to." He glanced at the gilt clock ticking away on the mantel, then said, "I've intruded on this reunion long enough—but I would like us to meet tomorrow. My mother has written you inviting you to dine with her and my father at Antoine's tomorrow night, Miss Cannon. Here—I've got her note somewhere—" He searched in his pockets and found a small envelope sealed with pale grey wax. "Of course you are included, Tom."

"I'd better not commit myself," Tom said. "The eve of the election, you know. There'll probably be last-minute meetings—and my nervous state would prevent me being a very good guest."

"You'll be here a while?"

"In New Orleans? I think not. Gabriele has seen to the greater part of our business—and I long to get home."

"So say we all," Alex said, so softly that Gabriele thought she must have misunderstood what he said. He bent and kissed her hand. "Shall I escort you to watch the parade and rally at Jackson Square, Miss Cannon? We can walk to Antoine's from there."

"Tom, did you say you'll be engaged?" Gabriele asked.

"Yes," Tom said.

"Then, yes, thank you—"

"I'll call for you at six," Alex said. "Jordan will be with me—poor fellow, I think he will be one of the happiest men in New Orleans when the last ballot is finally cast."

"How is Mr. Scott?" Gabriele asked. "I had a few letters from him—he seemed very involved with the business—"

"Yes, he and my mother have been putting in very long hours all fall. I sent word to her many times that I should be happy to return and take over my share of the burden—but she could never seem to think of anything I might do." He picked up his gloves and began to put them on, smoothing the black leather over his long fingers. "Ah, well, one cannot be a grasshopper most of one's life and then suddenly expect to be taken for an ant, can one?" He smiled, and Gabriele felt a small twisting pain in her heart. "Until tomorrow?"

"Yes," Gabriele said.

"Here, I'll walk down with you," Tom said. "Gabriele, let's have lunch up here—there's so much I want to tell you—we'll be by ourselves."

"Of course," she said.

He did have a great deal to tell her; she learned more about the political crisis facing them in that two hours

with Tom than she had learned the previous six months.
One topic she learned absolutely nothing about: Tom said
not one word about the identity of the person he had
visited that morning, nor did he mention Veronique.

Chapter Eleven

STANDING BETWEEN ALEX AND JORDAN, A THICK WOOL CLOAK
protecting her from the damp chill rising up from the river
beyond Jackson Square, Gabriele leaned over the wrought-
iron balcony rail of the Pontalba Building, watching the
torch-lit parade snaking its way by, heavy smoke from oil-
soaked flambeaus hovering over the marchers like a black
veil.

"It's like Mardi Gras," she said. "Except they're not
masked—"

A man carrying a sign bearing Breckenridge's image and
name held it toward the balcony, shouting up to them as
he passed by. "Breckenridge! Breckenridge!" People
crowding the kerbs took up the cry, a *mélange* of voices cut
through by a sudden scream from a rocket set off on the
levee. A second scream followed quickly, and then a
shower of sparkling fire-bits opened, brilliant green and
silver against the night sky.

One glittering Roman candle after another exploded in
a luminous display: blue and gold and scarlet patterns
thrown across the curtain of the sky. Then someone in the
crowd below passed out sparklers, and soon their lights
flickered like fireflies caught in summer, still glowing in
their jars.

"So much light," Alex said. "Let us hope it is symbolic
of the voters' minds—"

"I don't think we can expect a miracle," Jordan said. "We are in our present fix because the darkness of unreason has clouded even the finest minds—one election can hardly solve what decades of debate and legislation hasn't."

"I agree," Alex said. "Nor, I think, could a dozen elections solve the issues of this campaign. Slavery and secession—you could hardly find a better pair of weapons to destroy the union if our nation's worst enemy had forged them—"

"That sounds as though you are against secession, Mr. St. Cyr," Gabriele said. "It is the nearest thing to an opinion I have heard from you!"

"It is not so much what I am against, Miss Cannon, as what I am for," Alex said.

"And that is?"

Alex turned his back on the scene below and leaned against the rail. The backglow highlighted his high cheekbones and lit up flecks of gold in his dark eyes, like mica scattered in stone. "Let me see if I can quote it exactly—" He paused a moment, eyes looking straight ahead, and then began speaking in a low tone.

" 'When in the course of human events, it becomes necessary for one people to dissolve the political bands which have connected them with another, and to assume among the Powers of the earth, the separate and equal station to which the Laws of Nature and of Nature's God entitle them, a decent respect to the opinions of mankind requires that they should declare the causes which impel them to separation . . .' "

"But that's the Declaration of Independence!" Gabriele said.

"Yes," Alex said.

"I don't understand—are you saying then that you believe the South is wrong—that it may not secede?"

"Not at all," Alex said. "Secession is a re-enactment of the events surrounding that Declaration—the South wishes to dissolve its political bands with the Union if it does not receive better treatment—it is prepared to form a separate nation—well and good."

"Then you support secession," Gabriele said. "Mr. St. Cyr, you confuse me."

"Let me make myself clear," Alex said. "I had a great deal of time to read and think while at Olympia—and I read many of the letters, the journals and other papers, of the men who wrote the instrument I just quoted, and who, as they so bravely state, pledged their lives, their fortunes, and their sacred honour to giving it birth. Not a hundred years ago—and already, a large piece of that Union will break away." He looked down at her, his expression so grave that she felt suddenly much colder, and clutched her cape around her as though to ward off the wind.

"Now—let us say that the election goes against the South, which forms a new nation. In how many years, do you think, will some segment of that union become dissatisfied—feel oppressed—and start the entire process again?"

"Surely we would have common interests, Mr. St. Cyr!"

"So did the colonists," Alex said. "My reasoning may be specious—but when we consider how reluctantly a stronger federation was formed—and how soon the effects of it came under fire—I think we may be well on our way to a system of city-states like the Greeks."

"You can't mean that," Gabriele said. "Mr. Scott, bolster my arguments, I am quite caught by surprise!"

"You appeal to the wrong person," Jordan said. "The history of western civilization is the story of the rise and fall of empires, you know that as well as I do, Miss Cannon."

"Then carry your argument to its end, Mr. St. Cyr. Do you mean that, say, Felicity, along with close neighbours, might form its own small state?"

"That would be carrying my premise to the extreme, I agree," Alex said. "But if the South secedes, I would expect further dissolution on both sides of the line—and in our lifetimes."

"I still don't see where this is leading," Gabriele said. "You are stating ideas, offering arguments—I have not yet heard a point of view!"

"If you mean do I think this right or wrong—I make no judgement on that," Alex said.

"You make no judgement—does that mean you don't care? You foresee this—this further dismemberment—but you do not care?"

Alex moved abruptly, standing away from the rail and looking down at the crowd. "What difference would it make, Miss Cannon?" He waved his arm, encompassing the fireworks, the bands, the milling throng. "This scene is repeated all over the nation tonight—it culminates a season of such scenes—all those people, Miss Cannon, having and supporting opinions—and to what avail?"

"To what avail? At least they will have stood for what they believe!"

She watched Alex's eyes change as her words hit him, and felt again that small twist of pain. He waited a moment before he spoke; she thought he meant to defend himself, and with growing dismay heard what he finally said.

"I remember saying to you once that when I am with you I always seem to say the wrong thing—or to say what I think is my right thing in a way that upsets you—or disappoints you."

"It is only that I don't understand you, Mr. St. Cyr," Gabriele began.

"That is evident, Miss Cannon. I accept full blame." He looked over at Jordan, who had walked some distance down the rail. "Let me speak quickly, and then we shall go meet my parents at Antoine's. Until I spent so much time at Olympia, I had not realized how tranquil life can be when one simply—removes oneself from the fray. If the Union holds—obviously, there will be no fray. If it does not—well, there are many places I can go."

Gabriele stared at him, certain she had missed something—did he really mean he could walk away from a crisis that dominated the lives of everyone else? She heard someone speaking—her own voice—spilling out words.

"I'm very sorry, Mr. St. Cyr, that although you admire the men who founded this nation, you do not admire their dedication to their cause."

That dark curving eyebrow, questioning her.

"You don't emulate them," she said. "You have as much as said that if the South leaves the Union—you will leave the South."

He opened his lips, then closed them again. Offering Gabriele his arm, Alex called to Jordan to join them. Then quickly, speaking close to her ear, he said, "Please try to understand me, Miss Cannon. I don't think the North has the right of this—it is just that I think it has the South in a position where we cannot—stand. If we stay in the Union —we are oppressed. If we leave it—we are signing our own warrant of execution."

"But you could be wrong," Gabriele said.

"Of course—"

"Thank God, then, that you will not support your position, Mr. St. Cyr. We have enough people working against us—we don't need you."

Walking between Jordan and Alex toward Antoine's Gabriele regretted every moment of the hour just passed. What a mood to take to a dinner party, when she could think of nothing agreeable, and wanted only to be back at her hotel. And then, as they paused at the intersection of Chartres and St. Ann, waiting for a tag-end of the parade to go by, Gabriele saw a familiar figure ducking into an alleyway, and could not suppress a sudden cry.

"What is it, Miss Cannon?" Jordan asked.

"I—thought I felt my bracelet slip off my hand," Gabriele said. "But here it is—" She held up her arm and shook back the folds of the cape.

"Let me go a little ahead of you and Miss Cannon, Jordan," Alex said. "There's something I want to see to—"

"Of course," Jordan said. "We'll follow at an easier pace."

Alex immediately moved off, walking so fast that he soon disappeared in the mists. Gabriele and Jordan walked in silence for half a block, and then Jordan spoke.

"The life seems to have gone out of everything, doesn't it, Miss Cannon? Or does it just seem that way to me?"

"No—strangely, despite all the excitement we just saw— I know exactly what you mean, Mr. Scott. The same feeling comes over me from time to time—a sense of futility— I find myself wondering why I bother to go about my little duties, why I bother to read and form opinions—as Mr. St. Cyr says, it won't change anything."

Jordan looked down at her, the earnest gaze reminding her of happier occasions when their conversations did not run in such narrow channels, nor meet so many dams. "I'm not sure that Alex's feelings are as extreme as he makes them sound, Miss Cannon—"

"If they are, he might change them tomorrow—they called him Quicksilver at college, don't forget. But I can't worry about Mr. St. Cyr and his chameleon nature, Mr. Scott. There is no reason for me to do so—and I don't." She stepped closer to Jordan to avoid a pile of garbage on the kerb. "And what of you, Mr. Scott? Where do you find yourself?"

"Unhappy," Jordan answered. "And angry."

"That is not like you," Gabriele said. "You are always so even-tempered, so—controlled."

"My feelings are common to many young men my age, I imagine," Jordan said. "Our lives are before us—but if secession comes, and war follows—then they will belong to someone else."

The passion in his voice surprised her, and then she remembered the assessment she had so recently made about this very predicament, and the difficulty it would cause Jordan Scott.

"Your head and heart do not agree, do they?" Gabriele said. She sighed, thinking how hard it is to live in a soul divided against itself.

"You understand me," Jordan said. "Odd—that makes

me feel a little better, although it doesn't change my dilemma."

"Of course I understand you," Gabriele said. "You have lived among us, worked here—you know we are not all irrational monsters bent on war. And if you have to fight the South—you will not like to."

"I will have no choice," Jordan said. "That is what worries me—frightens me, really. How will I reconcile my feelings? How will I make head and heart agree?"

"If I knew that," Gabriele said, "I could make my own peace."

"Here's Antoine's," Jordan said, steering Gabriele across the street. He stopped at the restaurant door. "Have you ever met my aunt?"

"No—nor Mr. St. Cyr," Gabriele said.

"He's easy to know," Jordan said. "Lively, a man who enjoys life—but my aunt is—different. It's strange, Miss Cannon, but I sometimes think that she would be—could be—less determined in her opinions if she lived in Boston among people who think more as she does than she is here, when almost no one she knows holds the same views."

"Of course," Gabriele said. "When we are under siege, we defend every position. But if you are warning me not to provoke her—believe me, Mr. Scott, there is no need. The very last thing I want this evening is dissension—to be truthful, if I were not obligated here, I would ask you to see me home. As it is—"

"As it is, we will steer past treacherous passages, Miss Cannon, and make for a conversational open sea."

They followed the head waiter to a private dining room opening off a long hall. Alex stood in the open doorway: his posture seemed stiffer than usual, and Gabriele wondered if already he and his mother had found some subject upon which to disagree.

I have never felt less like being at someone else's table than I do tonight, she thought as she went forward to meet the St. Cyrs. A woman with ash blonde hair and light blue eyes rose as Gabriele approached her, and held out her hand. A simply cut dinner dress of grey satin, accented with necklace, earrings, brooches and bracelets of sapphires and pearls, enhanced Mrs. St. Cyr's fine features and slender form while not detracting from the pale colouring of her eyes and hair.

"Ah, Miss Cannon," she said.

The man standing at the hearth with his back to the room turned at the sound of her voice, and Gabriele had to quickly smother her surprise at seeing a duplicate of Alex's face. Older, of course, the smooth skin marred by lines. But that same little twisted smile, that same dark curve of eyebrow—not the eyes, she thought as she met his gaze. Alex draws everything he sees into him—his father's eyes are like the black surface of an obelisk, reflecting nothing, shutting everything out.

"You do us great honour by dining with us, Miss Cannon," Hector St. Cyr said, coming forward to bow over Gabriele's hand. "We are very fond of your brother, and hoped to have him with us tonight, but Alex tells me Tom is still politicking—" His tone made it clear what he thought of Tom's choice, and Gabriele felt blood rush to her cheeks.

"My brother—is very dedicated," she said. "He is trying to take my father's place, you see—"

"And doing it admirably well," Alex said. "Here, Miss Cannon, won't you sit here?" He held a chair for her on his mother's right, and took the one across from her himself. Hector St. Cyr sat opposite his wife, with Jordan placed next to Gabriele.

"So," Mrs. St. Cyr said, "do you take an active interest in politics, as your brother does, Miss Cannon? Alex has given us to understand that you have had a fine education —and argue as well as any man."

"I am interested in anything that affects my life as much as government does," Gabriele said carefully.

"You separate government and politics—that is interesting," Mrs. St. Cyr said. "So many people don't."

A waiter came in to open the champagne set in a cooler at Hector St. Cyr's elbow; as he filled their glasses, Hector glanced across the table at his wife. "Julia—you promised us a pleasant evening. By definition, that must exclude a discussion of either government or politics."

"Under ordinary circumstances, perhaps I would agree with you," Julia answered. "But the fate of our nation will be decided tomorrow—can any conversation ignore that fact?"

Hector raised his glass and sipped, then smiled at his guests. "I should be delighted to try," he said. "And I imagine some of the others would, too."

"Miss Cannon," Julia St. Cyr said, "would you prefer to leave politics off our menu tonight? We shall be guided by you."

"I believe this to be a situation in which everyone's views are either already known or easily guessed, Mrs. St. Cyr," Gabriele said. "Since it is unlikely any of us can change anyone else's opinion—and since we are such an intimate group—perhaps we could speak of more—harmonious things."

"If that is your pleasure, Miss Cannon—of course I shall not mention the election again." She picked up her menu and studied it, seemingly oblivious of the silence stretching around her.

The first course arrived, and they began to eat, but despite the elegance of the meal and the excellence of the wines, the party never jelled. Someone would begin a topic, someone else would attempt to carry it on—but the silence which now seemed a member of their group proved stronger than any effort to speak.

I shall be sitting at this table eating for the next ten years, Gabriele thought. And then the door burst open and a man ran into the room, cap clutched to his chest, face red and breath coming hard.

"Mrs. St. Cyr—the ships—fire—come at once—"

"What? Pierre, what are you saying?" Julia St. Cyr leapt to her feet, pushing her chair back and crossing the room with short, quick steps. The train on her dinner gown caught on the chair, and she shook it impatiently, not breaking her stride as the chair crashed to the floor.

"There's a fire at the docks. Two, maybe three, of your ships already burning."

Julia St. Cyr looked around the room wildly, then turned to her son. "Alex—get the carriage. I must go—"

"I'll go, Mother," Alex said, springing to his feet. "Jordan and I will take care of this—you stay here with Miss Cannon."

"I'll do nothing of the kind," Julia said. "Get the carriage, Alex. Or I'll run."

"Do as your mother asks you, Alex," Hector St. Cyr said. He had not moved, but sat savouring the wine the waiter had just poured in his glass. "An excellent claret, Miss Cannon. The 1844—it's the only one a gentleman can drink."

Gabriele stood, holding the edge of the table for support. "I—I'd better go back to my hotel," she said. "And let you take care of this crisis—"

"I'll escort you—" Jordan began, but his aunt quelled him.

"She can ride in the carriage as far as the docks," she said. "And then I'll get out and you can see her home."

"But—"

Again that cold gaze—and then Alex in the door, announcing the carriage. A flurry of movement, a bustle through the hall—then out on the street—into the carriage, Gabriele and Alex on one side, Jordan and Mrs. St. Cyr on the other, Pierre hanging on behind.

The horses picked up speed, heading down St. Louis Street toward Decatur Street and the Scott-St. Cyr wharves. Blanketed by her thick cloak, Gabriele peered from under its hood and saw the clouds of smoke billowing up ahead. The ships themselves were still hidden by warehouses, but the underside of the clouds, glowing orange with reflected fire, hinted at the inferno raging there.

As they drew nearer to the wharves, a growing crowd

impeded their progress, and the coachman picked up his whip, cracking it over the milling spectators and yelling, "Let us through! Clear a path, now—let us through!"

Breckenridge buttons flashed from lapels, and as the horses plunged through the crowd, Gabriele realized that most of these people had come from the rally, eager to add one more spectacle to those they had already seen. In a last spurt of speed, the team pulled the carriage into the open area in front of the shipping offices, and they could see the masts of the burning ships. Flames reached up to them, now leaping, now falling, but sending up a steady stream of smoke that signalled the coming destruction.

Four ships burned now, and although they had been cut loose from the wharves to drift out onto the river and lessen the danger to other vessels and to the warehouses clustered on the shore, flying sparks landing on ship decks and the roofs of buildings kept fire-fighters running from one place to the other, training great hoses fed by pumps drawing water from the river itself.

A man separated himself from the crowd when he saw their carriage, and ran toward them, shouting Alex's name.

"What happened, Jacques?" Alex demanded, springing down from the carriage and grasping him by the arm. And then Gabriele recognized the man Alex called Jacques. This was the man she had seen in the alleyway the day she followed Tom—Hector St. Cyr's factor—a free octaroon. Of course! Alex had enlisted him to help Veronique. She sank back, hardly comprehending what she heard.

"An explosion," Jacques said. "And then minutes later another one. The *Ocean Belle* first. Then the *Sea Queen.*"

"Did a boiler go? My God, just look at this!" Alex swept an arm toward the flaming ships bobbing on the river's surface. Pieces of burning sail broke off to float toward the water like wings of fire, vanishing beneath its surface in a sudden eruption of smoke and steam. Cargo barrels, some on fire, some unscathed, littered the river, and now and then a dull explosion from inside one of the burning ships told them that some volatile container had gone up in flames.

Jacques looked from Alex to Julia St. Cyr. "It must have been deliberate."

"Deliberate! You mean someone started it?"

"Looks like it," Jacques said. "The first mate on the *Belle* swears he smelled dynamite. And the engineer of the *Queen* was in her boiler room when she caught fire. All there still safe and sound—until the whole ship went."

"But why would anyone fire our ships?" Alex said. "Who hates us as much as that?"

As if in answer to his question, a low rumble came from the crowd. Indecipherable at first, the sound soon took form, and they could make out the words. "Traitors!" the crowd chanted. "Traitors to our cause!"

And then an echo of the jubilant cries from the rally just past—"Breckenridge! Breckenridge! Breckenridge!"

The crowd closed ranks around the carriage, and Gabriele sank back into her cloak's safe folds. Her eyes went to the river, where the four ships had drifted together, huddled as though drawn by a great net of fire.

"Get the ladies out of here," Alex ordered. "Jordan, come here."

Jordan sprang from the carriage, landing in the midst of the crowd. Gabriele could see fists shaking threats into his face, and she shrank back against the seat, her face pale inside her dark hood. She could no longer see either Alex or Jordan, they were lost in the crowd. And now the coachman cracked his whip in the air over the heads of the crowd clustered close to the carriage wheels, making the men fall back, momentarily halted. But then, in a mad surge, they engulfed the carriage, hands reaching toward the reins. The whip came down again, and again, opening cheeks, cutting across hands. The horses plunged forward, hooves making a path through the bodies pressed around them. For one moment, Gabriele stared into the face of a man who climbed up on the carriage step and clung there. Then the coachman veered the carriage hard to the right, and he fell back into the crowd, vanishing in a mêlée of arms and fists. The carriage, as though now freed from the weight that had restrained it, spurted forward. One last thin line of men before it—and then the open street.

Julia St. Cyr turned and looked back at the scene behind them. The glare of the fire, the streamers of black smoke—running figures like puppets dancing on invisible strings—"So that is what hell looks like," she said, and then collapsed against her seat.

"Mrs. St. Cyr—are you all right?" Gabriele asked. She thought of the way Hector St. Cyr had looked as his wife had run to her ships: eyes opaque, mouth set in that narrow smile—and only the drumming of one finger on the table signalling any emotion at all. "This is so terrible—"

"A harbinger, I'm afraid, of things to come," Mrs. St. Cyr said. She sat up, straightening her shoulders and holding her head high. "We'll take Miss Cannon to the St. Louis Hotel, Joseph. And then drive me back to the wharves."

"Yes, Mrs. St. Cyr," the coachman said. He seemed unperturbed by the wild scene and their escape from it, as though such turmoil were a natural part of his day.

Even Julia St. Cyr's demonstration of feeling had passed; she had gone back behind her mask, and the eyes that watched Gabriele showed curiosity, nothing more. "You are surprised at this violence, Miss Cannon?"

"I am grieved by it," Gabriele said.

"Ah, well, it was bound to come," Julia St. Cyr said. "Though I confess I did not expect it so soon—well, here we are, Miss Cannon. We have got you home safe and sound. I shall report that fact to my son and my nephew—they both have a great concern for your welfare, as I am sure you are aware."

"They are—very good friends," Gabriele said. Gratefully, she let the hotel doorman help her down, thinking that if she could last just a few minutes more, she could make it safely to her room.

"I am sorry for your trouble, Mrs. St. Cyr. I hope it will not prove too severe a loss."

"We will hardly go under because of a few ships," Julia St. Cyr said. "In fact, this disaster may in the end be a blessing after all, for it forces me to a decision I should have been bound to make."

"Good night, then," Gabriele said. "And thank you for dinner. I—"

"Enjoyed it? Yes," Julia said. Then she signalled to the coachman, leaning forward in her seat as though to urge the horses on.

Gabriele stood watching the carriage for a moment, then hurried into the hotel. She wanted to see no one, not even Tom, and when Lucie let her in, Gabriele heard with relief that neither Miss Emma nor Tom had come in.

"Lots of noise and commotion in the streets tonight," Lucie said as she helped Gabriele undress. "One of the porters, he say there's a fire at the river—you hear about that?"

"Yes—the ships belong to Mr. St. Cyr," she said.

"They *do*?"

Gabriele's face stopped any further questions. At the point of complete exhaustion, she felt that if she had to say one more word to anyone about the events of the evening, she would not be able to bear up. Asking Lucie to order a glass of warm milk, she sat by her fire, slowly sipping the milk when it arrived, and letting the warmth of both soothe her raw nerves. Then she got into bed, afraid she would still lie awake, but through sheer fatigue and discouragement falling almost immediately to sleep.

She woke the next morning to the low rumble of voices coming from the suite parlour. Lucie told her Mr. St. Cyr had arrived very early, and was having breakfast with Tom.

"Hurry, Lucie," Gabriele said. The fear that had closed around her as she watched the ships burn and heard the hatred shouted by the mob gripped harder: something more had happened, else why would Alex be here?

Tom and Alex rose when Gabriele entered the room,

coming toward her with anxious faces whose expressions
confirmed her fear.

"What is it?" she cried.

"I hardly know how to tell you," Alex said. He moved
into the light, and Gabriele saw the bruises that dis-
coloured his ivory skin, and the bandaged cut just above
one eye.

"You're hurt!" she said, and sank into a chair, her white
face framing eyes wide with shock.

"Now I've upset you," Alex said, coming to kneel beside
her. "These are not nearly so bad as they look—and I
imagine the ruffians who gave them to me are wishing they
had left well enough alone."

"But what happened, Mr. St. Cyr? Is your mother all
right? When she left me, it was to go straight back to the
wharves—"

Alex glanced at Tom. "Mother is—fine," he said. "Back
in control." He rose and went to the window, not looking
at either Tom or Gabriele. "In fact, in even more control."

"Tell me," Gabriele said. "Please."

Alex swung around, standing with his hand shoved in
his pockets and his feet braced as though for another
fight.

"We had a meeting as soon as the riot was over—Jordan,
Mother and I." The twist of a smile pulled at Alex's
mouth. "Mother voted Father's shares—and here is what
we decided. The remaining ships sail for Boston within the
week. Mother and Jordan will leave on the last one—I
may join her if that is my wish."

"Join her—do you mean—go to Boston?"

"Yes."

"But—but what of your father?"

"My father goes to Olympia tomorrow," Alex said.
"And I doubt very much that he will leave there again. He
does not require a large kingdom, you see—only the small
one left to him to control."

"How can you—choose between them, Mr. St. Cyr?
This is too hard, too cruel—"

Alex's eyes fastened on Gabriele's face, and in that moment she saw the tiniest portion of the pain he bore. She stretched her hand out almost unconsciously, and looked imploringly at Tom. "Oh, Tom, surely Mrs. St. Cyr will come to her senses—"

"She believes that she has," Alex said. He moved to the breakfast table and picked up his cup, staring into it as though he could see the future there. "I never dreamed my prediction of dissolution into smaller and smaller units would come about so soon—but here is my kingdom, split into the smallest possible parts. My mother takes her half to Boston—my father removes his to his country retreat."

"And you, Mr. St. Cyr?" She felt pulled apart, yanked from a world she recognized into a strange and terrible place. Tom's hand closed over hers, and she clung to it as she waited for Alex to speak.

"There's a ship bound for France sailing in three days' time. When I leave here—I shall book my passage."

"I wish you would reconsider, Alex," Tom said. "Come back to Felicity with us—give yourself time to think."

A light flared in Alex's eyes, the merest flame of hope—but then he shook his head, and his eyes went dark again. "I have had more than enough time to think, Cannon. If I had spent that time properly—I should very likely not be in this dilemma now. No, I shall not impose this disorder on the lives of my friends. I will take myself off to Europe —don't try to dissuade me, Tom. My mind is firm."

"Our door is always open to you," Tom said. "Isn't that so, Gabriele?"

She hesitated only an instant, but she saw it register in Alex's eyes. He is remembering how disappointed the views he expressed last night made me—he does not trust that this terrible disaster has pushed such small feelings aside, she thought, even as she added her assurances to Tom's.

"I cannot think ahead far enough to even dream of being once again in that happy place," Alex said. "I must put distance between myself and all this—conflict. I count on you to understand."

"Send me your address as soon as you know it," Tom said. "I won't let you just walk out of my life!"

"I couldn't," Alex said. He gathered up his hat and gloves, so overcome by emotion that he could say no more, only hold Tom's hand and stare into his face.

"I'll leave you," Gabriele said. "Such old friends—you should have these last moments alone—"

"Miss Cannon," Alex said. "May I write to you, also?"

"But of course, Mr. St. Cyr—"

"And you will write back?"

"I always do," she said.

She left them together, going into her room and reading the same page in a book over and over again until she heard the parlour door close. Thank heaven we go home soon, she thought. She let the book slip to the floor, closing her eyes, fleeing the room, leaving it and New Orleans far behind. In her mind, she was already at Felicity, riding Brandy through autumn-painted fields. She could see the yellow and orange and red foliage blazing against a blue sky. She could see the big sweet gum tree showering leaves as they rode beneath it, a glowing crimson cascade. She could smell the layers of leaf-smoke in the clear, bright air—and now they took the turn that brought them to the house itself, and she saw it shining in the sun, pristine, tranquil—safe.

From Tom Cannon to Gabriele Cannon, January 26, 1861

Dear Gabe,

Well, it is done. Louisiana has officially seceded from the Union, and, in the words of former Governor Alexandre Mouton, president of this convention, we are now a "free, sovereign, and independent Power." I have never before been present when history was being made, but I felt that this morning. All around me, men were half-weeping, half-cheering. And then Governor Moore entered our chamber, the Pelican Flag of Louisiana preceding him. The chaplain offered a prayer, and blessed the flag. You could almost feel the crowd come together—seventeen delegates had voted against secession, but by the time the Ordinance of Secession was signed, the vote stood at 121 to 9. I won't say I don't have misgivings, and I believe Governor Moore orchestrated the results somewhat by the action he took a week before he convened, which you may already have heard of. At any rate, he announced at the opening session that just over a week before he had seized two Federal forts below New Orleans, the US Arsenal at Baton Rouge, a Federal revenue cutter, and other Federal property. He asked for our vote of approval—if he had been refused, we might as well have packed our bags and gone home, and that first vote, 119 to 5, pretty well reflected the way it all went. Still, I can't blame Moore. After all, his inaugural address a year ago predicted that the South could no longer tolerate its treatment in Congress at the hands of the North —and everything he foresaw has come to pass.

I shall go to New Orleans before coming home—the general feeling is that the seceded states will soon formally organize a government—and once that is done, the next step would appear to be war.

My stay in Baton Rouge has not been all work and no play. Our friends have been kind to me, inviting me to dine with them. Two nights ago I had dinner with the Bienvenus, who asked to be remembered to you and to Aunt Mat.

> Your loving brother,
> Tom

From Alex St. Cyr to Gabriele Cannon, February 22, 1861

My dear Miss Cannon,

I received your letter this morning, and upon reading it found my mood, which has been as wintry and dull as the weather, lighten. I laughed as I have not laughed in weeks at your account of the drama of the Robins' Escaped Pig—the idea of the dignified Dorothea being dumped out of the swing as the pig ran under it should, I suppose, have distressed me, but had quite the opposite effect. I read your letters as I read novels—pulled into a different place and time, becoming engrossed in the stories of people who until now have been only names for me. Speaking of novels, I spent some time in England just after Christmas, and had the opportunity to meet Mr. Dickens, whose work you so admire. I picked up a set of his books and he kindly autographed them to you —they were posted from London before I left there, so you should receive them soon. I hope they are happy additions to your library.

You ask me to describe Paris for you, and then ask so many detailed questions about the city that I quite believe you when you say you have already toured it with Hugo and Balzac! I should be a poor guide compared to them, I fear. There is another French writer to whom I think you should be introduced—he is Gustave Flaubert, whose novel *Madame Bovary* caused a sensation when it was published here four years ago. I am going to send it to you today, at the risk of Mrs. LeGrange's disapproval, for it is considered by many to be highly immoral, and therefore not at all suitable for you to read. But I trust your intellect and your discrimination, Miss Cannon, and shall be interested to know what you think of the poor heroine of this book.

I go to the Comédie-Française on Tuesdays, which is the night when all the glamorous people go. Such a spectacle! If one does not care for the play, one can watch the audience—the ladies in particular, following the example of the Empress Eugenie, wear gowns cut so low that the style is referred to as *décolletage à la baignoire,* which in some instances means only the lady's shoulders and throat are seen rising above the opera box. And I go to the opera—I heard Verdi's *A Masked Ball* the other evening. Interestingly enough, it was to be premiered in New York this month—the 11th, I believe. So you shall probably see it in New Orleans before many seasons have gone by . . .

Miss Cannon, a dreadful thing has happened to me. I am in the City of Light and I go about it in a black fog. I am serious, so serious that my companions find me dull, and when I offer as an excuse the portentous things that are happening in my own country, they ask me why, if I am so concerned about them, I am in Paris? A very good question, one I cannot yet answer. This round of plays and operas and dinners and drives to villas on the city's outskirts does not seem to please me—but it is an accustomed routine, one I can perform in my sleep. Perhaps I am asleep, and am waiting for something or someone to wake me. Reading your letter, I thought that perhaps I should take it like a tonic every morning, letting its freshness and vigour enter my own blood, until I can emerge from this—miasma—and take hold of some purpose once more.

Whom do I fool, Miss Cannon? I have never had purpose, I have fled that word and all it implies. I embarrass myself, that is the long and short of it, but I am too practical to think some impulsive gesture will make my life have meaning—and too unhappy not to wish for a *Deus ex machina* to propose an answer.

You will be sorry you invited this correspondence, Miss Cannon, but I am very glad that you did. I find I cannot lie to you, nor can I lie to myself in your presence. And strangely enough, you are very near me, Miss Cannon. Nearer than the people I dine with twice a week.

Burn *Madame Bovary* if it offends you. But you have a brave mind, and I should insult it if I did not send you this remarkable work.

With very best wishes,
Alex St. Cyr

From Jordan Scott to Gabriele Cannon, April 14, 1861

Dear Miss Cannon,

Our correspondence during the months since I left New Orleans so precipitately has meant more to me than I can tell you. Now, I fear, it must come to an end, at least until the hostilities between our two countries are resolved. How strange to think of you as a citizen of another nation! And yet, since the Confederate States of America exists, I suppose you are.

And since, by the time you receive this letter, I will be an officer in the Union navy, it is clearly impossible for us to continue to write. I would not even know how to tell you to get letters to me—I cannot give you my military address, nor would I want you to write me in care of my family. They are so upset by the events of the last week—first the formation of the Confederate States and then the firing on Ft. Sumter by that entity, that I cannot add to their distress by having them relay letters from you. We expected that the Southern states would band together, but I think few of us expected the gauntlet to be so quickly thrown as it was with the aggression against Ft. Sumter. I wonder if General P.G.T. Beauregard, who ordered that attack, is regarded as a hero in Louisiana. I imagine so—when native sons perform distant acts of war, only the glory penetrates to the people at home, with none of the horror—

I beg your pardon, I do not mean to criticize a gentleman whom I believe I have heard mentioned as an old friend of your father's—I am badly confused, Miss Cannon, and wish that duty were not so strong a part of the Scott tradition. I do not have the luxury of choosing a more peaceful role—my entire family assumes I am as eager to be part of this war as any other patriot, and one part of me surely is.

But another part remembers the landscapes and people of Louisiana, and is sad that now I am not only physically separated from them, but emotionally as well. I had begun to feel very close to you, Miss Cannon—which is a little hard for me to understand, because I thought that such closeness would come only if a man and woman loved each other in a way that led to marriage. That is not the feeling I have for you, Miss Cannon. I suppose what I feel is friendship—or agape, that Greek word that describes a sympathy, an empathy, between two people that may in the long run be even longer lasting than romantic love.

I shall guard that feeling as though it were a sacred flame, trusting that the unhappy events which now divide us will not last forever, and that when we next meet, we may then pick up where we left off.

Believe that I shall pray for the safety of all of you at Felicity, and for the safety of that happy house. And I humbly ask, Miss Cannon, that if your thoughts ever turn to Jordan Scott, you remember me with kindness and trust.

Yours very sincerely,
Jordan Scott

From Gabriele Cannon to Alex St. Cyr, April 15, 1861

Dear Mr. St. Cyr,

You are too kind! The richness of having a set of Mr. Dickens' works, and autographed to me! They have an honoured place on my shelves, but I must confess that I keep *Madame Bovary* hidden away. I have only just begun it, but it does seem to be an extraordinary work. I shall give you my opinion of it as soon as I have finished reading it, and have had time to form one.

Life in Paris sounds most attractive to me, I must admit. There is excitement here, of course, because of the Confederate States being formed and because of Ft. Sumter—of which, I am sure, you will have read—but it is a scary sort of excitement, too, because the home-guard units which formed right after Mr. Lincoln was elected have stepped up their pace—the patrols to watch for runaway slaves enlist more men every day—in all, the atmosphere of our usually tranquil region is tense and anxious. Tom is home, which is good, but he is in such demand at meetings and conferences that I hardly see him any more.

Well, enough of this. Let me tell you another story of country life, just to prove to you that not all is politics and war! . . .

Chapter Twelve

THE RHYTHMIC THUD OF MARCHING FEET STRIKING THE SHELL drive in front of the house brought Gabriele out onto the upper balcony where she stood watching Tom drill the home guard. Spring sunshine, still pale and soft in late April, bathed the marchers with an almost veiled light, delicately gilding the long barrels of their rifles, staining their faces with a faint wash of gold.

She leaned forward and breathed in the perfumes of April scenting the air: wisteria hanging in great purple and white clusters on vines wrapped around tree trunks and arbours, ligustrum blooms starring the thick hedge that bounded the far end of the lawn, and in a long bed set in a sunny spot in the formal garden, roses making a tapestry of colour and sweet fragrance.

The very lushness of the landscape, the richness of the vegetation responding to the call of the sun after its winter sleep, the birdsong coming from every tree, made the figures on the drive below incongruous, as though they had wandered into this setting from some other terrain.

Tom, turning around to lead the men up the drive, saw Gabriele and waved his arm in greeting. She gave an answering wave, and then, as the attention of the men swung to her, went quickly back into the house.

Since the news of the attack on Ft. Sumter had arrived, the volunteer companies, loosely organized after Lincoln's election in November, had begun to drill in earnest. Gabriele and Aunt Mat had to accustom themselves to strange men who had never set foot inside Felicity's gates arriving every day to consult with Tom, who more and more showed he had the stature to fill his father's shoes.

The sight of uniformed men bearing arms was now a familiar one all over Louisiana, with a number of companies adopting the colourful pantaloons and tight-fitting jackets made popular by the Zoaves of the famed Italian Expedition of the Thousand the previous year. But Tom, observing that if anything would improve a Yankee rifleman's marksmanship, it would be having popinjays as targets, steered his own company into more sober hues.

The company drilled until just before noon, then gathered around Tom to hear him put a serious question before them. Would they volunteer for twelve months service in the Confederate Army, responding yes to Governor Moore's call just three days ago for five thousand Louisianians to bolster the Southern forces? The topic had been in their minds and on their lips since the call had come, and the same arguments that occupied citizens all over the state occupied the men of the Teche.

If Louisiana were attacked, how would she defend herself with her soldiers fighting on battlefields far away? The question had first been raised in March: even before the same delegates who had convened to vote secession formally ratified the permanent Constitution of the Confederacy on March 21, a call had come from Confederate Secretary of War Leroy Walker for seventeen hundred men to be used with other Southern troops to man forts throughout the Confederate states. And by April 8, President Jefferson Davis, in a response to President Lincoln's refusal to the attempts of the Confederate Peace Commission to find a compromise of their difficulties, requested more troops of each seceded state, including three thousand from Louisiana. When Moore's call for five thousand more came so quickly on the heels of Davis', grumbling reached new proportions.

"We'll be bled dry," some Louisianians complained. "Why should we leave ourselves defenceless to protect states so far away?"

But others believed that the new Confederation must show a united front to the common enemy, arguing that if Union forces were kept busy enough on battlefields further North, Louisiana would gain time to strengthen her defences.

The men in the company gathered around Tom divided themselves fairly equally between those who believed the company should remain to form a home guard and those who believed it should join other volunteers training at Camp Walker, which had been established on the site of the old Metairie Race Course in New Orleans.

Today they must decide, and as Tom stood on the top step of the short flight leading up to Felicity's front gallery, all eyes fixed on him. Although not having quite the seventy-five men Moore requested for each volunteer company, this number to be divided into sixty-four privates, eight non-commissioned officers, and three commissioned officers, still, with sixty-three men it was very near full strength, and Tom had no doubt that if the men chose to enter the Confederate Army, there would be more than enough volunteers from the Teche region to fill its ranks.

After all, despite all their protests, these men came from families which had never neglected their duty. The Acadian militia had marched from the Teche country to join Spanish Governor Bernard Galvez in his attack on the British-held forts of Manchac and Baton Rouge during the American War of Independence in 1779, and when Jean Lafitte's pirates put their guns and their lives at General Andrew Jackson's disposal in the Battle of New Orleans in 1812, Acadians had been found there, too. Nor had these men's fathers shirked service in a neighbour's war—many of them, including his own uncle Louis LeGrange, had helped Texans in their war for independence from Mexico, and had lost their lives, as he had, in the attempt. There is no lack of courage here, he thought, nor any lack of will to support a cause.

He held up a hand for silence, and gradually the men stopped talking, last-minute efforts to enlist support for a particular view abandoned as the time to vote drew near. Now they stood at their ease, leaning on their weapons or cradling them loosely in their arms. It would be a miracle if two men have the same sort of gun, Tom thought. These guns brought ducks sailing down through a winter sky, or felled a buck as he fled through the swamp, and each was as individual as its owner. But what the weapons lacked in conformity was more than made up for in the deadly eyes of the men who used them: these men might come out of fields as did the Minute Men of Concord, but they were experienced marksmen one and all, and so might make an army yet.

"I think we all know how quickly our situation is worsening," Tom said. "Lincoln's naval blockade has already begun—and surely the Union navy will move quickly to close the Mississippi River to all shipping bound to or from New Orleans—and, I fear, Berwick Bay, where the Atchafalaya finds entrance to the Gulf, as well."

"Does that mean they'll go after New Orleans itself?" a man called from the rear. A stir of talk went through the troops, and Tom again held up his hand for silence.

"I can't believe the Yankees will be satisfied with blockading New Orleans only—surely they'll have to take her to render her useless."

"But what about those river forts?" someone asked. "Fort Jackson and Fort Phillip?"

"Beauregard says they must be strengthened if they are to prove adequate against anything more lethal than a child's sailboat. Whether his suggestions will be followed in time—"

"Tell us the truth, Cannon," a man in the front said. He stepped out of the ranks and approached the steps. "What real chance does the South have against a foe with the North's industrial power?"

"No one can answer that with any certainty," Tom said. "But men with military experience say that much depends on the length of the war. If it can be over quickly—then our lack of industrial capacity might not handicap us as badly as it would in a long campaign."

"Then I say we answer Moore's call!" someone cried. "Go to Virginia and beat them back to the Canadian border!"

"That's right!" someone else shouted, and other voices took up the cry, until the lawn reverberated with their cheers.

At first some men hung back, indecision written on their faces. But then the common mood seized them, and within minutes, the entire company had resolved to leave for Camp Walker as soon as their departure could be arranged.

Gabriele, playing a new piece by Louis Gottschalk, heard their shouts over the music and went quickly to the parlour window, where she stood watching them throw their caps in the air and clap each other's shoulders in wild jubilation. Then Tom looked up and saw her, and broke away from the men around him, running through the front door and down the hall to the parlour.

"Here," he said, going straight to the open piano and searching through the sheet music in the cabinet beside it. "I want you to play something for us, Gabriele." He beckoned to her, pressing the music into her hands as she drew near. Then, standing beside her, his hands resting lightly on her shoulders as she found the first chords, Tom began to sing.

At first he sang alone, his clear tenor floating through the open windows, across the gallery, over the heads of the men outside. Then they took up the song; soon, all were singing. Gabriele's own light soprano came in at the chorus, her voice breaking with emotion at first, but then becoming firm and strong as she sang Daniel Emmett's song introduced in New Orleans at the Varieties Theatre the winter before, and taken up all over the South as its own tune:

> Then I wish I was in Dixie—Hooray! Hooray!
> In Dixie's land I'll take my stand,
> To live and die in Dixie.
> Away, away, away down South in Dixie.

As the last note faded, Gabriele reached up and took Tom's hand. "Aunt Mat and I shall go to New Orleans with you," she said. "To get you outfitted and start your military career in style."

"I should like that," Tom said. "We should probably see Guillot while we are there—consolidate some of our holdings—perhaps move investments abroad . . ."

"I wonder how long he will stay in New Orleans," Gabriele said. "You remember he had begun selling off assets even last year."

Tom looked out the window at his men, now milling about at ease. "There will be a small exodus, I imagine, as the threat of war becomes more real. And then there will be those already planning how to profit from this conflict —vultures feeding on the misfortune and misery of others, eager to forswear their own families if need be to line their pockets with gold."

"Oh, I hope you are wrong, Tom! It is bad enough to have the country divided—but to have this dissension divide us from old friends as well—"

"That is perhaps the most terrible effect of this kind of war," Tom said. "It makes enemies of brothers, and puts a sword between those who once shared their lives." He sighed, for a moment resting his hand upon Gabriele's head. Then, straightening his shoulders and unconsciously assuming a military stance, he said, "But there's nothing for it. We have our loyalties well placed, Gabriele, and all we have to do now is follow where they lead."

"I wonder where Mr. Scott's loyalties will lead him," Gabriele said. "I hope the ship he is assigned to does not bring him to the Gulf—though I don't suppose we shall ever know even if it does."

"I find myself more worried about Alex," Tom said. "Scott's role in this war follows his family's tradition and the duty it demands—but Alex seems to have very little from which to choose."

"His father is a member of the Washington Artillery," Gabriele said. "I am sure Mr. St. Cyr can join that if he decides to stop moping in Paris and come home."

"You speak so sharply, Gabe," Tom said. "I thought you had sympathy for Alex's unhappy position—after all, it is not the war he tries to avoid, but the terrible choice his mother has presented to him."

"It is a choice he would have had to make at some point, if he is ever to be his own man," Gabriele said. "Perhaps not one so drastic as abandoning one parent to follow another—but, still, Tom, eventually wouldn't he have had to decide? Whether to let that serious side we both admire become a larger part of his nature—or whether to finally squelch it, and lead a life marked only by frivolity and pleasure?"

"Of course you are right," Tom said. "And I have known that for a long time. I have not had the courage to admit, even to myself, that much of Alex's dilemma is one of his own making. He is not the only man, after all, torn between a mother's wishes and a father's desires! Something makes him put too much weight on that—something I may never understand."

I think I do, Gabriele almost said aloud. But then she closed her lips tightly, and bent once more over the keys. The rippling Gottschalk music followed Tom out of the room, and made a cover for the thoughts crowding into Gabriele's head. Motherless since infancy, her ideas of what a mother should be had come from books and from her father's veneration of her own mother's memory. Nowhere in that ideal was there room for a mother who would deny a child, and when she thought of Julia St. Cyr, and the coldness with which she treated her son, her heart went out to Alex as she imagined the pain he must have. And yet, he still cannot make that final break, she thought, absently beginning the piece over again. He stays in limbo, living with neither of them, choosing no cause. Nor could she blame him. In such a household, had he ever known love? Had either parent ever admired him, or praised him, or let him know that his presence made them glad? He has been greatly wronged, she told herself, finishing the last chord. And until he decides that he does not merit such treatment, his parents' behaviour will continue to give him pain.

The problem lay beyond her wisdom, and though Alex's unhappy position remained just beneath the surface of her thoughts, she knew that the solution lay, not with her, but with him. I am not a *Deus ex machina*, she thought. Mr. St. Cyr has to solve his own dilemma—and for his sake, I pray that he does so soon.

The pulse of New Orleans had quickened, as though the tempo of martial music had entered the City's veins, casting out for the present the lilting Creole rhythms that previously called her tune. Aunt Mat's pace quickened, too, as she bustled about the shops, gathering together not only those things Tom required, but items the blockade would soon put in short supply.

Not only shopping lists reflected the general military air: the entire city seemed to have no thought for normal commerce or social life; every activity focused on Camp Walker, where a steady stream of men gathered, pitching tents on marshy ground, and trying to establish a military routine under almost impossible physical conditions.

Even before the three thousand men destined for Camp Walker arrived, Camp Lewis had to be set up to take care of the overflow, and within a few short weeks, the impossibility of training men at Camp Walker became clear. Short of water and shade, infested by mosquitoes and always muddy, the camp offered nothing but its proximity to

New Orleans to recommend it, and already Governor Moore looked for another suitable site.

In the meantime, New Orleanians overlooked Camp Walker's deficiencies, journeying out to it as though it were a resort to dine in the officers' or enlisted men's mess, view the drilling, and watch the other military doings with awe and delight. Aunt Mat reported that ladies purchasing comforts of all sorts for the soldiers at Camp Walker thronged the shops, and the road leading to it became one of the best-travelled in the area.

For the first time in Gabriele's memory, the house on Esplanade was not the centre of hospitable activity as it had always been before. Tom, seeing to a myriad of details involving his volunteers joining the Confederate forces, had neither the time nor the inclination for social events, and Aunt Mat planned no formal calls or "at home" hours, saying that she and Gabriele had little enough time as it was to complete all she had set out for them to do.

With all of Tom's comings and goings, it was easy for him to disappear for hours with neither his sister nor his aunt being quite certain of his destination. Gabriele felt certain she knew: a cottage on an alleyway deep in the Quarter. On the fourth day after their arrival, she could stand it no longer. Waiting until she knew that Tom would be busy at a meeting of his company's officers all morning, she put on her bonnet, took up her parasol, and left the house, determined to find Veronique.

She traced the route to the alleyway with some difficulty: she had not been here for months, and several times she made turns that took her on fruitless detours. But finally she stood in the narrow brick walkway she remembered. Yes, there was the door she had seen Jacques Lamont, Alex's father's factor, coming from—she approached the green door slowly, thinking now that this venture could prove to be a terrible mistake. If Veronique is here, what shall I say? What shall I do? She hesitated, not knowing whether to stay or go, when a small sign placed in a window next to the door caught her eye.

"Modiste," the sign read. Only that, but those seven letters contained such a large dream that Gabriele hesitated no longer. Swiftly crossing the last few steps to the door, she lifted the iron knocker and let it fall resoundingly against the wood. She of course expected to see Veronique, and jumped back in surprise when an older woman opened the door.

"I—I'm looking for—are you the modiste?" Gabriele said.

"I am her assistant," the woman said. "Do you wish to see Mademoiselle Lamont?"

"Yes," Gabriele said.

The woman stood aside, allowing Gabriele to enter the house. She walked into a broad hallway that ran down the centre of the house, the french doors at its end giving onto a courtyard, with doors on either side opening into other rooms.

"In here," the woman said, pushing open a door on the right.

Gabriele went in, wondering what on earth she would say to Veronique. A woman sitting at a sewing machine pushing the treadle turned at the sound of footsteps—then the treadle stopped, the machine stopped, all noise stopped—all Gabriele could hear was a gasp of disbelief from Veronique.

"Gabriele!" she cried, rising and letting the garment she worked on fall to the floor. "What—what are you doing here?"

"I—had to find you, Veronique. I had to see for myself that you are safe and well." She hurried across the room and took Veronique's hand in hers. "Don't be afraid, I won't betray you! No one will ever know I found you. I promise!"

"But—how did you find me?" Veronique said.

"I—followed Tom," Gabriele said. "Last fall."

"You've known since then that I was here?" Veronique said.

Gabriele saw the quick panic in Veronique's eyes and

hastened to reassure her. "I have said nothing, not even to Tom." She let go of Veronique's hand and turned slightly away. "I won't say it didn't—hurt—to know he felt he could not trust me with this secret. But I said nothing."

"Oh, Gabriele, it wasn't a matter of trust!" Veronique said. "But such a dangerous secret—the fewer who knew it, the more likely it was to be kept."

"That is exactly what I told myself," Gabriele said. "And when I saw Mr. St. Cyr's factor at the fire—and realized he was the same man I had seen leaving here—then I knew that somehow Alex St. Cyr had involved himself in your—escape—and that Tom had an ally."

"There is so much to tell you," Veronique said. "And to show you! I know all kinds of laws have been broken, Gabriele, but I don't care! Mr. Lamont introduces me as his first cousin—which is why I am using his name—I have a circle of friends—good customers—such happiness as I would never have dreamed possible!"

"Have there been no alarms? No one linking you to advertisements and flyers asking for your return?"

"None," Veronique said. "I was not in New Orleans, at first—" She stopped, glancing at Gabriele, clearly not sure how much of the story Gabriele had guessed.

"I thought you must have gone to Olympia," Gabriele said. "When Mr. St. Cyr departed so quickly to see about his father's broken leg."

"He had broken it," Veronique said. "And pretty badly, too. I did go with him. But I returned here as soon as Tom and Mr. St. Cyr felt it safe for me—a matter of weeks."

"You had two stout champions," Gabriele said. "I suppose—I suppose you proved useful at Olympia—with Mr. St. Cyr disabled, he must have required great care."

"He has his own staff who know how to please him," Veronique said. "I spent much of my time mending the linens, freshening the lace, and the like. By the time I left there, even Mrs. LeGrange would have approved of the way the armoires looked!"

"It is strange," Gabriele said. "But Aunt Mat never even mentions your name—of course, I do not bring it up— why would I?"

"And why would she?" Veronique asked. "I myself think that Mrs. LeGrange is not certain whether she wishes me to be a slave or free—"

"Yes—she's not consistent, is she?" Gabriele said. "To treat you so differently all the while you were growing up —and then to expect you to sink beneath the surface of slavery—"

"Mr. St. Cyr—Mr. Alex St. Cyr, that is—helped me realize what different messages our hearts and our heads can send," Veronique said. "I think Mrs. LeGrange's heart tells her I should be free—but her head says I shouldn't. And so this—passive acceptance of my escape. If I am found—her head is proved right. If not—her heart wins."

"You—spent time with Mr. Alex St. Cyr?" Gabriele said, picking up a half-finished bodice and studying the sleeves as though she would be expected to duplicate them within the hour.

"Not in actual hours," Veronique said. "But he directed me in ways that filled my free time—showing me books in the library I should read, sending me into woods and fields to collect leaves and flowers—and helping me find the constellations at night."

"He tutored you, you mean," Gabriele said, feeling an unreasonable flash of discomfort.

"Yes—he said I must take my basic education farther before settling here if I were to convince people that I had been living abroad." The fear that filled Veronique's eyes banished any idea Gabriele had that her sojourn at Olympia had been the idyll it sounded. Alex St. Cyr trained her to survive, Gabriele thought, and went to Veronique, taking her into her arms.

"You are every inch a cultivated lady, Veronique," Gabriele said. "I understand that Jacques Lamont is quite sophisticated, but I am sure you fit into his acquaintance very well."

"He is kind enough to say so," Veronique said. "When I went to the first reception as his guest, I went with such trepidation! But everyone welcomed me so generously—oh, Gabriele, have you any idea what heaven it is for me to be here? To wake up in the morning knowing that even though my practical sense will make me work all day—I could still choose not to! To go to the Market and choose this vegetable over that one—this fish instead of that hen! To receive invitations and issue them! Oh, Gabriele!"

In that moment, Gabriele understood exactly what all this did mean to Veronique as clearly as though they shared one mind, one heart. "Oh, my dear!" she said, and when she kissed Veronique's cheek, her tears mingled with the ones already there. They clung together crying quietly, releasing the last remnants of resentment and envy on one side, and of guilt and frustration on the other.

The sound of the iron knocker against the front door sent their hands flying to their pockets for handkerchiefs to blot their tears, and by the time Veronique's assistant entered to announce that Madame Gautreaux had arrived for her fitting, both Gabriele and Veronique had recovered their composure.

"You are busy," Gabriele said. "So I won't take up more of your time. But may I come again?"

"Of course," Veronique said. Then, quickly, as Gabriele prepared to leave—"Don't say anything to Tom just yet, will you? I must think about it a while longer—whether he should know that you have found me."

"As you wish," Gabriele said. "But I really don't think he'd mind my knowing now—not when the whole plan has worked so well."

"Perhaps," Veronique said. Her customer entered and she said no more.

Gabriele hurried back home, so deep in her own thoughts that she did not even notice the crowds bustling around her. I will not tell Tom what I know since Veronique has asked me not to, she thought. She will think about it and see that no harm will be done if Tom knows I share their secret. She stopped in the middle of the sidewalk, unaware of the curious glances of people who had to then walk around her. But from Veronique's viewpoint, I suppose one harm would be done. To have me openly part of their secret would be to weaken what she sees as a special link to Tom.

After some weeks even Aunt Mat's industriousness finally demanded respite, and she ordered Tom to invite as many of his company as could come to a reception on a Sunday afternoon. "Nothing formal, but simply a good punch," she said. "And little cakes and sandwiches—we will send cards to young ladies of our acquaintance, and make the occasion a pleasant one for us all."

The date for the reception fell a few days after the first anniversary of Oliver Cannon's death, and Aunt Mat, coming into Gabriele's room, seeing her out of mourning for the first time, said, "Thank heaven our boys won't see you in mourning, Gabriele. They need cheering now—God knows when they will see this sort of party again."

I have emerged from a dark cocoon, Gabriele thought, watching her pale green muslin skirts swirl around her legs as she twirled in front of her long mirror. She studied her face. Its colour seemed fresher now, as though the heavy black of her mourning clothes had laid a film of grey over her skin that had now been removed. But something else is different, Gabriele thought, leaning closer to her reflected face. A more serious expression in her eyes—her cheeks a little thinner—the curve of her lips still full, but somehow not so ready to smile—I'm all grown up, she thought. A year ago when I dressed for the ring tourney I looked in my mirror and saw a child. Now she is gone—and in her place is this young woman—who I am not sure I really know.

Her heart beat a little faster: she could not determine whether the emotion stirring it could be called excitement or fear. She could not remember ever having felt this way before: as though she had traversed all the familiar territory left to her, and beyond lay only the unknown.

From downstairs she heard the first sounds of voices, and hastily picked up her fan. Whatever lay ahead tomorrow, this afternoon her course was clear. Be a gracious hostess to her brother's companions, and give them a good memory to take to camp. She started down the stairs, pausing to catch up her trailing skirts. Tom stood in the foyer, talking to a young man, his arm clasped around his guest's shoulders, his face alight with happiness. The guest stood with his back to Gabriele, but something about the way he stood, the gestures of his hands—Alex St. Cyr! He turned immediately, and only then did she realize she had called his name aloud. Still she could not move, and Alex had come halfway up the staircase before she could.

"Miss Cannon, I can't tell you how delighted I am to find you here."

"But what are you doing in New Orleans, Mr. St. Cyr? Your last letter gave no indication you intended to return."

"I sailed soon after that letter did," Alex said. "As for plans—I had no more than usual." He offered her his arm and escorted her down the remaining stairs. "If I had not seen signs of habitation when I passed your house just now, I should have missed this pleasant surprise, because just as you thought me still in Paris, I thought you would still be at Felicity."

"My company has joined the Confederate Army," Tom said, coming to meet them. "I wrote you about forming a company of the home guard—well, we are in regular service now, and soon leave to train at Camp Moore."

"To stay and defend the state?"

"I doubt it," Tom said. "Louisiana sends thousands of troops to Virginia every month—and the call has gone out for more."

"Is that wise? I took a French ship home, and so the blockade did not stop us—but the Union navy will soon cover every southern port, Tom, including New Orleans.

It seems to me troops should be kept to meet that threat —if the Mississippi River ports fall into Union hands—the war in Louisiana will be effectively over."

"You seem to know a great deal about military strategy, St. Cyr," Tom said. His tone was mild, but his posture, suddenly rigid, contradicted it, and Alex flushed slightly.

"I suppose it is a bit presumptuous of me to give advice when I am in no danger of having to follow it myself," Alex said.

"You are only saying what many people say," Gabriele said. "Be fair, Tom. You are not so sure sending all these troops out of Louisiana is such a good idea, either."

"True, I'm not," Tom said. "Which is why I took umbrage at what you said, Alex. Come, let us sit down and have a proper visit—such ages since we've seen you!"

"I can't stay," Alex said. "I'm due at a reception just down the block."

"What? Home a few days and already the invitations are flowing?" Tom said. He laughed, his joy in seeing Alex overcoming any other emotion. "Well, you will cut a wider swath than ever, St. Cyr, with the Parisian airs you will have acquired."

"Oh, I doubt Paris improved me," Alex said.

"But we must meet again," Tom said. "And soon! I won't let you go until we arrange it."

"You are busier than I am," Alex said. "Suggest a time."

"Lunch tomorrow," Tom said. "I have a dinner engagement tonight."

"Thank you, I will look forward to it," Alex said. He kissed Gabriele's hand. *"A bientôt,"* he said. "And look, here are your guests."

Several of Tom's soldiers strolled up the walk, the buttons of their uniforms flashing in the sun. Alex slipped out as the new arrivals entered, and Gabriele went forward to greet their guests.

Aunt Mat hurried in from the kitchen where she had been directing the cook, and then all three of them had every minute of the next few hours occupied seeing to the needs of their guests.

But although Gabriele's surface energies were totally dedicated to making the party go well, behind her almost automatic chatter her mind focused on one thing: how she had felt at the moment she realized that the man talking with her brother was Alex St. Cyr. As though a piece of her that had been lost had been found again. She could come no nearer to defining her emotions than that: even though she had not known it at the time, apparently when Alex St. Cyr left them the previous fall, he took something from her—now he had come back, and she felt whole.

But is that love? She did not know, had no way of knowing. She thought of Jordan Scott's last letter, when he told her that he realized now he loved her, not in a romantic way, but with a friendship so sincere he believed it better. Perhaps that is what I feel for Mr. St. Cyr, that agape of which Mr. Scott wrote. She felt Alex's presence all afternoon, knew what would make him laugh, and what he would find interesting, knew which of their guests Alex would seek out, and which avoid. But is that love? At the end of her reflections, she found herself no closer to the answer.

Both Aunt Mat and Tom went out soon after the last guest left, Aunt Mat to dine with relatives and Tom to meet friends. Gabriele saw them go with relief, refusing Aunt Mat's invitation to go with her, saying that she would have a light supper and go early to bed. The spring evening changed her mind: a whiff of sweet olive, newly blooming, scenting the night air with its perfume, drew Gabriele into the garden, and to the arbour where climbing roses grew.

She sat in the arbour's shadow, the glow of the street lamps touching only the tops of the trees, the moon not yet risen high enough to give much light. Hidden in the arbour, Gabriele watched people passing by, only their shapes visible behind the hedge that grew along the wrought-iron fence. Then she saw a figure she needed only the tiniest clue to identify: at that moment, the low hanging moon broke free from the cage formed by the trees, and rising, cast its light full on her.

"Miss Cannon!" Alex said. He stepped nearer the hedge, and Gabriele, after a moment's hesitation, went toward him down the gravel path.

"Good evening, Mr. St. Cyr," she said. "I am taking the air in the garden—it is so pleasant this evening—I could not stay inside."

"May I join you?" he said. "I'll understand if you think it better that I don't—"

"Of course you may," Gabriele said. "An old friend just back from Paris—I think we may suspend the rules. Here, I'll come open the side gate and let you in."

Who goes to meet him? she asked herself as she hurried toward the gate. The child he left last autumn—the woman just emerged—or someone in between them, a creature he helped form?

She opened the gate and stepped back as Alex came through, leading the way to the arbour, and taking her place on the bench inside. Alex stood just inside its entrance, hat in his hand, his body in an easy pose but one small muscle tightening the corner of his mouth.

"Well," he said, "and did your party go well?"

"Very well," she said. "And yours?"

"Mine? Oh, the one I attended—well, actually, it didn't." He turned and looked out into the garden, the moonlight painting shadows around his eyes.

"I'm sorry to hear that," Gabriele said.

"I—perhaps did not tell you and Tom the absolute truth," Alex said. "I went to a reception, yes—but one given by officers of the Washington Artillery as a farewell to the city. The regiment leaves for Virginia very soon— and I was fool enough to ask if I might—go with them."

"Mr. St. Cyr!"

Alex turned back to her, and she saw the one tight corner of his mouth twist in the old cynical smile. "You, too, are astonished, Miss Cannon. And so were they. It took me a long while to convince them that I meant what I said. And then—well, astonishment turned very quickly to embarrassment—at least, some of the members were embarrassed to refuse me—others took a certain amount of satisfaction in my—humiliation, and I can't say I blame them for that."

Gabriele had risen while Alex spoke, and now she came to stand beside him, one hand placed gently on his arm. "On what grounds do they refuse you?" she asked.

"Can't you guess?" And when she remained silent, he said, "My mother's—defection."

"You can't be blamed for that!"

"No, but I can be suspected," Alex said. He placed his fingers over her lips. "Don't waste breath defending me or attacking them," he said. "I have brought this on myself by coming very late to an opinion—like the little boy who cried wolf, I have said all too often that I did not care to choose between my mother and my father's positions— now the bill is reckoned and I must pay the price."

"But what will you do?" Gabriele asked. "Go back to Paris? Stay here?"

"I—haven't decided yet," Alex said. "Foolishly I had pinned my future on the Washington Artillery's flag—"

"You won't go away without letting me know?" she said, and felt a wave of dismay at the expression in Alex's eyes.

"Does that request mean you take a special interest in me?" he asked. "Because I must warn you—you do so at your own risk."

"Risk? Do you mean that you take no—special interest in me? After all those letters—the books you sent me—" And then she became angry, and flailed out at the barrier she thought he imposed. "You send me *Madame Bovary* and then speak to me of risk!"

Alex looked at her, his face closed into a mask. "Poor Emma. She risked everything—and lost. I only warn you not to do the same."

"I don't agree," Gabriele said. The heat in her cheeks rose to her eyes, making them spark green fire. "At the beginning of the book, Emma Bovary had no better life than that of a slave—at least she tried to escape it!"

"And you think her ultimate destruction did not show the futility of her efforts? That the system against which she mounted her feeble little rebellion had always been too strong for her to have any chance at all?"

"Futility does not come from trying to escape, Mr. St. Cyr," Gabriele said. "It comes from not trying. True, Emma's dreams came to nothing—worse than nothing, I admit. But the next woman would learn from her—would move with better wisdom—less folly."

"So if you were Emma Bovary—you would have taken that risk?"

The colour in Gabriele's cheeks deepened, but she stood her ground. "I do not know that my—rebellion—would have taken precisely the same form," she said. "But in spirit—yes, in spirit, I would be right there at her side!"

His arms came around her so suddenly that she had no time to think: one moment they stood separated by at least twelve inches, the next moment there was no space between them at all. She felt his lips on her forehead, her cheeks—and then she pulled away, staring at him as though she had never seen him before, saying nothing, letting her feelings spill with the tears in her brimming eyes.

"I—I apologize, Miss Cannon," Alex said. "I—I'm sorry."

Still she said nothing, and Alex, after one agonized look, turned on his heel, clapped his hat on his head, and almost ran down the path to the gate.

Gabriele sank back onto the bench, still staring straight ahead. She took a slow, steadying breath, then another, then a third. She waited for the emotion whirling through her to settle, so that she would know what she felt. Anger? Shock? She remembered the way his arms felt as they came around her, the touch of his lips—then the wholeness, the completion. Yes—he had felt it, too.

This is love, then, she thought. This whirling, this condition of being at one and the same time absorbed in another's identity, and yet more aware of myself.

She sat on as the moon rose higher, lost in happy dreams. They would meet tomorrow, and she would persuade him that loving him presented no risk. As though the last hour had given her a new pair of eyes, she saw how well Alex measured up to the standards she had formed last fall. Always loyal and honourable, capable of devotion, Alex does have purpose, something I never saw before. A more subtle purpose, one not easily discerned. But a purpose all the same. To somehow steer his way between Scylla and Charybdis, not adhering to either parent's life or views, but denying neither, too. And as if that were not enough—he means to do this nearly impossible task in such a way that they might all still love each other—or at least, not be hurt.

My love will help him, she vowed. He will learn that he can trust me, he will feel himself secure. And from the steady deck of the ship our love builds, he will steer between whirlpool and rocks, and bring us safely home.

Gabriele slept well that night; a good thing, as she would not again for weeks. Two letters arrived in the morning from Alex, one for Gabriele and one for Tom. Tom's said only that Alex had been called away from the city and that he would come see Tom at Camp Moore. Gabriele's was not much longer; long enough, however, to break her heart.

"Dear Miss Cannon," it read. "I can add no further apology for my behaviour than the one I offered last night, but I can ameliorate a situation I see fraught with potential pain by leaving New Orleans at once. Do not waste another thought on me, Miss Cannon. If I might ever have hoped to be worthy of you, I have that hope no longer. You made a great difference in my life, and I thank you for it.

> With sincerest wishes for your happiness,
> Alex St. Cyr"

Chapter Thirteen

WITH NATURE'S IMPERVIOUSNESS TO MAN'S VICISSITUDES, THE
June skies that hung over Felicity, powdered with a dust-
ing of clouds, seemed the same as those of the other summers Gabriele could remember. Roses smelled as sweet,
honeysuckle grew as thickly, and the first tomatoes picked
from the vine tasted exactly the same as those Gabriele and
Tom used to pick and eat as they walked down to the
bayou, seasoned only with salt from Tom's pocket and the
sun-warmth held within their firm, tight skins.

And although the dark space that opened in Gabriele's
heart when she read Alex's note did not become either
smaller or brighter as the summer days eased by, she knew
that she must preserve a cheerful exterior, one that would
not be contradicted by anything she wrote to Tom. And
so she filled her letters with the sort of vignettes and bits
of news that had so entertained Alex St. Cyr, blotting the
tears that sometimes fell on the page, and telling herself
that if Alex could not yet be worthy of her, he someday
might. He has not resolved the central problem, and the
Washington Artillery's refusal only confirmed what he already knows. He has to make a choice: events have forced
it. Except—he will not want to do that. He will not want
to make a choice dictated by a state of war. He will not
think it honest. Oh, what can he do?

That question, the one all her thoughts finally came to,

became a counterpoint to everything else in her mind. As she went about her daily routine, it would emerge and demand her attention. Where was Alex St. Cyr? And what was he doing?

Nor did Tom know. Alex did visit Tom at Camp Moore, shortly after the company settled in. He seemed a bit subdued, but they had spent a pleasant evening, Tom wrote. Alex had said something vague about perhaps going away—he had not said he would let Tom know his plans, and so far, he had not. But as soon as he himself knew anything, he would certainly let Gabriele know.

There had been no mention of Alex in any of his recent letters, which were filled with reports about Camp Moore. "It could not be more different from Camp Walker," Tom wrote. "Thank God!" Situated some seventy-eight miles north of New Orleans in piney uplands, the camp had almost no mosquitoes, fresh drinking water from Beaver Creek and the Tangipahoa River, and a well-drained campsite that lent itself well to the military requirements. The abundance of pine trees and fresh springs had made the area a popular resort for some years, and the quality of the air had given it the name "Ozone Belt." "Indeed," Tom wrote, "the creek and river bordering our camp are much more pleasant to swim in than is Bayou Teche, and at night, the temperature becomes so cool I am still sleeping under a light cover."

Other letters spoke of excursions from New Orleans, when the ladies came out to see their husbands, brothers, sons, and fiancés, and then the camp took on a holiday air, with bands playing, troops drilling, and the Confederate flag fluttering in the soft summer air. "The other night a young lady with a voice much like yours, Gabe, only not as sweet, sang 'The Bonnie Blue Flag' for us, and I must admit that no man had a dry eye by the time she finished."

Gabriele managed to keep her own eyes dry when under observation, but on her solitary walks down to the bayou, or when she sat alone sewing on the upper balcony, the loss of Tom's companionship told heavily on her, and she often gave herself up to tears. Everything reminded her of him—and increasingly, everything reminded her of Alex St. Cyr. The packets steaming past Felicity's dock, the path to the gazebo—he seemed to be everywhere, his presence often so strong that she quickened her step as though if she walked fast enough, she would find him just around the corner, or waiting behind a tree.

Until I can put him some other place, she thought, I will always see him here. Tom's letters helped her place him—she could see him marching between rows of pines, or swimming in the clear waters of a creek. Then he wrote that his company would soon join the Army of Virginia, and Gabriele turned to her history and geography texts to learn Tom's new terrain. She found the site of his Virginia camp on one of her father's maps: the neatly marked lines, the bright colours, reduced the territory they covered to an orderly and manageable size, but when Gabriele thought of the real distances involved, and the incredible events her brother and thousands of other soldiers prepared themselves for, then the maps' order seemed to mock the chaos in which they lived, and she turned from them, seeking refuge in her beloved Tennyson, or losing herself at the piano for hours.

She read the newspapers avidly, too, eagerly opening the bundle of New Orleans papers the packet dropped off and poring over their pages, searching for any reference to someone she knew. The names of Union ships taking part in the blockade meant nothing to her, except for the fact that Jordan Scott sailed on one of them. As she read of engagements between Union and Confederate ships, and as the effects of the blockade became harsher, she found it difficult to forget Jordan Scott's role in the war. He might retain a deep regard for her, might indeed consider her a well-loved friend—but his acceptance of his duty to the Union could not help but affect that bond. For the time being, at least, Jordan Scott had to be looked upon first as an officer in the Union navy—and secondarily as a friend.

And then one afternoon in mid-July her diligent reading

was rewarded. She had carried a newly arrived *Picayune* out onto the upper balcony, where she sat in a rocker pulled up into the shade. One headline caught her attention, and she held the paper closer, avidly reading the article beneath.

"Union gunboats captured six blockade runners off Galveston on July 4th. A seventh escaped: observers reported that the *Sir Lancelot* eluded the gunboats, due to evasive tactics and an apparently superior knowledge of the area's waters."

The article ran on for another several inches, but made no further mention of the *Sir Lancelot*. It did not need to: Gabriele knew as certainly as if Alex stood before her telling her so that the man at the wheel of the *Sir Lancelot* could be none other, and she clasped the paper tightly, staring unseeingly beyond the balcony rail.

It is just exactly the sort of thing he would do. Exactly. Fighting a lonely battle without the protection of a uniform—his exploits unrecorded, his courage unsung. He is not trying to prove himself to the Confederate army, Gabriele thought—but only to himself.

She did not see the trees and lawns before her, the squirrels chattering by the drive. She saw blue water, and a small white boat. A man with dark eyes stood at the wheel, dark hair blowing in the wind, hands strong as he turned the boat about.

She could feel herself pulled toward him, could feel the deck lift and fall under her feet, could feel, almost, the sea breeze fresh upon her face. She rose and stood at the balcony rail, clutching it as though it were indeed part of the steam packet Alex commanded. She felt pieces of her split off—one part of her journeyed with her brother Tom, another fluttered like a homeless bird, flying over an endless sea. Somewhere on the surface of that sea, Alex St. Cyr sailed. And though the sun that burned so mercilessly above her, heating up the earth and air until it seemed the whole world had been put into a vast oven, burned over Alex, too, the thought that they inhabited the same small area of the universe, and that the sky that bounded Felicity extended itself to form his horizons, did not comfort her.

She tried to fight the demon that held her in his dark grip, but the threat of death for Alex St. Cyr proved much too strong for her, and, vanquished, she crept to her room for a long and private weep. One other demon visited her there, demanding her attention, taunting her with its ugly knowledge.

Your youth is sacrificed to war, it said. All the beaux, all the dances, the pretty speeches and bouquets. Gone, all gone.

A selfish demon, a childish demon, but one to be battled with all the same. Because although the war has more tangible victims than youth and happiness, these are serious casualties still. And if those threatened with their loss are tempted to make light of them, the damage done can hardly be repaired.

Her father's memory rescued Gabriele that lonely afternoon. She visited his grave at sundown, laying a few crepe myrtle blossoms on his tombstone, and then sitting down on a marble bench nearby. He seemed very close to her here; if she closed her eyes, she could remember conversations they had had, she could see him smiling down at her as he gave her yet another tool with which to smooth her path.

"The hardest battles are not with things outside ourselves, but with those within that work to make us lesser beings than we truly are. Never get so caught up in those foes outside that you let the ones inside conquer you, Gabriele. Their victories are the only ones that really matter, and their defeat your only real task."

A stir in the air, not really a breeze, but a promise of a cooler night, touched her brow, bringing the scent of mint from a cluster growing thickly on the other side of the cemetery fence. A fledgling cardinal made a brave attempt at flying, skimming from the tombstone marking her mother's grave to a low branch near Gabriele's head.

She felt comfortable then, she could feel the continuity

of life assert itself. A kind of tranquil acceptance came over her, brushing the last traces of the afternoon's struggles from her soul, and leaving it healed.

When she finally went back up to the house, she had no sense of permanent victory, for she knew that today's battles were to be fought over and over again. But she had learned something during that hour at her father's grave, something that would stand her in good stead in the weary months ahead.

She did not have to understand all the chaos, the fearful events. She only had to face them. And that, she thought, unconsciously imitating her father's strong posture as she entered the house, I can do—and will.

July crept by, as though heat slowed the calendar. The newspapers reported skirmishes in Virginia, a series of movements much like a delicate dance in which each side issues an invitation which is tentatively accepted and then refused. But gathered under the command of General P.G.T. Beauregard, Confederate troops, including the Washington Artillery, and the Sixth, Seventh, and Eighth Louisiana regiments, massed at the vital railroad junction at Manassas, Virginia, and the importance of that site, added to a Confederate Congress set to convene in Richmond on July 20, finally overcame Union reluctance, and the first real engagement of the war in Virginia was launched.

Both armies consisted largely of hastily trained troops of little military discipline and less skill. The day-long battle pitted some 24,000 Union soldiers against a little more than 32,000 Confederate troops: at day's end, 418 Union soldiers had been killed, 1,011 wounded, and 1,216 were listed as missing. Fatigue took its toll—the Federal force began an orderly withdrawal back to Washington at four in the afternoon, but this soon disintegrated into a rout as unseasoned troops fled ahead of an expected Confederate pursuit. But Confederate losses—387 killed, 1,582 wounded, and 12 missing, added to their exhaustion, kept them from pressing their advantage. Although fresh units were on hand, the inexperienced Confederate officers did not know how to organize them, and so the Union troops escaped to the safety of the Washington defences.

If this battle created dismay in Washington that July 21, it created jubilation in Richmond, jubilation that resounded throughout the Confederacy as word of the victory spread. In New Orleans, a new wave of loyalty to the infant nation spurred more enlistments, and although black wreaths on doors reminded the city of those who had died at Manassas, the greater number of toasts were drunk to the victorious living, and to the Louisiana general who led them.

At Felicity, joy at the Confederate victory mingled with anxiety over Tom, and not until a letter from him reached them did Aunt Mat and Gabriele breathe easily again.

"He doesn't say—what it's like," Gabriele said, rereading the letter.

"I don't imagine he can," Aunt Mat said. Her agitation when she first read Tom's letter aloud had frightened Gabriele: her hands actually trembled as she opened the letter, and at one point, when Tom reported the death in battle of a boy from a neighbouring plantation, she could hardly read on.

"And of course," Aunt Mat said as Gabriele tucked the letter back in its envelope, "that was written weeks ago. There have been other battles since—"

Gabriele's face silenced her, and they knelt for evening prayers with a mixture of gratitude, hope, and fear that had become, Gabriele realized, their daily portion.

The smallest bit of good news became cause for thanksgiving: the arrival by packet of precious commodities, brought from Mobile or Havana via Lake Pontchartrain to New Orleans, and from thence by inland streams and bayous to the Teche country, could make them rejoice for days. Already, the Federal gunboats stationed at the mouth of the Mississippi River had slowed the bountiful flow of goods to and from New Orleans to a tiny trickle, and items Louisiana had long taken for granted were in short supply.

Soap, ladies' shoes, coffee and dry goods, along with fats, starch, and candles had soared in price, so that if they could be found, they were much too dear for most purses. And although Raphael Semmes' dashing feat of running the CSS *Sumter* right past the USS sloop *Brooklyn* at the end of June seemed proof that Confederate skill and courage could meet Yankee force with good effect, and although in the first ten months of the blockade of Louisiana, more than three hundred ships slipped past the Federal fleet, still, the longer the blockade lasted, the more terrible its effect, simply because human needs continue at the same rate regardless of the diminishing sources of supply.

Now Gabriele pored over the papers for news from two fronts: the war in Virginia, and the one waged between the Federal fleet on one hand and the blockade runners on the other. But all through the late summer, no mention of the *Sir Lancelot* appeared, and if it were not for a yellowing newspaper clipping, folded carefully away between two of her finest linen handkerchiefs, she might have thought she had dreamed she read that name.

The world seemed distorted: places insignificant as to size became important because of battles fought there, and men in their early twenties surpassed the fame of older and more experienced soldiers because of youthful daring and reckless deeds. Gabriele's horizons shrank, her days bounded now by Felicity's fences and by the roads leading to plantations and towns within a day's journey.

No longer did letters from friends in New Orleans and Baton Rouge or from plantations along the bayous and rivers invite her to houseparties and fêtes. For every man who left hearth and home to enter the Confederate service, there was a bevy of female relatives who abandoned their more frivolous occupations to knit for him, sew for him, hope for him, pray for him. The boys they had danced with in summers gone by had scattered across the

South, and as Gabriele read the newspapers and studied the maps on which she and Aunt Mat traced the course of the conflict, she found that she could not look at the name of a village or town without thinking of a friend's brother or cousin stationed there.

The war dominated every waking hour: there seemed no escape from it, for the simplest tasks of daily living were made difficult by its strictures, and the simplest wishes were frustrated by its demands. Worst of all was the tedium. Despite fêtes in support of the war, gaiety seemed a vanished element. No amount of dance music could make a young girl's heart sing when the young men who would have been her partners fought on distant battlefields, and since every gathering soon became an opportunity to compare scraps of news and to receive some reassurance from the worries of others, Gabriele soon dreaded the galas organized by Aunt Mat and the other women of the region, attending them as a duty, and hoping that her obedience to the seemingly trivial role she found herself occupying would count for something when the conflict finally ended.

Early predictions of a quick and victorious finish to the war gave way to more sober assessments of the South's position, and more than one leader, had he to do it all over again, might well have urged a different, and less belligerent, course.

But as though the summer skies of 1861 had been dominated by Homer's "red star that from his flaming hair shakes down disease, pestilence and war," as the summer drew to a close, the South prepared for a long siege, no less committed to its cause, but much more cognizant of its price.

As summer deepened, Gabriele slept restlessly, waking to humid heat that matched her spirits, and going about her tasks listlessly. The sewing in her basket looked mountainous, and suddenly distasteful. Her first enthusiasm for remaking her discarded clothes to give to needy others had long since left her; turning collars and cuffs and resetting hems was tedious work, and many an hour she longed for the frivolous needlepoint and embroidery with which she had once whiled away her time. But a dedication to duty and a sincere belief that this, too, helped the Confederate cause kept her at her work, although she could see no relationship between a dress for a husbandless woman down the road and the battles that same husband would soon fight.

Slaves at Felicity and on neighbouring plantations felt the tremors the war sent through the South: runaways became more frequent than usual, and although the pattern remained the same as always, with the runaways hiding out in the woods for a few days before negotiating their return, whenever a slave left a plantation, the alarm went out, and the patrols doubled their vigilance. Slaves who would not risk running away slowed down their work instead, and daily, the number reporting symptoms ranging from stomach aches to leg cramps rose.

"One of the best crops we've ever had, looks like, Mrs. LeGrange," Adams reported. "But if these slow-downs and illnesses keep up, I won't be able to keep enough hands in the field to work it."

"Do what you can to make them understand the Yankees won't arrive to free them any time soon," Aunt Mat said drily. "Though to tell you the truth, Mr. Adams, if I could get replacements—I'd send most of them to the North myself. Except for Letha and Jonas and Samson and Abigail—and some few others—they're not doing enough work to earn their keep."

"If those new laws hadn't been passed, I could let them have a dance," Adams said. "Break out some liquor and let them play until they got some of this discontent out of their systems—but it's not worth risking breaking the law, just to jolly the hands up a bit, so I'll have to see what sterner discipline will do."

"Nothing harsh, Mr. Adams, I won't have it," Aunt

Mat said. "You know my brother's feelings on that issue—and my nephew and niece feel just the same."

"I guess I can put some fear into 'em without going against you," Adams said. "But, Mrs. LeGrange—now's no time to be soft. The closer the war gets—the more disturbances we're going to have."

" 'Sufficient to each day is the evil thereof,' " Aunt Mat said. "Do the best you can—you can do no more than that."

Letha had her own views on the subject, views she shared with Gabriele one afternoon when they sat together shelling peas. Watching Letha's fingers popping bright green peas from the stiff pods, Gabriele thought of that long-ago discussion with her father when she begged him to free Veronique, and of that clause in the codicil of his will: "those who can bear the burden of being free."

"Letha," she said, "if you didn't live here at Felicity—where would you go?"

For a moment she heard nothing but the pop as a pod opened, followed by the rattle of peas into the pan. Then Letha laughed. "Law, chile, why you ask me a question like that? You know I'se rooted to this place just like them big oaks."

"If the North wins this war, Letha—you'll all be free. You'd want to go then, wouldn't you?"

Then Letha smiled, as though Gabriele's last words had opened a path into her heart. "So that's what's on yo' mind, chile. You thinking about freedom, and what all those people say." She leaned back in her rocker, the chair making a lazy song on the gallery floor. "I don't need some mens from far away to make me free, Miss Gabriele. I is free, free in the love of the Lord." She shook her head, her tignon making an arc of scarlet. "It's not up to me to tell him I cain't be a good person 'less he sets me free down here—I'se got to be a good person no matter where I is. I know that, Miss Gabriele. And so I is free."

"Oh, Letha," Gabriele said, jumping up and going to her old nurse. Her pan of shelled peas rolled one way, her basket of pods the other, but she ignored them both. Burying her head in Letha's lap, she began to cry. And as she felt Letha's big hand begin to stroke her, the familiar soothing touch that had calmed so many storms, she wondered at the power of the faith that made Letha so strong she had comfort for one whose life was free although she lived in slavery.

The one distraction during those long, hot days came from a distant relative of Mrs. LeBoeuf's who had arrived from New Orleans bearing with him a balloon and long experience in the aerial races that had become the rage in New Orleans the last several years.

"It sounds very interesting, don't you think, Gabriele?" Aunt Mat said after reading the invitation from Mrs. LeBoeuf to a demonstration of the balloon.

"Yes, of course," Gabriele answered. Her first impulse had been to beg off: Harold LeBoeuf's rash confidence in his charms had not diminished since he found himself one of the few young men remaining in the area, and she felt reluctant to place herself so near him for an entire afternoon. But the light in her aunt's usually tired eyes and the eagerness in her voice made Gabriele change her mind. I am not the only one who feels the heat and monotony, she thought, and Aunt Mat's duties are more numerous and more onerous than mine.

And so on the appointed day they dressed as for a fête: Aunt Mat had lightened her mourning for her brother to grey only when the first year had passed, but Gabriele wore a pale blue dress tied with deeper blue ribbons, with fresh white roses fastened at the waist and tucked beneath her bonnet's brim. The rare image of a dressed-up self in her mirror heartened her, and by the time they arrived at the LeBoeufs' plantation, where a throng of excited people filled the grounds, her spirits felt as though they already rode the silken wings of a balloon, and she pressed forward with as much enthusiasm as any of them.

The balloon, made of a linen and paper fabric gummed

for protection against moisture, stood out brilliantly against the pale blue sky. It had been dyed a deep violet, with designs of the Zodiac painted across it in silver. Long silk streamers ranging from the most delicate lavender to the darkest purple, interspersed with glittering silver ribbons, flowed from the wicker carriage suspended beneath, and below it, the machine that pumped hydrogen into the balloon finished its task, puffing the shimmering sides out to their fullest extension.

"It's beautiful!" Gabriele exclaimed. A sudden wish to be free of the earth and all its cares entered her. How would it be to sail above the tree tops, to skim over Bayou Teche and watch its waters sparkle far below? As though hydrogen filled her petticoats, making her, too, lighter than air, she felt detached from the scene around her. She heard the banter of the crowd, a burst of music from a band playing nearby. And just beyond the strange brightness that seemed to fill her vision, she saw movement, and colour. But for that one moment she felt lost in time, and space; within that gleaming capsule, she might find Alex St. Cyr.

Then a voice at her elbow, a hand on her arm—"Miss Cannon! How nice to see you," Harold LeBoeuf said. She turned to see him beaming at her, a tall, elegantly dressed man in tow. "This is my cousin Adolphe LeBoeuf," Harold said. "The balloonist, you know."

The balloonist bowed, the top of his head sweeping almost to the ground. His silk ascot, of the same shade as his balloon, also had Zodiac signs woven into the fabric; the strange symbols and the glittering excitement in the man's eyes increased Gabriele's feeling of detachment from the ordinary, and she stared at him, almost mesmerized by his dark gaze.

"I went up with him yesterday," Harold said. "He let me steer for a while—said I have a natural aptitude for such enterprises."

"And you, Miss Cannon," Adolphe said. "Do you wish to go up in my balloon?"

"I should like to very much," Gabriele said. "But my aunt has quite enough to try her without watching me vanish into the atmosphere—"

"It is much safer than it looks," Adolphe LeBoeuf said. "Although I will confess that I let people believe I risk my life every time I go up."

He continued to talk, gradually raising his voice so that a larger crowd could hear him, and putting on what Gabriele privately thought of as a performance rather than a conversation, so carefully planned did his pauses for effect seem, and so carefully rehearsed the details of narrow escapes that brought gasps from the ladies and envious glances from the men.

Harold comes by his dramatics and conceit naturally, Gabriele thought, moving away slightly and turning her attention on the balloon bouncing against its ropes. Two slaves leaned against a fence separating the lawn from the pasture beyond: as soon as the crowd's attention centred on Adolphe and his stories, they slipped beneath the lower rail into the field where they squatted within feet of the wicker carriage.

Now what are they doing, I wonder? Gabriele thought, but at that moment the musicians began another tune, a lively polka that set feet tapping and impelled some of the younger members of the crowd to start an impromptu dance on the smooth green lawn. "Dance with me, Miss Cannon," Harold said, offering Gabriele his arm, but she shook her head and went to stand at Aunt Mat's side.

"I wonder if those men are going to help Mr. LeBoeuf," she said, nodding toward the two slaves who still squatted near the balloon, their eyes never leaving its billowing sides.

Then Adolphe LeBoeuf began walking toward his balloon, back very straight, head very high, barely acknowledging the good wishes and cheers greeting him at every step. "He thinks well of himself," Aunt Mat observed. "He almost struts!"

"With good reason," Harold said, suddenly bobbing up

in front of them. "He's won more balloon races than any-one in New Orleans—"

A sharp cry, followed by shouts and a mêlée of voices, interrupted him. "But what are they doing?" Gabriele cried. "Oh, look! Those slaves—they're jumping into the carriage!"

"Let me through!" Harold shouted, trying to push past the row of people in front of them. He finally saw an opening and leapt through it, reaching the fence just as one of the slaves cut free the last of the mooring ropes, and the balloon began to rise in the air.

The other slave held Adolphe LeBoeuf around the neck, pulling his head back so that the purple ascot floated up and blew over it, making a mask. The silver zodiac signs sparkled in the sun like real stars; then the wind lifted the ascot, and they saw Adolphe's frightened face, reddened by the pressure against his throat, lit by wildly staring eyes.

Now the slave with the knife put it against Adolphe's throat and made a gesture whose meaning was all too clear. He said something the crowd could not hear, and then slowly motioned to his fellow slave to let Adolphe go. Struggling for breath, Adolphe staggered to the balloon's controls and began to fiddle with them. The balloon's ascent slowed, became steady, and the carriage, which had been swaying violently, swung less and less, until it hung beneath the brilliant purple and silver globe like a small appendage to a floating moon.

The crowd let out its breath in a mutual sigh, a soft suspiration sounding as though the balloon itself had sprung a leak that let its warm gases ooze slowly into the atmosphere. Harold, who had been staring skyward, whirled around and clambered to the top rung of the fence.

"I need some men with horses," he said. "My cousin's course will take them across the Teche some ten miles from here—he expects to touch down at the Goudeaus'— we need to have people waiting there."

"But won't he change it?"

"Won't they force him to go another way?"

Cries and questions added to the confusion; men were already running toward their horses, and someone else shouted over and over again that they must ride into the station and send telegraph messages up and down the line warning people to watch for the fugitives and their captive.

Now the balloon had become but a bright speck against the clouds piled up on the horizon. It shimmered, a small purple object hanging in the summer sky. Then it vanished behind a smoke-puff of thick clouds, and Gabriele felt all the afternoon's brightness vanish with it, leaving behind only heat and worry.

"I'm terribly sorry," she said to Harold as he dashed past her. "It's so dreadful—"

"They'll be caught," Harold said. He looked older now, with grim lines around his mouth that made a web of years. "The balloon won't stay up more than a few hours —and when it comes down, we'll catch them."

The crowd milled about, discussing over and over again the sudden events which had so changed the afternoon. Some, at the urging of Mrs. LeBoeuf, moved to the refreshment tables and stood sipping iced punch and eating small cakes, but most of the guests, with anxious glances at the cluster of slaves standing waiting with their horses and carriages, made hurried farewells and hastened homeward, oppressed by the same thoughts Aunt Mat voiced to Gabriele.

"An escape always stirs up the other slaves," she said, guiding Gabriele toward their hostess. "I don't know how they get word out so fast, but even before we get home, ours will know about this. Adams will have his hands full tonight, no question about it. I won't be much of an ally, but I'll be something. We'd best get home right away, Gabriele."

They said their goodbyes and had turned to leave when Harold hurried up to them. "You're not leaving?" he said.

"We must," Aunt Mat said.

"Then let me escort you," he said. "Felicity's in a direct line with the balloon's course—if it were to come down there, there could be all sorts of trouble."

"Now, stop frightening Gabriele," Aunt Mat said. "We've got Adams to protect us, Harold, and some loyal slaves yet. Besides, I wouldn't want to take you from your mother—she needs you here."

He followed them to their carriage, repeating his offer every step of the way, but finally they were settled and Jonas manoeuvred the carriage forward, steering it expertly through the other vehicles parked nearby.

"Well," Aunt Mat said, when they had reached the open road. "That's an afternoon that didn't end as I expected." She looked at Gabriele sharply. "Don't let your imagination run away with you, Gabriele. Harold likes to dramatize things, you know. I imagine that balloon'll be down before dusk, and it will all be over by suppertime."

"I imagine so," Gabriele said, then lapsed into silence, looking through her veil at the passing landscape, and thinking that its bedraggled dusty surface looked exactly the way her spirits felt. In all the commotion following the escape, she had heard no one comment on the slaves themselves. Did no one else sympathize, she wondered? Did no one else see the irony of their situation—now so free, sailing in such splendour above the earth, but only capture or death their sure destination?

She shook her head, trying to dislodge the unhappy thoughts settled there, but to no avail. When they reached Felicity, she went straight to her room while Aunt Mat went off in search of Adams. Nor was she surprised when Lucie tapped on her door with a message that Aunt Mat would dine in her room on a tray, and asked Gabriele to do the same: neither had a heart for conversation, and as Gabriele knew, in times of unrest, Adams liked to get even the house hands back to their quarters as early as possible, so that the guards he set could keep better watch.

The night seemed long enough to make at least three: Gabriele heard each quarter hour strike, and several times left her bed to go out on the balcony, searching the moon-lit skies in vain for the errant balloon. But though clouds tethered with moonbeams sailed past, she saw nothing more: a quiet and subdued Lucie brought her coffee but no news the next morning, and she went down to break-fast with an anxious heart.

Aunt Mat looked no better than Gabriele felt, but after breakfast they went up to the sewing room and bent to their tasks, the only sound breaking their concentration a query from one to the other about some garment and the reply.

Toward noon they heard a horse trotting fast up the drive: their sewing fell from their hands and they flew to the window, watching Adams come running around the house to greet the rider. They could not hear the words, but Adams' face frightened them, and with Gabriele quick behind her, Aunt Mat ran out of the room and down the stairs, throwing open the big front door just as Adams came up the gallery steps.

"They've found them," he said. "Just about where Har-old LeBoeuf said they'd come down—"

"Are they—safe?" Aunt Mat said.

"LeBoeuf's throat was cut minutes before they hit the ground," Adams said. "And the crowd waiting for them hanged the slaves not much later."

"God in Heaven!" Aunt Mat said, crossing herself quickly. She reached out a hand to Gabriele, and then suddenly sank toward the gallery floor, saved from a fall only by Adams' leap forward.

"Get your aunt's smelling salts," Adams said, half-carry-ing, half-guiding Aunt Mat toward the front door. Gabriele flew past them, running up the stairs and down the hall to her aunt's bedroom. Even as her hand closed on the vial of smelling salts standing on a table next to her aunt's bed, her eyes fell on a familiar picture set in the very centre of Aunt Mat's dressing table, where her eyes, seek-ing her own image in the mirror, could not fail to see it, too.

Gabriele did not remember her uncle Louis LeGrange. She had been only three years old when he died, but looking at the face in the picture, the delicate tints of the miniature still fresh, she had a sudden feeling of *déjà vu*, as though she had stood beside Aunt Mat, looking at this very picture, when word came that Louis LeGrange was dead. She shivered, crossing herself instinctively at the rabbit running over her grave, and pushing down thoughts of her brother's picture, at almost exactly this uncle's age, that looked back at her from her own dressing table, she picked up the smelling salts and went back downstairs.

Aunt Mat had already revived, but she allowed Gabriele to hold the salts under her nose and breathed deeply, then sat quietly waiting for the volatile spirits to take effect. "Well, Adams," she said, taking the arm he offered and rising carefully from her chair. "It's begun, I suppose."

"Begun, Mrs. LeGrange?" he said.

"The cracks in the surface," Aunt Mat said. "The fissures that break civilization's smooth finish and let all the ugly demons out."

"Feelings are running high, Mrs. LeGrange," Adams said. "Not that I hold with such summary action—"

Aunt Mat smiled, a smile so bleak and mirthless that Gabriele once again felt a shiver run down her back. "But then they never ask those of us who don't agree, do they, Adams?" And then, with some of her usual energy, she turned to Gabriele. "We must go to Mrs. LeBoeuf immediately after luncheon, Gabriele. Poor woman, what a terrible thing to have to deal with."

The mechanics of death had already begun to operate by the time they reached the LeBoeufs', and Gabriele soon felt useless. She slipped out of the hot parlour to the cooler gallery, standing against a column at the far end and staring unseeingly into the garden. She tried to let her mind go blank, to become an empty void like the endless blue sky stretched so tightly over the earth, shutting summer's heat into that confined space. But images rose in front of her—a silver and purple balloon, manned by a man with a bleeding throat. Two dark bodies, swaying slowly from twisted ropes.

If only Tom were here, she thought. He could make me feel better. Or Alex. But Tom was on his way to Virginia, travelling further from them every hour. And Alex had vanished, disappearing as completely as though he had taken a balloon to the outer reaches of space, to sail there like another Flying Dutchman on his ghostly ship.

She had never felt so alone as she did at that moment, nor so empty. And then she remembered what Aunt Mat had said to Adams that morning, and she could put names to at least two of the demons who had crept through that first violent break. One was called fear and the other was called loneliness, and if there were more to follow, she had better learn to deal with these here and now. Resolutely, she made herself remember whose sorrow they had come to assuage, and re-entered the house to offer whatever services might be required.

Darkness closed around the LeBoeuf house, and in the front parlour, candles glowed around Adolphe LeBoeuf's bier. And out in the barn, its purple and silver wings folded and dulled, the balloon sat in an empty stall, its promises of glory forgotten, and its carriage stained with blood.

Chapter Fourteen

"Do ask someone else to play so I may dance with you," Harold LeBoeuf said, leaning over the big vase filled with a blaze of autumn leaves and gazing into Gabriele's eyes.

"I should be a poor hostess indeed if I asked a guest to play so that I may dance," Gabriele said, leafing through the music to find another lively tune.

The opening chords of "Monsieur Banjo" drowned out Harold's next words: he waited a moment more, and when Gabriele kept her attention on the music in front of her, he shrugged and walked away.

"It's too bad Gabriele doesn't care for Harold," Mrs. Robin said to Aunt Mat behind the cover of her fan. "I know he's a little younger than she is, but he looks splendid in his uniform—and he certainly won't even look at anyone else."

"Gabriele seems proof against Cupid's arrows," Aunt Mat said. "Heaven knows she's had enough suitors in this last year—gentlemen from all over the state, some of them quite persistent—"

"I thought for a while that she might be interested in Mr. St. Cyr," Mrs. Robin said, her eyes betraying the curiosity lying behind her lightly spoken words.

"Did you really?" Aunt Mat said. "I saw no sign of that. Though I suppose he is the sort to turn a young girl's head. He's handsome enough, and with that dashing kind of grace—"

"He reminded me of your Louis," Mrs. Robin said. "Something of the same air—"

A twist of pain distorted Aunt Mat's face, and her friend reached out her hand. "Forgive me, Mat. I don't mean to bring up an old sorrow—"

"Louis has been dead over fifteen years," Aunt Mat said. "You'd think I could hear his name without feeling pain—" She shook her head, her eyes on her niece's face. "But I don't know—a man like Louis—once you've loved him—you can't get him out of your heart somehow, no matter how hard you try."

"Then it's just as well Gabriele did not fall in love with Alex St. Cyr," Mrs. Robin said. "You know what a weathervane he is—changeable as the climate!"

"I'm glad Gabriele isn't in love with anyone," Aunt Mat said. "I wouldn't want her marrying somebody about to march off to war." She stopped when she saw her friend's face. "I'm sorry, I know Dorothea is to marry next week—"

"Yes, and her groom will have but three days before he goes back to his troops. But she says this is what will make her happy, and who am I to deny her that chance, Mat?"

Aunt Mat bent and kissed Mrs. Robin's cheek, her lips brushing against a tear that glistened there. "Well, I suppose Dorothea must take her happiness where she finds it, my dear." But as she went away to supervise the serving of the supper, she took comfort in the thought that thus far, there were no signs Gabriele would do anything so rash.

From her seat at the piano, Gabriele had seen her aunt and Mrs. Robin talking: their looks and gestures gave them away, and she knew they talked about her. Mrs. Robin is matchmaking and Aunt Mat is being polite, but I can see from her face that she doesn't want to hear what Mrs. Robin is saying—there, she is leaving now, thank goodness, Mrs. Robin can make a match for someone else.

Her fingers crashed down on the keys of the final chord,

and the couples dancing on the parlour's bare floor broke into applause. Aunt Mat came into the doorway, inviting them into the dining room where the supper was laid, and as the crowd moved slowly toward the door, Harold Le-Boeuf slipped up beside Gabriele.

"Promise to have supper with me," Harold said. "There's a wonderful October moon—we can sit on the gallery, Miss Cannon—it's lovely out there."

"I'm sorry," Gabriele said. "But I can't." She walked past him, knowing that he stared after her as she went through the door. Aunt Mat's eyes flickered from Gabriele to Harold, and then back to her niece's face. For a moment, she looked as though she might speak, but then she sighed instead, and turned back to consult with Jonas about the carving of the ham.

"It's such a pleasure to be at a party in this grand house again," Dorothea Robin said to Gabriele. "Paul says he feels as though this party is for us, for everyone is congratulating him and taking such an interest in our plans." She looked up at the young man beside her, and Gabriele, seeing the look he gave Dorothea in return, felt suddenly shut out.

"Yes, it's so wonderful that you are getting married," Gabriele said. They don't even hear me, she thought, moving through the crowd. And why should they, when their time together is so precious and so brief? Dorothea and Paul's was but one of a dozen or more weddings to be held this month: mothers all over the region were drawing on all their ingenuity to stage celebrations befitting a daughter's marriage despite the shortage of time to prepare.

War heightens everything, Gabriele thought, taking her place at the punch bowl and ladling Aunt Mat's famous syllabub into silver cups. Some of these marriages, like Dorothea's and Paul's, would seem right no matter when they were held. But others would surely not have been undertaken in peacetime, when glamorous uniforms have been put aside for less flattering garb.

She thought of Alex, sailing the Gulf waters under the

great October moon. How far away he is—and really, I only think I know he is somewhere out there, running the blockade. He could be anywhere—I don't even have his letters, as I did last year. Nor does he have mine.

As though to underscore the thought forming in her mind, she heard a snatch of talk from nearby.

"Your letters encourage me mightily," a soldier said to his supper partner. "They don't come regularly, you know—I won't have one for weeks, and then a courier brings them all in a batch."

Gabriele didn't try to hear the girl's reply. Her mind, stimulated by the soldier's words, seized on a new idea. I can write to Alex, she thought, excitement rising in her like the drift of candle smoke floating up into the air. And I will.

She began that very night, and after that did not miss a day. Putting her thoughts on paper seemed to bring Alex closer, and each time she finished a letter, her faith grew stronger that he would indeed return. The daily letters soon made an impressive stack, locked away in her desk drawer. She often took them out and read them over, finding herself surprised sometimes by how much they revealed.

If I am never able to give these to him, she thought, tucking them back into place, and if he never learns all these things about me, these letters will still not have been written in vain. For they are helping me see into my soul, they are keeping track of all the changes I have made. Like any journal, they are recording where I have been, and where I am going, and what I have observed along the way.

Aunt Mat thought she noticed a new seriousness in Gabriele, a new dedication to her work. She sewed for hours without complaint, and joined her aunt on errands of mercy in the neighbourhood, taking food to the sick and offering comfort to those families who had already lost a son, husband or brother to the war. It was as though each day must be filled with purpose, so that when she sat down at night to write her letter would reflect hours well spent in tasks that, if they did not deflect the effects of the war, at least made their burden easier.

Gabriele's life became confined to a circumference not much beyond Felicity's fields: only when she rode Brandy did she seek a wider range, rambling down plantation roads or galloping on a fine, clear stretch until she could feel the cobwebs blow out of her head. These rides restored her; they became a source of renewed energy and quietly cheerful moods, so that if the weather soured, and she could not ride, she moped until the rain let up, and she and Brandy could take to the road.

She's growing up, Aunt Mat thought. Turning into a woman Oliver would be proud of, if only he could see her. If Aunt Mat had not been so burdened with the plantation, she might have ascribed her niece's occasional pensiveness and sudden tears to their true cause. But needing Gabriele's support more every day, she closed her eyes to any sign that Gabriele's heart had room for anything or anyone other than duty toward Felicity and prayers for Tom.

And so the autumn passed. Some few events lifted themselves above the routine: on November 6, Jefferson Davis, who had been serving as Provisional President, was elected to a six-year term as head of the permanent Confederate government. His presidential message to the new session of the Confederate Congress on November 19, quoted widely in the Southern press, had an optimistic spirit: the year so far "is such as should fill the hearts of our people with gratitude to Providence," he said, pointing out good crops, satisfactory military operations, an increasingly effective army, and hope on the financial front as reasons for confidence.

Militarily the year had been characterized by sporadic skirmishes, advances and retreats, turn-about victories and defeats. Neither the Federal government nor the Confederate one seemed closer to its goal: the Union had been broken, the new nation was not yet free. On both sides, families had suffered the loss of husbands and fathers, brothers and sons. For them the war was over. For thousands more, it had yet to begin.

An otherwise quiet Christmas season at Felicity had but one memorable event for Gabriele. As she sat at her piano on the last day of the year, trying to play the old Christmas favourites with some semblance of joy, Letha came into the room, a small, sealed package in her hand.

"For you, Miss Gabriele," she said, handing the package to Gabriele and standing stolidly by.

Gabriele turned the package over and saw her name, written in a familiar hand. "Where did you get this?" she said, half-rising from the bench.

"One of them boats on the bayou," Letha said. "Man come up to the house, give it to me." Letha eyed the package, then looked directly into Gabriele's face. "Miss Gabriele—he say not to tell anyone else about it. But if that package means trouble—I'se going to have to tell yo' aunt."

"It doesn't mean trouble, Letha," Gabriele said. She could not keep her eyes from shining, or her mouth from a joyful smile. She tucked the package into her pocket and closed the piano. "I'll just take it to my room to open it—"

Letha's hand closed over her arm, keeping her there. "Miss Gabriele—you goin' to tell me who it's from, you know. Else I got to tell yo' aunt."

"Later, Letha," Gabriele said, shaking off Letha's hand. She almost ran from the parlour, feeling Letha's eyes following her until she disappeared from view at the curve of the stairs. The moments before she could open the package seemed the longest she had ever had to endure, but at last she reached her room, turned the key in the lock, and settled into her rocker, pulling it into the window to save lighting the lamp.

A letter fell into her lap as she ripped the seal from the package, and she read it first, hardly stopping to comprehend it, but going quickly to the very end before beginning it all over again.

"My dearest Gabriele," the letter began. "I will not apologize for addressing you thus: to impose upon myself the conventional restrictions when your face has been my constant vision, your smile my constant joy, your eyes my constant inspiration, and your concern for me my constant hope these last trying months is to ask more than I am ready to bear.

"There may be men more foolish than I, but I doubt it. When I think of the great gift I threw back in your face the last night we met, I wonder that I have sense enough to get through one day—but there, I shall not berate an impulse I did not then understand. I thought I did not want you to love me because I did not deserve your love. Not until I had spent hours alone, thinking in ways I have never thought before, did I see how presumptuous and arrogant such a position was.

"Who am I to dictate to you in matters such as love? You, whose every breath brings happiness to those about you—whose gentle care and loving heart made your brother Tom the envy of every man he knew. It is I who am the novice, who must be schooled in the ways of love. Too late I realized I had found in you the perfect tutrix—too late I realized what I had almost lost. I say almost because I believe I can trust your loyalty as well as your love. I do not think you will have abandoned me, my dearest one—I can only hope and pray that I am right.

"I have long wanted to write these things to you, but until I could be certain the letter would reach you, I forbore. Now I can send you this letter, as well as a memento which represents but a minuscule part of what I will someday give you, and is only the most minute token of my very great love and esteem."

With fingers she could hardly make obey her will, Gabriele opened the small tissue-wrapped package to find a gold locket on a fine gold chain. Pearls rimmed the locket, and it had an amethyst set in its centre. The workmanship matched that of any jewellery Gabriele owned, and she lifted it from its wrappings, feeling its solid weight in her hand.

She pressed the small spring that released the catch and opened the locket, drawing her breath in sharply as she saw the two miniatures inside. Alex—and herself. She stared at their two faces, feeling suddenly as though she had somehow acted in another life, and had given this small portrait to Alex as a pledge of her love. A simpler life, a surer life, where all these doubts did not cloud her decision, and she had only to listen to her heart.

Still holding the locket, she picked up Alex's letter and read on.

"You will be surprised, I know, when you see the portraits the locket contains. And I pray you will not be offended. As to how these miniatures came to be, the answer is as simple as the designs of love can make it. The afternoon of the ring tourney, when I knew your attention would be fully engaged, I hired an artist to sketch you, and to later paint this miniature so that I might have an image of you with me always. I cannot make myself apologize for this liberty; it has meant far too much to me to have your dear face so near.

"And now I come to the part that is the hardest for me —to answer the questions I know must be in your mind. Did I love you so long ago? And if so, why did I not speak then?

"The answer to the first question is this: I do not know whether I can identify the emotion I felt for you from our first meeting as love—love, it seems to me, must grow as one's knowledge of the other person grows. Love comes from shared moments, shared ideas. Now I can say I love you, for that early attraction has had a base upon which to stand, and time to explore all the avenues you have so generously opened into your mind and heart. But surely, when I saw you standing in Felicity's hall, I felt—how can I express it, Gabriele? I felt that I had come home, although that was the first time I had stepped through Felic-

ity's doors. Tom had of course talked about his home and
family a great deal—I think he sensed that I had not had
the same sort of experience, and yearned to hear as much
as he cared to tell me of his. When I saw your face, it was
as though all the sweetness, all the happiness, that Tom
told me of had gathered itself to centre on you. Came
from you. Is you. I was much shaken by the strength of
my feelings—and so I'm afraid I adopted my usual mode
of somewhat cynical sophistication, thinking it would protect me against this sudden sentimental attack.

"Did you see through me? I should so love to know!
And other times, when I treated you as Tom did, thinking
perhaps what I felt after all was the kind of love I would
have given to the sister I never had. What a liar I am, and
how hard I tried to fool myself! Until I could hide from
the truth no longer, and knew that no matter what, I must
tell you of my love.

"Which brings me to the second question—why did I
not speak earlier? When I learned of the many suitors trying to court you in the months following your father's
death, I berated myself over and over again, telling myself
that he who does not pursue his dearest wish with his
whole heart deserves all the misery its loss might bring.
Pride held me back then, Gabriele. I did not believe it fair
to thrust such a serious decision upon you then—your
grief was still too fresh, your father's loss still uppermost in
your heart and mind. And by the time I might have spoken—well, you know the situation then. Pride again, of
course, but this time a little better placed. The scorn and
insult heaped upon my family would have touched you,
too. What sort of love is that, that would expose his beloved to such pain?

"But now I have hope again, for my enterprise is not
entirely without success. There are quarters in which the
name Alex St. Cyr is spoken with respect: thus is my small
private objective met while I pursue the greater ones more
relevant to the South's cause.

"It is with great reluctance that I part with your portrait, but I do not wish it to be found on me if my enterprise ever comes to an unhappy end. I do not expect it to —rather, I wake each morning believing that the passage of another day will bring me that much closer to reunion with you, and I go to sleep each night confident that the sweet dreams of you which accompany my slumber will at some future time become true.

"My messenger departs very soon now, and I must hasten to give this to him. Please believe that I love you above everything in the world, and that you and your concerns are constantly in my heart.

"Devotedly, Alex."

There has never been such a letter, Gabriele thought, raising it to her lips. Just think, after all these weeks of writing letters to him, I finally have one from him to answer. Her fingers ran over the locket's surface, gently caressing Alex's face. I feel dishonourable keeping this from Aunt Mat, she thought. And yet if I tell her, she will have so many questions—it will be as though I have invited her into our own private place.

No, I won't tell her, and I will make certain Letha does not. Alex is very far away, and he will be for a long time yet. If he returns—*when* he returns—that will be time enough to make our love public, and endure the interest of our friends and relatives that, while kindly meant, can make lovers feel as though the world is truly a stage, and everyone is waiting for them to take their place.

And so, reluctantly, but knowing that she must, she locked both letter and locket next to the stack of letters to Alex that she added to each day. Now, she thought, slipping the key back into its hiding place, I must go ask Letha not to tell Aunt Mat—I must make her see that it is all right not to, even if in my own mind, I am not that sure.

She found Letha at the linen press counting sheets, and as she spoke, her voice unconsciously slipped back into the intonations of her childhood, when Letha took delight in granting Gabriele every wish her heart could make.

"Letha, I have a favour to ask of you—"

"If'n it's about the package I brung you, I don't want to hear nothin' about it," Letha said.

"It's just that I don't want you to tell Aunt Mat."

Letha's eyes fixed Gabriele, seeing past her anxiousness into her heart. "That package—Mr. Alex sent it, didn't he?"

"Oh, Letha—"

Letha came forward and put her arms around Gabriele, pulling her close. A familiar smell of starch and vetiver, a memory of this woman who had been mother and nurse and guardian and guide, swept over Gabriele, and she clung to Letha's neck, sobbing.

"I know whose letters and packages from Paris last winter made you smile," Letha said. "And that package done been addressed in that same hand."

"He's so far away, Letha! And in terrible danger every day—I don't want to have to talk about him—I don't want Aunt Mat watching me, and all the ladies of the neighbourhood clucking over me whenever I look the least bit sad—"

"Now, chile," Letha said, her big hand patting Gabriele's head. "I guess we all got enough to worry about without me spoiling your little bit of joy. If'n it makes you happy to keep Mr. Alex a secret—you go right ahead. My memory ain't as good as it used to be, and Miz LeGrange, she's always fussing at me for talking more than I ought to anyway. I won't say nothin'."

"Oh, Letha, thank you!" Gabriele said. She kissed Letha's cheek, a smile breaking through her tears.

"Hold on, chile. You got to promise me somethin', too." Letha's right hand closed around Gabriele's, holding it palm to palm. "You got to promise me you won't never do nothin' foolish, like runnin' off to meet that young man somewheres."

"I would never do that!"

"I don't think you would," Letha said. "But folks do

strange things when times get hard. You promise me any-how, Miss Gabriele."

"All right—I promise."

"That's good," Letha said. "Something you got to re-member—love is one thing, but promises is another. You're a Cannon, and Cannons, they don't ever make promises they don't mean to keep."

"I'll keep it, Letha," Gabriele said. She hugged her old nurse, her spirits completely restored. "And anyway—he's going to come here someday, Letha, just you wait and see. He'll ask for my hand properly—and then what a wedding we'll have!"

"That'll be a glad day, Miss Gabriele," Letha said. "A glad day indeed."

Her mind at rest, Gabriele went back to her room and took out paper and pen. Her answer to Alex's letter grew beneath her hand, and although she knew that the letter's destination was no further than that locked drawer, still, she felt that somehow, its message would wing silently and swiftly across the miles that separated them to Alex's wait-ing heart.

A letter arrived from Mr. Guillot in the middle of Febru-ary, advising Gabriele that she should come to New Or-leans to consult with him about the sale of some of their property. "I believe we have waited as long as is judicious," the lawyer wrote. "And in all confidence I must tell you that I will not be in New Orleans much longer—if I am to oversee the sale of these assets, then negotiations must be accomplished very soon."

"Mr. Guillot does not seem sanguine about New Or-leans' future," Aunt Mat said, handing the letter back to Gabriele after reading it.

"He is only carrying out decisions Tom and I made be-fore Tom went off to war," Gabriele said. "I will feel much better knowing that the work is finally done—will you come with me, Aunt Mat? I plan to leave in two days' time—"

Her aunt's expression stopped her, and Gabriele realized that the usual order of their lives had been reversed. Instead of asking Aunt Mat's permission to make the journey, she had informed her of her plans. She almost spoke, thinking to put the proposition in its old form. But then Aunt Mat smiled.

"You are all grown up, Gabriele. Making your plans like a regular woman of business—no, I won't go to New Orleans now. The weather is terrible, and I'm needed here. Will you open the house, do you think?"

"I won't be there that long," Gabriele said. "The St. Louis Hotel is quite comfortable." She anticipated her aunt's next comment. "But, Aunt Mat—I shouldn't travel alone?"

"Of course not," Aunt Mat said. "Mrs. Robin's cousin, the one who spends the winter with them, you know, might be glad of a little journey." She looked at Gabriele, raising her eyebrows the least little bit. "We should give her a little something, of course. Poor dear, she really has nothing of her own."

"Will you send a note asking her, please?" Gabriele said. "While I make my arrangements?"

"I'll write now," Aunt Mat said. She rose and kissed Gabriele. "You're a diplomat, my dear, like your father. And I'm very glad that you are."

She said no more, but went to her desk and began her note while Gabriele sought out Jonas. *Aunt Mat is glad I am able to be more responsible for myself, but she appreciates my consulting her,* she thought. *Thank goodness we understand each other so well—it would be perfectly wretched if she refused to let me grow up!*

Jonas rode away through pouring rain to book Gabriele's passage on the packet to New Orleans, and Gabriele went to her room to sort out the clothes she would take. *This is the worst possible time for a journey to New Orleans,* she thought. *It can be freezing one day and balmy the next—whatever I take, I probably shall not be suitably dressed.* But then the excitement of the prospec-

tive journey infected her, and she hummed while she went
through her armoire, thinking that even if the purpose of
this trip was business, still, it made a happy disruption of
the dull winter routine.

The journey from New Iberia to New Orleans over the
inland route seemed both strange and familiar: the landscape slipping by on either side of the bayous and rivers
looked just the same, but the burden of responsibility now
resting on her alone, made Gabriele feel as though she
undertook the trip for the very first time.

Miss Hebert, Mrs. Robin's cousin, proved an agreeable
companion. She did not intrude herself upon Gabriele, yet
always appeared ready to provide conversation and company should Gabriele want it. "It's sad, really," Gabriele
wrote in her daily letter to Alex. "I can't help but think
that such agreeableness comes from the necessity of living
off the bounty of others, and not necessarily because Miss
Hebert's disposition is so easy in itself. But we get along
quite well, and she is delighted that she will be free to visit
old friends in New Orleans while I see to my affairs. I wish
I could consult Tom before all this is made final, but he
trusts my judgement, and I shall just have to hope that his
trust is not misplaced . . ."

Gabriele and Miss Hebert settled into a suite at the St.
Louis Hotel, and while Miss Hebert sent cards around to
her friends, Gabriele made an appointment with Mr. Guillot, and then went to see Veronique. Walking briskly down
Chartres Street, she perceived the difference in the passing
scene. Where not too many months before the French
Quarter had been filled with gaiety and life, now she
passed empty shops and signs that already the city felt the
pinch of war. There seemed to be more aimless people on
the street, as though whatever purpose their lives had had
was now forgotten. And although music and laughter still
spilled from behind café doors, Gabriele fancied that even
these bright sounds seemed touched with a hectic fever.

When she sighted Veronique's shop, she almost turned back, so fearful was she that Veronique, too, had changed.

But when she pushed the door open and heard the silvery tinkle of the bell, reassurance flooded through her, for here, all was the same. The same stacks of fabric, the same busy sounds. Whir of sewing machine, snip of scissors. "Veronique!" Gabriele called. "It's Gabriele—where are you?"

"Gabriele!" Veronique appeared in the doorway leading into the other room, standing a moment with her hand over her heart, and then coming forward quickly to take Gabriele into her arms. "How you startled me, Gabriele! But when did you arrive in New Orleans—are you here for long?"

"Yesterday afternoon late—and only for a few days," Gabriele said. "I'm here on business—Mr. Guillot is ready to sell some property for us—and I have to approve of his plans."

"I was just going to have coffee and calas," Veronique said. "Let's go into my parlour—we can catch up all the news."

Veronique's living quarters, occupying the other half of the cottage, though simply furnished, had a certain flair that Gabriele attributed to Veronique's own sense of style. An arrangement of dried flowers in a bright blue pitcher, an intricate quilt used as a wall hanging—everywhere Gabriele looked she found something to delight her eye. "It's perfect, Veronique," she said. "Like playing dolls, it must be, to have this sweet little house—your own business—"

"It all goes so well that I haven't stopped holding my breath," Veronique said. She brought a tray of coffee and rice cakes and set it on the table in front of Gabriele.

"And you are so stylish!" Gabriele said. "Look at that detail on your collar—you make me feel quite dowdy and countrified."

"Nonsense," Veronique said. She studied Gabriele's costume. "All that jacket needs is an adjustment of the lapels

—trim added to the sleeve—if you have time while you're in the city, I could do some small alterations for you."

"Of course it would be lovely to be in style," Gabriele said. She picked up her cup, watching the light shine through the translucent porcelain. "But it seems somehow —wrong—to bother about the set of a collar or the trim on a sleeve when Farragut's fleet sits in the Gulf like a great whale about to swallow us up!"

"And yet—this winter has been one of New Orleans' gayest, according to my customers," Veronique said. "Balls, plays, concerts—all going forward at an astonishing pace."

"There have been an unusual amount of entertainments in the country, too," Gabriele said. "Aunt Mat says when there is widespread trouble, as there is now, people want to cling together—to reassure themselves that they are doing as well—or at least no worse—as other people are."

"Mrs. LeGrange continues in good health?" Veronique said. As always when she mentioned that name her face showed her tension.

"You know Aunt Mat. She has never been presented with a duty she could not carry out, or a responsibility too heavy for her to carry. She is busy from early morning until bedtime—but she seems to be in excellent health."

"Does she ever speak of me?"

"Never," Gabriele said. "Oh—yes—just a few weeks ago —your name did come up, in connection with something so foolish—so almost—repellent—that I'd quite forgotten it."

"What?" Veronique asked.

"Colette is to have a child at last," Gabriele said. "Sometime in the late spring, I believe." She saw Veronique's face and shook her head. "I am too stupid—I should not have brought this up."

"No—not at all. That is all behind me—it is just that the sudden mention of her name—reminded me of something I hope one day to completely forget."

"It's really nothing," Gabriele said.

"Tell me."

"Oh, very well! But it is so silly—it seems that Colette has—blamed you for her inability to have a child."

"Me!" Veronique said. "I have not even been at Felicity for over a year!"

"She accuses you of using voodoo against her—says you escaped by means of those black arts—oh, Veronique, I told you it is all so foolish!"

"But she believes this," Veronique said. "You must understand that, Gabriele. She believes what she says."

"What difference does that make?" Gabriele said. "At any rate, she boasts that charms the *traiteur* at the Robins' made warded off your evil spell, and that is why she now carries a child."

"How do you know this?" Veronique said. "Who would have told you?"

Gabriele blushed and looked away. "You know my bad habit of listening to conversations not meant for my ears, Veronique. I heard Abigail and Aunt Mat talking—and naturally, when I heard your name—I listened."

"I'm glad you did," Veronique said. "I shall have to—protect myself."

"Protect yourself? Against what?"

"Gabriele. The charms the *traiteur* woman made—they would be against me, don't you see?"

"But they have no power!"

"My head says they don't," Veronique said. "My heart isn't so sure."

She refilled their cups, absently stirring a spoon of sugar into hers. "I realize how absurd this sounds to you, Gabriele. And I am appalled myself at my reaction, that I can't just—laugh at such nonsense." She fingered a small gold cross hanging from a fine chain around her neck. "I think I have rooted the last legacy of slavery from my soul —and it rears up again."

"Veronique—please don't make more of this than it is," Gabriele said. "Colette is a very emotional woman who enjoys bringing attention to herself. She says whatever will keep everyone stirred up—I assure you, she has created such a commotion that we will all be thoroughly relieved when that baby arrives!"

"You're right, of course," Veronique said. "I shall think no more about it." She rose and went to a delicately carved desk in the corner of the room. Opening it, she removed a slender stack of letters tied with a scarlet ribbon. She untied the bow, riffled through the letters, selected one and brought it back to the table. "Here's a letter from Tom that came last week," she said. "He says that he wishes you knew my whereabouts, and hopes I can find some way to get word to you." She looked up at Gabriele and smiled. "So we are all together in our secret now, Gabriele. I will write to him and tell him that you discovered me a long time ago."

"We heard from Tom just before I left home to come here," Gabriele said. "I always feel better when I get a letter—until I remember how long it has taken to reach me—and how much will have transpired since he wrote it."

"I know," Veronique said. "It is—very hard, having so little information as to how—how his life goes." She looked up at Gabriele. "And Mr. St. Cyr? What of him?"

"I—do not know," Gabriele said. Then, in a rush of need, she fell upon Veronique, sobbing against her shoulder and clutching her hand. "He runs the blockade, Veronique—he is in such danger! You mustn't speak of it to anyone—I should not have told you, but the secret lies so heavily on my heart!"

"Do you ever hear from him?" Veronique said, the concern in her voice making Gabriele's tears flow even more.

"He wrote to me at Christmas—but I have heard nothing since—oh, Veronique!"

They stood together, Veronique's sobs now mingling with Gabriele's. How foolish all the barriers are, Gabriele thought. Slave and mistress, black and white—in everything essential, we are exactly the same.

* * *

At the close of their meeting that morning, Mr. Guillot handed Gabriele a copy of the previous day's *Picayune* with an article circled in red. "I thought this might interest you, Miss Cannon," he said, "since it mentions an old acquaintance of yours."

She took the paper and glanced at the headline: "Former New Orleans Resident Among Federal Prisoners To Be Released." And then, her heart beating faster, she read the article beneath it, hardly able to believe the news it held.

"Lt. Jordan Scott, who will be remembered by many as the nephew of Mrs. Hector St. Cyr (née Julia Scott of Boston, Mass.), is on the list of Federal prisoners to be released under the terms of the Feb. 19 order of the Confederate Congress. Lt. Scott, who has been held at Ft. Jackson since his capture earlier this year, will be sent with other naval prisoners to one of the ships in Commodore David G. Farragut's fleet.

"Other prisoners with local connections are . . ."

The paper fell from Gabriele's hand, the rest of the article unread. "I wonder—if it is possible to—see him?" she asked Mr. Guillot.

"At Ft. Jackson? I suppose it could be arranged," Guillot said. He looked at Gabriele with the remembered mixture of legal formality and human warmth. "Would you like me to see if I can set something up?"

"I—yes," she said. "It would have to be very soon. I won't stay in New Orleans long—"

"His release will be effected soon, in any case," Guillot said. He rose and bowed. "I will see to this right away, Miss Cannon, and send a message round to your hotel as soon as I have something to report."

As he escorted Gabriele to the door, he said, "I've meant to ask you—did your aunt ever find her slave?" He glanced at Gabriele. "What was her name? I can't recall it—"

"Veronique," Gabriele said. "And no—Aunt Mat never did—get her back."

"Ah, well," Mr. Guillot said. "As I told Mrs. LeGrange when the woman first escaped—a young female octaroon would have excellent chances of remaining free." He sighed, his eyes measuring Gabriele's response. "One hopes she did not leave one sort of slavery for another— sorry, Miss Cannon, I have a bad habit of thinking aloud. Well, good day—you'll hear from me soon."

"Thank you," Gabriele said, ducking her head as a gust of wind blew down the street. She walked the few blocks back to the St. Louis Hotel, telling herself that Mr. Guillot could have no real information about Veronique, that he only probed because his intelligence told him there had to be some connection between Tom and Gabriele's frustrated plans to free Veronique and her subsequent escape. She resolved to keep her mind on the business she and Mr. Guillot had just concluded, thinking that if she sat down and wrote the details to Tom, she could keep the possibility of seeing Jordan Scott at the back of her mind.

But when she reached her suite at the hotel, and thought of the hours that must pass before she could hear anything from Mr. Guillot at all, her agitation increased, and when Miss Hebert returned from her own morning out, she found her hostess pacing restlessly up and down the parlour floor.

"Do you like cards, Miss Cannon? We could play double solitaire—"

"I don't think I could sit still long enough, Miss Hebert," Gabriele said. "I have had—news about an old friend this morning—he is a prisoner at Ft. Jackson, soon to be released."

"A Yankee, Miss Cannon?" Miss Hebert said, her pale eyes wide.

"A gentleman from Boston," Gabriele said. "His name is Jordan Scott—"

"Julia St. Cyr's nephew!" Miss Hebert exclaimed. "Oh,

it is the talk of New Orleans, Miss Cannon—at least in the houses I visited today."

"What is?" Gabriele said. "Lt. Scott's imprisonment?"

"The split of the family," Miss Hebert said. "The father has been at their plantation for almost a year—and Mrs. St. Cyr herself has completely allied herself with the Yankee cause—"

"I am aware of all that," Gabriele said, and instantly regretted the effect on Miss Hebert of the stiffness in her voice. "I'm sorry, Miss Hebert. You come to all this fresh —whereas for my brother and me, this family's disruption is an old, sad tale."

"People love to divert their minds from their own problems by talking about those of someone else," Miss Hebert said. "But you say Lt. Scott is to be released? Well, I am sure his mother rejoices!"

Oh my, Gabriele thought, what a weathervane Miss Hebert is, swinging this way and that with the prevailing breeze. I shall have to be careful not to take her into my confidence if I do visit Lt. Scott, for it would be all over New Orleans by nightfall.

And when a message from Mr. Guillot did arrive, detailing the arrangements he had made for her to see Jordan Scott, Gabriele immediately devised another reason for leaving the hotel, and pressed Miss Hebert until she agreed to invite a friend to dine with her in the suite at Gabriele's expense.

There, Gabriele thought, as the carriage drove her away. A good meal and good wine should keep Miss Hebert so pleasantly occupied until bedtime that she will have no curiosity as to where I have been and whom I have seen— and then, with the meeting so imminent, she turned her mind to Jordan Scott.

How long ago his last letter had come! Only ten months in actual time had elapsed, but what a distance of the mind! He will not be the same man who wrote that letter, Gabriele thought. He cannot possibly be. He has been in battle—captured—imprisoned. Now he is to be set free. He will rejoin his ship and re-enter the fray. His ship will form another link in the chain that keeps us locked away from things we need—he will give the orders that set cannon firing on Southern ports and Southern ships—he is an enemy of my brother, of the man I love—I should never have conceived this idea of seeing him!

The carriage slowed as it approached the first guard post, and Gabriele heard the coachman give the sentry the password. It is too late, she thought, leaning back against her seat. I have crossed the point where I could turn back —I shall have to go through with this as well as I can.

Think of him as he was, she told herself. His eagerness to learn everything he could about Felicity, and about the way we lived—his honesty when confronting any issue— his real concern for me. Still, as the carriage rattled through the last barrier and entered the fort, she asked herself: why am I really doing this? To what purpose this brief visit to a man I shall probably never see again? Something impels me, something I cannot name . . .

And when a soldier ushered her into the small room where Jordan waited, she saw that same question in his eyes.

"Miss Cannon," he said. "I am—surprised to see you."

"I am somewhat surprised myself," Gabriele said, taking the chair the guard moved forward for her. "I understood we were to be left alone?"

"If you wish, ma'am," the guard said, bowing and backing out the door. They heard a bolt slam home, and Gabriele shivered, pulling her cloak more closely around her.

"I happened to be in New Orleans on business—and Mr. Guillot, our attorney here, showed me the article about your impending release," Gabriele said. "I asked him to arrange for me to see you—as you see, here I am."

"I am very glad to see you," Jordan said. "Though— somewhat confused." He took the chair opposite her, straddling it with his arms resting on its back. "How lightly I asked you to preserve our friendship before I went to war!"

"It—makes a difference, then?" Gabriele said.

"I hardly know. You see, I had not been in a war before—"

Jordan looked so miserable, so very like the young man who had endured the gauntlet of many a Creole parlour before he had learned to run with skill, that Gabriele could not help but laugh. And after one startled moment, he joined her. The strain of the last months fell away, the grim little room faded, and they were as they had been before—two young people eager to be friends.

"Oh, Lt. Scott, of course you have not been in a war before! We none of us have—we hardly know how to behave! I know your duty leads you to perform acts hostile to the cause my brother defends—but somehow I cannot really connect you to the Union navy—I see you as Sir Tristram, I suppose, a role I much prefer!"

"How strange that you should hit on just that idea," Jordan said. "For when I think of you—when I think of Felicity—I see it as a distant, magic place, just like Camelot."

"It is a grim Camelot now," Gabriele said. "Shortages everywhere, the region stripped of men—" She stopped and shook her head. "No, I do not wish to speak of the present, Lt. Scott. There can be no good for us there. I'd rather talk about the happy past—I'd rather remember the somewhat harum-scarum girl I was than the dutiful lady I've become."

"I think of that harum-scarum girl often, Miss Cannon," Jordan said. "The first person I ever knew who dared me to play a little, and to see that no matter how grown-up we are, one part may remain a happy child."

Gabriele's eyes filled with light, as though she had just stepped from darkness into the sun. "Yes—yes, I know. I cling to that careless girl, Lt. Scott, when duty is wearisome and loneliness seems more than I can bear—I go to where she is, and I find you and other friends waiting for me there." She stopped, trying to swallow back her tears. "It comforts me a great deal, when I think this war will destroy everything good and true, to know that all of its firepower and mighty armies cannot take those memories away."

"I wonder if that is all we shall ever have," Jordan said. He placed his hand near hers, then moved his so that he touched her. "A place to retreat to when ugliness closes over me—"

"If we can preserve it—and the regard we have for one another—I think we can prove something important," Gabriele said. And then she knew what impelled her here, knew the answer to the question they both asked. "Lt. Scott—I just realized—" She struggled to put words to the thought that blazed through her mind. "What made me come here—what made you glad I had—goes beyond any friendship we may have. Something larger—a desire to prove that even war cannot overcome our best instincts— that our will to love is greater than the flaw that makes men hate."

"Yes—I feel that, too," Jordan said, his hand covering hers. "Some stubbornness that will not allow my better nature to be lost in this chaos called war."

"Your better nature could never be lost," Gabriele said, not minding now the tears that filled her eyes. "Yours is one of the best I have ever met—remembering it and your friendship has warmed many a dark, cold hour this past year."

They said little more: he could not ask about Tom, and Gabriele avoided any topic that might lead to Alex's name. But the memory of Jordan's hand on hers, the happy light in his blue eyes, would help keep strong Gabriele's belief in the ultimate triumph of good over evil. At the end of the visit, just before the guard opened the door, she turned to Jordan and said, "I am going to hope and pray that the day will come when we will once more welcome you to Felicity, Lt. Scott."

"Accepting that invitation will be one of the first things

I do when this war is finally over and we can all go on with our lives," he said.

"Please God that will happen soon," she said.

"We are totally united in that wish," Jordan said. He kissed her hand, holding it in his for a long moment before letting her go. And then he stood at attention as the guard entered to escort Gabriele out of the fort.

As the carriage left the fort behind and took the road back to the city, Gabriele considered the hour just passed. Her visit with Jordan had done her a great deal of good, and she believed he felt the same way. We are no closer to a resolution of the issues that divide us, she thought. But I think we have proven to ourselves and to each other that we have found a way to exclude our friendship from the ravages of war.

Chapter Fifteen

SPRING ARRIVED AT FELICITY BRINGING BAD NEWS FROM NEW Orleans, where Captain David Farragut's fleet pressed ever closer, and a rash of fevers and illnesses at home. Along with the usual stomach complaints and respiratory ailments came a siege of malaria: the plantation medicine box, its supplies severely strained by the blockade-created shortages, had very little quinine left, and as more cases occurred, Aunt Mat grew more and more concerned.

Already she and Samantha relied upon medicines made of available herbs to treat a variety of intestinal complaints; following the instructions in a circular sent out by the Surgeon General of the Confederate Army to hospitals across the South, they made compounds and elixirs based on plants and leaves gathered in the fields and swamps. The circular suggested using the twigs, bark and pith of sassafras as a substitute for quinine, but though Aunt Mat followed directions faithfully, there could be no question that the patients who received quinine recovered, and that most of those who did not died.

"Three new cases this morning," she reported to Gabriele at lunch one day. "And not enough quinine left to see us through the day."

"Can we get some from another plantation? Perhaps the malaria is not as bad everywhere as it is here," Gabriele said. She lifted her fork and then put it down again. The silver she and Aunt Mat used was all that had been left in the house when Adams took all their jewellery and the rest of the silver and hid it a month ago. Except for a ring her father gave her she would not remove from her hand, and Alex's locket, which no one ever saw, Gabriele had nothing left, nor did Aunt Mat, whose only ornament now was the cameo brooch that opened to reveal a lock of her husband's hair.

Her empty jewel cases, the silver cabinets stripped of the vast array of platters and tureens and bowls they had always held—of all the changes that had occurred on Felicity during the last months, they were the most unimportant—but they affected Gabriele's morale the most.

She could bear the extra work—and heaven knew there was plenty of it. Some slaves had slipped away from Felicity as soon as news of Farragut's successful passage into the Mississippi River reached the Teche. Others had been pressed into service at the mine being developed at the newly discovered salt dome at Avery Island, twenty miles away. House hands found themselves working the fields now, and Aunt Mat, with Abigail at her side, tended to the kitchen garden herself. With Aunt Mat's example before her, Gabriele took each new duty in her stride. She learned to wield a hoe almost as well as Abigail, and when Samson didn't return from the fields in time to milk the cows, Gabriele did that, too.

But when evening came, and the day had finally ended —then she longed for just a sign that the life they fought for had not already gone. Sitting in the bare dining room with Aunt Mat, eating plain food by the glow of one candle, she felt that they somehow let beauty slip away from them, as though the merest shadow of war could overpower her light.

"It is not that I mind necessary privation," Gabriele wrote in her daily letter to Alex St. Cyr. "My hardships are so small compared to those of most people that I should be ashamed to complain. But to hide our jewellery, to put the silver away—we are giving in to barbarism, Alex, for we are assuming the worst about the Yankee soldiers, if they indeed come. By acting as though they will steal from civilians, and break the rules by which even wars are fought—it is as though it has already happened, and this is what I hate."

But everyone hid their silver and jewels: no lady appeared wearing anything but the simplest chains, and ladies who had heretofore taken little interest in the war so long as their own relatives were safe became vocal about the Yankees, repeating tales of pillage and destruction until a miasma of fear lay over the land.

The onset of malaria further depressed the region's mood. Too many graves in the cemeteries of both masters and slaves held victims who had succumbed to the disease despite ample supplies of quinine: now, with almost none on hand, Aunt Mat knew that before this siege had run its course, she could see at least a dozen more of Felicity's slaves dead.

Now she looked at Gabriele, automatically instructing her to eat her meal. "You have a duty to keep your strength up, Gabriele. We all do."

"Yes, Aunt Mat," Gabriele said, and picking up her fork, began to eat.

"About the quinine—you know, I believe the Robins have a good supply. I seem to remember Mrs. Robin saying that Mr. Robin had obtained some this past winter— I'll go over there right after lunch."

"What will you offer them?" Gabriele said, breaking a piece of biscuit and dipping it into the small pool of cane syrup on her plate.

"Offer them?" Aunt Mat said. "Why—I hadn't thought—"

"I don't think they can be expected to just give you some, Aunt Mat. Quinine's worth its weight in gold right now—not that they'd want gold! What is there to spend it on?"

"But what can I give them in exchange? We have so little ourselves, Gabriele!"

Gabriele bit into her biscuit, thinking that at least Letha's light hand with the baking hadn't changed. "Whiskey, I should think," she said. "Mr. Robin's probably run out a long time ago—you know how parsimonious he always was about his cellar—not much wine and what there was not very choice. He never kept much whiskey, either —I imagine they'd trade you quinine for that."

"Gabriele—you shouldn't speak so about a friend—"

"Oh, Aunt Mat, what does it matter?" Gabriele said. "New Orleans is on the point of being captured—does it matter if I think Mr. Robin's supply of wine and whiskey is too small?"

"You object to hiding silver and jewellery," Aunt Mat said, rising. "And I object to letting down our guard on our tongues and minds."

She swept out of the room, leaving Gabriele with the remembered feeling that she must now repent. Bother! Gabriele thought, finishing the last bite of biscuit. I won't. Thank heaven Mr. Robin is stingy when it comes to wine and whiskey—otherwise, we'd have nothing they want, and Aunt Mat would come home empty-handed, no matter how much she considers Mrs. Robin her greatest friend.

When Aunt Mat returned from the Robins', her first words proved Gabriele right. "I confess to being completely astonished at my reception," she said, removing her bonnet and handing it to Abigail. "You would have thought I'd come to rob them—really, Gabriele, I have never seen that side of the Robins before!"

"You've never been in a war with them, either," Gabriele said. "Did you get the quinine? Jonas is terribly ill—"

"Yes, I got it," Aunt Mat said, holding up a jar. "But what a bargain Mr. Robin drove! I ended up giving him twice the amount of whiskey I thought fair—"

"Thank heaven Papa stocked his cellar with a liberal

hand," Gabriele said. "We won't miss the whiskey, Aunt Mat—and God knows we need that quinine now."

Aunt Mat waited until Abigail had left the room, then came and clutched Gabriele's hand. "Gabriele—there still isn't enough for all the slaves who are ill—"

"Enough? That looks like a fairly good amount, Aunt Mat."

"Yes—enough to see—some of them through. But if I give it to everyone—they may all still die."

Gabriele jerked her hand away and took a step back from her aunt. "You can't mean what you're saying—that you are going to *choose* who shall be given the quinine? Aunt Mat—you are going to *choose* who should live?"

"Gabriele—please—try to understand," Aunt Mat said. She came towards Gabriele, one hand holding the quinine, the other groping as though to find her way. "Is it better to let all of the sick die? Or to save those few who have the best chance?"

"Tell me this, Aunt Mat," Gabriele said. "Among those who have the best chance—would men who can work in the fields be at the top of the list?"

Aunt Mat's eyes did not falter, nor did her rigid posture break. "They are the strongest. It is only natural to assume that their own resistance, combined with the effects of the drug, will see them through."

"So—the others are left to die?"

"The others will be given the sassafras substitute the Surgeon General recommends, Gabriele. We will pray that that remedy, and any natural strength they may have—will help the rest of the sick—pull through."

Gabriele waited a moment until the wave of sickness that swept over her had passed, and until she could speak without choking on each word. "Aunt Mat—I hope that I have been—dutiful to you in all things since my father died." The smallest nod of Aunt Mat's head told her to go on. "But I cannot—support you in this."

"I don't expect you to," Aunt Mat said. "When Oliver made me your legal guardian until you are twenty-one, he protected you from just such hard decisions—and left them to me." She drew herself up even taller, her back so rigid that its shadow appeared defined by a finely drawn line. "And just as you try to be punctilious in carrying out your duties to me—I try to be punctilious in carrying out mine to him."

"Aunt Mat! Do not put this—terrible choice on my father's head. He would not for a moment have made it!"

"Do you know that, Gabriele?" Aunt Mat came to her, and took her chin in her hand. The hand felt cold, dry, the skin hanging loosely away from muscle and bone.

"I don't *know* it—"

"Then say nothing more. My task is difficult enough without having to listen to the emotions of a sentimental girl." And then Aunt Mat left the room, the rustle of her skirts signalling her swift departure down the hall. Gabriele heard the back door open and close, and knew that her aunt made her way to the Quarters.

It isn't right, it can't be, she thought, creeping wearily up the stairs. Lucie waited in her bedroom, dozing in a chair. She woke when Gabriele entered, standing and rubbing her eyes.

"You look plumb done in, Miss Gabriele," she said. "You better take care of yourself else you get sick, too."

"I'm all right," Gabriele said. "You're tired, too—run along, Lucie. I don't need you tonight."

Gabriele could not conquer the demons that beset her that night: fear and loneliness, anger against the war—herself—Aunt Mat. She slept in snatches, and when the first faint light pushed away the night, she rose and dressed and went to the stables, where she saddled Brandy and rode her long and hard. They stayed out until after sun-up, coming back to find Aunt Mat and Abigail already at their work.

Aunt Mat said nothing about the condition of the stricken slaves, nor did Gabriele ask. Over the next few days, she saw certain of them up and about again, Jonas among them, who soon returned to work. She knew that

not all of the sick recovered, but she did not need Aunt
Mat to tell her that. Well into the next week, at the end of
the day, the mournful wails of slaves bearing yet another
body to its grave rose up from the trail leading from the
Quarters to the cemetery where Felicity's hands buried
their dead. And though Gabriele longed to know if any of
those who died had been among those Aunt Mat chose to
live, she did not ask. She knew that she could never have
made the choice Aunt Mat had made—but she knew, too,
that by such an acknowledgement, she had relinquished all
right to judge.

"You take the berries on up to Letha," Gabriele told the
small Negro boy who stood beside her, a bucket brimming
with blackberries in either hand. "I'm going to walk for a
while."

"Mind you look out for snakes, Miss Gabriele," the
child said. "I seen a water moccasin sunnin' on a log just
now, waitin' for someone to come along."

"I'll be careful," Gabriele said.

She watched the child move slowly up the path that led
from the marshy land bordering the bayou to the pastures
and fields above it. Soon he disappeared behind a clump of
trees, and the particular silence of early afternoon settled
over her. The buzzing of insects, the occasional call of a
bird, the rustle of the light breeze passing through oak
and pine and cypress trees—all of these blended, not so
much disturbing the silence as enriching it with Nature's
own voice.

She lifted her face to the sun, hoping that its warmth
could break through the thin shell of ice which seemed to
separate her from all emotion. She could see through this
shell, could hear every word spoken. But none of it mattered. New Orleans had fallen in late April, Baton Rouge
had been occupied in May. She could muster up no feeling
about either of these events; she simply did not care. Two
things only did she care about, and she could control neither of them.

They had not heard from Tom in weeks. The last letter arrived in late March, but it had been written at the beginning of February, and its terse phrases, so unlike Tom's expansive correspondence from Camp Moore, made it the letter of a stranger. Over and over again, Gabriele read the few paragraphs, searching for some word that would make her brother alive for her. She found nothing, and turned to newspaper reports of the war in Virginia in an effort to piece together the world her brother now inhabited. But black marks on a map and days-old accounts of battles already concluded had no more reality than did the battles in the novels of Sir Walter Scott: Gabriele felt as though she were suspended at one end of a crevice in the earth and Tom were suspended at the other. Beneath lay a chasm of fear and death, between them spread only a vast and empty space.

Nor had she heard from Alex St. Cyr since his letter at Christmas. As far as Gabriele knew, Alex might lie on the bottom of the Gulf of Mexico, the wreckage of his vessel strewn about him. Reports of the Federal navy's slow but certain progress up the Mississippi River, and the battles at Fort Jackson and Fort Phillip, presented her with a vivid backdrop against which she could imagine Alex, but pictures of that small packet surrounded by heavy-plated gunboats and swift sloops only made her despair all the more. It seemed to her sometimes that the whole of the river below New Orleans, and all of the Gulf of Mexico within reach of the Louisiana shores, had become a trap, a whirlpool of fire and cannon smoke that would surely suck any who ventured against it into its fatal depths.

At other times she sought refuge in memories of New Orleans and Baton Rouge as she knew them in summers gone by. House parties at plantations on the west bank of the river at Baton Rouge, with ferry rides to parties in the town itself. A tour of the state capitol building, looking up in awe at the stained glass window set high above the stairway that wound up three storeys from the marble floor of the central hall. And once, sitting in the gallery in the House chambers, listening to her father speak.

She could weep for these memories, she could weep for the innocent life they symbolized, but she could not weep for anything else. The dread that greater cause for tears lay ahead paced alongside her each hour of the day, and so like women across the South, Gabriele threw herself into every task that presented itself, as though if she kept busy enough, the dread would seek an idle, and therefore easier, victim.

At times, however, the very busyness of her days brought the war home more plainly than anything else, and she worked with fear tugging at her fingers and making her breath come fast. Today, for example. Those buckets of berries would be turned into preserves and jam against the coming winter: while Letha might serve some at supper, and save a bowl for breakfast tomorrow morning, most would go into the big copper preserving kettle, and would then join the other jars in the pantry as another line of defence against the increasing strictures the fall of New Orleans forced upon them.

"At least we can live off the land," Aunt Mat had grown fond of saying, but the words meant as reassurance only frightened Gabriele more. To know that they depended for their sustenance on what they could produce here meant that her world had shrunk to the narrow circumference of Felicity's fields. As though she inhabited an island that drifted ever further from communication with a wider world, Gabriele drew inward. And at times, when the steadiness of the routine and the limits of her life grew too tedious to bear, she wished for anything that would end it, even if the anything proved to be the much-dreaded arrival of Federal troops.

Now she closed her eyes and leaned back upon her arms, seeking to escape her dreary thoughts in the warmth of the sun on her uncovered head and the soothing touch of the cool water. Both soon lulled her, so that she lost herself in the breeze, the sunlight, the flowing bayou's caress.

Time passed, she could not have said how much. Neither awake nor asleep, aware of her surroundings and yet not part of them, she heard a voice call her name without connecting the sound to any meaning. Then she heard a loud whistle, very close at hand, and opened her eyes to see a small packet only feet from the dock, with a man and a woman standing in the bow.

She scrambled to her feet as the man called her name again, and then, as she recognized him, stood frozen, unable to move or speak, as Alex leapt over the packet rail onto the dock and took her into his arms while behind him a man made the vessel fast, looping a rope around one of the dock's corner posts and pulling it tight.

She heard him say her name over and over again, making of the three syllables a love poem. "Gabriele. Gabriele."

He drew her to him, kissing her forehead, her cheeks, and finally her lips. She heard a sound she could not place —a pounding. Her heart, of course, her heart. Another sound—her voice, whispering his name. "Alex. Oh, Alex."

Then neither spoke, only clinging to each other, his fingers tracing the line of her cheek, lightly touching her lips, clasping her hand tightly, breaking through the veil of ice that enveloped her, setting her emotions free.

As though there had been real ice, and its melting water had turned to tears, Gabriele began to cry, burying her face in Alex's soft shirt and letting all the hard minutes and desolate hours of the last months flow gently away.

"You're breaking my heart," Alex said, kissing the top of her head. "Please, Gabriele, don't cry. I'm here now, I'm safe—and look who is with me!"

She remembered for the first time since she had seen him leaping from the boat that a woman had stood beside him on the deck. Lifting her head, she brushed at her eyes with her hand, and peered with tear-clouded vision at the silent figure still waiting there. A dark shawl draped around her head half-covered her face, but the ivory skin gleaming beneath its folds, the golden eyes framed by dark hair, revealed her identity immediately.

"Veronique!" Gabriele said. The dock seemed to move beneath her feet, and she leaned heavily against Alex, still staring at Veronique.

"Are you all right, Gabriele?" Alex said. His worried voice and the deep concern in his eyes steadied her, and she moved a step away toward Veronique, who had not moved from her place on the packet deck.

"I have been so worried about you!" Gabriele said. "Wondering how you were faring—"

Veronique's head moved slightly beneath the shawl, but she did not speak.

"She's had a bad time of it," Alex said. "We should get her up to the house—I'll tell you everything then."

"Of course," Gabriele said. She forced herself to stand straight, willing the slight giddiness that made the air shimmer and the boat blur to go away and leave her head clear and her legs strong. One, two, three calming breaths —she shook her head and smiled at Alex. "This is the loveliest surprise I've ever had," she said, "but it did strike me all in a heap for just a moment."

"I'm sorry," he said. "I should have given you some warning—"

Now her fingers touched his lips, closing them gently. "Shh," she said. "If I had had any warning, I should have done nothing but stay at this dock, waiting for you."

"Gabriele—"

"Later," she said, and for the first time in months, heard promise in that word.

Alex lifted Veronique from the boat, holding her in his arms as the vessel's captain called through the open window, "Good luck, Alex! If I can ever help you again—if I'm still afloat, I'll come as quick as I can."

"Just remember you didn't drop me here," Alex said.

A wide smile split the captain's face. "*Mais,* don't worry

about that. Time I go round that bend—I don't know who you are."

A crewman took a blunt-end pole and shoved it against the dock, pushing the boat out into the water. Smoke puffed up from the stacks, and the paddle wheel began to turn, churning a creamy wake behind it. The three of them stood watching the boat find the deeper channel in the middle of the bayou, and then move forward, the current·urging it along.

None of them spoke until only the wake on the bayou's brown surface showed that a boat had passed. Then Alex said, "I hope I haven't put Veronique in worse danger, bringing her here. I didn't know what else to do."

"Worse?" And then Gabriele remembered. Veronique was a runaway slave. And nothing in Aunt Mat's demeanour gave Gabriele hope that she would treat Veronique any more gently than the law allowed.

"What will Mrs. LeGrange do, do you think, when she sees Veronique?"

Veronique's eyes opened, and she reached out a hand to Gabriele. "My shop—my home—gone, Gabriele. All gone."

"This is terrible!" Gabriele said. "And you're ill, Veronique! You need care—"

"Gabriele," Veronique said in a voice so low Gabriele had to bend close to hear her. "Does coming back to Felicity mean that I am once more—a slave?"

"Don't even think of that," Gabriele said. "Try to rest, Veronique—I'll talk to Aunt Mat. I don't know what I'll say—but I'll think of something."

"If there had been any other place to go, believe me I'd not have brought trouble here," Alex said, walking beside Gabriele up the sloping path from the dock to the plantation road. He paused, shifting Veronique to settle her more comfortably in his arms, and then setting forth again, walking as easily as though she weighed nothing at all.

"Not come here? Oh, Alex!"

"If I had been alone—but once I came upon Veronique —well, despite the risk I ran bringing her back, it seemed better than just leaving her there."

"Is it very bad in New Orleans?" Gabriele asked.

"Terrible," Alex said. "Turmoil—panic—the militia abandoning the city, leaving the civilians with no defence—" He shook his head as though to clear his mind of the pictures hovering there. "Never mind. I'm here and you are glad to see me—"

"Glad!" She pressed his hand close to her cheek, and then kissed the palm. "That one small word cannot begin to describe what I feel, Alex. To see that you are—alive. Oh, Alex!" Her tears fell on his hand, still pressed to her cheek, and he bent and kissed her eyes.

"And Tom?" he said. "What news of Tom?"

Veronique stirred in Alex's arms, and opened her eyes, gazing at Gabriele. The intensity of that golden gaze frightened her: how quickly Veronique's life had gone from its smooth, straight path to this convoluted road!

"We've heard nothing since March," she said. "And that letter had been written long before we received it. He's in Virginia still—at least, that's where he was then." She could not bear the sympathy in Alex's face, nor the fear in Veronique's, and looked away. "Of course there is a great deal of fighting there—" She shook her head. "I pray for him constantly, as I did for you." She turned back to Alex as she spoke, and saw the sudden brightness that filled his face at those words.

"Your prayers were answered, then," Alex said. "For despite everything, I am here. And so will Tom be, Gabriele. We must all believe that he will."

They had reached the grove of oaks, and Alex stopped, his eyes surveying the serene landscape now surrounding them. Entering this grove, Gabriele always felt transported to an older place. Something about the very air—filtered through the thousands of green leaves that sheltered the earth from the sun—felt cooler, and had a scent compounded of all the green things that grew within the grove's protection. Wild violets and honeysuckle, green moss filling crevices between the thick roots of the trees—the air captured their essence, held it close within the stillness of the grove.

"It is still here," Alex said. "This peace I remembered—this tranquil place."

Now Gabriele looked at him, really seeing all the changes time and war had made. Alex appeared leaner, with muscles lengthened and firmed. His skin had a weathered look, the ivory tint burnished by the sun, and his dark hair had glints of reddish-gold where sun and salt spray had lightened it. The old laugh lines still curved up from his mouth and radiated out from the corners of his eyes, but new lines spoke of emotions once strangers to his face, and a tautness she had not seen before thinned the fullness of his cheeks.

"You've been in the worst of it, haven't you?" she said.

Something flickered across Alex's eyes, a memory of violence. "I'm here," he said. "That's all that matters."

A woman's figure appeared on the back gallery, and Gabriele braced herself for the hour ahead. All of Tom's duplicity, and hers, would be revealed now, as well as Alex's role in Veronique's escape.

"Surely the nearness of the war will put all this in perspective," Gabriele said, almost to herself.

Alex looked and saw Aunt Mat. "I'm ashamed to confess it—but until I saw Mrs. LeGrange—I gave hardly a thought to what she must feel when she learns we all conspired against her."

"I know," Gabriele said. "But our concern for Veronique was well-placed, Alex! And look how well she managed!"

"Wait—she's coming toward us," Alex said.

Gabriele looked up to see Aunt Mat walking away from the house toward the trees, one hand shielding her eyes. "Gabriele," she called. "Is that you? Who is with you?"

With a swift glance at Alex, Gabriele stepped out into the sunlight. "It's Alex St. Cyr, Aunt Mat," she said. "And he has brought someone home with him—he has brought Veronique."

"What?" Aunt Mat said. Her hand went to her heart as though she must hold it to keep it in place. "He has brought *Veronique*?"

"Yes, Aunt Mat." Gabriele signalled to Alex to stay back while she went forward to meet her aunt. "It's a long story, Aunt Mat. One we shall be glad to tell you. But Veronique is quite ill—she was in New Orleans when it fell —could we put her to bed, Aunt Mat, and then tell you everything?"

Aunt Mat turned her eyes to Alex, standing in the shelter of the first rank of trees. Her eyes swept from his face to Veronique, lying so quietly in his arms. Disgust filled her face as, without a word of greeting to Alex, she turned back to Gabriele. "He dares bring her here? He dares flaunt his—possession of my property in my face?" Aunt Mat's voice, low, controlled, but so venomous that if Gabriele did not know her aunt spoke she would have thought that sound came from someone else she had never seen before.

"Aunt Mat!"

"Now that it is not safe in New Orleans—or wherever he has kept her—he comes *here*?"

"You can't believe—what you are implying, Aunt Mat. You can't—"

"Why, Gabriele? Why can't I believe it?" Aunt Mat whirled around and confronted Alex, who had moved closer to them. "You offer to buy Veronique one day. I refuse. The next day she escapes. And the day after that— you remove yourself to Olympia, not to return for months! Then you sail to Paris—and during all this time, there is no sign of Veronique! Mr. Guillot warned me that she would undoubtedly find friends—I could have told him she would not have far to look."

Alex had gone so white that Gabriele held her breath, waiting for the storm of words that must come. But when he spoke, he said little, and that in a calm, cool tone. "I regret that anything in my life would lead you to form such an opinion of me, Mrs. LeGrange. Right now, Veronique is badly in need of medical attention. If she is not to receive it here, I shall have to take her elsewhere."

"Take my property again? Indeed you will not, Mr. St. Cyr." Aunt Mat stood aside, her cheeks centred by two circles of red, her lips held so tightly she could hardly speak. She pointed to the office door at the end of the back gallery. "There—take her there. And then leave Felicity, Mr. St. Cyr."

"Aunt Mat!" Gabriele said.

"What do you expect me to do, Gabriele? Welcome him?" Aunt Mat's eyes raked over Gabriele's face. "I see that you do. Well, I am hardly so foolish as to do that."

"He has himself escaped the greatest danger, Aunt Mat! You can't turn him away—you've no right!"

"I am your legal guardian, Gabriele. I suppose that gives me the right to refuse to allow Mr. St. Cyr to stay here."

If Alex had not been there before her, Gabriele could never have summoned up the courage to say what she then said. But the months of separation, the injustice of Aunt Mat's accusations, and the fear that kept Veronique silent in Alex's arms combined and made one pure force that moved through her and made her speak. She drew herself up and stared Aunt Mat down. "You forget that I am part owner of this house—this land—and that you are maintained by my brother and me, Aunt Mat. Alex St. Cyr is Tom's dearest friend. And he is the man I love. Under the circumstances, there is no possibility of his being sent away."

She waited for a torrent of words, hoping she could maintain her stand. But after one moment of shocked silence, Aunt Mat turned and almost ran into the house.

"Carry Veronique into the office, Alex," Gabriele said. "Please—don't say anything! I couldn't bear it."

"But, Gabriele—"

"When Veronique is better, she will assure Aunt Mat

that her—suspicions are completely wrong. Oh, Alex, that she should think such things about you!"

"I can't stay," Alex said, following Gabriele down the gallery to the office door. "The fact that what Mrs. LeGrange says is not true does not change the fact that she considers me capable of such—dishonourable behaviour."

"Don't say that," Gabriele said. She held the door open and let Alex go through, then helped him settle Veronique on the cot. "Everything has happened too fast, Alex. Aunt Mat will calm down, she will hear the truth—"

"The truth will clear me of that dishonour—but it will not clear me of another charge—that of aiding a slave escape."

"But so did Tom!" Gabriele said. "And kept going to see her, and never said a word—if I had not followed him one day, I wouldn't have known what had happened to Veronique until just a month or so ago."

Alex's face had changed as he listened to Gabriele; the first rush of anger had faded, to be succeeded by a look at one and the same time sober and secretive. "I think we'd better—leave Tom out of it."

"Leave Tom out of it? But Alex—his participation vindicates you! It proves that you did this to help Tom, don't you see?"

"I'm not sure that would please your aunt any more than her version of Veronique's escape," Alex said. He took her hands and looked into her eyes. "Gabriele—since you know so much—surely you know Tom's in love with Veronique?"

A faint moan from the cot drew their eyes to the woman lying there. "Gabriele," Veronique said, and again Gabriele had to bend close to hear. "Please—don't let Mrs. LeGrange know—know that Tom and I—please, Gabriele."

A stillness seemed to settle over Gabriele, entering her heart and quieting the passions that had raged there. She could not betray her brother and Veronique, not when Tom could not be here to protect his beloved from Aunt

Mat's certain wrath. When he came home—if he came home—then the secret could be told. But now? She could not buy her happiness by selling Veronique's.

"No—I won't tell her, Veronique. Now rest. I'll sit with you until Samantha comes."

Veronique slipped into sleep again, and Gabriele went into Alex's arms. "But if I can't tell Aunt Mat about Tom —she will not believe it did not all happen as she said! And she will then use every weapon to keep us apart! Oh, Alex, it is too cruel!"

"We cannot betray Tom," Alex said. "As for the rest— let us get past these first hard hours, Gabriele. Then we can think more clearly—"

They heard footsteps coming down the gallery and Gabriele sprang away from Alex, bending over Veronique. Aunt Mat, followed by Samantha, came into the room. She brushed past Alex as though he did not exist, and spoke coldly to Gabriele. "Samantha will see to Veronique, Gabriele. Which leaves you free to see to your—guest."

Her voice whipped against Gabriele's face, and with flaming cheeks, Gabriele darted past Alex and out into the fresh May air. He followed her quickly, and together they walked toward the *garçonnière*.

"I will sleep for a few hours before moving on," Alex said. "I am exhausted—and I know that Tom would want me to."

"You can't leave," Gabriele said. "There has to be a way to work this out."

"Gabriele—please. Let's get through today—this afternoon. I am so—tired."

"Of course you are—and I keep you standing here when you should be in bed." She opened the door to the *garçonnière* and went inside, unlatching shutters to let in air. "Luckily we keep all the guest rooms ready," she said. "Since the situation in New Orleans began to get bad, we've had an almost constant stream of people fleeing that area coming through here on their way to relatives in the northern part of the state—poor things, they come with no more than they can carry—and now I suppose the exodus will be much worse." She picked up the pitcher from the dresser and moved to the door. "I'll send Lucie down with water and something for you to eat," she said.

"I'm falling asleep where I stand," Alex said. "When I wake up—"

"I'll be sitting in the wisteria arbour just outside," Gabriele said. She rose on tiptoe and kissed him, putting her arms around him and holding him, thinking that if at that moment he had been able to take her away with him, she would have forgotten everything, including the promise she made to Letha not to ever let love triumph over what duty demanded.

Gabriele returned to the house only long enough to find Lucie and send her down to the *garçonnière* with Alex's tray. Lucie listened to the instructions, her eyes signalling she had something to say.

"Miss Gabriele—is it true Veronique's come back?"

"Yes," Gabriele said.

"Mr. St. Cyr—he brung her?"

"They both got out of New Orleans just ahead of the Union troops," Gabriele said. "They're lucky to be alive—and very glad to be here."

"Veronique won't be glad," Lucie said. "She done been free—" She looked at Gabriele slyly. "Maybe Mr. St. Cyr —he take her away again."

"And maybe you should see to your own duties instead of wasting time," Gabriele snapped. She waited until Lucie went away, then slipped back outside, taking refuge in the wisteria arbour while she waited for Alex to wake up.

If she kept her thoughts only on the first moments of Alex's arrival, then she could be like the sundial in the garden, marking only the happy hours. But even the fiercest concentration on the way he looked when she first saw him, the touch of his lips, the strength of his arms around her, could not keep the darker images at bay. Aunt Mat's angry face; Alex's, white with shock; Veronique, imploring Gabriele to keep her secret. And herself, defying her aunt, throwing her dependency in her face in the rawest terms.

Oh, Papa, I am not much of a Cannon today! she thought. If only you were here . . . But he is not here, and if there is any way out of this, you must find it, she told herself, sitting up and blinking back her tears. There must be some way all these conflicts can be resolved—now what? She rose and paced beneath the sweet-smelling vines, eyes not even seeing the lavender and white blossoms spilling over the arbour, aware of nothing but the problem she wrestled to solve.

First I must decide what it is I want, she thought. That's easy—I want Alex here. Now—is what I want possible? Not under the present circumstances—we can't tell Aunt Mat Alex only helped Tom, and as long as she believes that Alex—seduced Veronique—he cannot remain here, not unless I am to bring matters into open conflict. Very well—if he cannot remain at Felicity, then he must stay someplace near—another plantation? No—that will not do. He cannot be idle—there will be enough talk as it is. So the sooner he slips beneath the surface of ordinary life, the better it will be.

And then it came to her. The salt works at Avery Island needed every able man they could get. Not just hands to work the mine, but men to help Captain Avery supervise the operations. Only last week Adams had returned from taking several slaves over to work and had said Captain Avery was desperate for assistance, that between commanding a company of the home guard and running the mine, he had more than he could possibly do.

Alex can go there, Gabriele thought. It is twenty miles away, which is twenty miles further than I want him to be —but at least we can meet—and in time, when Aunt Mat sees that he is not—dishonourable—the rift between them can be mended—and she will realize how falsely she accused him.

I owe her that much, Gabriele thought, even if she is

being difficult and hard. It is not to my credit that I have rarely even thought of Aunt Mat's life—what it must be like to run a house that belongs to someone else, care for children not her own. And especially when those children put their own wishes above hers! How ruthlessly Tom behaved, if I think of his helping Veronique escape from Aunt Mat's point of view. He took not only her property —but robbed her of the income she earned from Veronique's work. And no matter how I feel about it—Aunt Mat does have a right to her view. Not about Alex—never that. But she has thought ill of him before—now what in her makes her so suspicious? She knew his father, she seems to have liked him! And I have heard people say that Louis LeGrange was anything but a serious man. Well, that is idle speculation. I must get on with my plan.

By the time Alex appeared, she felt that it was as good as done, and she ran to meet him with a radiant face. "Oh, Alex, I have it all worked out!" she said. "You can work with Captain Avery on the Island—there's a salt mine there now, he is supplying most of the South."

A beam of light bore through the thick sycamore leaves overhead, turning Gabriele's hair to a blaze of red-gold, touching Alex's face, highlighting how much he had changed. How serious he is now, she thought, going into his arms. How purposeful. Loyalty, devotion, honour— and purpose. Alex met her standards in full measure now, and she clung to him, knowing that no matter how hard the weeks ahead might be, she now had the strength to see them through.

"I'll go talk with Captain Avery right away," Alex said. "Tomorrow, if I can borrow a horse."

"I would hide all of them if I thought that would keep you here, but I know we must smooth things over with Aunt Mat—"

"Shh," he said, drawing her to a seat beneath the arbour. "Let me live for at least this afternoon in a world my dreams have made—one with only two inhabitants, Gabriele—me and you."

"Yes," she said. "Oh, yes!"

She looked at their hands, so closely intertwined. How curious, she thought, that my hand, more familiar to me even than my face, should look so different when held by his. Already she knew the contours of his palm, could trace the small scar that crossed it, and recognize it by the line of calluses on its ridge.

"Now tell me everything," she said. "If you knew how I have worried!"

"I hated that more than anything else," Alex said. "Not being able to write to you except that once—you did get that letter?"

She reached beneath her dress and pulled the locket into view. "Neither it nor this are ever far from me," she said. "The miracle of hearing from you—I only have to think of my joy at that moment to be happy again."

"Happy," Alex said. "Yes, it can still exist." He brought her hand to his lips and kissed it, then kept it clasped near his face. "My happiness in those long months at sea lay in remembering every word you had ever spoken to me, every glance you gave me, every moment—there is nothing I wouldn't have braved knowing that at the end of it, I could come back to you."

"But you were in constant danger—oh, Alex, was it very bad?"

"Not for the most part," he said. "Running the blockade is like any other risky occupation, I suppose—though having nothing to compare it with, I don't really know. But there are long flat stretches in which monotony sets in, and then peaks of action in which everything compresses—an hour is a minute, a minute is too short to divide—and then it is over, and you are once more alone with the sea."

He stopped when he saw Gabriele's questioning look. "I had a small crew, of course. I could not have managed by myself. Brave men, each of them, who deserve recompense far beyond what I have been able to give them."

"Are they—alive?"

"When I last saw them they were."

"And where was that? You must begin at the beginning, Alex."

"Yes," he said. "At the beginning." He opened her hand and stroked the palm, his eyes fixed past her head as though he were reading out of a book. "When I was certain that the battle for New Orleans was about to be launched, I slipped up the river and offered my vessel to help bolster the Confederate fleet." He sighed and shook his head. "It didn't take me long to realize that I would have served the Confederacy better by keeping my ship out in the Gulf where she might have survived to fight later with better effect."

"We have heard that the river defences could hardly have been worse," Gabriele said. "The biggest gunboat not finished—Ft. Jackson and Ft. Phillip manned by inexperienced troops—"

"It was chaos," Alex said.

"Governor Moore should never have allowed so many soldiers to leave Louisiana," Gabriele said. "Such a drain must have weakened our defences—"

"The South has only so many men, Gabriele. Whether they are sent closer to the Union lines to try to hold the land forces back, or whether they are concentrated at ports —their number is the same."

"Does that mean you think we are not strong enough to win?"

"No one can say that yet. But if you had seen what I saw at those forts meant to defend New Orleans—militiamen without a single round of ammunition for their small arms —crews abandoning their posts the instant their vessels were hit—and a steady stream of well-placed fire from Federal gunboats that made short work of our fleet."

"But surely all our armies are not so demoralized!"

"Of course not. Still, New Orleans has fallen and Baton Rouge is occupied. The blue line creeps further upriver— and when the Union navy controls the Mississippi River, the war will be over in this part of the South."

"We have other river forts—"

"Yes, Port Hudson near Olympia is reputed to be strong, and people seem confident that Vicksburg will hold." He put his arm around her, and she leaned against him, feeling his deep sigh. "But even if those forts stop Farragut—he must still be pushed back into the Gulf if we are to regain lost ground. And I am afraid history's lesson is that it is much easier to hold in the first place than to take back what's been lost."

"And the *Sir Lancelot*—is she gone?"

"But how do you know my vessel's name?"

"An account in the newspaper last summer—a fight near Galveston on the fourth of July. It said a packet by that name escaped—I knew it had to be yours."

"What a different challenge I faced then, Gabriele! Still, one element of the ring tourney held true. All that I did I did to win the love and respect of my own Queen of Love and Beauty—"

"Which is yours for all of our lives," she said. "Oh, Alex, thank God you have been spared!"

"I came close to not being," he said. "We fought as long as we could—until we took a hit in the boiler. The boat was blown to bits and my crew and I escaped with our lives —which is more grace than many poor fellows had that day."

"I wonder if Jordan was there—and if so—how he fared," Gabriele said.

"Jordan! What makes you think he might have been?"

"I saw him, Alex—"

"You saw *Jordan*? Where?"

"In prison at Ft. Jackson—in February, just before he was to be released. I was in New Orleans—and Mr. Guillot saw an article listing the names of prisoners who would be exchanged. He arranged for me to see him—and so I did."

"How was he? This is extraordinary, Gabriele! He must have been at New Orleans—must have been with Farragut's fleet the whole time I ran past it—"

"I know. I prayed so hard that you two would never meet in battle—"

"I suppose we'll never know if we did," Alex said. "But Jordan, for heaven's sake! And he was well?"

"He seemed just the same," Gabriele said. "Quiet—but very glad to see me. It was—a little awkward at first, Alex —but by the end of our meeting, we both felt that we had been able to salvage our friendship, and might even be able to continue it, once the war ends."

"Seeing what I saw in New Orleans, I would say that it is not the battles that will make permanent rifts but the behaviour of people on both sides when hostilities of a different nature are carried on in defeated cities, and among the vanquished."

"We have heard stories," Gabriele said. "Not a great deal yet—but some."

"The mobs of New Orleanians wreaked enough destruction," Alex said. "They took advantage of the chaos that broke out when word reached the city that the Union ships had passed the forts defending her, and plundered warehouses and shops, setting fire to all they could not carry away—of course, the city officials set fires, too, burning cotton and other goods to keep them from falling into enemy hands. But the looting—the pillage—this came from people who took advantage of their city's grief—it was from such a horror that I rescued Veronique."

"Oh, Alex!" Gabriele said. "How terrible—did you go to her shop?"

"No—I had ducked down an alley to bypass a fire— stumbled on a stone—caught myself against the side of a cart—peered under it and found myself looking right at Veronique."

"I can't bear it," Gabriele said. "Oh, Alex, suppose you hadn't come!"

"I hope I would have remembered to look for her," Alex said. "As it was—we did pass her shop—" He stopped, looking past Gabriele beyond the gazebo door.

"And?"

"Burning," he said shortly. "A trail of fabric and half-finished garments making a path of destruction into the street—"

"Poor Veronique," Gabriele said. "Her lovely shop—her home—"

"She's lucky to be alive," Alex said. "I've pieced the story together—it seems that late in the winter, the woman who helped her and lived in the house with her died. Then, before Veronique could replace her—the war came. She tried to find Jacques, ask him to help her—but he of course had long since gone up to Olympia with my father—and Veronique knew no one else but her customers, who at that point had more on their minds than the modiste who made their dresses."

"All alone to face that—oh, Alex, Tom would hate it if he knew what helping her escape had come to in the end."

"He could hardly have foreseen this madness," Alex said. "Remember how happy Veronique was, and how successful her life, before all this began."

"But why did she go out instead of hiding? That seems so foolish!"

"She didn't even know the forts had fallen, Gabriele. She'd had some respiratory ailment and had kept to her house for over a week. The day I found her, she had gone to the Market for food—she reached it just as the crowd mobbed it, smashing stalls, taking everything they could carry. She turned to go back home—but someone grabbed her. A lot of the men had been drinking their stolen liquor —now they had someone to torment."

"Oh, Alex!"

"They roughed her up pretty badly—no telling how bad it might have been—but thank God, something distracted them, and they let her go while they pursued something else."

"Did no one try to stop them? Tom would be wild if he knew!"

"Stop them? Stop a madhouse? Burning bales of cotton

—soldiers milling through the crowd seeking direction—if Fate had not sent me down that alley—"

"We should never have seen her again," Gabriele said. "When she tells Aunt Mat, Alex—and Aunt Mat realizes she has you to thank for Veronique's life—"

"Will that change Mrs. LeGrange's mind that I set Veronique up in the shop in the first place? And went to find her purposely, to protect what I considered mine?" A shadow crossed his face, and Gabriele knew he, too, heard Aunt Mat's ugly words.

"She will know the truth one day, Alex. She must!"

"But for the present, the damage is done," Alex said. "I should have taken her up to Olympia, I suppose—and then tried to make my way here. But I could think of nothing but you, Gabriele—and reaching you just as fast I could."

"I can't imagine how you did," Gabriele said. "Federal troops and ships everywhere—"

"The chaos made it easier than you'd think. I'd been living on my boat, of course, so had nowhere to take Veronique, and the Quarter wasn't safe—so we went to the old house and hid there until nightfall. Then we made our way north of the city until we reached a place where I felt it safe to cross the river."

"Without a boat? How did you manage it?"

"I'm ashamed to say I simply took one," Alex said. "Found a skiff and used it. And then, once we were on the other side, set it adrift, trusting the current to take it back."

"And from there?"

"I hired a farmer to take us to the beginning of the inland passage, found a captain I knew—and got him to bring us here."

"Thank God! Oh, Alex, thank God!"

She lifted her face to his kiss, knowing at that moment what power finally sends all the demons back to their dark caves, tails curved over their backs in defeat. Love conquered each of them—childish pride, selfishness, loneliness and fear. Here in Alex's arms her struggles with herself had their reward, and when she saw the same sweet knowledge in his eyes, she knew he had his, too.

A figure appeared at the end of the arbour, and Gabriele moved away from Alex, rising and peering to see who it could be.

"Why, it's Lucie," she said. "And look at her face— something's wrong—oh, Alex, I hope Veronique's not worse!"

She went to meet Lucie, almost afraid to find out what put such fear on Lucie's face. "What is it?" she said. "What's wrong?"

"Colette—she done had her baby," Lucie said. Her eyes shifted toward the house, and then rolled back to Gabriele. "But it been born dead—and Colette, she say it's 'cause Veronique put a curse on it the minute her foot touched this ground."

"That's ridiculous! Veronique doesn't believe in all that!"

"Colette—she believe," Lucie said. "Look there, Miss Gabriele."

"What is it?" Alex said, coming to stand beside Gabriele.

"Colette had her baby—but it's—dead."

"Colette? Isn't that the woman who fought with Veronique?"

"Yes—and now she's accused Veronique of putting a curse against the baby—of killing it!"

"Come look," Lucie said again. She stood looking through the arbour at the first row of slave cabins some two hundred yards away. Alex and Gabriele looked where she pointed, and saw a crowd milling about in front of one of the cabins: the women's wails came faintly to their ears, and as they watched, a woman came out of the cabin carrying a bundle. She walked into the centre of the crowd, and they gathered close, making a tight dark knot. Then one of the men shook his fist at the sky and yelled words Alex and Gabriele could not understand. But in the next in-

stant, their meaning became all too clear. Gathering
around the man Gabriele now recognized as Zeke, and
following his pointing arm, the crowd of slaves started
running toward the house.

Chapter Sixteen

"We must go to Veronique," Gabriele said, tugging at Alex's arm.

"You go up to your room," he said. "I'll go to her."

"They won't listen to you," she said.

"Will they listen to you?"

"We're wasting time," she said. "I'm going with you, Alex."

He grabbed her hand and drew her along, her feet taking two steps to every one of his as she somehow matched his pace. The door to the plantation office seemed miles away—she could hear the shouts of the slaves as they burst onto the lawn—and then the door there before them, with a figure looming on the threshold. Abigail.

"Go find Mr. Adams, Abigail," Gabriele said. "And hurry!"

"Ain't no time to find him," Abigail said, looking past her.

They turned to see the slaves surging toward them: Zeke led them, a thin metal blade gleaming in his upraised hand.

"Get back!" Alex commanded. He shoved Gabriele and Abigail into the office and then slammed the door, shouting at them to lock and bar it.

Gabriele heard the bolt slide home and cowered against the door, her ear pressed to it. At first she could hear only a cacophony of noise, but then it settled into a cadenced shout: "Veronique—*die*! Veronique—*die*!"

Louder and louder it came, until the entire room seemed to resonate with it. Closer and closer, until the crowd must be upon Alex, must have his back against this very door—she strained to hear his voice, and could just make it out above that dreadful chant.

"Get back! All of you! Get back!" Alex yelled, but the slaves only chanted louder.

"Veronique—*die*! Veronique—*die*!"

And then, booming over it all, a woman's voice, strong and imperious. "GET BACK FROM THAT DOOR!" And then again, closer now—"Get back, I tell you!"

"Aunt Mat!" Gabriele said. "Oh, God in Heaven, Abigail, it's Aunt Mat!"

She saw Abigail cross herself and automatically followed suit even as she rose and struggled with the lock. "We must help her," she said.

"Listen," Abigail said, gesturing to the door.

Silence. No sound at all from beyond the door. Nothing except the low whistle Veronique's breath made as it left her body in a slow, ragged stream.

Then Aunt Mat again, coming closer, taking up a position next to Alex. "What is all this? Zeke, what's gotten into you?"

A murmur of voices that rose threateningly—and then silence again.

"I asked Zeke," Aunt Mat said. "Well, Zeke?"

"That Veronique—she done kilt Colette's baby," he said finally.

"I never heard such nonsense," they heard Aunt Mat say. "How could that poor sick girl in there kill anyone, Zeke? She's so ill I'm not at all sure she'll live, much less harm anyone else."

A muttered phrase from Zeke that Gabriele couldn't hear.

"Voodoo!" Aunt Mat said. She made the word sound both ridiculous and wrong, and Gabriele felt a shiver down her own back, remembering the times from her childhood when Aunt Mat quelled Gabriele and Tom with one look and with one word, spoken in just that tone. "Voodoo!" Aunt Mat repeated. "Maybe you'd better explain that to me, Zeke. This is a Christian place, and I don't hold with those devilish goings on, as you know very well."

A stream of broken words, a murmur impossible to hear. Then it stopped. A beat, and Aunt Mat spoke. "That's a pack of lies and you know it, Zeke. Veronique doesn't believe in voodoo any more than I—any more than any of you should. Voodoo comes from the devil, and anyone who trifles with it may find themselves in the way of great harm. Colette is the one who fools with voodoo, Zeke. I won't say her baby died because of it—but I will say that you'd better get her to forget all that, to remember her Christian prayers and ask God to forgive her for all the trouble she has caused—"

Gabriele could almost see Aunt Mat's eyes sweeping the slaves before her, making certain each understood the gravity of the situation before going on to the next. "You all come storming up to this house brandishing knives and shouting for blood—and you should be seeing to the baptism of that baby. Has anyone thought about that?"

Feet shuffled, and as though that movement released them, the slaves found their voices. But this time the sound was conciliatory, and Gabriele knew they had no spirit left for violence.

"All right," Aunt Mat said. "Now, Zeke, I understand what grief will do. So I want you to go back to your cabin and we'll forget all this. So long as it *is* forgotten, and you get it through Colette's head that voodoo has no power on this place."

"Yes'm, Miz LeGrange," Zeke said.

"I'll bring a little dress down for the baby to be buried in," Aunt Mat said. "And I'll christen it first—" She sounded suddenly tired, and for the first time since Aunt Mat arrived on the scene, Gabriele heard Alex speak.

"You heard Mrs. LeGrange," he said. "Now go."

Gabriele stepped to the window that looked out onto the gallery and watched the slaves disperse. Not until they had left the lawn and reached the top of the path to the Quarters did she nod to Abigail to unlock the door: as soon as it swung open, she flew across the threshold into her aunt's arms.

"Oh, Aunt Mat! I was never so frightened in my life—"

"Gabriele! What are you doing here?" Aunt Mat's eyes went from Gabriele to Alex, and back again. "Never mind that now. Mr. St. Cyr, we've got to move Veronique upstairs. They're calm enough now, but whether this will subside or not I can't tell."

"I'll do anything I can," Alex said.

"Begin by carrying Veronique up for me," Aunt Mat said. "Abigail, you go make up the daybed in my dressing room—we'll put Veronique there."

"Yes,'m, Miz LeGrange." Abigail started from the office, then turned and fell to her knees, grasping Aunt Mat's hand. "That Zeke—if'n he harms one hair on your head, Miz LeGrange, he got me to answer to."

"We've had enough threats of harm today, Abigail. I'd rather you pray for Zeke and Colette and their poor dead baby—"

"Prayers is for the dead," Abigail said, getting to her feet. "Sometimes the livin' has to look after theyselves." She took hold of Aunt Mat's hand again. "Please, Miz LeGrange. That Zeke, he look like the fight, it gone out of him—but when Colette gets hold of him again, she going to stir him up all over."

"I'm hoping a christening and a burial will make both of them remember in Whose hands their souls lie," Aunt Mat said. "Now go on, Abigail, we've no time to waste."

Veronique woke as Alex lifted her, staring past him at Aunt Mat. "I'm sorry for all this trouble," she said. "I—should never have—gone."

"You'll have time to think about all that while you get well," Aunt Mat said. Her voice had no colour, as though she had her emotions under such tight control that no feeling would ever break through again. "All right, Mr. St. Cyr—take her up, please. Abigail—go quickly now. We've a great deal to do if we're to get that baby christened and buried by sundown." She glanced at Gabriele, the first time their eyes had really met since Gabriele's defiant speech. "I'll need your help, Gabriele."

"Yes—of course," Gabriele said. She still felt stunned, the rapid events of the day seeming to be part of an avalanche that gathered force and speed as it came toward her, threatening at any moment to engulf her fragile strength. Alex vanished inside with Abigail behind him, but just before he disappeared, he looked back at Gabriele, and what she saw in his face gave her the support she needed. "Tell me what to do," she said. And when Aunt Mat had told her, she went about her duties grateful that now, at least, there was something real to do.

The next hour passed swiftly. Jonas went out to the slaves' cemetery to dig the grave while Samson nailed together a small wooden coffin, carefully tacking the scraps of white brocade Gabriele gave him around the sides.

They gathered in the parlour for the services, Zeke carrying his infant up to the house in its coffin, with the other mourners following behind. Samantha had cleaned and dressed Colette, and tied a fresh tignon around her hair, but when two slaves made a chair of their arms and carried her in, despite her ordered appearance, she brought the jungle into the room. Her eyes, glazed with grief and pain, came alive only when fixed on the tiny coffin set on a carved chair. Then they sprang into violent life, roaming the room, staring at each face, as though Colette were a wounded animal tracking her child's predators to their lair.

Alex slipped into the room, standing at the far edge of the crowd. Again he sought Gabriele's face, sending her messages of love and strength.

If Aunt Mat noticed his entrance, she gave no sign. "It's time to begin, Gabriele," she said as she went to stand at the coffin's head. She held a bottle of holy water in one hand and a clean linen towel in the other: nodding toward the piano, she waited until Gabriele had taken her place there before beginning to pray.

"Our Father, Who art in heaven—"

Gabriele took up the words, and then Letha, followed by Jonas and Lucie. One by one, the slaves began to pray, until only Colette sat silent, mouth bitten into a small, taut line.

When the prayer ended, Aunt Mat opened the bottle of holy water and poured a little into the palm of her left hand. "I'm going to baptize Zeke and Colette's baby now," she said, raising her voice so all could hear. "Zeke—what is the baby's name?"

"How come you sprinkle a dead baby?" Colette said. "That baby ain't never seen the light of this world. That baby strangled in my womb by a witch—a she-devil—" Her voice, dulled and flattened by the weight of her pain, made her words all the more terrible.

Gabriele watched Aunt Mat's face and saw the same quick revulsion she herself felt. But when Aunt Mat spoke, she betrayed no such feeling.

"If you're not up to this service, Colette," she said quietly, "it's all right if Zeke takes you home."

Aunt Mat's eyes locked onto Colette's, forcing the dark wildness in them to retreat. She held the holy water toward Colette, dipping the fingers of her right hand into it, then leaning forward and making the Sign of the Cross on Colette's forehead. "May the mercy and peace of Christ be upon you," she said. And all around her came the chorus, "Amen."

Colette, her eyes still on Aunt Mat's face, reached out her hand, dipped it into the holy water in Aunt Mat's palm, and slowly crossed herself. And then, as though Aunt Mat's eyes were a scroll she could read and be instructed by, she dipped her fingers once more and touched them to her baby's head.

Gabriele could see Aunt Mat's shoulders relax, and her

face ease. People shifted their feet and released held-in breath, and as Aunt Mat stepped forward to baptize the baby, Colette motioned to Zeke to lift it from the coffin, and put it in her lap.

"I don't got no name for him," Colette said. "There warn't no time—"

Aunt Mat opened her prayer book, looking at the page the ribbon marked. "Today is June 5," she said. "The feast day of St. Boniface. Shall I christen him Boniface, Colette?"

"Who Boniface? I don't never hear that name."

"A great martyr," Aunt Mat said. And then, seeing Colette's confusion—"Someone who dies for what he believes."

For a moment, something struggled behind Colette's eyes, and Gabriele imagined she saw a glimpse of the same violence that had beamed out of her face when she entered the room. Then Colette threw back her head, and a great sigh came from her lips. "He be Boniface," she said.

Aunt Mat poured more holy water into her hand, dipped her fingers into it, and then made a cross on the baby's head. "I baptize thee Boniface in the name of the Father, and of the Son, and of the Holy Spirit, Amen," she said. "And into Thy hands, O Lord, we commend this spirit. May his soul and the souls of all the faithful departed rest in peace. Amen."

"Amen," they all echoed. "Amen."

Gabriele could hardly see the piano keys for the tears in her eyes, and as her fingers found the opening chords of the hymn Aunt Mat had chosen for her to play, they suddenly had a will of their own, moving to other keys and beginning to play a melody that even Gabriele did not recognize at first. Only when the slaves began to sing did she know what song some inner voice had chosen to take the baby home.

"I looked over Jordan and what did I see, Comin' for to carry me home—A band of angels comin' after me, Comin' for to carry me home—"

And as she took up the words, blending her voice with Letha's deeper one and coming in under Lucie's high soprano, she could not help but consider her aunt's great strength. She has maligned Alex, yes—but I see now that those harsh words sprang from her resolve to take care of everyone under her charge. Me—Veronique—these slaves. Where would we have been without her today? For that matter, where would we have been without her all these years?

She looked up to see Alex watching her, and made the slightest motion of her head toward her aunt. She did not know if he read her message—she was not even sure just what she felt. But it would not be as simple as she had thought—herself and Alex on one side, Aunt Mat on the other. I will have to pick my way carefully if I am to be true to what I know is the right thing to do, she told herself. Not giving an inch when it comes to loving Alex —but never again offending Aunt Mat as I did today.

"I want to see you and Mr. St. Cyr, Gabriele," Aunt Mat said as they walked back to the house from the cemetery. "It has been an exhausting day, but I'd prefer to get everything said and start with a fresh slate tomorrow. So come into the parlour, and we'll try to get this—situation straight."

Then she walked ahead of them, not giving the slightest sign of the fatigue that must dog her every step. They followed her to the parlour, taking the chairs she indicated, feeling still the remnants of the emotions that had so recently filled the room. Aunt Mat sat opposite them, fanning herself slowly, taking a long time before she began to speak.

"I learned a long time ago that the only past it is fruitful for me to explore is my own, Mr. St. Cyr," she said. "So I will not ask you how it happened that you helped Veronique—escape. You are the only person who can deal with that—whether you do or not is of course up to you." She closed her fan, tapping it against her palm, the rhythmic movement setting the pace for her slow speech. "So—let me deal with what does concern me. And that, to put it most simply, is the money you cost me when you took Veronique."

"I offered to buy her—" Alex began, then bit back whatever else he had meant to say.

"And I did not wish to sell her," Aunt Mat said. "The money I speak of is the income I gained from Veronique's being hired out as a dressmaker—since she belongs to me, my brother of course made that money over to me."

"How much would it have come to?" Alex said.

"I can't give you an exact figure now, Mr. St. Cyr. But it would not be difficult to look over my accounts and make an estimation.".

"Please do so at your earliest opportunity," Alex said. "I am not in a position to pay you immediately—but I promise you, Mrs. LeGrange, that money will be yours if it is the last thing I do." Alex could not keep his voice calm; Gabriele saw that he had not even considered that kind of loss to her aunt, and that even as she had begun to see their collusion in Veronique's escape in a somewhat different light, so did he.

"I will render you a bill, Mr. St. Cyr," Aunt Mat said. "And considering the avenues open to me as a consequence of your action—that is mild, indeed."

"I know you could take me to the law," Alex said. "I—appreciate your forbearance."

"Forbearance? Mr. St. Cyr! Do you think for a moment if only you were involved I would hesitate? It is Gabriele I am protecting, not you."

"Gabriele?" Alex said. "What can you mean?"

"Do you think I don't know who helped you? Veronique could never have gotten away from that house alone! Who begged for her freedom in the first place? Who insisted that Oliver had promised to set Veronique free? I saw through the whole scheme the minute I knew she had run away—and as for her enlisting you, Mr. St.

Cyr—in view of your offer to buy Veronique, how hard
would that be?"

"I am—astonished," Alex said.

"You should be sorry," Aunt Mat said. "On your knees
thanking God you did not bring the worst sort of scandal
tumbling around Gabriele's head. Uniting with you in
such a business! Ignoring her upbringing—her family's expectations—and now, to add to all that—you bring Veronique here!"

"I could think of no other place," Alex said. "Except
perhaps Olympia—and—I did not want to go there."

"Why did you not stay in New Orleans?" Aunt Mat said.
Her fan swirled open, moving rapidly through the air.
"Your mother arrived on General Butler's heels and reopened your house—I am sure such a pronounced Abolitionist would have been glad to give Veronique a home."

"What? My mother?" Alex leapt from his chair, so agitated that Gabriele rose and went to him, gently putting
her hand on his arm.

"Aunt Mat—what is this you're saying? Mrs. St. Cyr in
New Orleans? How do you know?"

"Mrs. Robin's sister arrived there yesterday," Aunt Mat
said. "She got out the week after Butler arrived to take
command of the city—he and Mrs. Butler arrived on May
1—and Mrs. St. Cyr's ship docked four days later."

"I—did not know this," Alex said. The salubrious effects
of his few hours sleep earlier that afternoon were not
strong enough to overcome the emotions battering him
now, and he sank back into his chair, head in his hands.

"What could bring Mrs. St. Cyr to New Orleans now?"
Gabriele said. "A city in turmoil—"

"A city in her country's hands," Aunt Mat said. "A shipping business to be revived—" Aunt Mat shrugged. "From
her point of view, Julia St. Cyr has every reason to return
to New Orleans."

"But to flaunt herself—the difference in her position
and that of her old friends—" Gabriele said.

"You will find, I'm afraid, Gabriele, that Julia St. Cyr will neither be the first nor the last to let commercial instincts overcome finer ones. Before the summer is out, I expect many people in New Orleans will do business with the Federal occupiers—in times of great crisis, pragmatism very often seems far more beneficial than sentimentality and ideals."

"Then Alex cannot go to New Orleans—even if he were not in danger of his life if the Union found him and tried him as a blockade runner—he could not be in the same city with—her," Gabriele said.

"I thought you had informed me that Mr. St. Cyr would remain here," Aunt Mat said. She speaks to me as though I am a stranger, Gabriele thought. That is just: my behaviour in her eyes is that of a stranger; certainly it does not reflect what she expects of me. "I—should not have—been so rude," Gabriele said. Alex stirred, lifting his head and looking at Aunt Mat.

"I blame myself, Mrs. LeGrange," he said. "My sudden appearance created a—a kind of whirlwind, I suppose. We both got caught up in our own feelings—we did not consider anyone else."

"Well, I'm glad to hear that you both realize that," Aunt Mat said. "Gabriele, I believe I heard you describe Mr. St. Cyr as the man you love?"

"Yes," Gabriele said.

"And do you think that the recklessness Mr. St. Cyr seems to inspire in you is a sign that this 'love' is mature enough, and steady enough, to support the demands of matrimony?"

"He does not inspire me to recklessness! Oh, Aunt Mat, quite the contrary!" Gabriele said. But she could see the trap she and Alex had put themselves in. By refusing to drag Tom into the whole miserable business, they must take all the consequences themselves.

"You may not consider your behaviour reckless, Gabriele, but I do." Aunt Mat raised her hand and ticked off Gabriele's sins on her fingers. "First you help Veronique escape when you knew very well that I did not want to let her go. Secondly you lied to me over and over again about her whereabouts, simply by omitting to tell me all that you knew. When I think of the hypocrisy you have practised all these months, Gabriele, I am sorely worried about your soul. Third, you engage in a correspondence with Mr. St. Cyr that apparently is not the innocent exchange of letters your brother assured me you told him it was. Fourth—"

But by the time the fourth finger was raised, Gabriele had dissolved into tears, leaning her head against the back of her chair and sobbing hopelessly.

"Mrs. LeGrange," Alex said, rising and standing in front of Aunt Mat. "I wish you would allow me to take full responsibility for all of these—these apparent violations of your code."

"I would be quite happy for you to do so, Mr. St. Cyr," Aunt Mat said. "For then it would lie where it belongs." She rose, too, holding her fan like a sceptre. "You are a worldly man, and Gabriele is an inexperienced girl. True, she has matured a great deal since her father died two years ago—but it is perfectly clear to me that in matters of the heart—she still weaves fairy tales."

"I would give everything I ever hope to own if I could convince you that my love for Gabriele is true, Mrs. LeGrange," Alex said.

Aunt Mat said nothing for several minutes, only walking away from Alex to stand in front of the portrait of her brother hanging opposite the one of his wife. "My brother played a larger part in my life than he would have had my husband lived, Mr. St. Cyr. His principles, the way he carried them out in his daily routine, have been a beacon for me during many dark hours." She turned and looked at Alex, and Gabriele, who sat watching them, so drained that she felt almost nothing at all, saw the look strike Alex's soul. "It is not me you must please, Mr. St. Cyr. It

TWILIGHT OF THE DAWN 335

is Oliver Cannon's principles you must measure up to. You come to such a rigorous standard late, whether or not you can do it—or even want to—I do not know. But I know this. As long as there is breath in my body, I will oppose your marriage to Gabriele until you demonstrate that you are the kind of man her father would have willingly given her to."

Two flags of colour appeared on Alex's white cheeks, and Gabriele saw the effort with which he held back the proud, angry words that rushed to his lips. When he did speak, it was in a rapid, clipped tone, as though the guard he had put on his tongue raised only enough to let the words through. "I go to Avery Island tomorrow, Mrs. LeGrange, to seek work at the salt mines there. Although I have served the Confederacy in one way—I have not yet worn its uniform. But if Captain Avery will have me—I will enlist in his company. Neither of these enterprises seems to have the potential for glory—but I shall do my best within their limits to rise to the standard you have set."

Aunt Mat looked up again at the portrait, as though to confirm the opinion of her brother's character that she held. "Glory, Mr. St. Cyr? I do not speak of glory. I speak of duty—of the quiet courage that sees to it that every responsibility is carried out with diligence and care—of the compassion that considers the consequences of our choices to all they impact. You misunderstand me if you think the Cannons seek glory, Mr. St. Cyr. My brother had his share of fame—but no act of his ever had that as its end."

"My tongue does fail me when I need it the most," Alex said. "I shall have to rely on deeds—"

"Yes," Aunt Mat said. "You shall." She pulled her watch forward, snapping it open and shut as though to mark the end of their meeting. "Well, I've said all I have to say. Except this. Gabriele—"

"Yes, Aunt Mat," Gabriele said. She could not look at

either Alex or Aunt Mat. And though she kept her eyes
away from her father's portrait, she did not have to see it
to feel the calm strength of his gaze, the serene confidence
with which he met the world. I have failed you, Papa, and
failed myself. This is the lesson Aunt Mat wants me to
learn—and although my heart rages against it—although I
don't want to recognize the justice of what she says—I
must master myself, or the love I give Alex will not be
strong, and steady, and sure. She straightened her shoulders a little, and made herself meet Aunt Mat's gaze.

"You reminded me in no uncertain terms who owns Felicity," Aunt Mat said. She held up her hand against anything Gabriele might have said. "Now—for seventeen
years now I have had the full responsibility of this house,
knowing that someday the stewardship would pass to
someone else—perhaps Tom's wife, perhaps you. It occurs
to me that if you wish to exercise the privilege of owner-
ship, as you did today, you should assume the responsibilities, too." Her hand went to her belt, where the great ring
of household keys hung. "Shall I turn these keys over to
you today, Gabriele? And with them the duties they represent?"

"No—no—I—wouldn't know what to do—Aunt Mat,
please—" If anything remained to strip Gabriele of any
pretension to maturity, Aunt Mat's offer completed the
task. Gabriele's small store of knowledge about the work-
ings of the household seemed more insignificant than ever
when placed against the enormity of Aunt Mat's duties,
and she regretted at that moment every hour she had
stolen to be with Tom, or to ride through the fields on
Brandy's bare back, when she should have been learning
how to care for every inch of this house, and all its contents.

"Then you are not ready for marriage, either, Gabriele,"
Aunt Mat said. "Unless you expect a husband to live in
chaos, and children to be brought up like flowers growing
wild in a field." She came and took Gabriele's face in her
hands. "Child, child. You are not bad—but you are care-

less and wilful. The scrapes you got into as a little girl had consequences no more serious than scratched arms and skinned knees—but now, as I hope you understand, the consequences of carelessness and wilfulness are far more severe."

"I know. Oh, Aunt Mat, I'm sorry—I never meant to make us all so unhappy!"

"Of course you didn't, and I am willing to believe that Mr. St. Cyr acted with no such purpose, either. But wilfulness and carelessness take their toll even among gentlemen of the world—now, you both will have to pay the price."

"We are agreed on that," Alex said. "If I could ride to Avery Island tonight, I would do it!"

"Nonsense," Aunt Mat said. "You'd be stopped by the patrols a dozen times and further exhaust yourself. Sleep, then make a new start tomorrow, Mr. St. Cyr." She kissed Gabriele's forehead. "I shall expect you to stay by my side tomorrow, and every day after, Gabriele, until you can run this house as well as I can."

"Yes, Aunt Mat," Gabriele said.

Aunt Mat moved toward the door, turning just as she reached the threshold. "I won't exempt myself from fault in all this. Certainly I could have been more rigorous in making you assume your proper duties, Gabriele, instead of sitting by while you took over business decisions better left to men, and allowed you to ignore the domestic sphere. But having lost one home—I'm afraid I became too attached to this one. I did not want my kingdom encroached upon. It is as simple as that."

As though this confession had been far more than she intended to say, Aunt Mat almost ran from the room. They followed her footsteps down the hall and up the stairs until they vanished.

Then Alex came to Gabriele and took her into his arms. "My darling girl," he said. "You have had to endure too much today."

"I just can't—sort it all out," she said, leaning wearily against him.

"I know. We must both sleep—in the morning, I'll go to Avery Island—"

"Take Jupiter," Gabriele said. "He hasn't been ridden nearly enough since Tom left."

"Not Tom's horse," Alex said. "I have a superstition about that—"

"Then any of them," Gabriele said. "Samson will help you." She spoke by rote, not thinking, not really hearing what she said. Images whirled through her mind—Alex running toward her—Veronique collapsing in his arms—the slaves, surging up to the house—Aunt Mat, facing them down. And then the poor baby, birth and death coming to him at the same time. "I'd better go up. I need to cry for a very long time, Alex. And I want to do that alone."

"Will I see you before I go?" he asked.

"Yes," she said.

She felt a difference in his kiss: was he not as sure, not as confident that they were meant to be happy after all? He walked with her to the bottom of the stairs and stood there while she went up. The last image she had of him was his face turned up to her, the expression a mixture of love and regret.

The tears started even before she reached her room. When she heard someone else crying, for a moment she thought her tired nerves betrayed her, and that she heard herself. Then she realized that the sound came from across the hall, and that Aunt Mat cried behind that closed door.

Tears make a poor lullaby: Gabriele slept, but badly. She rose before the sun and dressed, going out to the wisteria arbour to wait for Alex to wake up. The blossoms appeared faded in the pre-dawn mist, their fragrance tainted by the smell of leaves decaying on the moist earth. She and Alex had only minutes alone before he left: he would not wait for breakfast, saying that he had no time to waste.

Gabriele stood on the gallery watching him ride away, trying to tell herself that twenty miles was not so very long a distance, but knowing a wider space had been put between them that would be far more difficult to cross. But I will never cross it standing here, she thought, and turned and went inside to find Aunt Mat.

Chapter Seventeen

THE DAYS FOLLOWING ALEX'S DEPARTURE FOR AVERY ISLAND
seemed to belong to another calendar: June should be
serene, untroubled, her mood set by the placid skies overhead. Instead, a maelstrom of rumour disrupted the
month, as word of Federal actions in New Orleans began
to come through.

General Butler issued his first proclamation to the people of New Orleans immediately upon his arrival: it declared New Orleans under martial law, and asked citizens
to renounce their allegiance to the Confederacy, and to
"renew their allegiance" to the United States. Street assem-
blies were forbidden, but businesses were to register and
remain open. When some shop owners refused to sell to
Yankee soldiers, Butler made an example of one, arresting
him and confiscating all his goods. And one by one, the
city's newspapers were seized and closed, as they defied
Butler on one issue or another.

By far the worst tales had to do with the infamous General Order 28, which "ordered that . . . when any female
shall, by word, gesture, or movement, insult or show contempt for any officer or soldier of the United States, she
shall be regarded and held liable to be treated as a woman
of the town plying her avocation."

The reaction to that order of the people gathered in the
Robins' parlour one hot June night was identical to the

reaction of people all over the South: Butler, in one sweeping announcement, had vindicated all of their worst ideas about the Yankee invaders, and had earned the General himself the nickname "Beast."

If New Orleanians thought by this insult to deter Butler's behaviour, they found themselves wrong. When John T. Monroe, the city's mayor, mounted heated opposition to the "Woman's Order," Butler felt pushed too far. He removed Monroe as mayor, committing him to Fort Jackson for an indefinite stay.

Any number of other prominent citizens had already been arrested and imprisoned, either at Fort Jackson, on Ship Island in the Mississippi Sound, or, in some rare cases, all the way to Massachusetts. With a skilful hand, Butler imposed threat here, fear there, at the same time organizing indigent citizens to clean up the stagnant canals, scrub the streets, and run fresh water through the neglected sewers, giving one benefit New Orleans could not dispute: under Butler, it became one of the cleanest and healthiest cities in the land.

Even before Lincoln lifted the blockade of New Orleans on May 12, the free market had been reopened, and food distributed to a starving people. With the lifting of the blockade, the city could once more trade with Northern ports—and already, citizens were finding reasons that would justify their doing just that.

"The city is in a vice," Mr. Robin said. He looked around his crowded parlour, assessing the sentiments of his guests. "The people of New Orleans had to trust their defence to the Confederate military—and now the troops are gone, and the civilians are left to bear the brunt of the defeat." He sipped from the glass at his elbow, and then went on. "What it comes to—do you cooperate with the conquerors and thus hang on to what you can so that when they've gone you've something left to begin again—or do you recklessly throw everything away?"

"Recklessly! What happened to loyalty?" someone exclaimed. "There's more involved here than property, Robin—"

"Easy enough for us to say, sitting safely here," Mr. Robin said. "But when they are no longer so safe—"

"The Yankees won't get to the Teche country," another man said. "Our troops are regrouping at Camp Moore—they'll launch a counter-attack—"

"None of that changes the situation of the people in New Orleans," Mr. Robin said. He glanced at his sister-in-law, who sat silently close by. "You left everything, Nell. What happened to it?"

"It's been confiscated," she said. Her face seemed calm, and her voice held steady, but the rapid motion of her fan gave a better reading of her emotions. "A trumped-up charge about something or other—and it's gone, all gone."

"And if you had it to do over again—would you still abandon everything?"

His sister-in-law gazed around the room, looking not at the people, but at the heavy silver candelabra on the mantel, the rich brocade draperies at the windows, the thick Aubusson rugs on the floor. "No," she said, so low that her listeners had to read her lips. "I'd stay and—protect it."

Mr. Robin looked around with an air that seemed almost triumphant. "And so you see," he said, "it depends upon one's point of view. What one person might see as cooperating with the enemy, another might see as a form of—guerilla warfare, in which property the enemy would otherwise take is kept safe from their depredations."

"You split too fine a hair for me, Robin," one of the men said. "If the Yankees come here, they'll find me at my plantation gate, armed with every weapon I've got. And they won't cross through it until they step on me."

"I am not advocating compromise," Mr. Robin said. "I haven't yet decided what my own course will be, if it comes to such a hard decision." He reached out and took his wife's hand. "But with Jaime in the army, I am left to protect my wife and daughters and grandchild the best way I can. I spend much time thinking over all these things, trying to fathom where my duty lies. More and more, I believe it lies first with those whose dependence upon me is the most natural."

"Six months ago I'd have called you a coward and we'd have had to draw guns on it," a man said. "But after they hanged Mumford—"

A murmur went around the room at the mention of that name. Already, only weeks after his death on June 7, Mumford had become a martyr to some and a foolish patriot to others. Although his action late in April had inspired all who heard about it, when he ripped from its standard the United States flag just hung at the US Mint and tore it into bits, the death sentence so quickly executed brought second, and soberer, thoughts.

One can be loyal in one's heart, many decided. Mumford would have done far better to remain in his house, ignoring the flag's presence, than to make such a spectacle of his opposition that Butler must punish it. And as Butler's punitive ways extended to churches and schools, as banks fell and business houses struggled to hold on to a tenuous existence, the mere act of surviving took its toll. At the same time Butler's behaviour made New Orleanians despise him and all he stood for more vehemently than ever, that same behaviour put so many obstacles in their paths that they had time, most of them, to do little more than see to the reduced condition of their lives.

Stronger hatred was reserved for those who openly consorted with the Yankee occupiers: no name could be insulting enough to give them, no snub sufficiently severe. And so the seeds of discord, present from the very beginning, when some Louisianians supported moderation and others cried out for the extreme, sent out roots and began to grow. Those who for one reason or another suffered loss and privation for the privilege of remaining true to the Confederate cause judged harshly those whose dedication seemed weak. Rifts that would last for generations opened, and the cracks in the surface Aunt Mat had recognized the afternoon Adolphe LeBoeuf's murderers were summarily hanged spread now. Whole pieces of civilization dropped off into an abyss, the bonds that had held them together rotted and no longer in place.

In the midst of all this turmoil, Alex established himself on Avery Island with almost no notice at all. The few people who took enough time from their own concerns to question where he had been since the outbreak of the war found their curiosity easily satisfied: Captain Avery, well-respected in the area, let it be known that St. Cyr's loyalty and service to the Confederate cause could be put next to that of any, and the matter dropped.

Between his duties at the salt mine and his duties with the home guard, Alex had little time to come to Felicity. The South depended upon the salt found at Avery Island for the greater part of its supply, and to take hours away from work to see Gabriele had importance for no one but Alex and her. As the summer wore on, Gabriele realized that while their situation had improved, the frustration of being relatively close to Alex and seeing him seldom was almost as great as that she suffered when she did not know with any certainty where he was. One relief only, and that she knew she should be forever grateful for: she no longer feared for his life.

As Veronique grew stronger, she took over Gabriele's work in the sewing room, freeing Gabriele to take more of her duties from Aunt Mat. Veronique lived in the house now, in a small room on the third floor.

"It is not safe to send her to the Quarters," Aunt Mat said. Indeed, Veronique avoided the other slaves: except for Lucie, Letha and Abigail, she had no contact with any of them, keeping to her room when she was not at work, and taking air on the gallery when no one was about.

Although she seemed glad to see Gabriele in the brief moments they had together, Gabriele felt that the person she sat with and talked with had very little relationship with the Veronique she had known in New Orleans. Her fire has gone out, Gabriele thought. And whether some spark stays alive under its blanket of ashes remains to be seen—when Tom comes home.

She would not say, if Tom comes home. With her worry for Alex's safety relieved, her entire store of it went to Tom, and as the dispatches became increasingly more grim, it became more and more difficult for her to even mention his name.

In this spirit she welcomed the most difficult and tedious task, learning that the more unfamiliar it was, the better a mental respite it proved.

She came down one morning to find Letha waiting for her with a barrel of cooking pears. "Miz LeGrange say you the one to talk to 'bout them pears," Letha said. "If'n they don't get put up today, I won't be responsible for their condition."

"Then let's get to it right away, Letha," Gabriele said.

"I'se got all that meat to salt down," Letha said. "And Miz LeGrange, she's off to the Robins'—they got somebody sick, and sent for her early this morning."

"As if Aunt Mat doesn't have enough to do here," Gabriele said. "If Mrs. Robin had ever properly trained a nurse, instead of relying on that *traiteur* woman—" She stopped, letting the number of pears the barrel contained register on her mind. "Well, that's not getting these pears done, is it? Ask Jonas to carry them out to the kitchen, please, Letha, I'll just go get the receipt."

She left the room, trying to keep her face from showing the dismay she felt. Letha's expression had not changed, but Gabriele knew her opinion of Gabriele's skill in the kitchen. It had been formed when Gabriele was five years old, and had attempted her first biscuits. She had left out the shortening, and only her father had eaten the hard little rocks that came out of the oven. Letha had sniffed and fussed that anyone would prefer such fare over her own light bread, and the memory of Letha's disdain had kept strong Gabriele's determination to master culinary arts. But between Aunt Mat and Letha, she had had little opportunity to try any but the most trivial teacakes or Christmas pies: the thought of actually transforming the barrel of fruit into a neat row of preserved pears intimidated her, and she went slowly to her aunt's desk for the recipe book, giving herself a stern talking to at every step.

By mid-afternoon, the sternest lecture in the world could not encourage her. At least a third of the pears were still to be cooked, and although the ones she had finished looked every bit as good as those Aunt Mat and Letha put up in years gone by, she had neither the strength nor the will to complete the task, and sinking onto a low stool set in the open doorway of the kitchen, she buried her head in her syrup-stained apron and cried.

Veronique, coming around the corner of the kitchen, almost stumbled over Gabriele before she caught herself. "Gabriele! What's wrong?" she said. She picked up Gabriele's hands. "You've burned yourself—and look at these cuts! What are you doing, for heaven's sake?"

"P-putting up pears," Gabriele said, sobbing harder than ever.

Veronique looked past her into the kitchen where a heap of pears waited to be peeled. "Fire's going out," she said. "But I guess it doesn't matter—you don't look fit to do any more."

Gabriele heard the compassion in Veronique's voice and felt her spirits ease. The burns did hurt, and the cuts did smart, and her back felt that it would break in two, worn through by the band of pain that had set in at lunchtime and pulled tighter and tighter every minute since. She'd finish tomorrow—the pears couldn't get too spoiled—but then she remembered Aunt Mat's eyes as they had looked that night in the parlour, when Alex first arrived, and a hotter fire burned in her cheeks than the kitchen's heat put there.

"Of course I'm going to finish," she said, struggling to her feet. "I just wanted to catch my breath a minute—but I don't have that much left. I'll be through in no time."

"I'll help you, then," Veronique said. "Now, don't argue, Gabriele. I know you're keeping silent to protect Tom—and I know the price that silence costs. Helping put up a few pears is small enough return."

"Then of course you may help," Gabriele said. "Though you may be sorry you asked." She pushed her hair out of her face and retied her apron, making a firmer knot at the centre of the bow. "Oh, Veronique—when I think how I used to just spoon preserves on my plate without a thought as to how they got there—and tear the lace on my petticoats and stain my clothes—if this war is ever over, even if this work isn't mine to do—I'll never forget how hard it is. Never!"

"Tom would tell us that even a terrible machine like war opens a few new paths as it makes its destructive way. I suppose small realizations like that are one of them, Gabriele."

"I wish we had word of Tom, Veronique! It's so hard, not knowing where he is—how he is—"

"Yes," Veronique said. She picked up the paring knife and began peeling a pear, letting the long, thin strip of skin fall into the bucket where Gabriele collected the parings for the pigs. "It's all hard. Remembering to call you Miss Cannon whenever Mrs. LeGrange is near—remembering to walk with my eyes on the ground again—not to hold my head high."

"That will be over, too, Veronique!" Gabriele said. "When Tom comes—"

Veronique's eyes met hers, and that other word hung between them. If.

As the summer wore on, Aunt Mat seemed to move more slowly. Or perhaps it is just that my pace has picked up, Gabriele thought. She went about her duties with more confidence, having to ask for less and less advice. There came a day when Aunt Mat, sampling the chicken and okra gumbo Gabriele had made, put down her spoon and said, "This is better than mine."

Each small victory took Gabriele nearer her goal of proving to Aunt Mat—and to herself—that this time, she had really grown up. At the same time, the events of the larger world made her gains seem futile. What difference did it make if she learned to run a complicated household, when their very way of life seemed doomed? Letters trickling into the region from family and friends in New Orleans and its environs spoke of a whole new régime: the Federal government had taken over plantations where planters refused to swear loyalty to the Union, more and more slaves ran away every day—as one lady wrote, "It is as though I went to sleep in a well-ordered house and woke to find that what I thought a nightmare was the reality, and all that went before a dream."

Alex rode in one morning with the announcement that he could spend the whole day. "Do people have picnics any more?" he asked.

"We shall," Gabriele said. She went to the morning room where Aunt Mat worked. "Alex is here," she said. "And I would like to spend the day with him. That means neglecting a number of things I meant to do. But I will stay up late tonight, and rise early tomorrow—I will get caught up, Aunt Mat, if I may just have this day."

Aunt Mat put down her pen and looked over her glasses at Gabriele. She had said little about Alex the last few weeks: he did not visit them often, his manner towards her could not be faulted when he did, and the reports she heard of him made her realize that Captain Avery's regard for Alex was based on a sure foundation. She had been a little surprised at how easily Gabriele had accepted her dictum, and now, presented with the opportunity to show her that self-discipline and a dutiful attitude bring a reward, she agreed at once that Gabriele deserved a day off.

"Send Mr. St. Cyr down to your father's cellar," she said. "If he is Hector's son, he will know how to choose your wine."

"We thought we'd go near the bayou," Gabriele said. She tried to keep from blushing, but felt the heat in her cheeks that told her she failed. "If you want Lucie to come with us—"

"I imagine you can manage to stay out of trouble, Gabriele," Aunt Mat said. The faintest glimmer in her aunt's eyes awakened a response in Gabriele's heart. Why, I do believe she's softening, she thought, and went off to tell Alex the good news.

She could not identify the precise moment when she knew he had come to tell her goodbye. One minute she sat beside him on the top of the Indian mound, feeling the sultry stir of air lift her hair, happy to be with him, not thinking beyond the afternoon—and the next minute she sat in a cold, dark place, feeling already the loneliness and fear born of losing him.

"You're going away," she said. "Aren't you?"

"How did you know?" he said.

"Then it's true—oh, Alex!" She had resolved that her behaviour would be up to the strictest rule; he had sensed that, and although he touched her hand, once brought it to his lips, he had not held and kissed her. He would wait for her. Rules meant nothing in the face of this loss. She went to him, clinging to his neck, feeling his kisses on her eyes, her cheeks, her lips.

"Where are you going?" she said, drawing back.

"They need salt at Vicksburg. A man arrived on the Island yesterday, sent by Governor Pettus. We'll start putting a big shipment together tomorrow, and send it out within the week."

"But why do you have to go, Alex? Why can't Mississippi's governor send for it himself?" She heard the petulance in her voice and thought sadly how quickly adversity made her act like a child. "I'm sorry. Of course you must go if you're needed."

"I know the route, Gabriele. Inland by wagon to the Atchafalaya—and from there to the Mississippi River above Baton Rouge—and then on to Vicksburg."

"How long—will you be gone?"

"At least a month," he said. "Perhaps longer—"

"Not longer! Oh, Alex, not longer!"

"I can't make promises, Gabriele. About loving you—yes. But not about when I'll return."

She stood up, closing her eyes and feeling the essence of the land surrounding them, the summer heat, the water threading its way southward. *Just so have I stood all the summers of my life—I have felt this same hot sun, have smelled that honeysuckle and sweet clover—have fished in that bayou—even learned to swim there. And all the time, I marched toward this day, this hour, this minute, when I learn, once and for all, that I have no control over the most important thing in my life.* She opened her eyes and saw Alex watching her; his anxious look broke through her pain, and she cried, "If this is what it means to be responsible, to be grown-up, I don't want to be either, Alex!" She knelt beside him, catching his hand. "Take me with you. Please!"

"Gabriele—you don't mean that." He put his free hand against her face, as though she were a child he tested for fever. "Sweetheart—I will be back. I just can't say when—"

"Why can't I go with you? I could meet you after the wagons left the Island—who would care?"

"You would," Alex said. "And so would I."

"We could find a priest to marry us," she said. "Oh, Alex, think of all the time we would have! All the way to Vicksburg—" She bent to kiss him. "Not a grand tour of Europe, I grant you—but if it's all we can have—oh, Alex, take me with you! I am so tired of being here alone."

His lips came down on hers, stopping words. The part of her that had been waiting all these long months since she first knew she loved him to cross all barriers and be truly his responded to his kiss; her consciousness of the world around her, so keen only moments before, slipped away. There was nothing but Alex. And that was all she wanted there to be.

She felt him shudder, and pull away, holding her at arm's length with shaking hands. "Gabriele—please—"

Two words only, but they told her how close she had

come to courting disaster for them both. "I—I'm sorry," she said. She could not look at him now, she saw her disordered hair, her rumpled dress in his eyes, and turned away.

"Don't be sorry, my darling," Alex said. He put a gentle hand on hers. "Never sorry that you love me—"

"How could I even suggest such a thing?" Gabriele said. "I have learned nothing—I am still careless, still wilful—"

"No," Alex said, his lips against her hair. "You are in love."

She leaned back against him. "Aunt Mat says I must love strongly and steadily and surely—but I don't feel any of those! I feel—ready to kick off all rules—break them—make new ones—" She turned to look at him. "Is that the way love makes people feel?"

"It is the way it makes me feel," Alex said, "but despite your aunt's view of me, I am not experienced enough to know if everyone is affected the same way."

"At least you are experienced enough to stop madness when you hear it," Gabriele said.

"Now that we are—calmer," Alex said, "let me tell you that refusing you—was one of the hardest things I have ever had to do."

And now we are on the other side of it, Gabriele thought. The day has had its peak—in the hour or so we have left, we will both tread carefully, for we know what caverns loom beneath us. She kissed Alex's cheek and rose, going to the tree where she had hung their basket. "I'm hungry, aren't you?" she said. "Get the wine out of the bayou, will you, and I'll lay out our food."

When they got back to the house, she asked Alex to wait while she went up to her room. "I've something to give you," she said, "something that belongs to you."

She went upstairs and unlocked the drawer where all the letters she had written to Alex still lay. Tucking them into a glove box, she went downstairs, handing him the box and watching while he removed the lid.

"I wrote these to you those awful months when all I

knew was that you were on your boat, dodging the whole
Federal fleet—I meant to give them to you before—but
when I read them over—oh, Alex, when I read them over,
right after you first came—I realized how much better the
girl who wrote them was than I am now! She doesn't get
cross and fuss over things—and she would never have—
have—" I won't cry—I won't—

"I shall take these letters and read them and treasure
them, every one," Alex said. "But the girl you describe is
the girl I see before me, who is much too hard on herself
and must stop it, right now. Or I shall have to love her all
the more to prove to her just how—dear she is."

His voice broke, then, and the rest of what they had to
say to one another was said with kisses mingled with tears.
Gabriele rode part of the way with him, stopping where
Felicity's boundaries ended, and watching him trot away
into the dusk. Then she turned and made her own slow
journey, hearing another barrier between her and Alex fall
into place with every step Brandy took.

A yellow leaf drifted silently through the cool September
air, touching Gabriele's cheek and then suddenly spiralling
upward, caught by an errant breeze. Gabriele reached out
her hand, but the leaf danced beyond her reach, and she
paused and gazed after it, waiting until the breeze released
it and it continued its fall before she walked on down the
path.

Now in late September, the first front had finally come,
breaking the back of summer's heat and putting heart into
them all. During the last weeks of August and the first half
of September, when each morning brought another day of
sultry, smothering heat, the weather became the scapegoat
for the entire burden of their lives. "I have never seen such
a summer," Aunt Mat would comment to Letha as they
measured out the food for the day's meals. "No wonder
we are all so dispirited and weary—the mere act of breathing almost wears me out."

"It's some hot," Letha would agree. Later, they would

blame the heat for the disturbances in the Quarters, the fist fights that broke out among the men, the quarrels that kept the women in turmoil. Children fell before another siege of fevers and stomach complaints, and both Aunt Mat and Gabriele added tours of sick duty to their already lengthy list of tasks.

As the heat continued, Gabriele felt herself confined to the house because of the sheer impossibility of leaving it: even at dawn, the still warm earth sent trails of steam up to meet the sun, and a metallic sky made a glaring backdrop for its burning rays. A call had gone out for winter clothing, and when her other tasks were finished, Gabriele joined Veronique in the sewing room, where they made vests and leggings out of Oliver Cannon's old coats and trousers for the soldiers to wear under their ragged uniforms in the coming winter. The material, thick and rough against her skin, made her hotter than ever, so that as she worked she had to stop frequently to mop sweat from her brow and dry her hands.

The heat became tangible, walling off the occupants of the house from one another; each kept to her own space, fanning the air around her, maintaining a small perimeter of coolness. Gabriele saw that isolation as a benefit: lately Aunt Mat had seemed to want to talk about Alex St. Cyr, and Gabriele could not bring herself to do it.

She made a decision and we have abided by it, Gabriele told herself. If now she softens—if now she believes there might be another side—it doesn't matter. It is too hot, and I am too tired, and we are all unbalanced anyway, to think anything will ever be the same. She felt detached from everyone and everything around her. Even when neighbouring families came to call, or she and Aunt Mat stirred themselves to make a round of visits, Gabriele sat in the midst of the chatter as though she did not understand the language, and had no desire to learn.

She detected similar apathy in others: conversations began energetically and then trailed off: topics once considered a normal part of any social interchange acquired dangerous undertones, so that the mildest question about a son's welfare or a relative's condition could result in strained silence or an emotional response.

People seemed secretive about all sorts of things: political opinions were not announced quite as openly as before, and occasionally a family would disappear from the region, quietly moving what belongings and slaves they could reasonably take to safer ground, leaving everything else behind. Only very small landowners chose this course: those who owned thousands of acres now promising a bountiful harvest felt tied to their land as never before. Because although only the sugar of planters loyal to the Union would be accepted and sold in New Orleans, that condition did not mean much to the desperate men across Louisiana. Even taking into account the fees paid to the factors who took the sugar to New Orleans and handled the sale, enough would remain to make a doubtful conscience a luxury many were willing to afford.

Because Gabriele closed her ears to any talk of business, going about in an apathetic fog that distilled all but the most direct remarks, she did not know what Aunt Mat and Adams planned to do with Felicity's sugar, once the cane had been cut and ground at the mill. She had none of her usual interest in the progress of the crop, and the rows of blue-green cane filling the horizon did not excite her as they once had done. Something had drilled a hole in the bottom of the vessel that held her life securely; she felt everything important to her draining away in a slow but steady stream, and she waited helplessly for the final emptiness she knew must come.

But then came a morning when she stepped out onto the balcony to feel the fresh kiss of a cool wind on her cheeks. It lifted her hair from her neck, blowing strands around her face and touching her bare skin with smooth fingers. Although by noon the day had heated up, it began to cool down again in the late afternoon, and Gabriele went to bed that night knowing that the faint surge of energy she felt would be followed by others, and that before too many days had passed, she would forget the lethargy heat and depression between them made, and could begin to rebuild her courage and her hopes.

Now she walked faster, peering through the dusk at the white headstones gleaming palely behind the screen of low-hanging oak branches and trailing Spanish moss. She meant to spend time at her father's grave, as she had done occasionally throughout the summer. She took her loneliness there, confiding to the cold marble all the things she had no one else to tell. In the hours spent among the graves of her ancestors, Gabriele discovered how strong the presence of the dead could be: not only her father, but her mother, seemed to come to her here, and when she returned to the house, she always felt comforted and renewed.

Today fresh fears harassed her. Only yesterday Adams had come back from a trip into New Iberia with news that Baton Rouge had been plundered and despoiled by Union forces after the battle there. And when Aunt Mat had protested that surely even Union soldiers had better discipline than that, and even Union officers adhered to the rules of war that spared citizens and their belongings, Adams had shaken his head and said, "It wasn't regular troops that did it, Mrs. LeGrange. At least, not the worst of it. That Butler, he released a couple of hundred convicts from the penitentiary and made 'em enlist in the Union army. They took their feelings out on that town—as if it already hadn't been shelled and burned during all the fighting. They say they ripped portraits to pieces, smeared molasses all over everything, broke mirrors, smashed china—and of course ran off with all the silver and jewellery they could find."

"God in heaven!" Aunt Mat said. "And did no one do anything?"

"You might as well put your hand up to stop a gale force wind," Adams said. "Terrible thing is—the Confederates held, you know. The Yankees weren't a match for our men, even if they had more and better weapons. If the

Arkansas engines hadn't kept breaking down—if they hadn't had to finally abandon her—set fire to her and watch her float burning down the river—"

"If, if!" Aunt Mat exclaimed. "But it did break down, and apparently that ended any hopes of our army saving poor Baton Rouge. When I think of all my friends who live there—what a sweet, pretty town it is—"

"Not any more," Adams said. "Trees cut, at least a third of its buildings burned—"

"And all in the name of freedom and union!" Aunt Mat said. She had looked around the morning room, eyes lingering on each piece of furniture, each painting on the walls. "What manner of man would rip a portrait, Adams? Or smear molasses into fine brocade?"

"An angry one," Adams said. "One who thinks to hisself that if he has to be miserable and risk his life and limbs, no one else is going to be any better off."

"For the first time since my brother's death, I am glad he did not live to see his worst fears come true," Aunt Mat said. "To know that he had not been able to stop this—" Aunt Mat had closed her lips and bent over her work, and Adams had gone away, leaving behind him dark pictures and terrible images that still clung fast in Gabriele's mind.

She quickened her step, wanting to feel the timeless peace of the cemetery close safely around her. Ducking under a branch, she approached the gate, unlatching it and stepping through it, and then closing it behind her. The creak of the hinges and then the solid click of the latch startled a pair of doves pecking in the dusty grass, and they flew up past Gabriele, wings beating about her head in a flurry of fear. She jumped, too, and then moved forward, heading for the bench placed near her father's grave.

And then she saw him, the man sitting there, his back to her, and his head bent low. "Papa!" she cried, in the brief instant before fear seized her, and she turned and ran toward the gate, hand outstretched to unlatch it.

"Gabriele?" The voice, low, hesitant, belonged to no

one she knew—a bare breath of a voice, as though her name proved too heavy a word for it to sound. And again —"Gabriele?"

An intonation, then, that she did know. She stopped, hand touching the rusting gate, keeping perfectly still while the rustle of leaves told her that the man had risen and moved toward her. She waited until she felt his hand on her shoulder, then turned, tears streaming from her eyes, to embrace him. "Tom," she said. "Oh, Tom."

Even with her eyes closed, her hands told her the changes in his face. She could feel his cheekbones, mark his fatigue by the hollows under his eyes. She opened her eyes and gripped his shoulders. The left one felt strange— thick, padded—but no arm beneath it. The sleeve, pinned so neatly over the bandage that did not disguise his loss. Her eyes went back to his face. "Your letter—said a minor wound—"

"I didn't lose it then," Tom said. "Just weeks ago. At Baton Rouge."

"At Baton Rouge—we thought you still in Virginia—" She took a breath to steady herself, and then took Tom's hand in hers. "No matter. You are here with me, and you won't ever have to leave Felicity again." He looks so pale, she thought, so tired and worn. I must tell Aunt Mat, and get Jonas to help me bring Tom home.

"Sit with me, Gabriele," Tom said, leading her toward the bench. "I came here first—I didn't know, you see, how all of you fared—if you were safe, well—" He looked at their father's grave, and at their mother's at its side. "But there were no new graves, so then I knew—at least I'd find you all still here."

"Oh, Tom!" Gabriele said. She had choked back her first quick tears when she saw Tom's empty sleeve, but now she could keep them back no longer. Pulling his face against her shoulder, she stroked his hair, watching the runnels her tears made down her brother's cheeks. "It's all so awful, isn't it? A terrible, dreadful war—and Alex says fast coming here—"

"Alex! Is he here?" Tom said, sitting upright and looking at her with the first sign of real life.

"Not now. But he has been—and he'll be back. He's on his way to Vicksburg, with salt from the mine at Avery Island." She saw incomprehension in Tom's eyes, and felt a chasm open between them again. All the things he had been through since they had last met, all the events of her life, and in the life of the region—these did not come between them, nothing could do that. But as though the happenings of each day they had been apart had been like the silt the Mississippi River carries with it to its mouth, dumping it and making new earth, so too did their lives have extensions, territory unexplored by the other, with much of it already a no-man's land where none would be invited to enter, and few would choose willingly to go.

"I've been gone a long time," Tom said.

"Yes," she said. She took his hand and opened it, tracing the lines of the palm. "Remember when the conjure woman told our fortunes, Tom? She said this line meant you would have a long life, and die in your own safe bed."

"I almost proved her wrong," Tom said, and Gabriele heard the bite of bitterness cut off the final word.

"Silly superstitions," she said. "Like all that voodoo—" The word brought dark pictures crowding to her mind, and she shivered, moving closer to Tom. "Veronique is back," she said. "Alex brought her."

"Veronique!" He jerked away from Gabriele, staring down at her. "Alex brought her?" He lifted his hand to his forehead and brushed it across his eyes. "I can't take any of this in, Gabriele. I've been on a wagon for days—and the last miles on foot—"

"You're exhausted," she said, springing to her feet. "Stay right here, Tom, while I get Jonas. He'll come help you— we'll have you settled in your own bed in no time—"

"Yes," Tom said. "Sleep—if I can just sleep—"

She looked back once as she darted up the path from the cemetery. He sat still as stone, so still that a squirrel sat on the other end of the bench, grey tail pluming up around him. As though Tom is already part of that safe quiet place, she thought. As though he feels at home there.

Chapter Eighteen

TOM SETTLED IN SO QUICKLY THAT GABRIELE, CARRYING HIS breakfast out to the gazebo one morning early in October, had difficulty remembering exactly when he had arrived home: then the date, October 5, jarred on her, and she realized that it had been two months to the day since Tom was wounded, and two weeks since he had come home.

Dr. Delahaye, called by Aunt Mat to examine Tom, pronounced him a lucky man indeed. "For," he said, "he found a good surgeon, one who at least managed to keep the wound clean. Losing one arm isn't the worst of it for a lot of those poor fellows—infection sets in, then gangrene, and they're lucky if they don't lose their lives as well."

They all had to grow accustomed to hearing Dr. Delahaye's view repeated: to families whose men would never come home again, or had already returned more maimed than Tom, an arm, and particularly a left one, seemed a small price to pay, and Tom, more sensitive than ever, detected the mixture of envy and goodwill in the greetings of visiting neighbours and withdrew into a reserved and somewhat hostile silence.

"I should have hung around and let the Union cannon blast off a leg, too," he said to Gabriele after Mrs. Robin and Dorothea left one afternoon soon after he returned home. "How they can blame me because Paul Levert is dead is more than I can see—but it's clear they do."

"Oh, Tom, of course they don't blame you," Gabriele said. "You mustn't think that—"

"I don't think it," he said. "I feel it." He spooned up the *couche-couche* Letha had just fixed, and then licked the faint rim of milk it left around his lips. "I know I'm not being reasonable—but I don't have the strength to be right now. So until I do—I'd prefer not to see visitors, Gabriele."

"We don't have many anyway," Gabriele said. She stood in the gazebo doorway, feeling the fresh crispness of the October morning. Tom's attitude surprised her, and hurt her, too. She had thought that once he felt better, he would be her companion again. He'd had Jupiter saddled and started riding again before he'd been home a week, but when Gabriele said she'd join him, he'd made an excuse and ridden away alone. Nor did he seem to want her company during the hours she spent sewing and knitting, when she could just as easily have brought her work to his room, or to the gazebo, or to any of the places where Tom spent his days. He appeared at meals, but had little to say: occasionally he would comment that he had rediscovered some favourite author, and anticipated rereading all of his works, but usually he ate in silence, excusing himself as soon as he decently could, and retiring immediately to his room.

Aunt Mat seemed intimidated by Tom, and unsure of how to act with him. She retreated, too, into a kind of formality that seemed very much the way she treated Adams; to listen to a conversation between Tom and Aunt Mat, no one would know they were even related, much less that they had shared a life.

Then Adams asked Tom to help with the harvest, suggesting that he supervise the work in the fields while Adams managed the sugar mill. Tom seemed no more interested in that than he appeared to be in anything else, but he said yes, and now after breakfast each morning disappeared for the rest of the day, eating his lunch somewhere in the open, and coming in only when the hands no longer had light enough to work.

Yesterday the last of the cane had been cut and hauled to the mill, and today Tom could be idle: Gabriele had rehearsed over and over again how she would put her plan to him, and suggest that they spend the day on the bayou, but the sight of his closed face disheartened her, and she turned away to go back to the house without saying a word.

Once again his voice stopped her, and just as there had been almost nothing familiar in the voice that called her name that first day Tom was home, there seemed nothing familiar now. If I did not know Tom calls me, I would say that voice belonged to a bitter and angry old man, she thought. As she turned back to him, she saw her brother in a different light, and wondered why she had not seen the extent of the change in him before.

Deep lines framed his mouth, and the muscles of his neck looked like cords pulling tight against his skin. The skin itself, splotched with pale new patches where powder burns healed, glowed with high colour, but despite that sign of health, a closer look revealed that the colour had been painted on his face by hours of marching in the sun, and that Tom at twenty-two had the weathered, windworn look of a man twice his age who had spent the greater part of his life before the mast or breaking prairie sod.

"What?" she said.

"I don't mean to be such a trial to your patience," he said.

"It's not my patience that hurts," she burst out. "Tom— I love you. I can't bear to be shut away from you—as though you cannot trust me with your memories—your own pain."

But his eyes looked past her, and she knew he did not hear a word she said. She glanced over her shoulder, and saw a wagon come to a halt at the foot of the front stairs.

A woman climbed down from it, then reached up to remove a small bundle that she tucked under her arm as she watched the driver turn the wagon around and head back up the drive.

Gabriele looked back at Tom, and the light in his face made a needle of hot steel she could feel pierce through her.

"It's Veronique," she said, because she could not stand silent in the face of that look.

Still Tom did not hear her: he walked slowly forward, making straight for where Veronique stood. Had Gabriele not jumped aside, he would have walked right into her, so intent were his eyes on his course.

I won't spy on them, Gabriele thought, running into the gazebo and picking up Tom's tray. She held it tightly, watching the knuckles of her hands go white and counting to one hundred as slowly as she could make her tongue move. Then she whirled around and stared at the place where they had met, but as she had expected, it lay quiet and empty, the only movement the light dance of hanging moss, the only sound the repetitive coo of a dove.

At supper that evening Tom seemed as impassive and removed as ever until Gabriele saw the pulse jumping in his neck, a steady beat of excitement that took all the suppressed tension in his body and let it escape through that one small drum. His attention still focused somewhere out of the room, but tonight Gabriele knew its target. And so when he finally spoke, coming in at the end of a comment Aunt Mat made about the prospects for the sugar harvest, Gabriele felt no surprise at his words.

"Veronique has told me that you blame Gabriele for her —escape," Tom said. He put down his fork and looked at Aunt Mat. "Gabriele had nothing to do with it, Aunt Mat. I never even told her where Veronique was. She found that out by herself." He waited, but when Aunt Mat said nothing, he went on. "I arranged her escape, Aunt Mat. And as for St. Cyr's part—when he saw how desperate I was—"

"Desperate! Did Veronique's freedom mean so much to you, Tom? That you would take my property—deprive me of income—?"

Tom's fist came crashing down on the table, making the glass at the side of his plate jump. "Property! Don't use that word in connection with Veronique, ma'am!"

"Tom—have you gone mad?" Aunt Mat said. "Veronique is a slave—she belongs to me. You steal her—you connive against me—and you see nothing wrong in that?"

"I see a legal wrong," Tom said more quietly. "But I see no moral wrong."

Aunt Mat glanced at Gabriele, then back at Tom. "I may as well say what I am thinking, Tom. Not that it will have much effect—but I will say it anyway. What I hear in your voice makes me think that you are contemplating a very great moral wrong—and that saddens me more than the theft."

"Do you mean that you fear I love Veronique?" Tom said. His voice came from some dark place inside him, that place where he went to hide with pain. Gabriele felt a chill down her own back, and when she looked at Aunt Mat, she saw that her aunt, even though she had expected this blow, had been hit hard.

"Tom—be careful," Aunt Mat said. "There are words that once they are said—they take a life of their own—not only can we not get them back—but they may end by ruling us."

"If you mean that once I have said out loud that I love Veronique, I will feel obliged to live by my words, do not give yourself any trouble about it, Aunt Mat," Tom said. "I have loved her too long and too sincerely for anything to change my feelings—except perhaps to make them deeper."

Aunt Mat's face had gone white, so white that her skin looked paler than the linen collar at her throat. "And what —do you plan to do about this—feeling, Tom?" she said.

"What most people in love do," Tom said. "I will marry her."

"You—can't," Aunt Mat said. "The law—" But then her voice dwindled to nothing and she sat staring at Tom as though he were her executioner and the axe were about to fall.

"Law! There is no law any more, Aunt Mat. The Union excuses its appropriation of property on the grounds that this is best for those loyal to its cause—those who resist excuse their behaviour on the grounds that they do not have to honour those who rule them by force."

"There is a law," Aunt Mat said. "A higher law than anything a legislature makes. You cannot marry a woman of another race, Tom. And nothing you say or feel can change that."

"Maybe not," Tom said. He stood, pulling his napkin through its silver ring. Gabriele's eyes went to the ring, remembering nursery days when she and Tom used their napkin rings as hoops for their circus animals to leap through, or as wheels for miniature carriages. "But what I do can change it."

"You would do this to the Cannon name, Tom?" Aunt Mat said. "Bring dishonour to it?"

The look he turned on his aunt then was one Gabriele hoped never again to see on her brother's face. As though he would stop at nothing to do as he wished, no matter how much pain and destruction that meant.

"Dishonour? Because somewhere in her veins Veronique has some small part of what we call 'Negro blood'?" He walked around the table to stand over Aunt Mat. "Tell me, Aunt Mat—if Veronique cuts herself and the blood flows from the wound—does it separate itself into white and Negro streams?"

"That is a specious argument, Tom—"

"She is whiter than many of the Acadians, Aunt Mat! Lighter in colour—fine-featured. But because their colouring has another origin—they are accepted and she is not. Explain the reason of that to me if you can."

"I cannot reason with a man who thinks with his heart," Aunt Mat said. "I have never had the training and education that you and Gabriele have had, Tom, but at least I know that." She rose, too, supporting herself on the back of her chair. "Something else I know. Already your action has had serious consequences. I blamed Gabriele and Mr. St. Cyr for something in which she had no part—and in which he apparently was pressed by friendship and perhaps even concern about your lack of judgement to act. When I think of the things I said to him!"

"Don't put the blame for your suspicions on me," Tom said. "You attributed bad motives to St. Cyr from the first —when he asked to purchase her, you said some very ugly things, Aunt Mat."

"Which you have never forgotten," Aunt Mat said. "Or, I suspect, forgiven."

She sighed, looking from Gabriele to Tom. "Well, all things come to an end in time," she said. "I have thought for some months that my tenure here had run its course. Gabriele has become quite efficient—and now that you are home, Tom, the rightful owners might as well assume full responsibility for this place."

"Aunt Mat," Gabriele said. "Please—don't make a decision now. We are all—upset—"

"My decision has been made for me," Aunt Mat said. "I cannot maintain a position of authority in a household where my deep-felt wishes are ignored." Her hand went to her belt and unhooked the great ring of keys. "Here, Gabriele," she said, handing them to her. She stood away from the chair, standing tall and straight, her hand going back to her now-empty belt. "You know, I can feel a weight slipping from me already. Just think—for the first time in many years, tomorrow I can sleep in." And then she turned and left the room before either of them could recover enough to say good night.

"Well," Tom said. He came to where Gabriele sat, staring at the keys in her hand. He patted her shoulder, then pulled out the chair next to her and sat down. "I didn't mean to bring the world down around your head,

Gabriele. I never expected Aunt Mat would do something like that."

"What did you expect her to do?" Gabriele said. She had never thought of Tom as reckless, or careless about the consequences of what he did. But to rush in and tell Aunt Mat he not only loved Veronique but intended to marry her—ignoring law, ignoring his aunt's feelings—and Alex and I took the blame for what he did and never said a word! she thought.

"You're angry, too, aren't you, Gabe?" Tom said.

"Angry? Oh, Tom!" She shook her head, thinking something she had never expected to—that she wished Alex had not brought Veronique. "You come in here, shock Aunt Mat—now don't give me that look, Tom, of course she's shocked."

"And you? Are you shocked, Gabe?"

"Do you care?" The moment she had snapped at him she regretted it. "I'm sorry—I know you care about me—and I know you care about Aunt Mat. If I'm going to be fair—I have to admit that I understand how your feelings for Veronique can make what Aunt Mat and I may feel or think very unimportant—because that is the way I feel about Alex."

"But in your case—you did what Aunt Mat asked," Tom said. "Why didn't you tell me Aunt Mat blamed you for Veronique's escape? When Veronique told me—I couldn't get over the fact that you've kept quiet all the time I've been back."

"Tom—you've hardly spent an hour with me!" Gabriele said. "You haven't invited confidences—quite the contrary! You didn't even want to listen to me talk about Alex—"

"I've been a self-absorbed wretch," Tom said.

"You have a right to be a little self-absorbed," Gabriele said softly. "I didn't mind you not paying more attention to me when you first got back—I thought I understood—but, Tom, I've missed you so!"

Then, for the first time since he had come home, Tom held Gabriele the way he used to do, letting her cry herself quiet against his chest, his one good arm making her old safe place. When she had stopped, he bent and kissed her, and then said, "I can't change the way I feel about her, Gabe."

"I know. But, Tom—how can you marry her? No priest would do it—you couldn't get a licence—it's not just that she's part Negro, Tom. She's still a slave."

"I know." He rose and went to the window overlooking the back lawn, rubbing the stump concealed by the neatly pinned-up sleeve. "I'm an idiot. All Aunt Mat has to do to stop me is to keep Veronique enslaved. And after the way I lost my head tonight—that's exactly what she'll do."

"Does it—does it hurt?" Gabriele said, looking at his empty sleeve.

"Not what's left," Tom said. "It's what's gone that bothers me."

He came to her and kissed her. "Never mind. It'll stop hurting or I'll get used to it, Gabe."

"I don't know what to tell you about Veronique," Gabriele said. "It seems hopeless, Tom."

A small smile flickered across Tom's face. "My favourite kind of cause. Well, I'm off to bed. Adams and I have an early meeting in the morning—we've got to figure out a way to sell that sugar without trading with the Federal occupiers and we're running out of time."

"I'll be up early, too," Gabriele said, jingling her keys.

She sat alone a while longer before going up to bed. The keys lay on the table in front of her, each one a reminder of the responsibilities she now had. This key for the linen press, that one for the storeroom—the little gold one for the wine cellar, the smaller brass one for the tea caddy. Sighing, she stood and picked them up, feeling as she did so the weight Aunt Mat had dropped settle upon her.

Aunt Mat did not come down for breakfast the next morning, and when Gabriele went upstairs to see her, she found her still in bed. "I'd forgotten how wonderful it is to lie in bed, knowing that someone else has already stirred, and that day will indeed begin without my pushing it," Aunt Mat said. "I haven't indulged myself like this since I was a girl."

"You should do it more often," Gabriele said. "I'll look in on you later. As you know better than anyone—I've a long list of things to do."

Gabriele did not see Tom until late that afternoon: he stayed closeted with Adams most of the morning, had lunch alone, and then disappeared. Gabriele took a book out to the gazebo as twilight began to fall: these brief moments of respite would become scarcer in the busy harvest days ahead, and she snatched this one eagerly. She heard a horse's hooves and looked up to see Tom riding Jupiter in the field that stretched between the Quarters and the lawn.

He reached the top of the field, turned, and started down it again, pelting along toward the road. Just as they were about to pass beyond Gabriele's field of vision, they stopped, Tom's jerk on Jupiter's reins so violent that Gabriele could see the stallion's head rear back and Tom's body bounce forward against his neck.

"Now what?" she thought, half-rising and peering in the direction in which Tom stared. Then another horse and rider came into view, riding as hard toward Tom as he had been riding before he stopped. Gabriele could not make out the rider's face, but Tom could: she saw her brother slide off Jupiter's back and start running toward the other man. And then that rider, too, leapt from his horse and ran toward Tom, meeting him in mid-stride and flinging his arms around him.

"Alex," Gabriele breathed. "Oh, thank heaven, Alex!" She dropped her book and dashed through the door around the gazebo and down the path that led to the field. Dry weeds brushed against her skirts and tangled vines caught at her flying feet as she ran, breath coming so hard and fast she had none left to call his name.

The two men still stood as one: only when Gabriele was

within yards of them did Alex look up and see her. The sorrow in Alex's face changed instantly, and he took one arm from around Tom's shoulders and stretched it out to her. As she closed the space between them, and Alex's arm pulled her to him, she felt as though she were the one who had been on a long journey, and was finally safely home.

She could not speak, nor could he, but their eyes spoke for them, and when Tom turned and saw her, his eyes mirrored what they both felt. To be here, to be alive, to be together—these, finally, had more importance than any other concern. The world and all it offered could be no vaster than the breadth of their love for one another, the war and all its threats no more powerful than their trust. Tom is whole again, Gabriele thought, now that Alex is here. She lifted her face for Alex's kiss. And so am I.

Then came the burst of talk, the questions and explanations tumbling over each other, the constantly repeated exclamation from Tom or Alex—"I can't believe you're here!"

"We must both start at the beginning," Alex said. "But before I say another word, I must see to my horse. Poor fellow, I made him cover the distance between Avery Island and Felicity as though it were a race course—"

"Go with Tom to the stable," Gabriele said. "And I'll go back to the house and get a meal ready." She looked at Alex's horse and saw the saddlebags. "You will stay, won't you?"

"For a few days," Alex said. "Avery said I needed some time away—and believe me, he got no argument."

"I'm glad you're here, Alex," Tom said. "For all the usual reasons plus one more. I only learned yesterday that all the blame for Veronique's escape fell on you—in my anger at Aunt Mat for thinking such terrible things about you—I said all kinds of things that, although I meant them, should never have been said to her."

"Your aunt is an extraordinary woman," Alex said. "I admire much about her—but I confess that when she gets an idea in her head, no matter how mistaken it might be, she cannot be shaken out of it."

"Well, I've made a mess of things," Tom said. "Told her I loved Veronique and plan to marry her—"

"My God, Tom!" Alex said.

"I do love her," Tom said. "But you both know that."

"Yes," Alex said.

"And I do want to marry her. Only—of course I know the obstacles as well as Aunt Mat. If I had thought for a moment before I spoke—but I didn't, and now I'm really afraid."

"Of what?" Gabriele said.

"Adams mentioned that Aunt Mat had sent a note to him last night asking him to check and see if he could find a buyer for a female slave," Tom said.

"What?" Alex said.

"Oh, no—" Gabriele cried.

"Don't you see? It's the one sure way she can stop me—" He held his hand against his eyes as though to block out a picture he did not want to face. "I've been telling myself that if I think calmly about all this—I will see a way out of it."

"I'm still paying Mrs. LeGrange for the loss she sustained when Veronique escaped," Alex said. "Or I'd offer to buy her myself."

"Aunt Mat wouldn't sell her to you, Alex, no matter what you paid," Tom said bitterly. "No, if she does sell Veronique, it will be to someone who lives far away from here—or will take her away. I can't let that happen! I just can't!"

"It won't," Alex said. "Tom, Mrs. LeGrange might not go any further than that note to Adams. You know how upset she must have been—perhaps in the clear light of day she changed her mind."

"Aunt Mat? Not on your life. No, I shall have to take Veronique away from here—but this time, I'm going with her."

For a moment, Gabriele felt that the world around her

—the high, clear blue of the sky where the sunset had not yet stained it, the deep green-black of the oaks at the edge of the field, the lightly waving field grasses making a monochrome of ivory-gold—had started spinning, whirling her around and making her dizzy so that she clutched Alex's arm in an effort to stay upright. Then she took a breath and the world steadied. "Tom—you can't."

"I have to."

"But where would you go?" Alex said. "Think, man!"

"I have thought. Ever since Adams told me what Aunt Mat asked. And I have the perfect plan."

He sounds so calm, Gabriele thought. Which tells me that we cannot talk him out of this: his mind is firm.

"Well," Alex said. "What is it?"

"I'm not sure I should tell you," Tom said. "If you don't know it—Aunt Mat can't accuse you of conspiring with me."

"The damage has been done there long ago," Alex said. "And although I saw some signs of a softening toward me —I put your friendship above any consideration for your aunt." He looked at Gabriele, apparently reassured by what he saw in her face. "I'm glad you don't think me ruthless, Gabriele," he said. "But if anything were needed to convince me that our world is gone and that we must do what we can to build a new one, what I saw and heard on this trip gave me all the evidence I need. Plantations in shambles, unharvested crops in the fields—the roads filled with people abandoning everything they had, heading away from the devastation in the occupied part of this state—" He stopped abruptly, looking out over the field. "I took advantage of the opportunity to see my father on my way back from Vicksburg," Alex said.

"How is he?" Gabriele asked.

"The same bon viveur. He pretends there is no war— doesn't read the papers, refuses to let it even be mentioned. When I tried to tell him that he sits not three miles from Port Hudson, and that if the Yankees continue to press for control of the river there will surely be a battle there, he got up and left the room."

"That is astonishing," Gabriele said.

"Not really. He has Jacques, as he always has. And Jacques has sense enough for ten men like my father. Already he has transferred as much of my father's money to France as he can—and he's waging a campaign to get my father to go there."

"To France? Leave his plantation, and just go?"

"Olympia means nothing to him," Alex said. "So long as my father has his comforts he does not really care where he is—and Jacques assures me that he could live quite well in Paris."

"There is the problem of getting out," Tom said. "Has Jacques solved that, too?"

Alex stared at the ground, idly poking his boot at the soil. Then he looked up, and Gabriele saw the dark shadow pain cast in his eyes. "It seems my mother has offered him safe passage," he said. "In return for Olympia and the New Orleans house."

"But part of both are yours!" Tom said. "At least they will be. Even your mother can't deny the dictates of the Napoleonic Code, Alex."

"She doesn't wish to. Only that part not entailed by my inheritance would go to her—which would make us joint owners," Alex said. "A prospect I relish no more than she."

"Will he actually do this?" Gabriele said.

"Why not? As my father sees it, it should not matter to me which parent holds the rest of the Louisiana property as long as it all comes to me when they both die. In the meantime, he assures me, my mother has the shipping line flourishing again—there is no end, apparently, to the people willing to do business with her, regardless of how loyal they were to the Confederacy not so long ago. He sees my refusal to be reconciled to her as a luxury I cannot afford— and as a final testimony to his own good will, he says I may go to Paris with him and Jacques. He believes Jacques could easily put me in the way of a few good things—and then, when the war is over and New Orleans is herself again—why, I may come back if I wish!"

Until the end of this speech, Alex's voice remained calm, almost colourless, as though the tale he told had happened to someone else so distant from all of them that the story could have no real interest. But now his voice broke, and he looked at Tom and Gabriele with a face so grief-stricken that Gabriele put her arms around him, whispering words of love and comfort into his ear.

"At least the Yankees will leave Olympia alone, if your mother owns it," Tom said. "After seeing the devastation in Baton Rouge, I think that's no small thing. It will be yours one day, Alex, and at least it will still be in one piece."

"I gave up being hostage to property when my mother first left and my father retired to Olympia," Alex said. "They can do with it as they wish—so long as they leave me alone."

"You're not alone," Gabriele said. "And if I have anything to do with it, you never shall be again."

"Which is why the fate of Olympia does not concern me," Alex said. "All I want is right here—" He held out his hand to Tom. "To love Gabriele—to have you as a friend."

"Yes, that is what it comes to," Tom said. "Which is why —never mind. It's getting dark, we'd better go in. We'll go put the horses up, Gabriele, and meet you inside."

Walking back to the house, Gabriele remembered what Aunt Mat had said to Adams, the day after Harold LeBoeuf's cousin had been killed by the slaves. A crack had opened in civilization's surface, letting all the demons out. The crack has widened, she thought. It is now a gap, a chasm. And even if there are no more demons, even if already they roam the earth, the chasm itself is dangerous, for it opens wider every day—and soon it will be wide enough to swallow us up.

* * *

Aunt Mat did not come down to dinner, which did not surprise Gabriele. *She does not want to face Tom—and if I am honest, I am very glad she won't be with us, for now we can speak freely about all these problems that confront us, and that seem so impossible to solve.*

As she left her room to go down, she heard Tom coming down the stairs that led to the third floor, but even when he caught up with her and they walked together down the hall, she did not ask him if he had been to see Veronique. She had not allowed herself to form an opinion about Tom's attachment since she first knew it to be real: Tom was her brother, whom she loved above everyone but Alex St. Cyr. She would no more judge him than she would deny him anything he wanted that she could give. *But I can see Aunt Mat's point of view—I can understand how she feels. And, oh, if she persists in selling Veronique, which, the more I think of it, is the most logical thing for her to do—and Tom runs away with her— then what will she do?*

She stole a glance at Tom, trying to see something in his sober face that would give her a clue as to why he would risk everything he used to consider important to be in love with Veronique. *Of course he has always been fond of her —when she came here she was so little and she amused us so much! The way she always clung to Tom—and defended him against anyone who said the slightest thing.* She stopped suddenly, one foot poised to take the next step down.

"What is it?" Tom said, pausing, too.

"Nothing," Gabriele said. "A rabbit ran over my grave."

She knew now why Tom loved Veronique, the reason more powerful than her beauty, more forceful than her charm. In all their childhood games, Gabriele and Tom had been the courageous knights, with Veronique the damsel in distress. Veronique could not climb trees as Gabriele did, or fence with Tom. How many times had Tom vanquished his sister to rescue Veronique? How many crowns of clover and ivy had Veronique woven and placed on Tom's head? A game, a childhood game, but its pattern operated in him still.

How strange, she thought as she preceded Tom into the dining room. All these years I thought I could not get romantic notions out of my head, that I yearned for the world of King Arthur and Camelot, and all the while—it was Tom.

She took her place at the foot of the table while Tom sat at the head. Alex sat between them, face alight with happiness as he looked from Gabriele to Tom. "I know we face some hard times," he said. "But somehow I think that we're going to win out."

"Yes," Tom said. "No matter what."

As though they had agreed to temporarily push the problems confronting them beneath the surface of their minds, their talk in the early part of dinner rested on happier days, and for the first time in a long while, young people laughing made the dining room a bright and joyous place.

Over coffee, Alex turned and said to Tom, "Don't tell me if you'd rather not. But I would like to know what happened to you. If you don't mind."

"I suppose I should talk about it," Tom said. He stirred sugar into his coffee, staring down at his hand. "I haven't —except to Veronique."

"Don't, if you'd rather not," Alex said.

"No. I want to." Tom settled back in his chair, quiet for a moment as though considering where to begin. "I had been in Virginia, under Beauregard's command. And when he left there to take over the defences of the upper Mississippi River below Memphis, I jumped at the chance to go with him. I'd almost recovered from a minor wound, and by the time we got there, it had healed." He glanced at his empty sleeve and away again, and Gabriele realized she did not even know what that first wound had been. "Then Ft. Pillow went, and Memphis fell—the main body of troops stayed at Vicksburg, but I got sent to

Camp Moore. Four thousand of us left Vicksburg by train at the end of July—the 27th, I think—to join the force preparing to strike the Yankees at Baton Rouge."

Tom paused so long that Gabriele finally spoke, leaning toward him and looking earnestly into his face. "Don't tell more than you want to, Tom."

"I—I want to tell it," Tom said. "I have to diminish the strength of those pictures—the force of those screams—" He picked up a place knife and began to toy with it, drawing lines in the damask cloth with its tip. "Remember my letters from Camp Moore, Gabe? When I first went there a little over a year ago? It didn't seem the same place when I returned. We got there the evening of the 28th—and then we had to wait for the *Arkansas* to clear out the Yankee gunboats around Baton Rouge. We had no shelter —it rained constantly, but the heat never let up, and within a few days close to a thousand troops were sick from fever and dysentery—we left a graveyard full before we ever began to march."

The point of the knife bore harder upon the smooth surface of the cloth, drawing a row of small crosses and then beginning to make a long straight line. "Finally our commander, General Breckinridge, got word that the *Arkansas* was headed downriver, and so we started out." The knife stopped, wavered, and went on, making two parallel lines now, as though the cloth were a map and Tom marked a route. "Two days of it—I guess a third of the men had no shoes, and walked on sand so hot it blistered their feet the first hour out. Few had a whole uniform, but we all had a full pack—but no water. I can't describe the heat—the thirst. Men broke through the scum on stagnant water and drank it—of course they sickened from it, and I'd say that by the time we reached the edge of Baton Rouge, Breckinridge had left only twenty-six hundred men."

Tom stopped and picked up the goblet of water at his place, drinking it off in one swallow as though just the memory of that march could recreate his thirst. He set the

goblet down and looked at Alex and Gabriele. "I'll tell you
one thing—some of the troops looked like skeletons, most
looked like rag-bags—a lot of them could hardly walk. But
every rifle shone, with every part clean and in perfect order."

I can't hear this, Gabriele thought. I thought I couldn't
bear not knowing what he suffered—but knowing is
worse. She moved in her chair, as though to rise, and
Alex's hand came down on hers.

"Go on, Tom," he said quietly. "We're here."

Gabriele closed her fingers around Alex's hand, squeez-
ing it so tightly that she could feel the signet ring he wore
bite into her flesh. "Yes," she said. "Go on."

"We marched all night," Tom said. "Even when dawn
came, the ground fog cut visibility so badly that we could
hardly see what lay ahead of us. And when the shooting
did start, the fog kept the smoke from rising, making conditions even worse." Now Tom's voice had slowed so
much that there seemed to be a beat of silence between
each word. Gabriele, remembering the lethargy her own
fits of depression caused, could almost feel the thick, grey
fog clinging to Tom's soul, making a screen through
which he could not see the sun.

"What company were you in?" Alex asked.

"Captain Oliver Semmes' battery," Tom said. The knife
point drew rambling lines now, a maze of aimless begin-
nings that twisted and turned back on themselves.
"There's no order, you know. Not in a battle like that. We
were all tired—by ten in the morning, thirst was the worst
enemy, and troops on both sides had broken and run.
Colonel Henry Allen went down, badly wounded, and I
guess that did more damage than what the enemy did. The
men loved him so—they stood around crying, and a lot of
them just threw down their arms."

"But all of this was in the city itself?" Gabriele asked.
She tried to imagine the quiet, tree-lined streets of Baton
Rouge overrun with soldiers and full of the debris of war.

"All through it," Tom said. "A lot of people had built

bomb shelters where they went when the first shells went off. Others left the city, heading south—" He stopped talking completely, staring at the knife in his hand and then up at Gabriele and Alex. "You'd be setting up a mortar in someone's front yard—the door would be wide open behind you and flowers blooming all around. I could even smell food burning from houses where they'd left so fast they hadn't pulled the pots off the fire."

"It's terrible," Gabriele said. "Just terrible—"

"The Yankees weren't in much better shape than we were," Tom said. "We managed to drive them back to the river—and even though their gunboats kept pouring shell, grape, and canister into the streets, the troops wouldn't come back up that hill."

"Then we—won," Gabriele said.

Tom's mouth twisted; he gave the most fleeting glance at his empty sleeve. "Oh, yes, we won," he said. "Held the town until we learned the *Arkansas* wouldn't be coming after all. Breckinridge had pulled the troops back to the suburbs, where at least there was water in cisterns. Some of us went back to destroy everything the Yankees had left behind. If we'd had wagons, we could have carried it all off. As it was—we burned it."

"But—when were you hit?" Gabriele asked.

"I wasn't," Tom said. "A shell had fallen into a commissary tent at one of the Federal camps—somehow, it hadn't exploded. We—didn't see it. So when I fired the tent, the heat made it blow up." Again the twisted smile that took the brother she knew and replaced him with a bitter stranger. "Not a very heroic way to lose an arm, is it? Destroying food that so many people needed—"

"Hush," Gabriele said, going to him and pulling his face against her breast. "Hush." She felt him shudder as he released his breath on a long sigh.

"It's all so pointless," Tom said. "Men dying in Baton Rouge, and in New Orleans, not a hundred miles away—thousands have already taken the loyalty oath and are going about their business as though there isn't any war at all."

"It's the plundering I find incredible," Alex said. "When I arrived in Vicksburg, and they told us how the Yankees pillaged Baton Rouge before they left it—is there no discipline? No honour?"

"Those were not regular troops," Tom said. "Butler had released convicts from the penitentiary—enlisted them. We can lay the pillage at their door."

"That's where you're wrong, Tom," Alex said. "Any general who would use such troops is responsible for their actions even more than he is responsible for the actions of troops he trained. And what about the Negroes the Yankees are using? Williams worked thousands of them building that futile canal at Vicksburg—promised them their freedom, and then, when he and Farragut abandoned Vicksburg and sailed downriver at the end of July, Williams left the Negroes wailing on the levee, no freer than they had ever been."

"They'll be free soon," Tom said.

"The Proclamation, you mean," Alex said.

"Yes," Tom said. "Word came through just before I left to come home. Caused a lot of consternation—the people who took care of me have a sugar plantation below Baton Rouge, and by the time I left, a good third of their slaves had run away."

"What are you talking about?" Gabriele said. "What Proclamation?"

"You don't know about Lincoln freeing the slaves?" Alex said.

"No—"

"Late in September," Alex said. "Of course, he's been offering one form or another of it for months—and I understand he ran into a lot of opposition on some of the earlier ones that would have emancipated slaves gradually, with full compensation to their owners, and with colonization of those freed in Liberia or Latin America—but that's not the form the Proclamation finally took."

"What does it say, then?" Gabriele asked.

Alex laughed, and some of the bitterness Gabriele had seen in Tom's face sounded there. "It declares those slaves held behind enemy lines to be free—those in Union-held territory are of course being well taken care of, as you have just heard."

"You mean our slaves will be free but those in New Orleans and around it will not?"

"Yes. Ridiculous, isn't it? But it might stop the flow of slaves to the Union lines and keep them on the plantations where even the Union wants them to be," Tom said. "Oh, yes, now even General Butler realizes how valuable all those acres of sugar cane and cotton are—the plantations run by the Federal Army have opened the eyes of a lot of its officers to the peculiar nature of our agricultural system —in fact, they have persuaded any number of planters to take the loyalty oath and then keep their slaves just that— slaves."

"But—but they are fighting to free the slaves," Gabriele said. "Yet Lincoln does not free those behind Union lines?"

"Maybe someone can figure it out," Tom said. "I can't. I don't even try." He got up, rubbing his stump in a gesture familiar now. "No, I'm going to take Veronique and get out of here—start all over somewhere else."

"You really mean it," Alex said.

"Absolutely," Tom said.

Alex rose and went to Gabriele, taking her hand and looking steadily into her eyes. "Then let's go with them, Gabriele. There's nothing here for us—the Yankees will come—Felicity will be destroyed. Let's go now, while we can still leave."

"But—where are you going, Tom?" Gabriele said.

"To Texas," Tom said. "I have to go there anyway— Adams and I decided to send the sugar overland to Mexico. Although Maximilian has only a tenuous hold on the territory Napoleon claims for France, there are French troops near the border and French ships at Galveston. We can negotiate a sale there."

"That sounds like an ambitious expedition, Tom," Alex said. "You can't make it alone!"

"I'll take Jonas and Samson with me," Tom said. "And if they want to—they can stay and work for me out there. Not as slaves, of course—God, I hope to reach the day when I can forget that word! I'll hire them, as I would anyone."

"And when you leave—Veronique will go, too," Gabriele said.

"I'll send Aunt Mat money when the sugar is sold," Tom said. "If I thought she had right on her side, I wouldn't defy her. But she doesn't, it's as simple as that."

"The more I think about it, the better I like your idea," Alex said. "As light as she is, Veronique will be taken for a woman of Spanish descent—"

"Yes, and we'll have no problem marrying. Why would we?" He turned his attention to Gabriele. "You haven't answered Alex's question, Gabe. Will you come with me?"

"I—I don't know," Gabriele said. "To just abandon Felicity—and then there's Aunt Mat. How can I just go off and leave her, Tom?"

Tom put his hand on her shoulder. "Gabriele—I don't think you understand. People are fleeing northward already as the Union troops advance. This is war, Gabriele— fought on civilian territory, carried into civilian homes. When they come here—and after what I've seen, I know they surely will—there will be no way to protect you from war and its consequences. None."

"I still have to think of Aunt Mat," Gabriele said. "I know you are angry with her, Tom. And I am not that happy with her myself. I understand why she has said and done all that she has—but she came between me and Alex, and I can't forget that." She held up her hand as Tom started to speak. "No, let me finish, Tom. Papa's will entrusted her to our care. And I will not go against what he asked me to do."

"I suppose it's a matter of interpretation, Gabe," Tom said. "You believe to maintain her you must stay and see to it yourself. I don't. She will have money—she has money now, for Alex has been paying her back what she lost. She has friends—her husband's family still lives on Bayou Lafourche. She doesn't need me to sacrifice any more for her, Gabriele. And believe me, I won't."

"She has been so devoted to you, Tom. To us both! If you knew how she prayed for you—hoped for you—"

"I have thanked her for that," Tom said. "I know you think me cruel, Gabe. But Aunt Mat had her chance for life—and I must have mine."

"Is there no other way to have it, Tom? She objected to my having that chance as early as I wished—if she had not opposed us, Alex and I would have been married in June. But that is not permanent—I will be twenty-one in March, and she will have no power over me then."

"She has no power over you now," Tom said. "Except what you give her." He bent and kissed her cheek. "Well, think about it, Gabriele. I won't be leaving for a couple of days—you've time to change your mind." He bade them good night and left them alone.

Gabriele rose and went to poke up the fire. Alex came up behind her and encircled her with his arms. "Now I propose to run away and you refuse," he said. "All the way to Vicksburg and back I kept thinking what a fool I was to have said no—now I am willing to be one, and it is you who have found your senses."

"I—I can't say I won't think about this," Gabriele said. "But there are so many obstacles—you would have to desert the home guard, Alex! You'd be a traitor—how can we start a new life like that?"

"Men leave the army every day, Gabriele. Especially when the fighting is near their homes. Just walk away and don't come back. I'm not regular army—what difference does it make? If you really wanted to marry me, you'd do it. All this tells me is that you don't."

"Alex—don't say that. You know it isn't true!"

"Then say you'll go with me."

"It's not that simple for me, Alex. You've lost everything —you've nothing else to lose—"

"Except you."

"You won't lose me!"

"I'm afraid I might."

"We can marry in March!" Gabriele cried. "Stay here— and if the Yankees destroy Felicity—we can build her up again."

"You really don't understand, do you?" Alex said. "You act as though the troops will break a few things, steal a few chickens, ride through the fields—and then go. Gabriele, Gabriele, how can you fool yourself so?"

"I'm sorry you think I'm so—childish," Gabriele said. "Just because I don't want to abandon everything that means something to me—" Too late, she saw the pain in his face. "I don't mean I love Felicity more than you—" she said. But he had already turned away, striding toward the door.

"Alex—" she said, starting after him. He did not stop, he did not even turn his head.

Chapter Nineteen

Neither Alex nor Tom appeared for breakfast the next morning, and Gabriele made quick work of her meal, going up to see Aunt Mat before beginning her day.

"Sit and have a cup of coffee with me," Aunt Mat said. "There's a cup over there. And tell me how Mr. St. Cyr is —I could hear you all laughing at dinner last night. It did me good to hear life in the house again."

"He's—fine," Gabriele said. "He and Tom were of course delighted to be together again." She could think of nothing else to say about Alex that would not make her cry: grabbing for a new topic, she said the first thing that came to her mind.

"Tell me about living in Texas, Aunt Mat. You've never talked much about it—was it very hard?"

Aunt Mat raised her eyebrows, peering over her glasses at Gabriele. "Where does that question come from, Gabriele? I hardly even think of Texas any more—" Her hands dropped into her lap, and her gaze shifted past Gabriele's head. "No—that's not true. I think of it all the time. I was happier there with Louis than I had ever been before—or than I have ever been since."

"It must have been awful when he died," Gabriele said. "No wonder you left the ranch—"

"Oh, I would have stayed," Aunt Mat said. "Tierradoloroso—that's what we called it. 'The sweet earth.' "

"What a lovely name," Gabriele said. "Tierradoloroso—
but what happened to it, Aunt Mat?"

"I lost it," Aunt Mat said.

"But how? I thought you'd bought it with your share of
what your parents left you and Papa—I'm sorry, that's
none of my business."

"It's long over now," Aunt Mat said. "It still hurts—but
with an old, familiar pain." She poured herself more coffee
and held up the pot to Gabriele, who shook her head.
"No more? Well, then—how did I lose the ranch?" Aunt
Mat sighed, her eyes going to her husband's picture on the
dresser across the room. "Louis was a very . . . spirited
man, Gabriele. When he believed in something, he believed in it with all his heart and strength—and optimistic?
No one could ever convince him that something he em-
barked on might not—work out."

"No wonder you loved him, Aunt Mat!"

"Yes, I loved him," Aunt Mat said. "Maybe too much—
I'd never expected to marry anyone like Louis LeGrange,
Gabriele. I wasn't pretty, and I couldn't flirt the way other
girls could. Too matter of fact and straightforward—my
mother used to blame it on my father's German mother—
she said all the solemn traits had come down to me!"

"But Louis could see what others couldn't," Gabriele
said.

"I suppose," Aunt Mat said. "Don't think I didn't hear
the talk that went around—that he'd married me for my
money—his family had land, Gabriele, but nothing like
ours."

"People will say unpleasant things, Aunt Mat, even
when they're not true."

"When you are older, Gabriele, you will realize how
little it matters what people say, true or not true." Aunt
Mat lifted her hand, looking at the gold ring shining
there. "I'd rather have had this ring from Louis LeGrange
than a trunk full of diamonds from someone else."

Then if you loved like that yourself, why did you come
between me and Alex? Gabriele wanted to say. Because she

doesn't see Alex the way she saw Louis. Or maybe she does. And maybe some part of her is still angry that she lost him—so angry she can't let me be happy—it is almost as though she wants all of us to carry some of her pain.

"And being Louis, of course, he borrowed against the ranch and paid to raise a company himself," she heard Aunt Mat say, and realized she had lost the thread.

"You mean—he outfitted a company to fight in the war?" she said.

"Yes—it took every cent he could borrow, and of course I pleaded and cried and did everything I could to stop him —but it was like talking to the wind. Mexico would lose, he said, and then he'd pay off the debt." A spasm of pain twisted Aunt Mat's face. "Well, Mexico did lose. But by that time, Louis was long dead—and I had lost the ranch."

"Oh, Aunt Mat!"

"I—I didn't see how I could stand it—Louis dead, the ranch gone—if Oliver hadn't been here to offer me a haven, I don't know what I'd have done."

"To think I never knew what you had been through, Aunt Mat," Gabriele said. "I'm so sorry—"

"Nothing would have been different if you had, Gabriele. That chapter of my life closed when I crossed the Texas border. I brought few reminders—"

Abigail, Gabriele thought. And Veronique. Involuntarily, her eyes went to the open door. From the sewing room across the hall the sound of the machine could be heard, a faint whirr as the moving treadle pushed the wheel around.

"Aunt Mat," Gabriele began, but could not make herself finish the question that burned in her mind.

"What?" Aunt Mat said.

"Nothing—I was going to ask you something about dinner—but it's all right. I know what I want."

"I feel so lazy this morning," Aunt Mat said. "I don't think I'll get up at all."

"We must get Dr. Delahaye out to look at you," Gabriele said.

"Oh, no, I'm all right. Just—lazy," Aunt Mat said.

Gabriele left her then, thinking as she went back downstairs that Aunt Mat had never been lazy in her life. The fatigue she feels comes from everything that is happening here, she thought. Tom's love for Veronique—Aunt Mat's recognition that she treated Alex unfairly—that she has let go of her old authority and has nothing to take its place. She shook her head as though to throw off her own problems so that she could concentrate on finding some way to stop Tom.

I don't care if he loves Veronique, I don't care if they marry. But for him to run away—I know he thinks he has no other course, but there must be. There must. She stopped, cocking her head as though she had heard someone call her name. Wait—I'm wrong—he's not running away. He's going toward.

She sank onto the step, letting the thought sink in. Of course. It's all over here, that's what he believes. The fact that the Yankees haven't come yet means nothing to Tom. For him, it's gone. She looked down the stairs into the wide front hall. Each table, each chair, each picture on the wall, told a story to her loving eyes. This chair brought from Ireland by the first Cannon in 1798. That gold-leaf framed mirror carried from France by her mother's ancestors in 1789. She rose and ran down the last flight of stairs, then went to stand in the parlour doors. I may not be able to save any of this, she thought. But until I can let go of it—I will have to stay.

She thought of Alex, of the way he had looked just before he left her the night before. He, too, believed there was nothing left here, so he would not understand why she could not go. She might lose him—still, she could not change her mind. I want no bits and pieces of me trailing me when I begin a new life, she thought. I wish I were finished here—I wish I felt ready to leave it. But I don't. And if that means losing Alex—I would have lost him anyway. Because sooner or later whatever it is that binds my old life would have come between us. Maybe it's just as well it did so now.

Despair flooded over her as she made herself face what this decision could mean. But strangely, though her heart ached, it did not tell her she was wrong.

Alex found her in the cemetery at twilight, where she had gone to spend a quiet hour at her parents' graves. He sat beside her and took her hand in his. "I keep thinking I've gotten rid of all my old bad habits, Gabriele," he said. "Then another test comes—and I fail it as I did you last night."

"I do love you, Alex," she said. "And I want to marry you more than anything on earth. But I can't leave just yet. Something I don't even understand holds me here—as though I must spin the last of this thread before I begin a new skein."

"I know that now," Alex said, kissing her palm. "Tom and I talked late last night, Gabriele, and this is what we think we must do. Tom must go to Mrs. LeGrange and tell her that one way or the other, he means to take Veronique away with him."

"Alex!"

"It may force her hand, if she truly means to sell Veronique. But we'll be ready to leave for Mexico the day after tomorrow—she could hardly effect a sale so soon."

"We—then you are going—"

"But I'll come back," Alex said. "That's the other thing we—I—decided. I won't let Tom make that trip alone, even if he does have Samson and Jonas. But since you are not yet ready to leave—I'll come back." He took her other hand and bent closer. "We must go to Mrs. LeGrange, too, Gabriele, and tell her that we want to marry as soon as I get back. That should be late in November—so you can plan a wedding for anytime after, say, the 20th, with full confidence that I will be here."

"Alex—but what if she says no? She is still my legal guardian—"

"You must not let her say no, Gabriele." He brought her hands to his lips and kissed the fingers one by one. "I have thought about your aunt very carefully since yesterday, and I think that when she believes you are ready to make your own decision—can meet any argument she gives you with a quiet assurance that what you choose is right—she will gladly give over her responsibility for you."

"I hope so," Gabriele said. "Oh, Alex, I hate to talk about something so—private and wonderful with Aunt Mat! I hate to talk about it with anyone!" She stood up, opening her arms wide. "I want to feel the way I used to feel when I'd spring on Brandy's back and ride and ride until all the cobwebs blew away!"

He rose and stood behind her, arms around her waist. "Poor darling," he said. "You've had far too many cobwebs lately. But I promise you—we will marry when I get back. And the first thing I'll do is sweep every one of those ugly things right out of your mind."

They stood in silence, no longer needing words. Then Alex took her left hand and slipped a ring on the third finger, a circlet of gold set with a square-cut emerald surrounded by pearls. Gabriele stared at it, hardly able to believe her eyes. "Alex—it's beautiful—but where did you get it? Why, it's the loveliest ring I ever saw in my life!"

"I bought it in Vicksburg," Alex said. "I saw it and thought of your eyes—"

As though the ring had the powers of some ancient amulet, Gabriele felt suddenly sure that when she spoke with Aunt Mat, the obstacles would vanish, leaving the path to their wedding open and smooth.

"I'm glad you gave it to me here," she said. "Near Papa and Mama's graves—"

"I hadn't thought," Alex said. "I suppose a cemetery is a strange place to become engaged—"

"No—exactly right," Gabriele said. "I always feel so close to them here—every decision I've ever made here has turned out to be right. As though somehow their spirits touch me and keep me from going wrong." She pulled her cloak around her, feeling the bite of the wind. "Now let's go up to the house," she said. "And tell Aunt Mat."

They entered Aunt Mat's room to find Tom and Veronique sitting by her bed. Their faces told the story, there was no need to ask. They had made peace, the three of them, and when Tom stood up, the pain and anguish at last gone from his eyes, Gabriele already knew what he would say. "It's all right," he said. "Aunt Mat understands."

"Then may we hope that you will understand our wish, too, Aunt Mat?" Gabriele said, going to her aunt's side. "Alex and I want to marry as soon as he returns from Mexico—we have thought very carefully, and we see no reason why we can't."

"Nor do I," Aunt Mat said. She took Gabriele's hand and touched the ring. "Emeralds for hope—pearls for constancy—and a gold ring for eternity. Well, you've been very patient with me, Gabriele, you and Tom." She saw the glance Gabriele exchanged with Tom and smiled. "Oh, yes, I hung on much longer than I should have—I thought I could somehow keep you from making mistakes —or rather—keep you from doing things I thought—wrong."

"You were only giving us guidance, as you have done for so long," Gabriele said.

"But that was no longer appropriate," Aunt Mat said. "Only I didn't want to see it." She picked up the miniature of Louis LeGrange that sat now on the table next to her bed. "I've blamed myself, all these years, that I didn't—couldn't—stop Louis from borrowing against our land to indulge his own pride. Oh, yes, it was pride drove him to make a grand gesture like that—pride and—anger at me."

"Aunt Mat—" Gabriele said. "Don't tell us anything you'll be sorry for later."

"I need to tell this," Aunt Mat said. "I have to get it off

my soul." Her eyes went to her husband's face: seeing
Louis LeGrange's young, handsome image Gabriele
thought how hard it must have been for Aunt Mat to
grow old alone with memories that still brought bitter
pain. *And all the while I thought she had been so
happy . . .*

As though she read Gabriele's mind, Aunt Mat said,
"The first two years in Texas were the happiest I had ever
known. The ranch prospered, I was young and in love—
how that happiness lulled me! I became careless, I did not
keep up a daily battle against the old weaknesses of self-
doubt and jealousy that had so long plagued me—and
when the first big temptation came to indulge them both
—I fell."

"Are you sure you want to say all this?" Gabriele said,
taking Aunt Mat's hand. "It's all over and done with—"

"No, my dear, that's where you're wrong. The poison
those bitter days brewed has spilled over to touch your life
—and Tom's—as well as Veronique's and Mr. St. Cyr's.
God has long ago forgiven me—I now have to forgive
myself."

Gabriele sat quietly then, reaching out her other hand
and feeling Alex's warm grasp.

"It's not a long story," Aunt Mat said. "It concerns
Veronique's mother—a woman named Consuela, who was
mostly Spanish with a great-grandmother who was black."

Veronique's sharp intake of breath made them turn and
look at her: she gazed at Aunt Mat as though each word
were meant only for her. "Yes, I've always known who
your mother was, Veronique," Aunt Mat said. "I only—
pretended I did not—for reasons that shame me still.

"Consuela had a child by the overseer on the ranch
where she worked as a cook—that child is Veronique."

"Worked?" Tom said. "Then—was she not a slave?"

Aunt Mat held Louis' picture against her breast like a
shield. "No," she said, steadily meeting Tom's eyes. "She
was not."

"Not a slave!" Tom said. "Then neither is Veronique!"

"No," Aunt Mat said.

"But you have said that she is—you have *lied* all these years?" Tom rose and started toward the bed, but Veronique caught his arm and pulled him back.

"Tom—let her speak," she said.

"I did not want to tell my brother the truth when I first came, so I let him think that both Veronique and Abigail were slaves."

"What is the truth?" Gabriele said.

"The overseer would not marry Consuela—he left and went to work somewhere far away. She had grander ideas than staying on as a cook—raising a child by herself—so she wangled a job on our ranch." Aunt Mat leaned back and closed her eyes. For a moment, only the sound of wood sap hissing in the fire and a pine branch tapping against the window pane broke the close stillness of the room. Then Aunt Mat opened her eyes and sat upright, bracing herself for the rest of her tale.

"My mind told me that she had her eye on our trail boss—but my jealous heart told me it was Louis she wanted. She was so pretty—laughing and singing all the time—I—couldn't stand it. And so I told Louis she had to go." Aunt Mat's hand tightened on Louis' picture, and she kept her eyes on his face. "I couldn't have picked a worse time for a quarrel. We were already on edge because Louis wanted to raise a company and join the Mexican War—he was restless, bored by the routine of the ranch—" She shook her head, as though still trying to say no to an impetuous, high-spirited man. "I said all the terrible things plain women say when they pour their own self-doubt on their handsome husbands' heads. Until that day, I had not known I could even—think such things. Much less say them to the man I loved more than anyone on earth."

A log broke and fell in pieces, sending up a fountain of sparks, and out of the corner of her eye, Gabriele saw Veronique move into the shelter of Tom's arm.

"Well—after that—who could blame Louis for what he

did? He rode away without another word—borrowed the money—raised his company—and went off to—die." The last of Aunt Mat's control went, and she collapsed against her pillows, tears pouring down her cheeks.

"Tom," Gabriele whispered. "Come here."

He looked at her questioningly, but rose and did as she said.

"Take her hand," Gabriele said, as she took the other one in her own. She waited until Tom's hand came slowly forward and closed around Aunt Mat's. Then, bending over the bed, she said, "It's all right, Aunt Mat. You mustn't torment yourself any more. It's all going to be all right."

"All the years I've lied to Veronique," Aunt Mat said, pressing her handkerchief against her eyes. "But I was so—frightened as to what would become of her—"

"I still don't understand how you came to have the care of her," Gabriele said.

"When word came of Louis' death, I—went crazy, I guess. I couldn't face my part in it—I blamed Consuela. I went to her cabin and—scared her to death. The next thing I knew—she had gone—and left Veronique. And then after that—all of it happening so fast—I lost the ranch—and came to Oliver, the only home I had left."

"And let Veronique grow up along with us," Tom said. "Because she was not a slave."

"I kept thinking I could right the wrong I'd done," Aunt Mat said. "But every turn I took led to a worse place —then when I saw what letting you all be so close all those years had done—that you were well on the way to falling in love with her, Tom—well, that, along with Oliver's death—I got myself into a place so deep I saw no way of getting out of it at all."

Veronique came to stand next to Tom, placing her hand on his arm as though his touch would give her strength. "Mrs. LeGrange—do I look like my mother?"

Aunt Mat's eyes, startled, ringed with fear, met Veronique's. "I didn't—see it for a long while," she said. "But as you grew older—yes, yes, you do."

Veronique sighed as though her last question had finally been answered. "And so you still hoped to punish her—through me," she said.

Aunt Mat looked at her, her eyes going over each feature of Veronique's face. They could all see the battle truth and deception waged—and they saw the moment when truth won. "Yes—I see now—that is what I did."

"But you don't have to any more, do you?" Veronique asked.

"Never again."

"I'm glad," she said. She moved closer to the bed. "I never thought the day would come when I would say these words to you, Mrs. LeGrange. But it's all right. I understand what you did—and I forgive you."

Aunt Mat's face twisted as she fought the last bitter pain. Then she smiled and took Veronique's hand. "You'll be part of the family soon," she said. "I think you should call me Aunt Mat."

Two days later, Tom and Alex and Veronique, followed by two wagonloads of sugar driven by Samson and Jonas, left for Texas and the Mexican border. They rode through the mists of dawn, passing under trees where night still lay captured. Gabriele stood shivering in the chill, watching them vanish down the drive. Then, kissing the ring Alex had given her and touching the locket which now hung unconcealed around her neck, she went into the house to begin preparing for the day Alex would return, this time to find her waiting as his bride.

The whole atmosphere is different, she thought, as she stepped into the hall. Fires burn more brightly, the simplest food tastes fine—the cobwebs of deceit and doubt are gone, brushed away by the truth's great broom. One deception they had all agreed must be allowed: word would get out to the slaves that Veronique's true owner had at long last asserted a claim, and that she returned to him.

"In a way it is true," Veronique said, smiling up at Tom. "For my life belongs to Tom as surely as if he owned it—more surely, for it is a gift freely made."

"And gratefully received," Tom said. "How glad I'll be to be away from here, where between us we can build life as we want it to be."

They are on their way to doing that now, Gabriele thought. Tom would use part of the money the sugar brought to buy land and build a house large enough for Alex and Gabriele and Aunt Mat if they should ever want to come. "The rest I'll take in gold," Tom said. "And save that with the jewellery and silver I carry from Felicity to make sure that whatever contingency arises—it will be met."

Tom and Alex had gone with Adams to where he had hidden their valuables, loading the jewel cases and chests of silver under the sacks of sugar. "You see, Gabe," Tom said the night before he left, "I'm taking parts of Felicity to Texas—so if you decide to come, you'll find old friends waiting for you there."

She said nothing, thinking that when he told her he planned to take those treasures, he told her something else: he believed his dark predictions, he did not think she could possibly stay here. When Alex returned, it would be to marry her, yes—but after that, she thought he would try to persuade her to leave.

Will I go? she asked herself. She went into the parlour and opened the piano lid. She had not played in weeks—she could not remember the last time. Now she sat and let her fingers roam over the keys, falling finally into her father's favourite song.

" 'Believe me, if all those endearing young charms,
Which I gaze on so fondly today,
Were to change by tomorrow, and fleet in my arms,
Like fairy gifts fading away,
Thou would'st still be adored as this moment thou art,
Let thy loveliness fade as it will;

And around the dear ruin, each wish of my heart
Would entwine itself verdantly still.' "

Gabriele stopped singing, though she still played the
tune. Her father had kept his love for her mother alive, all
those years after she died. He had lived in happy memory,
Aunt Mat had lived in a bitter one—her father's life had
gone on—but Aunt Mat had stayed frozen in the past,
unable to keep it from looming much larger in her heart
and soul than did the present itself.

And if I cling to the old days when all signs tell me they
are gone—even if the memories are happy ones—if they
keep me from going forward—are they not as much a trap
as Aunt Mat's bitter ones? Her hands stilled on the keys,
she heard or saw nothing around her as she concentrated
on that thought. There is no cowardice in venerating the
past, as my father did. But there is cowardice in clinging to
it. She rose, closing the piano and going to stand before
her father's portrait. In front of that quiet, confident face
she could let herself confront her fears. It took a while for
the last and strongest one to emerge, but finally it crept
out into the light of Oliver Cannon's gaze.

I have kept hoping that something would happen, and
that I would not have to do the last hard thing, Gabriele
told her father's image. Now I know that what matters
isn't whether I really have to do it—it is to know that
whatever it is—I will and can. Something entered her soul
then, something she had never felt before. Not new
strength, and not yet will—then it came to her. What she
felt was trust in her own self.

When she left the parlour to go to Aunt Mat and make
her wedding plans, she did so with a happiness so new she
felt as though it had been created for her heart alone.
Aunt Mat saw the change in Gabriele the moment she
entered the room. When I told the truth it broke the last
knots that bound Gabriele to childhood, she thought.
Thank God, we've both grown up.

"And now we must get to work," she said to Gabriele.

"I've begun making out a list for the invitations—and Letha is hunting for the receipt for that good white cake your grandmother used to make." She looked at Gabriele and smiled a little sadly. "There will be no wedding trip to Europe as your father and mother had—but we shall think of a place nearby where you may have some time together, Gabriele."

"I have waited so long to be happy, Aunt Mat," Gabriele said. "But today I think I have learned what a mistake it is to believe we have to wait—happiness lies around us, just within our grasp. And to find it—we have only to trust that it is there."

Chapter Twenty

November 29 dawned clear and cold; when Gabriele woke, the fire in her room had long been burning, painting the ivory folds of the satin gown hanging nearby with rich hues of pink and gold. She lay for one minute more, the thought that had been the last clear image in her mind as she fell asleep the night before still fixed: this morning is the last day of my existence as Gabriele Cannon. When I wake tomorrow, it will be as Mrs. Alex St. Cyr.

And then she could lie still no longer, throwing back her covers and reaching out her hand for the bell-pull near the bed. Lucie appeared almost immediately, a tray of steaming coffee in her hands, the smile on her face saying that she, too, welcomed this temporary restoration of the old régime, when her time was spent tending to Gabriele and her wardrobe instead of working in the barns and fields.

"You and Mr. Alex got a beauteous day for yo' wedding," Lucie said. "It's as though the Lord hisself is making you a present."

"Oh, He is," Gabriele said, slipping on the dressing gown Lucie handed her and taking her cup from the tray. She looked around the room, happily noting the completeness of her preparations for both the ceremony and the wedding trip to follow.

Her mother's gown had not required much adjustment,

and what alterations it did need had been accomplished easily. Abigail had washed the yellowing lace veil, rinsing it in lemon juice and putting it out in the sun to bleach until it regained its pristine ivory hue. Even the satin slippers with seed-pearl buckles fit: seeing Gabriele gowned as her mother had been so many years before, Aunt Mat had hugged her, crying a little, but smiling through her tears as she assured her that surely her father and mother watched her from heaven, and wished her the joy they had found.

Even reports the first week of November of skirmishes between Federal gunboats and the Confederate gunboat *Cotton* some thirty miles east of Felicity did not affect their mood as they prepared for the wedding, and when the *Cotton* fought off her attackers, when the barricade the Confederates put across Bayou Teche held, and when the Yankee troops marching on Avery Island in mid-November to destroy the salt works were repelled, the Confederate loyalists in the region took heart that a holding action in the Teche country could expand.

Nor did the weeks before Alex returned seem as long as Gabriele had feared: Aunt Mat's list of things to be done kept growing, and Gabriele sometimes thought that it resembled Penelope's weaving, and that at night after the household went to sleep, Aunt Mat must undo some of what had been accomplished, adding the same tasks back to be done all over again.

Now all had been accomplished: in the absence of the household silver Aunt Mat used crystal punch bowls and platters, filling out what she lacked from neighbouring houses. And despite wartime shortages, Aunt Mat had managed to put together a wedding reception that, if it did not rival the glory of the old days, at least, as she said, would not put the Cannon tradition of hospitality to shame.

In a burst of energy that made her bustle around like her old self, Aunt Mat had made over a suit of hers and an afternoon dress into a travelling costume for Gabriele.

Now when she and Alex left for their wedding trip to Chretien Point, the plantation of their good friend Hypolite Chretien on the other side of Vermilionville, Gabriele would have a hunter green suit to wear, with a blouse and petticoat of ecru crêpe de Chine. Dorothea Robin Levert had contributed a bonnet of the same dark green as the suit, and Gabriele added to it pheasant feathers saved from a hunt with Tom.

Only Tom's absence on her wedding day wove a dark thread through the golden fabric of those days, but that could not be helped. Mr. Robin would give her away, and Felice Robin would attend the bride. Now as Gabriele put the finishing touches to her toilette she heard the carriages rolling up the drive, and a hubbub rose from the floor below as guests filled the house, their laughter and chatter rising like warm air to lighten the atmosphere and lift all fears and anxieties away. The guests might have to reclaim them when they departed at the festivities' end, but for now they marshalled all their faith, all their hope, and all their love, affirming with their grace and gallantry the principles upon which their lives were built.

Every guest gathered at Felicity that day knew that the Yankees occupied the entire Lafourche area, and that on every front, the Confederate armies found themselves more and more on the defence, their earlier threat of invasion blunted by the North. Every guest knew that this long prelude to their own involvement in the war drew nearer and nearer to its close, and the skirmishes between the *Cotton* and the Federal gunboats and between Yankee and Confederate troops at Avery Island were like the first waters rising above the levees in the spring: a trickle at first, they soon became a stream, then a wider flow, and finally, a flood that drove everything before it.

The isolation of rural lives had given them a strength different from that of their fellows in the cities. They knew, these people, that they must rely on themselves and their own resources to survive any blow; through fever epidemics, floods, droughts and hurricanes they had proved themselves, making a network of support that drew its strength from the constant willingness of those who belonged to it to make themselves available to all the others.

The family at Felicity needed only joy and laughter today, and for guests who had lost sons, brothers, husbands and fathers on battlefields across the South, joy and laughter could be in short supply. But as Gabriele peeked over the balcony rail at the scene below, she found not one gloomy visage or one anxious face. Some observers might see this gaiety as a foolish mask whose defence against trials and sorrows would prove futile indeed, but others might see what Gabriele saw: not a mask, but armour, made in the same spirit of the words of the verse from St. John worked on a sampler that hung on her bedroom wall. Its message, read unconsciously many times throughout the day as her eyes fell upon it, had entered Gabriele's heart, where it became one with all the other words and phrases cherished there. "Perfect love casteth out fear." The colours of the embroidery thread had faded, but the belief in the sentiment had not, and although some words lose power the more they are repeated, Gabriele had learned that these did not.

She and Alex stood protected today by all the armour love had at its command: to the guests at Felicity that day, these young people represented the triumph of all that is good in man and his condition over all that is wrong. One more step was being risked into the unknown, with no demand for guarantees or safe passage. Their marriage might last a month, a year, a decade. Alex might be killed by the first Yankee bullet to be fired at the Teche home guard; Gabriele might, as so many women around her, live on to bear a fatherless child. The strength in that house came not from ignorance of the hazards that lay before them, but from a recognition that life is always dangerous, and that those who wait until everything is safe will die before they have attempted even one dream. And so when the first toast was made, and the guests raised their glasses high, drinking to the couple's happiness and wishing them long life, they drank also to a larger vision, one in which each person present shared.

Now Felice Robin broke away from the crowd and darted up the steps to Gabriele, holding a bouquet of white camellias in one hand and one of deep pink camellias in the other. "Father DeBlanc is here," she said. "We're almost ready to begin." She followed Gabriele back down the hall to her room, where Lucie waited to pin on her veil. "You look so beautiful, Gabriele! Are you very happy?"

The door behind them opened and Aunt Mat came into the room. She had refurbished a grey silk dress made by a Paris house some years before, and though the style might be out of fashion, it suited Aunt Mat.

"I wonder if I might have a word with Gabriele alone," Aunt Mat said. "I have a little present for her."

"Of course, Mrs. LeGrange," Felice said, leading the way out of the room with Lucie behind her.

"I had some difficulty settling on a gift for you, Gabriele," Aunt Mat said. "You already own all your mother's jewellery, and mine will go to you, too."

"I don't need or want a present," Gabriele began, but Aunt Mat cut her short.

"What I have for you is not a present in the usual sense of the word," Aunt Mat said. "In fact, I suppose it seems an odd gift for a bride—" She pulled a long, slender box from her skirt pocket and thrust it toward Gabriele. And when Gabriele hesitated, she said, "Open it, child. Open it."

Gabriele loosed the silk cord that held the box closed and lifted the lid. There on a cushion of black velvet lay a gold-handled knife studded with emeralds and pearls. Its thin blade shone in the light, its sharp edge glimmering as though lined with diamonds.

"Aunt Mat—"

"You are puzzled, of course," Aunt Mat said. "But when

you hear the story behind this knife, you might appreciate it better."

"It is beautiful, Aunt Mat—but so very deadly looking!"

"As it should be. It comes down through the Cannons —legend has it that the first Cannon to possess it took it from a Spaniard at the time of the Armada. At any rate, I have written out the names of all the owners—you will find them on the paper underneath the velvet. My brother Oliver insisted I take this knife when our father died, although normally it went to the first born male. It would fit my new Texas landscape, he said." Aunt Mat stared at the knife for a moment, then back at Gabriele. "Since Oliver broke the tradition, I feel that I may, too, and give this to you rather than to Tom." She bent and kissed her niece. "Well, do with it what you will, Gabriele. It opens letters easily, I assure you, and is no laggard when it comes to a joint of meat."

"I shall treasure it always, Aunt Mat," Gabriele said. "The more because it is your gift."

She put her arms around Aunt Mat's neck and kissed her tenderly, wishing that some of the great happiness that filled her now could bloom in Aunt Mat's heart. Even as she put the knife away, she thought of that other gift Aunt Mat had given her, one she had made without knowing that she gave it. And that is the lesson about what hanging on to the misery of the past can do, Gabriele thought. If I can remember that—and never by my own bitter experience have to learn it again—I need no gift from anyone, ever again.

Mr. Robin waited for Gabriele at the top of the stairs: he escorted her down them, and they passed through the aisle the ranks of guests made, into the parlour where an altar had been arranged. Father DeBlanc stood before it, with Alex at his side. And then Gabriele saw no one else. She knew Father DeBlanc spoke the words of the service, for she saw his lips move. But the only voice she really heard belonged to Alex: she took her cue from him, and repeated the vows that would make her his.

Father DeBlanc touched their heads as he blessed them, and then Alex took her hand, placing the gold wedding band on each of her first three fingers as he repeated the words of the vow, finally sliding it into place on the ring finger of her left hand. "With this ring, I thee wed," he said. "In the name of the Father, and of the Son, and of the Holy Spirit, Amen."

Her eyes went to the ring, hardly seeing the delicate tracing of vines and leaves carved into the wide gold band. I must try to fix this moment, she thought. Try to remember everything I am feeling, every detail around me. But then people pressed forward, shaking Alex's hand and kissing Gabriele's cheeks, and she let that one single beat of time slip away, lost in the new impressions coming thick and fast.

Wishes of joy and felicitation, over and over again. Hands grasping hers, faces held close. Ladies who remembered her mother clutching her and telling her how like her Gabriele was. Men who revered her father kissing her and telling her how happy he would be. Letha moving through the crowd, directing Jonas and Lucie and Abigail. Scent of mulled wine, aroma of ham. Music playing, feet sliding across the floor. Then feeling Lucie's hands removing her wedding gown, putting the new travelling dress on in its stead. The hat, her gloves. A last glance in her travelling case—a hug from Aunt Mat—

Then at last in the carriage, blanketed with a great fur robe. Alex picking up the reins and slapping them lightly over the team's back. People standing on the gallery, waving as they drove away. Gates of Felicity shutting behind them, and ahead an empty road.

"We're getting away in good time," Alex said. "We should reach Chretien Point well before nightfall."

Such happiness filled Gabriele then that she thought if this day, the night ahead, were all they ever had, it would be enough. For once you know what real happiness is, she thought, touching her ring through her glove, it can never completely leave you, and you can never really be unhappy again.

The road, hard-packed after a dry fall, made a swift track for the horses, and they fairly sped along, passing through a landscape held fast in the crystalline air. Scarlet and yellow leaves blazed against the bright blue sky, while the drying stalks of cane strewn over the harvested fields made a dun-coloured carpet as far as they could see. The speed of the horses whipped up a breeze that blew against Gabriele's face, and she turned the collar of her cloak up to protect it.

"Cold?" Alex said, reaching under the carriage robe to take her hand.

"It's just the wind," Gabriele said. "But now I'm warm."

Even through the two gloves, his hand seemed to pulse in hers, as though already their new state had changed the way they touched. A solitary rider going the other way approached them, eyes resting on them incuriously as he closed the distance between them. *We were married today,* Gabriele wanted to call to him. *Not three hours ago.* The rider passed on by, and she turned to look after him.

"Isn't it strange," she said, "that something so momentous can happen—and so many people neither know nor care that it has."

"You think everyone should know, just by looking at us, that we are just setting out on a wonderful adventure," Alex said.

"I know that's silly," Gabriele said. "But I feel that surely the glow I know surrounds us should be visible to everyone else!"

"God forbid," Alex said, laughing. "Else we should never be let alone. And the very last thing I want this week is company."

Gabriele heard the way his voice dropped on the last few words, the sudden husky note. She raised her eyes to his, certain what she would find there. That same blaze of light, that same energy, which she had seen in Alex's eyes from the very beginning. She had at first mistaken that light for passion, but now she knew its source was deeper and stronger still. Alex's very essence was in that light—all the emotions he had denied through years of living with an inflexible and rigid mother and a too easy-going and irresponsible father burned steadily deep within him, ready to come into the open when the right key was finally turned.

I hold that key, Gabriele thought, and the last of her anxieties faded away. If Alex were to be her guide into the mysteries of love, then she would be his means of emerging from darkness into the light. Together they would be stronger than either one apart; together there would be no obstacle they could not vanquish, no challenge they could not overcome.

"And I," she said softly. "I wish to see no one but you."

When they arrived at Chretien Point, their hosts had anticipated just that desire. Mrs. Chretien greeted them, conveying Mr. Chretien's regrets that he had accompanied his cotton crop to the dock on the Red River, and would not return until near the end of their stay. "The children are scattered," she said in response to Gabriele's inquiries after her family. "The boys away at the war, of course—and the girls visiting friends."

"You are very kind to have us here," Gabriele said.

"Nonsense, child. It is our pleasure," Celestine Chretien said. "Now, I've put you in the southwest bedroom—it's a favourite of guests, because the view of the sunsets is so splendid. We're on the prairie here, and nothing breaks the vista for miles."

"It's a splendid house," Alex said as she led them up the stairs, followed by a boy carrying their baggage.

"My husband's father built it in '31," Mrs. Chretien said. "It's been a happy house—your presence here affirms it."

"We're going to pretend there's no war," Gabriele said. "For just this week."

"Oh, my dear, if that were but true!" Mrs. Chretien said, and kissed Gabriele on both cheeks.

Then she moved ahead of them to open a tall door, standing aside so they could precede her into the room.

A good fire burned in the fireplace, flames reflected in the black marble framing its face. Although the french doors were closed, the draperies had not yet been drawn, and they could see that the room gave onto a gallery, beyond which lay fields of picked-over cotton. Small bits of white still clung to the brown bushes, and beyond the cotton field stretched the promised view.

"It's a lovely room," Gabriele said. "We shall be very comfortable here." She walked over to a chair set in one of the windows, untying her bonnet as though being here with Alex was the most familiar thing in the world.

"I'll leave you to settle in, then," Mrs. Chretien said. "Bess will bring coffee up immediately, as I'm sure you are weary after your trip. I'm going to beg off dining with you, I do hope you don't mind. But I've only been up for a few days—I had some sort of ailment that kept me in bed. So I will dine in my room, and you of course may dine where you choose. Tell Bess, she will see to everything."

All the while Mrs. Chretien chattered on, Gabriele became more and more conscious of the room, the bed, the door that would soon close behind their hostess and leave her and Alex alone. She felt her heart begin to beat faster, and ducked her head so that neither Mrs. Chretien nor Alex could see the quick blush that painted her cheeks. Alex had his back to her as he listened to Mrs. Chretien: this back belonged to someone Gabriele did not know, had never seen before, certainly did not love enough to marry.

Panic fluttered in her throat, and she opened her mouth to speak. But before she could say a word, Mrs. Chretien came to her, kissed her on both cheeks, took Alex's hand and clasped it warmly, and then walked out of the room, closing the door firmly behind her.

"Wait—" Gabriele said to the solid panels.

Alex moved toward the door. "Shall I call her? Do you need something?"

"Yes—no," Gabriele said. She stood perfectly still, staring at him, watching him as he turned from the door and came to her.

"Don't you want to remove your cloak? Or are you still cold?"

"No—I—yes, here it is," she said, unfastening the clasp and letting him take the cloak from her shoulders.

A gentle tap at the door, and a soft voice called, "It's Bess, with your coffee."

"Coming," Alex said. He smiled at Gabriele and opened the door, swinging it wide to accommodate the large tray the woman bore.

"Mrs. Chretien, she say you might be hungry, too," Bess said. "She say most peoples don't eat at they own wedding."

"Mrs. Chretien is a wise woman," Alex said, eyeing the tray. "Please thank her for her thoughtfulness."

"Yes, suh," Bess said. "I do that." Then she backed out of the room, smiling and bowing until the door closed and they were alone once more.

"A hearty repast," Alex said, indicating the tray. A large plate held cheese and sliced ham, while next to it was a basket filled with biscuits and light bread. Three kinds of preserves, a bottle of wine besides the pot of coffee, and a dish with several baked sweet potatoes completed the meal. "With all those provisions, we might stay here for days."

"Yes," Gabriele said.

"Now I wonder if I just put the coffee pot and the sweet potatoes on this trivet near the hearth, if they wouldn't stay nice and warm," Alex said. He suited action to words, then turned back to the tray, picking up the wine and holding it to the light.

"A very nice red," he said. "But it should breathe before we drink it. Why don't I open it and set it aside for a while?"

"That would be—very nice," Gabriele said.

She felt mesmerized: the excitement of the day, and of all the days before it, the long drive through the cold, and now the warm room with its glowing fire lulled her, so that she felt encased in something very smooth and very soft and very thick that kept everything beyond this room far away.

Alex set the opened wine back on the tray and came back to her.

"Can you think of anything else we must do now?"

"No—"

"Except this," he said, kissing her forehead. "And this," kissing her cheek. "And this—and this—and this," as his lips kissed her other cheek, then her throat, then her lips.

He made the centre now, the core of this smooth, soft, thick case that held her safe and fast. She could feel herself sinking ever more deeply into that core, moving farther and farther away from a world where reason and thought held sway. Only feeling his lips, his fingers, his hands. Him.

"Oh, Alex," she whispered, sighing against his neck. "I'm so glad I'm married to you."

There was no answer, but there did not need to be. Once again, a moment became separate from everything that had gone before it and everything that would come afterwards. Rich coffee odours blended with the sharp, clean smell of Alex's skin; she could not tell the difference between the cool, smooth crêpe de Chine of her blouse and his cool, smooth fingers—she could feel their two lives merge, blend—become one.

And later, as the last pink band of sunset faded to lavender, then grey, then went as dark as the rest of the sky, she curled against Alex, sipping the wine he poured for her, thinking that what they had now belonged to them forever, and that though she could not have known it, each day of her life had prepared her for the wonder of being Mrs. Alex St. Cyr.

* * *

Gabriele returned to Felicity from Chretien Point determined to make the first Christmas she and Alex spent as
man and wife as memorable as it could possibly be, despite
the ever-present threat that the lessening of activity on the
battlefields which winter always brought would burgeon
again with the spring. And if she felt as she put pine and
holly branches around the house and supervised the setting up of the tree that she performed a farewell rite, she
did not let that dampen her spirits. I shall live for today,
she thought each morning, and rejoice that I have Alex—
there is nothing more I need.

They felt Tom's absence of course, and when a letter
arrived from him on Christmas Eve, Gabriele read it with
increasing joy. "They're safe," she said. "Safe and well—
settled on land near San Antonio—Tom says a river runs
through it, and that it has both hills and a fertile plain—
and they are *married*! At a little church dating from mis-
sion days." She handed the letter to Alex, thinking that
this good news made their Christmas celebration complete.

And so when families from nearby plantations and from
New Iberia came to Felicity on New Year's Day, they
found a happy young mistress receiving guests at her husband's side, and more than one of them told Gabriele how
much like her mother she was.

Talk of the New Orleans social season dominated the
conversation at first: "Operas!" one scandalized lady announced. "Plays and dances! How can they revel when
New Orleans is in enemy hands?"

"General Nathaniel Banks, who replaced Butler, seems
more willing to be conciliatory than the Beast," someone
said. "And after all, when at the last count over sixty-one
thousand people in New Orleans had taken the loyalty
oath and been restored to full citizenship in the Union—
well, I suppose those people feel they have nothing to
regret."

"Regret?" said Mr. Robin, looking at the assembled

guests. "I should imagine that like all of us, the people of New Orleans live with regret, both those who have taken the oath and those who will not do it."

"Do you mean we were wrong to secede, sir?" a man cried. "I will not hear such talk, not even from a friend like you."

"Right—wrong—the lines have blurred so that I can hardly see them any more," Mr. Robin said. "I still believe we had a right to leave the Union—but history teaches us that there are some rights which so oppose each other that when they meet in conflict—the supporters of both of them lose."

"I don't understand you," someone said. "If you asked the Yankees, they'd say they're winning. And if things keep on as they are—they probably will. And yet you say they'll lose?"

"We all will," Mr. Robin said. "Civil wars, unlike wars mounted against an outside foe, deepen all the smallest divisions among sections of a nation until they widen and will take generations to cross." He reached out a hand to his wife, and drew her nearer. "I am not young enough to wait generations for the wounds this war has made to heal. And so I have sold my plantation and will be taking my family away in a matter of weeks."

A murmur of shock greeted his announcement, and questions came at him from every side. "We did not make this decision lightly," he said. "But if I am to salvage anything from what my family has taken years to build—I must cut my losses and get out."

"But where will you go?" Gabriele said to Dorothea. "Oh, we will miss you!"

"We go to Texas," Dorothea said. "I am not certain just where—Papa of course knows—to tell you the truth, Gabriele, with Paul gone—it doesn't matter to me where I am."

"Tom is in Texas," Gabriele said. "We had a letter from him on Christmas Eve. He has bought land near San Antonio—he says it is very pretty there."

"Perhaps," Dorothea said. She touched Gabriele's cheek. "Be happy," she said. "While you can."

Then someone came up to speak to Dorothea, and Gabriele moved a little distance away, standing in an alcove made by a bay window and looking at the scene before her. The ladies' dresses still glowed as richly in the candlelight, the warm scent of nutmeg and brandy from the large bowl of egg nog on a table nearby still hung in the air as sweetly, and the sounds of laughter and excited chatter still rang throughout the reception rooms. But just as the tips of the greens strung along the staircase and hung over doorways had begun to turn yellow as they dried, Gabriele could feel the chill that would wither her memories of these holidays, making them less and less real, until the day would come that such gaiety and frivolity seemed only echoes from a distant and long-dead past.

She sought out Alex then, taking him by the hand and leading him into the other parlour where musicians had begun to play. "Ask them to play 'Then You'll Remember Me,'" she said, and saw a responsive light come into his eyes.

"That's the music we first danced to," he said.

"Yes," she said. "I have never danced to it with anyone else since."

He spoke to the fiddler, then held out his arms to his wife. She went into them, matching her steps to his, and they waltzed away down the long polished floor, nodding to others to join them in the dance.

Gabriele caught sight of the two of them in a tall mirror as they danced by: for a moment, she saw nothing in the background but the brocade of the draperies behind them, and a glittering crystal sconce mounted on the wall. Then another couple moved into view: the girl wore a pale blue satin dress but the man wore a uniform of Confederate grey, with a sabre dangling from his side.

The war is everywhere, she thought, shutting her eyes and letting Alex guide her. The Robins move away from it, I close my eyes—but it is coming, it cannot be avoided or stopped—

She heard a strange sound somewhere nearby, and opening her eyes, looked about for its source. It came again, a low, strangled sort of cry. "Alex?" Gabriele said. "Did you hear that?"

"Yes," he said. They stopped dancing and moved toward a chair set in the window, its back facing away from the room. He walked around it, then suddenly knelt, an anxious expression appearing on his face. "It's your aunt," he said. "She's fainted. Catch Dr. Delahaye, Gabriele—he left only minutes ago, he should still be in the drive."

It seemed to take forever to reach the doorway, and then she felt as though her voice had no strength. She ran across the gallery and down the steps, crying at Dr. Delahaye to stop, to come back. Then he heard her, and wheeled his horse around, trotting back toward the house and dismounting, following her back to where Aunt Mat sat.

He bent over her, holding her wrist with his hand and putting his ear close to her chest. "Get her to her room," he said to Alex. "Get Abigail—she can undress her."

"But what's wrong, Dr. Delahaye?" Gabriele said. "She seemed perfectly fine this morning—"

"Mrs. LeGrange's heart has troubled her for some time," Dr. Delahaye said. "Though she made me promise I wouldn't tell you." He looked past Gabriele at Alex, carefully carrying Aunt Mat from the room. "Now—there's no help for it."

"But will she be—all right? Surely she's not really ill!"

Dr. Delahaye, already halfway down the room, paused and came back to Gabriele, taking her hands in his. "My dear child—her heart has been slowing down for a very long time now, and nothing I have done has assuaged it. This could be just another attack—or it might be the last one. You must prepare yourself for that, Gabriele. It would be foolish not to."

Then he went away, pushing through people crowding

around with inquiries about Aunt Mat, leaving Gabriele to deal with them as best she could.

"Excuse me, I must go to my aunt," she said. "I—excuse me." She flew up the stairs, conscious of the brown needles that crunched under her steps. All the fear and anxiety she had held at bay with Christmas carols and baubles on the tree descended upon her: she clutched at the rail, willing herself to be strong. Then she heard Alex call her name, and looked up to see him waiting at the top of the stairs.

"Don't be afraid, darling," he said. "I am with you."

How strangely light his words made her feel, how quickly serene. I had forgotten, she thought, in my fear for Aunt Mat. I am married now, and no matter what happens, I do not have to face it alone.

Alex did not leave her, but kept vigil with her throughout the rest of the day. They sat on into the night, unwilling to leave Aunt Mat's bedside, for although she had regained consciousness, and had spoken their names, she had lapsed back into a heavy slumber that Dr. Delahaye said did not mean returning health.

"I hate to see her like this," Gabriele said as she watched Aunt Mat's motionless form and listened to the stream of air entering and leaving her body on each hard-fought breath. "If there were only something we could do—"

"One thing you can do is to come get some rest," Alex said. "You won't make matters better by getting sick yourself." He put his arm around Gabriele and guided her to the door. "I'll get Abigail to sit with Aunt Mat—she's been camped outside the door since her mistress took ill."

Abigail, dozing as she leaned against the wall outside the door, roused as soon as Alex and Gabriele came into the hall. "Will you sit up with Mrs. LeGrange?" Alex said. "I need to get Mrs. St. Cyr to bed—"

"You go on, Miss Gabriele," Abigail said. "I'll watch with Miz LeGrange." She patted Gabriele's hand. "I'll call you if I has to."

She disappeared into Aunt Mat's room, and as they

went down the hall, they heard a low croon: Abigail, singing to Aunt Mat as though she were a baby.

Gabriele sank onto a low rocker when she reached her room, overcome with grief and fatigue.

"She's going to die, isn't she, Alex?"

"We don't know that," he said, coming to kneel beside her and take her in his arms.

"But she looks so awful—"

"She's very ill, Gabriele."

"Isn't it strange? Thousands of men die in terrible battles—but this one life still looms so large."

"We cling to the comprehensible, Gabriele. One death —we can grapple with that. But thousands in one day?" He shook his head. "I sometimes think, though, that this war has extorted a greater price even than those wholesale deaths, Gabriele—one not so visible, and therefore often ignored."

She heard the solemnity in Alex's voice, and saw the deep unhappiness that lined his face. Shifting in her chair so that she could pull his head against her breast, she stroked his hair, bending to kiss a tear that traced its way across his cheek.

"What price is that, my darling?"

"Innocence," he said, lifting his head so he could see her face. "Not just the innocence of the young whose childhoods have been detoured into treacherous paths— but the innocence of people like Tom, who has to struggle to hold to the principles his father taught him to revere."

"Surely Tom is just the same beneath the scars we see!" Gabriele said. "The same honourable man I grew up with—"

"Of course he values honour," Alex said. "Tom Cannon would no more do a dishonourable thing than you would. But he has seen too many men twist their values to fit the situation, or change the situation to make it work for them. He has seen too many birthrights sold for the tiniest portion of ill-gotten porridge, too many causes betrayed—"

"But you have seen the same thing!"

"Ah, but I did not go into this with the innocence of a man like Tom. I went into it guarded by cynicism, shielded by my basic mistrust in the nature of man—"

Gabriele put her fingers against his lips. "Shh. Don't talk like that, my dearest. You haven't been cynical for a very long time now—"

Alex's face changed, illuminated by a brightness much stronger than the light from the room's one flickering lamp. "I have you to thank for that, my love," he said. "Possibly the greatest gift you have given me, next to the right to share your life, is that while other men have marched into darkness, I have moved out into the light."

She went into his arms, feeling them close securely around her. Perfect love does cast out fear, she thought, lifting her face to his. It is not that I worry less about Aunt Mat—or that my concern for our future is less strong. It is just that for this moment, this space in time, all of that is secondary to what I feel.

Aunt Mat rallied during the night, and when Gabriele went in to see her toward noon the next day, she sat on a bank of pillows, hair freshly brushed and tied neatly under a ruffled and ribboned cap.

"Abigail loves it when I am too weak to lift a hand against her spoiling me," Aunt Mat said. "Where she dredged this cap from I don't know, but I told her it makes me look like something in a confectioner's shop."

"Letha won't be outdone," Gabriele said. "She's made you Floating Island for your lunch, and has threatened all of us if we dare go near it."

"I don't have the strength to protest," Aunt Mat said. She held out her hand to Gabriele, drawing her closer to the bed. "How good it is to know the plantation is in such capable hands, Gabriele. I've never told you how proud I am of you—it's a failing I have. I don't tell people my good thoughts about them enough, though they usually hear more than enough of the bad ones."

"Over the years you cared for me, Aunt Mat," Gabriele said, "I received far more sound guidance than anything else."

Aunt Mat smiled and patted Gabriele's hand. "Maybe so, Gabriele. But it's a humbling thing to find out how much better other people are than I am." She leaned back on her pillows, briefly closing her eyes. The mild winter sun, the brilliant blue sky framed by draperies half-drawn, the fire blazing on the hearth, made a cocoon of calm and peace, and Gabriele thought that finally, here was a place no demon would dare to come.

"Veronique, for instance," Aunt Mat said, opening her eyes. "I did not see how she could be so forgiving—after all the pain I had caused. But just before they left, she came to me and told me that of all the hard lessons she had learned, the hardest one had to do with conquering bitterness and rage. 'If I had given in to the first terrible anger I felt when I heard that I had never been a slave, in the end, I would have suffered most, for I would have let bitterness rule me—as it has you.'" Aunt Mat's grip tightened on Gabriele's hand. "Oh, Gabriele! When I heard those words—and saw how true they were! Well, it gave me something to think about, and pray about, for a long, long time."

"Your life has been guided by other things, Aunt Mat," Gabriele said. "By loyalty, dedication to duty—love."

"Oh, yes—all of those. But battling constantly with my old, dark foe!" Aunt Mat's gaze shifted to the bright day outside. "Well, I have finally vanquished that one, Gabriele. Now I must concentrate on the last one of all—though more and more, I look on him as a friend."

"Aunt Mat—you're better—you'll be well soon," Gabriele said.

Aunt Mat's eyes, filled with love, helped her tell Gabriele one last lie. "Of course I will, child," she said. "Now I think I want to rest."

Aunt Mat continued to improve, and when word reached them toward the end of the week that a Union attack on Galveston, Texas, launched on New Year's Day, had been soundly repulsed, they all took heart. Perhaps the New Year would bring a turn for the better: although reason told them that the Yankees must still take the Atchafalaya and Red Rivers, still, the lack of activity over the past several months lulled them, and when, in mid-January, the redoubtable Confederate gunboat *Cotton,* which had kept the enemy from progressing up the Teche, fell before overwhelming Union forces, and was burned and scuttled by her own crew, the blow seemed even harder since they had allowed themselves to hope it would not come.

"It's like pulling the plug out of a bottle," Alex said, unrolling a map of the state and spreading it out on the study table. He placed an inkwell at Brashear City, and a tin of sealing wax at Indian Bend. "If the Union troops who are camped at Brashear City come up the Atchafalaya —and meet other Union troops here at Indian Bend— they will draw our troops from Opelousas and Butte-à-la-Rose. Which means the outcome of the first encounter may well determine the entire campaign."

"Surely now that the state capital is at Opelousas, there will be large concentrations of our troops there," Adams said. "Besides, we have the advantage of knowing the terrain. Many of the men are drawn from this area—they'll be defending their own back yard."

"That would be an advantage if it were not for the other side of the coin," Alex said. "In New Iberia the other day they were discussing General Taylor's fear that since so many residents are leaving the Teche country, soldiers whose families are moving may go with them."

"But—what can we do?" Gabriele said. Involuntarily, she glanced over her shoulder at the rows of books lining the ceiling-high shelves. So accustomed was she to the ranks of volumes that she hardly ever took time to consider that each book represented a treasure-house of information, or beauty, or wisdom, printed and bound with all care to preserve the contents for the ages.

"Stand and fight," Alex said. "Or—leave while we still can."

"Aunt Mat couldn't possibly travel yet," Gabriele said. "And we can't leave her behind—"

"No," Alex said. "We can't." He stared down at the map, then moved the inkwell and sealing wax and rolled it up again. "Well, we'll just have to do the best we can." He went to Gabriele and put his arms around her. "Though if we stand and fight—I'll have to join a unit. Leave you here—"

Alex kept his face from her as he spoke, as though he did not want her to see what hid there. She went to him and took his face between her hands, turning it to her so that she could look into his eyes. And there she saw such sorrow, and such hurt, that she knew in one quick instant what raged in Alex's soul. All the love he bore her could not save this house, these things—in the face of the tide that inched its way toward them, even the greatest love in the world proved no barrier, and this he could not bear.

Alex's arms made the first barrier, she could feel them strong and safe around her. Beyond them she felt the room, and beyond that, the thick walls of the house. Lawns and fields, stretching wide around them. The bayou itself, a ribbon of defence. Then she felt the bayou vanish, felt the fields and lawns shrink. The brick walls crumbled, the rows of books tumbled from their shelves. All barriers gone, all defences shattered. Only Alex's arms, still around her. Only that.

Gabriele could not mark the exact moment at which she knew that Aunt Mat, despite her seeming continued progress, would soon die. But there came an afternoon when Gabriele sat by her aunt's bed, watching the play of firelight on her pale features, and knew with a certainty nothing could shake that the days of her vigil fast approached their end. As though Aunt Mat knew what Gabriele thought and felt, she opened her eyes and smiled. "Sing to me, child. One of the old songs your father and I sang in our youth."

Alex, coming to find Gabriele, stood outside the door listening to her sweet voice, tears rushing to his eyes as he, too, realized the change that had taken place within that room. He clenched his fists, his rage against his parents suddenly so violent that he would not have answered for his behaviour had either one of them appeared before him. That they would throw away the peace and joy and tranquillity promised in a home where love for others proved more powerful than worship of self had had enough bad effects as it was. But for him to know that except for his mother's selfish will and his father's equally selfish weakness he might have at his disposal the means to save Gabriele from the devastation so surely on its way seemed by far the worst price he had had to pay thus far.

Only a portion of the fortune my mother controls would have moved Gabriele and everything she loves to safety, if we'd had to sail across the ocean in one of the St. Cyr ships to do it, he thought bitterly. He could not be reasonable, he could not consider that although the loss of their remaining New Orleans properties when the city fell had been severe, the Cannons still had wealth, and might have removed themselves had that been their wish. He only knew, as he listened to Gabriele sing, that as her husband he did not have the resources to keep her safe, and that if he had married her with no fortune of his own, he now had to fight for what she had left, knowing that his efforts would not be nearly enough.

Alex had no illusions about what would happen when the Yankees came. The fact that certain properties were termed legitimate forage, and could be taken by Union troops in return for a receipt to be honoured at the end of hostilities seemed an open sesame to soldiers less schooled in the refinements of war. Seeing their officers legally take horses, mules, and other stock, the rank-and-file soldiers, particularly those who straggled behind the main march, found it easy to "liberate" anything they might fancy. And that, Alex knew, could range from a couple of chickens for the camp pot to a lady's jewels or her slave's body.

He could not seem to control the anger that gripped him, and he turned to go away, not wanting Gabriele to see him in such an agitated state. Then she began to sing another song, a lullaby Alex remembered from his own nursery days, when a black mammy crooned him to sleep with that very same tune. Then he knew the source of his rage, the fear that fuelled it. He heard in Gabriele's voice that special innocence, that trust, which burned so steadily at the core of her being, touching everyone and everything she met with its pure light.

Even Gabriele's strength might not shield that innocence in the face of pillage and destruction. Danger is one thing, horror another: Alex remembered well a woman of his mother's acquaintance whose face made all the right expressions to accompany her trivial chatter, but whose eyes stared out of some private hell. "She saw her husband killed," his mother said when pressed for an explanation. "In a particularly horrible way." No more, but that had been enough. Alex did not know how much Gabriele could endure before she broke, and the knowledge that he could not take her to a safer place while Aunt Mat lived put him in a private hell. War honours nothing, not even our natural concern for the dying, he thought. I no longer hope for Aunt Mat's return to health: my only thought is that since she is dying, let the end come soon. Or else her death will come too late to let us go.

There came a kind of hiatus, then, a time during which all of their horizons seemed to shrink and their world to be confined to the house, the walks around it, and, increasingly, Aunt Mat's room.

"She knows she is dying," Gabriele said. "It is as though she has made a list of things she wants to tell us, and is going through them, one by one."

Dr. Delahaye, when consulted, agreed that Mrs. LeGrange seemed to be in a steady decline: he gave her stimulants which resulted in a momentary brightening, but each time he came to see her, he told Alex and Gabriele that the end could not be long in coming, and that they must prepare themselves for it to happen at any time.

"I don't know which is worse," Gabriele said one afternoon toward the end of February when she and Alex walked in the grove of oaks. "Father seemed to die so quickly—the shock of his illness and death kept me numb, so that at first I hardly felt pain. Now, I feel as though I am already in mourning—and yet I still have to tell her goodbye!"

"You are mourning the life you have had with her," Alex said. "I'm sorry you have this grief, my darling—with all the rest you have to face."

"She keeps giving me things," Gabriele said. "This morning she gave me her embroidery scissors, that lovely gold pair her father brought her from London the year she was twelve. I—I try to dissuade her—but then she becomes agitated, and tells me she must leave things in order —" She stopped walking and looked up at Alex. "She asked about the war this morning. I thought maybe she had forgotten all about it—she lives so much in the past."

"What did she say?"

"She asked how long we had before the Yankees came. I told her I—didn't know."

"Not a great deal longer, I wouldn't think," Alex said. "The news from New Iberia doesn't change—still a jockeying back and forth up a few miles and back again from Brashear City. But both General Mouton and General Sibley expect an all-out attack as soon as the weather gets better and the roads aren't so impassable. A matter of weeks—"

"Then my decision will be made for me," Gabriele said, looking through the trees at the house.

"What decision, Gabriele?"

"The decision to leave this place. You remember how I went on about it—I couldn't leave Felicity and go to Texas —I had too much of life invested here."

"And now?" Alex said, drawing her closer in the circle of his arm.

"Now I have learned a great deal about giving things up," Gabriele said. "And I know now that even if I leave Felicity—I will not lose it unless I choose to."

"I don't understand," Alex said.

"I mean that as I listen to Aunt Mat talk about people and places from her youth, I can see in her eyes and hear in her voice all the love and closeness she had with them— it's still all there, don't you see? As though she hasn't really lost it at all." She took Alex's hand and pressed a kiss into his palm. "Even Uncle Louis—she has found him again, now that she is at peace with Veronique. That's what I meant about not giving Felicity up unless I choose to. Aunt Mat chose to give Uncle Louis up when she decided she could not bear the pain of remembering him. Felicity means too much to me for me to ever stop holding it in my heart, no matter how hard that might be at first."

"My brave girl," Alex said. He said nothing for a moment, then very quickly, as though he knew he must say it before he lost his nerve—"I'm going to have to stay closer to the militia unit now, Gabriele."

"What does that mean?" she asked, her eyes already dark with fear.

"I shall have to be away at least a few nights every week," he said. "And if the situation gets as bad as we expect it will—"

"You'll have to go," Gabriele said. She turned and put her head on his shoulder, unable to hold back tears which seemed always just beneath the surface now.

"It's my fault we're still here," she said. "If I had listened to you last fall—we'd be safe in Texas now."

"Shh," Alex said, though her words echoed his own thoughts. "Who is it that so often tells me we mustn't live in the mistakes of the past? If I had presented it differently —if we had not had so many other things going on—but, there, it's done. And we shall just have to—do the best we can."

"If my wilfulness cost you your—" But she could not say that last word. Please, God, she prayed. Please. Don't take Alex. Don't. She could hear her father's voice, see his loving face. You can't bargain with God, Gabriele. Pray to Him—trust in Him—and hold up your end because that is the only way to live. "I'm all right now," she said, lifting her face to his. "No matter what comes, Alex—I'm going to be all right."

They turned at the end of the walk and faced the black façade of the house: one tiny glow of light came from the office and one from Aunt Mat's room upstairs, beckoning them back. They had almost reached the house when a flickering light appeared behind the sidelights of the door. It danced unevenly, like the swamp fires that sometimes appeared eerily in the marsh, and Gabriele cried out in alarm.

Then the door opened, and Abigail stood on the threshold, the lamp casting its glow over her face, picking up her livid scar. "Mrs. LeGrange is asking for you," she said. "She say to hurry—she don't have much time."

They raced past Abigail, taking the back stairs two at a time, pausing at Aunt Mat's door to catch their breath before going inside.

"What day is it today?" Aunt Mat asked when they stood by her bed.

"The 24th of February," Alex said.

"Still winter," Aunt Mat said. "I thought I might last until spring—but I am so very tired."

"Nonsense," Gabriele said. "You're playing possum because you like being spoiled."

"Yes, and you have spoiled me, Gabriele. In a strange way—these last weeks have been some of the—happiest of my life."

"Shh," Gabriele said. "You must rest, Aunt Mat."

But Aunt Mat had already slipped back into a deep sleep, and Gabriele, after straightening the coverlet and adding wood to the fire, turned up the wick on the lamp and drew the draperies tight. Then, with Alex at her side, she took her place near her aunt's bed.

Aunt Mat did not wake again: her sleep became a coma during the night, and although she lived another three weeks, she lay still and silent as though her spirit already soared in another sphere, and only this shell must wait for the tomb.

The flames of the tall candles set at the head and foot of Aunt Mat's casket flickered as Gabriele pushed open the parlour door and went inside. Closed all winter, the room smelled like death: chill, empty air, scented only by the pot-pourri and vetiver Abigail had set about the room when she readied it for the funeral. And it was dark, so dark, even at noon. The weather had turned yesterday, and another storm had come roaring out of the north, beating rain against the windows and enveloping the house and grounds in a sheath of grey.

The hands had barely got the grave dug before the rain came; Gabriele heard Adams tell Alex that they had covered it with a tarpaulin, but she could imagine the weight of water collected on it pushing the cover deeper into the hole, until there was no protection at all, and the rain soaked the grave and made it a pond.

Someone stood at Aunt Mat's casket, a thin, dark figure that Gabriele recognized at once. Abigail, who had not left Aunt Mat's side except for the briefest periods since she lost consciousness, and who had performed all the final offices for her when she died. The scar on her cheek looked darker than usual, thrown into relief by the shadows the candles cast. Her eyes were fixed on Aunt Mat's face; even when Gabriele came to stand beside her, she did not look away, but kept that steady gaze directed at the woman lying there.

Gabriele watched Abigail, and suddenly, it was as though she saw two lives written in Abigail's face. Abigail had been given to Aunt Mat at birth, a nine-year-old orphan who had arrived at the Cannon plantation with a group of older slaves. Aunt Mat's life had been Abigail's life: no other love, no other loyalty, ever deflected one heartbeat of her devotion, and now, as she stood beside her mistress' coffin and said goodbye, Gabriele could almost feel a bond still stretched between them, as though Abigail knew that Aunt Mat would never be far from her side.

What years are locked away in Abigail's head, she thought. How many rooms, how many seasons. And then Abigail's grief seemed so private that Gabriele turned away, walking to the window overlooking the front gallery and peering out into the rain. If we lose Felicity, I shall lose all these rooms in which I can still see Papa—and Aunt Mat, she thought. I will never be able to sit in Papa's big chair in his study, and close my eyes, and bury my face in it, and smell his cigars and cologne. I will never be able to pretend that he will soon come, and tease me as he always did, and make things better just because he is there.

And Aunt Mat . . . A smile broke through her tears as she thought of Aunt Mat, feet tapping impatiently down the hall as she bustled through the day, head held sternly as she admonished Tom and Gabriele for some small sin— if Aunt Mat ever haunts anyone, what a busy ghost she will be, Gabriele thought, knowing even as the image formed that fatigue and sorrow had pushed her to the edge of hysteria, and that if she were to bear up through the funeral, she must rest.

But even when she undressed and got into bed, she could not sleep. The rain on the roof did not lull her the way it usually did, and the stillness of the house did not encourage rest. This was not the stillness of tranquillity; this was the terrible stillness of the eye of the hurricane, when the storm is turning and gathering up its forces for an even more destructive attack. Her eyelid jumped and her leg muscles felt as though they were bound with rope. When the door opened and someone spoke her name, she jumped and cried out as though she had been slapped.

"Gabriele, my dearest—what is it?" Alex said. He closed

the door behind him and came rapidly to the bed, taking her hands in his and rubbing them briskly. "You're cold as ice," he said. "And absolutely worn out—"

"I just need to rest," she said. "But I can't. I close my eyes and I can't sleep—they fly open again, Alex, and my legs hurt—"

He got on the bed beside her, holding her close against him and stroking her back. "Shh, darling. Shh. You've been up most of two nights—and all the strain of the weeks before that—"

"Oh, Alex, we can go now, can't we? Pack what we can and go to the ranch in Texas—it's spring, almost. We'll be in time to plant a garden—bluebonnets, isn't that what they have?"

She rambled like an exhausted child, sinking into a half-sleep, crying out, subsiding suddenly into a deeper quiet, and then rousing again.

And Alex, holding her, stroking her, wondered how he could tell her that the roads to Texas were closed, that Union forces and Confederate forces brought their thrusts and parries closer and closer to the arena of the Teche, and that his militia unit now formed a major block in the dike of Confederate defence: to leave would be not only dishonourable, but treason.

Chapter Twenty-one

ALEX, NOW PART OF THE TWENTY-EIGHTH REGIMENT LOUISIANA Volunteers, left for Ft. Bisland, some thirty miles below Felicity on the road to Brashear City, two days after Aunt Mat's funeral, and as she stood watching him ride away, Gabriele felt as though the last hope of life in the house rode with him. The weather had cleared, but the air still seemed to have that heavy quality: there was little connection between the dim interior of the house and the March winds outside, and in the days that followed Alex's departure, Gabriele went about as though preparing the house itself for burial. Letha would come upon her standing before an open china cabinet, holding a sauceboat or trifle bowl in her hand. Not even aware of Letha's presence, Gabriele would look at the object, sometimes setting it aside, but more often than not returning it to its place behind the cabinet door. Or she would pore over several books at the same time, turning through their pages, reading the inscriptions on the fly-leaves, once in a while taking a book up to her room, but again more often than not replacing it on the shelves.

"I'll help you pack things up, Miss Gabriele," Letha told her. "Mr. Adams, he can hide what you want to save somewhere—"

"There's so much," Gabriele said, waving a hand as though to take in all the rooms and the costly, beautiful things that furnished them. "How could I choose, Letha?"

"I don't know, but I think you ought to pick a few things out," Letha said. "Everybody say those mens, when they come through—they don't leave nothin' in one piece. Now, that little tea-set of your Mama's—I think you should save that out, Miss Gabriele."

With Letha's help, Gabriele did pack some items in heavy wooden crates: the Limoges tea-set brought from Paris, her grandmother's Belgian lace banquet cloth with two dozen napkins, her parents' portraits, nailed securely in crates Adams made: she even found it easy now to pick those books she felt so bound to that to lose them would be like losing part of her own soul. The Aesop's *Fables* her father had given her, with a note from him on almost every page. Aunt Mat's household book, that compendium of recipes and remedies, family lineages and birth and christening dates, that Aunt Mat had taken over as her responsibility when she came to live with them, adding to the entries in Honore Cannon's hand in the early pages her own record of the family's life. Of course the books Alex gave her—the set of Dickens; the *Madame Bovary; Idylls of the King,* her beloved Sir Walter Scott; and one other only, her mother's Missal and Prayer Book, which had come to Gabriele on her First Communion Day. She packed the books and then had Adams take the crates to a cabin set deep in the woods Tom used when hunting.

When Gabriele and Letha had finished, Gabriele found that as the days went by, she could walk through the house feeling very much as though she were a stranger there, and had no attachment to it at all.

Adams came in one morning with unsettling news: the storehouse had been broken into the night before, and at least half its goods were gone.

"Our people, Mr. Adams?" Gabriele said.

"Probably," Adams said. "They know the Union troops

are near—and they know about the Proclamation now. They know they're free."

"Then perhaps we should advise them to go," Gabriele said, slowly rising to her feet. "Call them together—give them all the news we have—and let them decide what to do."

"You really want more darkies roaming the countryside?" Adams said. "Think, Mrs. St. Cyr. With no way to support themselves, they'll have to turn to theft. We've got enough trouble with the Yankees without making more."

"Then what? We can't just let this deterioration of order grow!"

"I'll be swanned if I know," Adams said.

"Call them together," Gabriele said. "I have something I want to say."

"Mrs. St. Cyr—I'd think on that a while," Adams said. But her face told him she would not change her mind. "All right—I'll get 'em," he said.

Gabriele caught up a shawl and wrapped it around her shoulders, following Adams to the back gallery where she waited for the hands. There were only about a hundred and seventy now: since the war began, some had run off, some had been pressed into service on Avery Island, others helped build fortifications around the Teche. Fevers and other illnesses had caused some deaths, particularly among the older slaves, and there had been only a few births to swell their ranks.

Letha came bustling up to stand beside Gabriele, Abigail not far behind. "Miss Gabriele, you got no business out here. Let Mr. Adams talk to these people—"

"No, Letha. I am the only Cannon left here—I am the one who must do this."

The hands straggled up, their mood sullen. Gabriele stepped forward, raising her hand for silence although the crowd had not made a sound. "I want to tell you all I know about what's happening," she said. "Union troops are massing on Patterson where Ft. Bisland is—there'll be a battle there pretty soon, and although it's not possible to really know the outcome—we can guess. The Union has more soldiers, more guns—" She stopped as she thought of the identity of the only soldier at Ft. Bisland she cared anything about.

Some few hands shouted, raucous cries filling the pause, then subsided as Gabriele went on. "If the Union wins at Ft. Bisland, they'll push on through here. Word is that they've got to get up to the Red River—and this plantation is on their way. I can't really tell you how you will be treated, but you are free now—as you know—and I think if you meet up with Yankees—they will take care of you."

As though the crowd had waited long enough, and Gabriele's words had finally reached the fuse that would light them, the hands exploded. A bombardment of shouts, a thunder of cries—

"Go inside," Adams said. "I'll handle them."

"No," Gabriele said. "I'm going to see this through." She left the shelter of the gallery and stood out on the lawn not three yards from the first row of hands. Gradually they quieted, shifting their feet, looking at each other, but not at Gabriele.

"All right," she said. "Now—as I see it, you have two choices. You may leave now—and those who choose to do that will be given food and whatever else you can carry that might help you start a new life—or you can stay. If you leave, I've no idea what you will be going toward. If you stay—I am prepared to divide this plantation into plots that you may plant with crops of your own."

"Mrs. St. Cyr!" Adams said.

"I know what I'm doing," Gabriele said. She raised her voice. "Take the rest of the morning to decide. We will assemble again at noon—and do whatever we must." She turned back to Mr. Adams. "Let's go into the office," she said. "We have a lot to do."

"I'll say!" Adams said.

Behind them, the first excited murmurings of the crowd rose as the hands realized the magnitude of what Gabriele had said. Gabriele closed the door against the noise and took her seat across from Adams' chair.

"I know you think I'm crazy, Mr. Adams, but before you say anything—please hear me out."

"All right," he said, "but already I think I see the drift."

"I'm sure you do," Gabriele said. "We can't plant sugar now—I can't pay the hands, armies are going to be tramping through the fields—but why should those fields lie fallow, when they could be growing food? And maybe—just maybe—if former slaves are living off this land—it can stay out of Yankee hands."

"But are you going to *give* them land, Mrs. St. Cyr? Five thousand acres of the best earth around here?"

"No—we'll draw up long leases," Gabriele said. "Whether it will matter in the end I don't know—but it's the only thing I can think of to even try to save this place."

"It might work," Adams said. He pulled a list before him and ran his finger down the names. "I've got a good idea of the hands that would have the best chance farming by themselves," he said. "I'll go out and talk to 'em—see if I can advise them to stay." He stood up, looking down at Gabriele. "And the others—you going to let them ransack your house? Take those fancy things on the road to nowhere?"

"It doesn't matter any more," Gabriele said. "I'll keep enough to use while I'm still here—as for the rest—if they can carry it, it's theirs."

She stood up, smiling for the first time that day. "As a matter of fact, Mr. Adams, it tickles me just a little to think of some marauding soldiers bursting in here—and finding they've come too late."

"By God if that's not spoken like your father!" Adams said. "You can count on me, Mrs. St. Cyr. I won't desert you, no matter what."

"I do count on you, Mr. Adams," Gabriele said. "With my husband away—" But the strain of the morning proved too much: she could not mention Alex without tears, and

Adams, knowing she could not maintain her poise much longer, turned and left her alone.

When they met again at noon, the whole procedure went more smoothly than Gabriele had thought it would. Except for a few hands who couldn't make up their minds, most knew whether they wanted to leave or stay. Abigail's decision surprised Gabriele. "I'se leaving," she said. "Going to make my way back to where Mr. Cannon bought me from—see if maybe some of my people are still there."

"Are you sure, Abigail?" Gabriele said. "The roads are dangerous—"

"I'se got some people to go with," Abigail said. "Without Miz Mathilde—I just don't want to hang around here."

Letha was adamant. She would never leave. "Not while I got breath in my body to stay with you and help you, chile," she said. Lucie would stay, but she would no longer work in the house. Her man had chosen to farm: he needed her with him.

By the time the day ended, Gabriele could hardly keep her back straight as she interviewed the hands. When the last one left, and the door closed behind him, she turned to Adams. "I'm going to open one of Papa's best bottles of wine tonight, Mr. Adams. Come and have supper with me —I don't know how well French Bordeaux goes with sweet potatoes and hoecakes—but there's a first time for everything, I suppose."

And later, as they sat sipping their wine, the thick silence of the house close around them, Adams said, "I guess this is the worst part. This waiting. I served out West with Wells Fargo when I was a boy, you know. People'd talk about Indian attacks—and they'd always say the same thing. It was the waiting that was so awful." He saw Gabriele's face and stopped. "Sorry, ma'am. The wine makes my tongue loose."

"No, you're right, Mr. Adams. It is the waiting that's so awful," Gabriele said. "Nothing more to do, no way to know what's—happening."

"I've let the dogs out, Mrs. St. Cyr," Adams said. "And I've moved my things into the office. I'll sleep there from now on."

"Yes," Gabriele said. She bolted the door behind him, and then went up to bed. But not to sleep. When dawn came, she pulled her rocker to the window where she could watch the sky. April's palette painted it, pinks and ivories and mauves that made ribbons across the clouds. Gabriele watched a hawk find a rising wind and soar up the column of air. Lucky hawk, she thought. He can stretch his wings and sail far above this sad old earth—fly faster than misery, higher than pain. And then her thoughts flew to Alex, only thirty miles away as that hawk would fly, but as distant from Gabriele at that moment as though he were on the other side of the world.

What would it be like, when the Yankee attack came? She tried to imagine the soft air rent with shattered metal and whining with shells. And when a bullet struck a man, did it make that same soft thud as when it penetrated a deer's thick fur? Did the man let out his breath in that grunt of surprise, and did his eyes glaze as quickly, and his legs go slack? She thought of blood trickling from Alex's lips, and his face staring sightlessly at the sky. She closed her eyes and buried her head in her lap, but still the images came. Nothing would stop them, nothing would send them away. One pair of arms only were proof against them, one voice in her ear the only charm.

She sat in an agony of fear and pain, knowing in that moment something she had never realized before. If she did indeed lose Alex, that loss would be made worse than any she had ever had to bear because he who had helped her bear them would be the one she mourned.

The new régime began that morning: hoes flashed in the sun as hands tilled the fields, and the last of those who would leave Felicity departed through its gates, laden with treasures from all over the house.

"I need fresh air," Gabriele told Letha. "I think I'll go foraging for dandelions—a fresh salad would taste good."

"Take this Caleb with you, then," Letha said. "He's been under my feet all morning—his momma's out hoeing and she don't want him with her."

"Come on, then, Caleb," Gabriele said. "You can help me dig."

Caleb ran along beside her, thin black legs slicing through the tall grass. "What you got to dig 'em with, Miss Gabriele?" he asked.

"We don't need a shovel," Gabriele said. "I brought a knife, see?" She held up the Spanish dagger, and watched Caleb's eyes grow big.

"I never saw a knife like that before," Caleb said. "What you call that kind of knife?"

"It's a dagger," Gabriele said. "My aunt said its first owner used it to kill people—it's a whole lot tamer now."

"It could still kill somebody," Caleb said, walking a respectful distance away, his eyes fixed on the knife. "You be careful with that, Miss Gabriele. You could slice yo' hand clean off."

"All I'm going to slice with this is dandelion roots," Gabriele said, kneeling down next to a thick clump. Carefully, she eased the tip of the blade under the plant, forcing it down until she could prize the dandelion free. "Line your hat with those big leaves over there," she told Caleb. "And we can put the dandelions in it."

Caleb skipped across the grass, bare feet slapping against the cool earth. He stopped at the tree Gabriele had indicated and began plucking leaves, dropping them into his hat as he picked. Gabriele sat back on her heels and looked at him, appreciating the small moment of peace. Then a scream cut through the air, and Caleb turned to her, eyes wide and mouth making a bright red *O* of fear. He screamed again and sank onto the ground, the scream losing its force now, and becoming a high, thin wail.

Gabriele was on her feet and running hard before the

second scream left Caleb's mouth. "What is it?" she cried. "What's wrong?"

And then she saw it, the thick snake slithering away through the grass. She looked at Caleb, whose eyes seemed fixed on the ground. Her eyes followed his gaze—not the ground. His leg. He held it stuck out stiffly to the side, as though to put it away from him. In the centre of his calf Gabriele saw two small marks, with red blood oozing slowly.

"I'se going to die, Miss Gabriele," the child moaned. "That old snake, he bite me 'fore I even seen him—he's poison, Miss Gabriele. I'se going to die."

"You're not going to do any such thing," Gabriele said. Even as she spoke her mind thought of what she must do. There was no time to get Adams—she looked at the dagger in her hand. Thank God it's sharp, she thought, and placed her hand on Caleb's head.

"I've got to get the poison out, Caleb," she said. "And you must help me do it."

"How you going to do that, Miss Gabriele? You got a charm?"

"Not a charm, no." She braced herself, knowing that if he fought her, the blood carrying the poison would flow faster still. "I'm going to make a cut just over the place where the snake bit you, Caleb. And then I'll suck the poison out."

He jerked away from her, scurrying under the low branches of the tree. "I'se afraid, Miss Gabriele," he cried. "Don't cut me up!"

"I'm not going to cut you up, Caleb, can't you understand?" She got on all fours and crawled after him, holding the dagger in her hand. But one look at his terrified face as he backed up against the tree trunk convinced her that if Caleb's life depended upon his helping her, the snake would surely claim its victim.

She stopped, holding his eyes with her own while she tried to think of something she could do. And then she

remembered—something Tom had taught her—would it
work? It will have to, she thought grimly.

"Caleb," she said. "Look over there. Is that someone
coming?"

Caleb's head swerved, and Gabriele darted forward. The
flat edge of her palm caught him on the back of the neck,
and he slumped forward, sprawling face down on the
grass. Carefully, she turned him over, placing her ear over
his heart. The slow but strong beat reassured her, and,
breathing a quick prayer, she took off her sash and tied it
as tightly as she could just below the joint of Caleb's hip to
his thigh. Then, biting her tongue and making herself
hold on, she made two deep cuts over the marks of the
snake, waiting until blood ran fresh and fast before putting
her mouth to the wound and drawing blood and venom
out.

She felt Caleb stirring as she spat out the last mouthful.
Loosening the tourniquet, she reached out and helped
him sit up. "How do you feel?" she said.

He looked around, eyes still dazed. "Have I been
asleep?" he asked.

"For a little while," she said.

"I thought so," Caleb said. He looked at his leg, where
congealing blood covered the wound. "Did a snake do
that?"

"Some of it," Gabriele said. "I—did the rest." She saw
fear returning, and pulled him against her breast. "Don't
worry, Caleb. It's all over now. You're going to be fine."

He nestled against her, his fears easily vanquished by her
soothing words. Would that all our enemies were so
quickly put to rout, she thought. Then she looked at the
dagger lying in the grass. Its first blooding—no, not its
first—mine.

The day wore on, but after the excitement of the morning
Gabriele found it difficult to concentrate on her tasks. She
kept going to the windows, peering in the direction of Ft.
Bisland, trying to imagine what might be happening

there. Once she fancied that she saw something waving above the trees, a bit of black and white that might be a signal flag; another time she saw dark puffs of smoke rising from far down the bayou, and shuddered to think of boats burning there.

Then she heard a horse on the drive, and went out onto the balcony to see who it might be, surprised to recognize the horseman as Harold LeBoeuf.

Harold had been home a little over a week: assigned to a scouting party near Brashear City, he had suffered a leg wound and had lost the limb. Now, as he dismounted and came toward the house, Gabriele saw that he moved almost as rapidly as before. It would take more than a wooden leg to stop Harold, she thought, and went downstairs to greet him.

"I came to see if you want to go to Ft. Bisland with me," Harold said.

"Ft. Bisland? But—how could we?"

"In the hot air balloon," Harold said. "It's been in the barn all this time—and I know how to work it. I'm going to go tomorrow—I know St. Cyr is over there—and I thought—well, I thought you'd want to come."

"Oh, yes!" Gabriele said. "Harold—yes!"

"Good," Harold said. "I thought I'd bring it over here —launch it from the Indian mound so we'd go up straight and clear."

"Then stay the night here," Gabriele said. Impulsively, she leaned forward and kissed his cheek. "Oh, Harold," she said. "Thank you—"

"You're the only woman I'd have asked, Gabriele," Harold said. "I'll go get the balloon now—bring it back by wagon."

"Is there anything I can do?"

He paused and looked down at her. "Brace yourself, I guess. It's a war we're going to, Gabriele."

A narrow band of gold sliced the dark, marking the horizon where the sun would appear. Gabriele moved closer to the fire, and stretched her hands over its warmth. Here on the Indian mound the wind cut through her clothes, and she felt its chill fingers on her neck.

"We'll rise with the sun," Harold said. He had spent the late afternoon of the day before setting up the balloon and its apparatus on the top of the Indian mound. Now Gabriele could just make out the balloon carriage, looming dark against the gradual light of dawn.

"I'd better start filling it," Harold said. He hung a lantern on a branch near the balloon and beckoned to Gabriele. "I'll operate the hydrogen machine and you manage the balloon," he said.

Gabriele took her place at the balloon, picking up the smooth fabric, feeling the night dew wet on her hand. A steady hiss rose from the machine as Harold directed the hydrogen into the balloon. At first, Gabriele could feel no difference. But then the fabric in her hands began to swell and plump out, and soon it billowed away from her, and she was able to release it, and watch it rise above the carriage slung below.

Just as the top of the balloon stood free and full, the sun broke through the last fetters of the night, and touched it with beams of gold. The silver zodiac signs glittered like fallen stars, and a startled dove cooed anxiously at the strange object in its path.

"Ready?" Harold said.

"Yes."

Gabriele climbed the ladder while Harold held it steady and then dropped inside; when she was clear of it, he followed her on board, pulling the ladder in behind him.

"Poor Cousin Adolphe," Harold said. "Mother always thought he'd die of a broken neck, not a slit one."

"Hush," Gabriele said. "I don't want to think about it."

Harold leaned forward and loosed the ropes mooring the balloon from the stakes he had driven in the ground. For a moment, the balloon seemed to hang stationary, as though it had caught on a hook set in the sky. Then, with a lurch, it began to drift slowly upward, trailing its ropes behind.

At first, Gabriele watched the earth fall away: light pushed through the night mists, turning dark shapes into greening trees and picking out rail fences and footpaths. But then she looked at the sky around her, and caught her breath. They rode into the morning, keeping pace with the rays of the rising sun. The sky was now a pale peach, with one dark streak of rose slicing through it. Above the peach, a deep, clear blue, with a thin shell of a moon glowing white, anchored by the morning star.

"It's so beautiful!" Gabriele said. And then the balloon rose high enough for her to see all of Felicity and the plantations on either side. Bayou Teche ran along behind them, forming their eastern boundary, while the road that connected them to New Iberia on one side and Jeanerette on the other appeared as a winding ribbon, its dun colour pocked with dark clots of mud. Sunlight sparkled on ponds and coulées, mists blew into trees and dissipated in their branches, and in the pastures, calves nuzzled against their mothers while cow birds pecked at their feet.

They heard shouts from below, and peered down to see tiny figures on the bow of a fishing boat. The figures waved their arms in the air pointing at the balloon, and Harold threw back his head and laughed.

"This must be a sight! They'll think they're still dreaming—"

"I felt invisible," Gabriele said. "As though I had become part of the sky, and couldn't be seen at all."

"We can be seen, all right," Harold said. He moved the lever again, and then nodded at Gabriele. "Cut that bag of sand away," he said. "So we can go higher."

She pulled out a stout knife and sliced through one of the ropes that tied ballast beneath the balloon. Freed of some of its weight, the balloon rose almost straight up into the air, until they could see the entire landscape, from the clusters of trees and houses and spires marking New

Iberia to turns the bayou took at Indian Village and Irish Bend.

"It's like looking at one of those old maps," Gabriele said. "Where all the landmarks were drawn in—"

"Look how neatly they are contained in the peninsula of land at Irish Bend," Harold said, and Gabriele focused on the strip of green and brown earth surrounded on three sides by Bayou Teche as it made its sweeping turn.

A narrow band of woods ran across the bottom of the bend, further containing the land. Cane fields, some thick with dry stalks from last year's unharvested crop and some greening with the spring's planting, ran from the southern arm of the bayou to a swamp that filled the centre. On the bayou itself, level with the woods, a gunboat stood positioned, cannon blazing. And in between cane and bayou, stretching back to where the land opened up at the widest part of the bend, they saw rank after rank of men in blue.

"But—where are our troops?" Gabriele said.

"Look into the woods and canebrakes," he said, pointing. "That's where the firing is coming from."

From their height, they could not hear the sounds of battle, except, once in a while, a peculiar whistle which Harold identified as being made by the gunboat's Parrot shells. Men in blue would rise out of the ditches and furrows and charge toward the woods, only to fall as the hailstorm of bullets from Confederate guns hit them. At the rear of the field, a yellow flag waved, denoting a hospital and men with stretchers scurried toward it, lowering their burdens and then going back to the front for more.

"There," Harold said, "look into the canebrake—see those Rebels crawling through it? They're setting up something—" He gripped the edge of the carriage, leaning out and peering toward the battlefield. "Damn it, I want to be right there. To be this close—and not have my hands on a gun—"

The Confederate soldiers exploded out of the canebrake's shelter, smoke puffing up as they fired round after round into the forward Yankee brigade. "That's when those smooth bore rifles show their worth," Harold said. "It's like having four bullets to every Yankee one."

Gabriele's mind fastened onto the small puzzle Harold presented, and she turned from the scene below to look at him. "How?" she said.

"Each cartridge is charged with a bullet and three buckshots as well," he said. "So each shot is like four."

"Look there!" Harold cried. He grabbed Gabriele's arm and leaned so far over the carriage rail that it swayed. "They're attacking! Look at them come!"

Men in grey poured out of the woods and from behind fences, charging forward into the Union lines. Even from that height, Gabriele could see the blue ranks falter before they began to return the Confederate fire. Mounted officers urged their horses forward as they tried to rally the men, but in a matter of minutes, every horse had been hit, and the dead and dying animals served as barricades for the men who were left.

"Take me home," Gabriele said. "I—I've seen enough."

"But we don't know how it's going to come out," Harold said. "Come on, Gabriele—"

She stared at him.

"It's—not a play, Harold. Not something to watch for —amusement."

"Of course not! It's real—it's history happening! Our fates are being decided down there, Gabriele. Don't you want to stay and find out what they're to be?"

She shook her head and sank to the bottom of the carriage, leaning back against its side. Alex is down there somewhere, she thought. Maybe wounded, maybe dead.

She tilted her head upward so she could see the sky. Through the network of ropes holding the carriage to the balloon she saw a clear, unclouded blue. The sun burned higher now: she would guess it must be about ten o'clock, and wondered wearily when Harold would have his fill.

"Not until it's over," he vowed, and so the morning wore on. Once in a while Gabriele would stand and look over the side: the scene seemed always the same, with only the shape the ranks of men took changing. Blue men, grey men, running and firing and falling. Men clustering together, then separating, running toward different points, forming other clusters. The guns from the boat on the bayou, never ceasing their steady fire.

The balloon floated silently, drifting in a small circle of air. Harold showed Gabriele how to work the tiller so that they could stay in the same general spot, and thus freed, gave his whole attention to the battle below. He had a notebook, she saw, and jotted things down, drawing little sketches that marked the positions of Federal and Rebel units, and acting, Gabriele thought, as though this entire conflict were being fought for Harold alone.

"How can you?" she said at one point, gesturing to his notes.

"How can I write about a battle?" Harold said. "But people have always written about battles, Gabriele. Valiant Greek heroes and pure knights—you grew up on such tales."

"But—those were—poems," she said. "Stories handed down—"

"Someone had to begin them," Harold said. "Someone who watched it happen, watched the heroes die—and thought that there must be something that could be told about their dying that would—honour it."

"Honour it!" Her eyes went to the field below. There seemed to be less happening now; not so much movement, nor so much gunfire. She could still see soldiers, so at least they were not all dead. "Honour?" she said again. "Is that what you plan to do?"

Colour rushed into Harold's face, his usual bravado suddenly gone. "Someone has to—take notice, Gabriele. Write about it, sing about it—take those tiny moments in which a man's life ended and make them count for something. Don't you see that?"

An agony of pain went through her, and she made herself gaze at the field below. If she could see the spirits of the men who had died here, the air would be thick with them. Men still in their teens, the fuzz of their first man-hood clinging to their cheeks. Men who had survived every battle but this one, carrying into it the knowledge that past luck didn't matter, and that in each attack, the dice must be thrown all over again. Men who believed in a cause, and perhaps died more gladly. Men who fought because they were made to, and died in anger. Men who had been born to a state over which they had no control, and who viewed soldiering as one more detour on a road that seemed to have no destination.

"I do," she said. She felt a kinship with Harold she had never expected to feel, and put her hand over his. "I'm glad to know you do, too."

He bent and kissed her hand, then held it. "I hope St. Cyr is—all right," he said. "You're a brave woman, Gabriele."

Spirits, rising all around them. Air choked with life, filled with cries and weeping. "Not really," she said. "I think what looks like courage is just—that I don't know what else to do." She felt her lips make a smile, but knew her eyes belied it. "If he is—all right—it won't be because of me. And if he isn't—there's nothing I can do."

Harold squeezed her hand and looked at the field again. "It looks like it's about over, down there," he said.

"Did we—win?" Gabriele said.

She looked down, too, but on both sides, the field looked the same. Strewn with bodies and abandoned gear, Yankees gathering the survivors, Rebels falling back toward Jeanerette.

"How can I tell?" Harold said, and stepped around her to set the course for home.

Chapter Twenty-two

AFTER WEEKS OF ISOLATION, WHEN IT SEEMED AS THOUGH NO word from the world beyond Felicity would ever get through to them again, a barrage of rumours and sketchy reports assailed them. The Rebels had escaped the Yankee trap, and Taylor and his men had retreated to safety. The Yankees pursued them. The Yankees did not pursue them, but only followed the line of march through Franklin and Jeanerette, still intent on their Red River goal. The Yankees' casualties had weakened them greatly. The Yankees had reinforcements coming up from Berwick Bay.

And fast on the heels of the rumours, the flood of people began. Since early April, when it first became clear that a battle would be fought below New Iberia on Bayou Teche, those who could leave had done so, and the road past Felicity had been filled with horses and mules and wagons as families fled to central and north Louisiana, taking whatever they could carry, and abandoning the rest.

Now soldiers marched by. First Rebel units, heading toward Vermilionville and points above it on the way to Alexandria and the Red River beyond. The lawn would suddenly be full of them: hot, dusty men, needing water for themselves and the horses, needing food, needing respite under the shade of the oaks. Gabriele moved among them, handing out food and mugs of coffee, changing bandages for the walking wounded who were not yet out of the fray, listening to their tales of skirmish after skirmish as they fought a rearguard action to keep the Yankees well behind them.

"They've got a whole lot more men than we do," a lieutenant told them, sitting on the gallery with Gabriele one afternoon. "And they've got supplies and men to draw on, coming up from Berwick Bay. We've got to keep moving up toward Alexandria, where we can meet up with troops from Texas and Shreveport and take the Yankees on again." He paused and looked at the house behind him, then down at Gabriele. "I wish we could leave you some protection," he said. "Any army will take legal forage—but undisciplined troops will take anything they fancy, and destroy the rest just for meanness and spite."

"I think it's not always that," Gabriele said. She, too, looked at the calm face of Felicity, and then out at the spring green lawn. "If I had been in battle after battle—seen my comrades fall—barely escaped death myself—I think that if I saw this landscape, these serene houses, these fertile fields, I should think I had crossed beyond the realm of reason, and lived in a world conjured by my exhausted mind and despairing spirit—" She moved away from the lieutenant, searching for the right words. "I would either move through that world in a dream, hardly noticing what I saw—or I think I would want to smash it, make it as ugly as my own reality—" She stopped, bracing herself against the balcony rail, waiting for the silence behind her to break.

"I think, ma'am," the lieutenant said gently, "that the men who smash furniture and destroy houses are tired, and are dispirited. But the reason they do it is because they are led by inexperienced officers, who themselves do not have the discipline to control their men."

"That is the military reason," Gabriele said, turning to face him. "I'm not sure it's the human one." Then, gathering up her courage, making herself face yet another moment of risk, she asked the question she had asked of every

Confederate who had come within Felicity's gate. "Do you know my husband, Captain Alex St. Cyr? He's with the Twenty-eighth Louisiana Volunteers—with Taylor at Irish Bend."

"No, ma'am, I'm sorry, I don't," the lieutenant said. "But don't give up hope. It was a—mess out there. It will be a long time before they can account for everyone."

"Oh, no," Gabriele said. "Of course I won't give up hope."

Even as she spoke the word, she wondered what it meant. Long ago, hope meant a happy feeling of expectation, based on a certainty that good things would happen. She hoped her father would remember to bring her the French doll from New Orleans, she hoped the dress Veronique stitched would be exactly like the picture in Godey's book. What foolishness, to think that small flutter of anticipation, that delicious trembling on the edge of fulfilment, could be named hope!

Hope, she had learned, wore more sombre colours, and a sterner face. Hope must be tenacious, must somehow cling to her purpose no matter how strong the arguments reason mustered to do otherwise. Hope pulled back from the pit of despair, over and over again, until finally she lay beside it, exhausted and close to defeat, daring to look into the abyss.

"I wish you well, then," the lieutenant said. He tipped his hat and rallied his men, and soon they, too, disappeared, a dust cloud hanging briefly to signal their going before it settled and the road lay empty and still.

And then came a straggling patrol of Confederate troops that announced itself as the last. They drank water standing, munched the cornbread and ham Gabriele gave them as they marched back through the gates. They swung through them, turned into the road, and then vanished in the direction of all the troops before them, following the war.

"As though they had an engagement," Gabriele said, staring after them. "All of them making their way to Alexandria—Confederate and Union troops alike." She looked at Adams. "Does that make sense?"

"Taylor moves toward strength," he said. "And tries to draw Wietzel from his. Let's hope they're in too much of a hurry to bother us here."

Then they waited for the Yankees to come.

Toward mid-afternoon, Gabriele, sitting on the upper balcony, saw a lone blue-coated rider turn into their gate and trot toward the house. Her heart stopped, and for a moment she thought that perhaps it would never start again, and she would be delivered from this, but then, with a slight hesitation as it found its rhythm, it began again, a sure, steady beat.

"Letha," she called. "Get Mr. Adams, please."

Letha's head appeared in the open window behind Gabriele, eyes rolling with fear. "He done gone out to the bayou, Miss Gabriele. To catch some fish for supper, he said."

"Then I'll go down alone," Gabriele said.

"No, Miss Gabriele. I go with you," Letha said.

Gabriele ducked inside, and together she and Letha crept across the room to the hall, going stealthily down the broad stairs. As they descended the last steps, they could see a blue shape through the sidelights of the front door. And then they heard a knock as the great brass knocker rose and fell against the door.

"Letha—he's *knocking*," Gabriele said.

"Must be some of them has manners," Letha said. "You stay here."

She sailed forward, tignoned head held high, and unbolted the door. She swung it open, then stood so rigid that Gabriele's nerve almost deserted her.

"Why—why—it's Mr. *Scott*," Letha said. She looked up at Gabriele. "Miss Gabriele—it's Mr. *Scott*!"

"Jordan—" Gabriele ran forward, hands outstretched. "Oh, Jordan!" she said.

He took her hands and held them, looking into her face with anxious eyes. And then she saw the barrenness of the hall and the rooms beyond it strike him—"My God," he said, "what's happened? Have the troops already been through?"

"No—I—gave it all away," Gabriele said. "To the slaves —the hands, I mean—when they left." She shook her head. "It doesn't matter—Jordan, tell me—how in the world did you get here?"

"I command a gunboat," Jordan said.

"Then you were at Ft. Bisland—" Gabriele said. "Oh, Jordan, have you seen Alex?"

"It's why I came," he said. "Now hold on, Gabriele— here, sit down." He helped her to a chair and stood beside her, still holding her hand. "He's a prisoner—he's held at Franklin now, but he'll soon be sent to New Orleans for a military trial."

"Oh, no!" Gabriele said.

"He'll be tried as a blockade runner," Jordan said. "And the fact that he wears a uniform now won't help him, I'm afraid."

"Oh, Jordan—is there nothing you can do?" She rose, hanging onto his arm. "We're married, Jordan—almost six months ago—I've been wild with worry—oh, Jordan, help me, please!"

"Alex didn't tell me that," Jordan said. His eyes went past Gabriele to the place near the door where he had first seen her. "In fact, he tried to make me think he hadn't even been in touch with any of you—he didn't want to involve you, Gabriele."

"Involve me! As though I care! I'd do anything to save him. Anything!"

"Do you really mean that?" Jordan said. He glanced at Letha. "I'd like to talk with you alone."

"Let's go outside," Gabriele said. "It's all right, Letha. Why don't you see if you can scare up something to eat? Bring it to us in the gazebo—it's still pretty there."

Neither spoke until they were seated on the benches, looking through the screen of vines at the first blooming roses. "It's hard to think of war in a place like this," Jordan said. "You say you gave your things away—that was probably wise, Gabriele. At least then you had some—control."

"What can I do for Alex?" Gabriele said.

"I can help him away from the camp," Jordan said. "But I can't get him farther than that. If you can arrange for someone to pick him up—but Tom's not here, is he? Alex said he wasn't—"

"No—and I can't ask Adams to risk his life," Gabriele said. "What is needed, Jordan? Maybe Harold can help me—"

"A small boat," Jordan said. "God, I can't believe I'm planning this—but there have been enough demonstrations in the Scott family that blood ties don't hold—I may not be able to right the wrongs my aunt has committed, but I won't make them worse."

"A small boat—a sugar cooler would do," Gabriele said. "The Confederate soldiers put two men in them—I suppose a girl and a man can fit!"

"A girl—Gabriele, you can't!"

"Oh yes, I can," Gabriele said. She rose and held out her hands. "These hands are as strong as yours, Jordan, and the muscles in my arms as hard. I can row, I've rowed for years—and I know every inch of that bayou between Franklin and here. Tell me where to meet him—and I'll be there."

"And if you're caught?" Jordan said. He stood, too, looking down at her with a look she could not define. "I couldn't help either of you then."

"We'd ask for none," Gabriele said. "As long as we are together—oh, Jordan! I've been so afraid!"

The tears she had held back since he walked in the door found release now, and she took the comfort Jordan's arms gave her, thinking that if the war had cost them all many terrible losses, at least the friendship she and Jordan cherished flourished still.

"I shouldn't let you do it," Jordan said when her tears had stopped. He saw the flashing light in her eye and laughed. "Yes, I know—my letting you has nothing to do

452 Elizabeth Nell Dubus

with it. And really, there's nothing else we can do. To involve anyone else—especially someone who has been a soldier himself—well, that would increase the severity of the consequences if it doesn't—work."

"It will," Gabriele said, feeling a burst of energy that seemed to come from the ground beneath her feet. "It—has to."

"But he can't stay here," Jordan said.

"We neither of us will," she said. She took his hand and looked up into his eyes, remembering the first time she had felt that clear and honest gaze. "I can trust you with our destination, Jordan. We'll go to San Antonio, to Tom and Veronique. He has land there—and Jonas and Samson are there, too."

"A long and dangerous journey," Jordan said. That expression she had not been able to read returned, but now she knew it for what it was. Respect, admiration—and a true affection that would go with her during all those weary miles.

"With Alex there—it will seem like nothing," she said. "But first I have to save him—"

"Let's make our plans," Jordan said. He traced a rough map in the dust coating the floor, showing Gabriele the point at which she could meet Alex.

"Now when?" he said. "It must be soon, Gabriele."

"Is tomorrow morning soon enough?" she said.

"Tomorrow! Can you leave so quickly?"

"Why not?" Gabriele said. "There's nothing to leave." Now she knew that she spoke the truth. Whatever ties that had held her here had loosened: she had been set free. The souvenirs of this life lying in the cabin in the woods would go in the wagon—as for the rest, the few furnishings the hands had not carried away—let the Yankees have them.

Letha appeared carrying a tray, grumbling to herself over the meagreness of the food she offered them. "Letha, we've a lot to do today," Gabriele said. "Pack your belongings and wait for me in my room—and don't say a word to anyone, do you hear?"

"Yes'm, Miss Gabriele," Letha said. She looked as though she wanted to say something, but when Gabriele gave her a stern look she picked up the tray and scurried off.

"Are you taking her with you to Texas, Gabriele? Won't she slow you down?"

"Of course not. Anyway—even if she did, I can't leave her. Letha's my last connection to my early life, Jordan. The one who held me as an infant, helped me learn to walk—I can leave the house, I can leave the land. I can't leave her."

"I'd better get back to camp," Jordan said. He took her hand. "I—won't see you again."

"The war can't last forever," Gabriele said. "And when it is over—"

"I'll go back to Boston," Jordan said.

"Not New Orleans?"

"That's over for me," he said. He stared past her at the house, which in the soft light of an April afternoon slept peacefully, its ravaged interior hidden behind its calm façade. "Write to me in care of the Scott Shipping Lines in Boston, Gabriele. I'd like to know how you—all get on."

"I will," she said. She stood and walked with him toward his horse. "Maybe you'll come see us in Texas, Jordan. It's supposed to be wonderful there."

"You won't come back here?" he said. "When it's over, I mean."

"I don't know," Gabriele said. "But having left it like this—I have a feeling it's over for us, too."

She watched him mount and start down the drive, turning at the last to wave his hat to her before clapping it on his head. Then he slapped his horse lightly with his riding crop, and trotted quickly up the drive.

The moment he vanished through the gate, Gabriele ran into the house, slammed and bolted the door, and called Letha. "Send Caleb to find Mr. Adams," she said. "Tell him I need to see him right away. Now hurry!"

"Yes'm," Letha said, and hurried down the hall.

Gabriele went at once to the attic to find the costume trunk that had provided so much entertainment on rainy afternoons when she and Tom were growing up. Her mind had cast up the solution to the hardest problem: how to conceal Alex while she got them safely away. I'll use that yellow make-up, the stuff that made us look Chinese, she thought as she shoved aside a barrel to get to the trunk. And if our wagon is stopped—I'll say Alex has yellow fever, that he's very contagious—that will stop them, the Yankees have been afraid of yellow fever since they got to New Orleans: some of them have even asked for transfers to get away from it—they won't bother Alex when I tell them that.

Of course she would take Brandy—Tom had Jupiter in Texas—but there was Brandy's stable mate Vanilla—she'd use her as the other half of the wagon team. And I'll rub mud all over them and bind up their knees to make them look decrepit.

As she went down to meet Mr. Adams, she knew that she was letting her imagination protect her, that she made a game of a dangerous business to keep her spirits up. But if it works—I don't care, she told herself, and when she told her plans to Adams, carried all his protests before her on the strength of her confidence that they would work.

"I won't waste any more time arguing, Mrs. St. Cyr," Adams said. "I've seen enough of what you can do when you put your mind to it since your father died—I guess you can do this."

"If you'll take Letha and the wagon and the horses to the cabin," Gabriele said. "Stay with her until I get there with Alex—" Her throat closed around that word, and she saw quick sympathy in Adams' face. "I'd take you with us —but I thought two women with one sick man would attract less attention—"

"Don't worry about me," Adams said. "Matter of fact, this frees me, Mrs. St. Cyr. I wouldn't have gone off and left you alone—but I'm itching to join the Texas Rangers that have come over to help out. Knew some of 'em in my

Wells Fargo days. I reckon to get a few Yankees 'fore I'm done."

"I wish you luck," Gabriele said, eyes misting. "I don't know what I'd have done without you, Mr. Adams—"

"Aw, it's all right," Adams said. "Your Pa—he always treated me fair. You, too, Mrs. St. Cyr. You're a Cannon through and through."

"If you're ever out near San Antonio—come look us up," Gabriele said.

"Tell you what," he said. "If I make it through all right —I might come back and see what happens to Felicity. Let you know." He cocked an eye at the sun. "I'd better start rounding stuff up," he said. "That Letha—she know about this?"

"I'm not going to tell her about going to get Alex— she'd throw herself across the door and never let me out," Gabriele said, and saw Adams grin. "I'll just tell her we have to leave here before the Yankees come. She'll go, don't worry about that."

"That sugar cooler—you know where one is?"

"There's one down near the dock now—it floated down the bayou a couple of days ago and Caleb pulled it in for me. It seemed a shame to just let it go—"

"Good," Adams said. "We'd have wasted time going to get one at the mill."

Later, when it was time for her to go, Gabriele could hardly believe how easy it was to walk away. One moment she stood in her father's study, the aroma of books and fire-smoke enveloping her, and the next she stood in the open air, the door closed behind her for the last time. How easy, she thought, as she slipped down the garden path. No cracks in the earth—no cries from heaven—just a soft night wind stirring, just a pale, silent moon.

She paced herself as she walked through the grove of oaks to the field beyond it: it would take her the better part of an hour to reach the bayou, and several hours of rowing to reach the place where Alex should be. Excitement kept her from feeling fatigue, but it also tuned her nerves to their highest pitch, so that the slightest noise made her heart beat loud and fast. Field mice scurried away at her approach, and once the wing tip of an owl swooping down on its prey brushed her cheek.

Finally she saw the glimmer of moonlight on water that meant the bayou lay not far ahead: she quickened her pace and soon reached the bank. Sliding down it, her feet almost going out from under her on the slick mud, she reached the moored sugar cooler and climbed in. A thick oar lay in the bottom, heavy and rough in her hands. Carefully, she pushed away from the bank, using the oar as a pole until she reached the middle of the stream.

The current ran against her, and she made a few false starts before she found a rhythm that would guide the cooler in a steady path. Something splashed in the water, and she saw a long, dark form, scaly back just breaking the water, swimming against the current parallel with her. She felt more alone than she had ever felt in her entire life: her grasp on the oar loosened, and it almost slipped from her hand before she grabbed it, willing herself to find her nerve again.

Her eyes went up to the skies, and she saw the Big Dipper angled there. As though the stars could speak, could remind her of all the nights spent with Tom and her father, learning the constellations, calling them by name until they were old friends who saw her through the dark until the dawn came again, she felt courage flood through her. I can do this, she vowed. And I will.

Once she heard voices ahead of her, and dropped to the bottom of her makeshift boat, oar beside her, until the cooler drifted past and all was quiet again. She had no way to gauge the distance she had travelled, and when two tall pines, trunks crossed to make an X loomed up on the bank ahead of her, she almost panicked. That was the spot Jordan had told her to watch for: he would see to it that Alex hid nearby.

Flailing at the water, sure the noise must rouse every sentry for miles, Gabriele steered the cooler toward the bank, letting out her breath only when the thrust-down oar struck mud. She dug the pole in and heaved, and the cooler nudged the soft bank. Peering into the thick underbrush, she called softly, "Alex! Alex, are you there?"

For a moment she heard nothing. Even the bayou went quiet—and then a form emerged from the heavy blackness and crept toward her on all fours.

"Gabriele?"

She bit her tongue almost through to suppress her cry of joy. "Yes," she whispered.

He slid down the bank and climbed into the cooler, ducking down immediately, squatting close to the floor. "Gabriele—I can't believe it—when Jordan told me—"

"Nor can I," she said. "But we mustn't say a word—lie down, Alex, while I get into the middle of the stream."

The current worked with her now, and she felt the cooler surge ahead as she turned its nose toward home. Alex's hand came up and closed over hers. "I never thought I'd see you again," he said.

Her tears fell on him, warm and sweet. After all the fearful days and lonely nights, all the despair of not knowing how he fared—she had him back again. The blisters opening on her hands did not sting, nor did the muscles of her back complain. At that moment if she had had to row twice as far, and carry twice the weight of that unwieldy oar, she could have done it. Alex was here, and they were going home.

They stayed in the cabin all day, waiting for dark before setting out. Letha, after her first joyous welcome, left them alone. "I won't stray far," she told Gabriele. "But they's blackberries around here—I'se going to get us some."

The rough bed covered with a quilt did them as well as the softest down. "We need nothing but each other," Alex said, touching her face as though he still could not believe he held her once more.

"And friends," Gabriele said. "If it had not been for

Jordan—and Adams, too." She let out her breath in a long sigh, thinking how lucky they were.

"Yes, Jordan's made me proud to be a Scott again," Alex said. "I'll repay him, someday. Though nothing could ever be enough."

"I don't think life works like that," Gabriele said, settling more closely against him. "I don't think we repay each other for favours—I think we often just—pass them on to someone else. You helped Veronique—Jordan helped us—don't you see? A chain of good deeds, Alex—a circle of trust going around and coming back again."

"Then I hope you live in such a circle all your days," Alex said. "I don't want pain or fear or horror to ever touch you again."

"How can they?" she said, kissing his hand. "I have you."

When Letha stole back to the cabin, and peered through a crack in the wall, she saw them asleep in each other's arms, heads curved toward each other, faces smiling and at peace.

"Like two babies," she said, wiping away a tear. "Miss Honore, I promised you when you died I'd see that chile through—now don't you worry—that promise, it's still good."

They left just after nightfall, Alex lying in the bottom of the wagon, wrapped in a blanket that he could pull up over his head, his face jaundiced and lined.

"You look awful enough to scare anyone," Gabriele said, surveying her work. "Now remember to shiver like anything if we're stopped—I want them to think you're dying of yellow fever and leave us alone."

Letha sat in a corner of the wagon, her skirts spread over one of the crates. The others they covered with old sacks, throwing loose clothing around to further conceal the crates. Then Gabriele climbed up to the driver's seat and picked up the reins, clucking softly to Brandy and Vanilla, guiding them carefully over the rough track through the woods.

They travelled until almost midnight: keeping to wagon tracks that wound through pastures and cut-over fields had slowed them, but at least they had travelled alone. Occasionally, a light flickered off in the distance, and when this happened, they stopped until sure the glow came from a house or cabin, and not from a lantern held in a Yankee soldier's hand. Alex took watch while Gabriele slept next to Letha in the wagon bed: she had thought she would not sleep, but she did, waking in the early dawn with stiff limbs and an aching neck.

"The most ticklish part lies ahead," Gabriele said as they jolted along after a meagre meal. "This track comes to an end, and we'll have to turn and go toward the main road."

"Should we wait until night?" Alex said from the wagon-bed.

"No, I think we'll attract less attention travelling during the day—the road is full of refugees, one wagon more shouldn't matter."

"Where are we?" Alex said.

"Past New Iberia," Gabriele said. "We passed a milepost that marked Dulcito a few minutes ago."

"And when we get to the main road?"

"We'll follow it for a while before we can turn west. And then—then we can head straight across the prairie to the Sabine."

"I wish I could do something active!" Alex said. "Lying here while you run all the risk—"

"There's not a price on my head," Gabriele said.

She set the horses in motion, and they subsided into silence. Only the creaking of the harness, the rattle of the wagon wheels, the soft sounds of the spring morning—Gabriele made the turn into the main road, anxiously looking for danger signs, but saw none. The road was empty, and only a long trail of smoke hovering over it blocked the way.

"Is that smoke?" Alex whispered.

"Yes—I can't see where it's from—" The wagon rounded a curve, and Alex heard both Letha and Gabriele gasp.

"A house," Gabriele said. "Burning—cover your head, Alex. Don't say a word."

She looked at the burning house, flames making bright curtains at its long windows, roof beams arching against the sky before they crashed into the inferno below.

A man threw buckets of water against the flames while a woman filled more from the pump in the yard. Near them stood three children, huddled together, eyes stark, faces drawn.

Gabriele set her eyes ahead, urging the horses on. Behind her she heard Letha praying, and her own lips moved: "Hail, Mary, full of grace—"

Now, as though the burning house had been a gateway to a new landscape, Gabriele saw the debris scattered along either side of the road. Women's clothing caught on fences and draped over shrubs. Broken china, shattered mirrors, bits of bric-à-brac lugged a few miles and then discarded. A child's rocking horse—a doll.

"Lor', Miss Gabriele—I never seen such," Letha said.

"I'm glad I emptied Felicity," Gabriele said. "I'm glad there's nothing but a tomb of our life there—if they burn it, they will only set the funeral pyre."

The devastation she saw on every side heartened her rather than otherwise: every bit of evidence as to what fate awaited the people of the Teche convinced her how wise they were to leave.

They had but a mile to go on the main road before they could once more take to safer tracks when she saw a small troop of Yankee soldiers marching toward them, a cloud of dust swirling up from their feet.

"There are soldiers coming," Gabriele said quietly. "Alex, cover yourself and start shaking. Letha, don't you dare say a word!" She glanced at Letha and saw her face. "They won't hurt us, Letha. I promise."

"I wish I had my rolling pin," Letha said. "Somethin' I could use—"

"Shh!" Gabriele said. "They're almost here."

As the soldiers drew closer, she could make out a sergeant leading them, with four enlisted men behind. For a moment, she thought they might go on past. But as they came abreast, the sergeant held up his hand. "Halt!" he said. He strode over to the wagon. "You, too."

Gabriele reined in the team and waited silently.

"Where are you going, miss?" the sergeant said.

"To my uncle's near Youngsville," Gabriele said. "My Pa was overseer at a plantation back there—but he died of yellow fever yesterday. My brother's got it, too. He's 'most dead."

"Yellow fever!" one of the soldiers said. "Hey, let's move on, sergeant."

"Just a minute," the sergeant said. He put his hand on Brandy's back. "If you had to pick one of those horses—which one would you choose?"

"They're both pretty mean," Gabriele said quickly. "Only reason Pa had them was because they're so hard to ride."

"The chestnut looks sweet enough," the sergeant said. He went up and opened Brandy's mouth, peering inside. "Doesn't seem mean to me," he said. He reached up to unfasten the reins. "I'll give you a receipt for her, of course," he said, winking at his men.

In a flash, Gabriele was off the wagon, her dagger drawn from her belt. She grabbed Brandy's head and jerked it around, and pointed the dagger right at Brandy's heart.

"What the devil!" the sergeant said. He grabbed her wrist and threw her back into the weeds at the side of the road. "You little witch!"

His hand again went to Brandy's harness, but then a voice cried out, "Stop! Stop, I say!"

Slowly, the sergeant turned around as Gabriele got to her feet and stood with the dagger still grasped in her hand. A Yankee officer mounted on a black horse stood at the side of the wagon, sidearm drawn. "All right, sergeant. What's going on?"

"She—she tried to kill—that horse," the sergeant said.

The officer dismounted and approached Gabriele. Removing his cap, he gestured toward Brandy. "Is she yours?"

"Y-yes," Gabriele said. She felt a trickle of something on her chin and touched it. When she drew her finger away, it had blood on it, and she licked her lip and felt where her teeth had bitten through.

"You'd rather see her dead than—borrowed?"

"I raised her," Gabriele said.

The officer looked at the sergeant. "On your way," he said. "Don't let this happen again, Anders."

"Yes, sir," the sergeant said. He moved ahead of his men and called out an order, his voice still filled with rage.

Not until they were out of earshot did the officer speak.

"I admire your spirit, miss, but not your restraint. Not all our troops are as disciplined as we'd like them to be— you shouldn't provoke them."

"I couldn't help it," Gabriele said. "I just—couldn't."

"What are you doing out here anyway?" the officer said. He went to the wagon and peered inside. "What's the matter with him?" He reached toward Alex's blanket, taking a corner in his hand.

"Yellow fever," Gabriele said.

The blanket dropped, and the officer jerked away. "Yellow fever! You should be in quarantine!"

"I'm trying to get to family," Gabriele said. "Our Pa died yesterday—he was overseer at a plantation up the road—"

The officer reached out and took Gabriele's hands, turning them over so he could study the palms. He looked from the broken blisters to her weary face. "How far do you have to go?"

"The other side of Youngsville," Gabriele said.

The officer hesitated, then shook his head. "All right. Go on, then. But if I were you—I'd get off the main road."

"I will," Gabriele said.

She climbed back up on the driver's seat and picked up

the reins, unconsciously straightening her back and holding her head high.

The officer swung back onto his horse and trotted along beside the wagon. "How far before you can turn off?" he said.

"About a mile."

"I'll escort you," he said.

"I—thank you, sir," Gabriele said, ducking her head to hide her tears.

The officer said nothing, but rode to the front, staying several yards ahead. His blue back bounced up and down, a blur of colour to Gabriele's tired eyes. The surge of adrenaline that had carried her through those terrible moments had died, leaving her completely exhausted. Not one more thing, she thought. I cannot manage one more thing.

And then they reached the small break in the shoots of cane that marked the opening they looked for. Gabriele steered the wagon carefully over the narrow ditch and into the rutted track while the officer watched.

"I have a sister with eyes and hair just like yours," he said. "You don't see that much, around here."

"No," Gabriele said. She turned in the wagon seat, deliberately raising her hand and saluting.

The captain smiled. "Good luck," he said. Then he wheeled his horse and rode away, moving from a trot to a canter and then vanishing in his own dust.

When two days had gone by and they had seen no Yankees, Alex washed off his make-up and took his turn driving the team. They made better time now, travelling through country as yet untouched by war, the only signs of it other travellers journeying like themselves to a new home.

The closer they got to the Texas border, the higher their spirits rose. Even Letha took heart and decided that they would reach Tom after all. They talked about the new place, and the house Tom would have built. "You'll see, Letha," Gabriele said. "It's going to be like going home."

The legends Gabriele had grown up with about her own people blew across her mind, flying pennants that told of conquest over hardship, and the constancy of love. Her hands, callused and scarred, had convinced a Yankee captain that this was no pampered lady, but a woman capable of work. She looked at them, seeing them for what they were. Tools to build with, tools to make all they dreamed of true.

She heard Alex shout something as he grabbed her hand. "The Sabine!" he cried. "We've reached the Sabine."

Gabriele stood and gazed at the wide brown river drifting slowly past reed banks. Sunlight glinted off its surface, breaking into shimmering pieces of light. A breeze stirred up, ruffling leaves, blowing through Gabriele's loose hair. A bird flying high against the sky—a rabbit jumping up from her nest—

"It's like the morning of the new world," Gabriele said. "Made for you and me—and with all our lives ahead."

"There's the ford," Alex said, pointing to a shallow crossing.

As the wagon came out on the far bank, water rolling from its wheels and dripping off the horses' coats, Alex reached into his shirt pocket and pulled out a small cloth bag. "This is for you," he said, handing it to Gabriele.

"What is it?" she said, holding out her hand.

In answer he loosed the knot that held the bag closed and poured a stream of fine, black earth into her palm.

"From Felicity," he said. "I thought you might want it —as a promise—and a pledge."

Earth from Felicity, a memory of her fields. The house rising above them, massive, secure. As though the crumbs of dirt, warm and powdery in her hand, were a lodestone for her heart, Gabriele felt it take direction. It settled into a circle of time, a ribbon winding round. All the blood of all those ancestors, particles flowing in her veins. All their hopes and dreams built up and then laid waste and through her and Alex, built up again. A continuity of love and purpose, meeting here.

She took Alex's hand in hers, and felt the earth from her palm rub into his warm skin. Then together, his arm lifting her, they leapt down onto Texas soil.

Tales of Bold and Reckless Romance

They were dazzling American beauties...transported to the breathtaking shores of Europe.

CRYSTAL RAPTURE
Sarah Edwards
_____ 90704-4 $3.95 U.S.   _____ 90705-2 $4.95 Can.

PASSION'S TEMPEST
Emma Harrington
_____ 90937-3 $3.95 U.S.   _____ 90938-1 $4.95 Can.

DESERT ENCHANTRESS
Laurel Collins
_____ 90864-4 $3.95 U.S.   _____ 90865-2 $4.95 Can.

SAPPHIRE MOON
Peggy Cross
_____ 91308-7 $3.95 U.S.   _____ 91309-5 $4.95 Can.

PASSION'S SONG
Carolyn Jewel
_____ 91302-8 $3.95 U.S.   _____ 91303-6 $4.95 Can.

The AMERICANS ABROAD Series
from St. Martin's Press

Publishers Book and Audio Mailing Service
P.O. Box 120159, Staten Island, NY 10312-0004

Please send me the book(s) I have checked above. I am enclosing
$ _____ (please add $1.25 for the first book, and $.25 for each
additional book to cover postage and handling. Send check or
money order only—no CODs.)

Name _____

Address _____

City _____ State/Zip _____

Please allow six weeks for delivery. Prices subject to change
without notice.

AA 1/89

THE *NEW YORK TIMES*
BESTSELLER BY
THE AUTHOR OF
THE SHELL SEEKERS

"BREATHTAKING...
A book you will want to
keep, to read and re-read!"
—*Grand Rapids Press*